MURDER AT THE TOWER

N.R. Daws spent thirty years as a civil servant, mostly in security and counter-terrorism. He is a hiker, skier, lover of history and travel, as well as a long-standing fellow of the Royal Geographical Society. He was awarded an MBE for charitable services in 2006. An alumnus of the Curtis Brown Creative writing school, he achieved Highly Commended in the Blue Pencil Agency First Novel Award 2019, where he met his agent, Nelle Andrew. His first novel, *A Quiet Place to Kill*, was published by Thomas & Mercer in 2021.

Also by N.R. Daws

KEMBER AND HAYES SERIES
A Quiet Place to Kill
A Silent Way to Die
A Perfect Time to Murder

MRS LYDIA BRAMBLE SERIES
Murder at the Palace

MURDER AT THE TOWER

N.R. DAWS

ORION

First published in Great Britain in 2026 by Orion Fiction,
an imprint of The Orion Publishing Group Ltd.
Carmelite House, 50 Victoria Embankment
London EC4Y 0DZ

An Hachette UK Company

The authorised representative in the EEA is Hachette Ireland, 8 Castlecourt
Centre, Dublin 15, D15 XTP3, Ireland (email: info@hbgi.ie)

1 3 5 7 9 10 8 6 4 2

Text © N.R. Daws 2026
Trademark © Historic Royal Palaces 2026

The moral right of N.R. Daws to be identified as
the author of this work has been asserted in accordance
with the Copyright, Designs and Patents Act of 1988.

All rights reserved. No part of this publication may be
reproduced, stored in a retrieval system, or transmitted
in any form or by any means, electronic, mechanical,
photocopying, recording, or otherwise, without the
prior permission of both the copyright owner and the
above publisher of this book.

All the characters in this book are fictitious, and any resemblance
to actual persons, living or dead, is purely coincidental.

A CIP catalogue record for this book is
available from the British Library.

ISBN (Mass Market Paperback) 9781 4091 9986 1
ISBN (Ebook) 9781 4091 9987 8
ISBN (Audio) 9781 4091 9988 5

Typeset by Deltatype Ltd, Birkenhead, Merseyside
Printed in Great Britain by Clays Ltd, Elcograf S.p.A.

www.orionbooks.co.uk

For George Henry Ward.
Our first grandchild and future reader.

Please note that while the notable locations in this story are real, the characters and events are fictional.

Cast of Characters

Mrs Lydia BRAMBLE – Lady Housekeeper of Hampton Court Palace
Kitty – her loyal housemaid
Reverend Thomas WEAVER – Chaplain of the Chapel Royal at Hampton Court Palace
Detective Inspector COLE – from Scotland Yard

Reverend Augustus DENCH – Chaplain of the Chapel Royal of St Peter ad Vincula
His household:
  Esther – his chambermaid
  Anonymous – his housemaid
  Anonymous – his parlourmaid
  Anonymous – his cook

Mr Jasper CHANT – Organist of the Chapel Royal of St Peter ad Vincula
Dr William BURFORD – Physician at the Tower of London

Stuart TREADLE – Chief Yeoman Warder at the Tower of London
Lance Corporal BOLTER – Steward in the Royal Fusiliers

Captain Jeremiah FRY – Royal Fusilier garrisoned in the Tower
Mrs Catherine FRY – his wife
Beth – the Frys' housemaid
Sir Stephen LOVELL – good friend of the Frys
Lord FRY – Captain Fry's father (mentioned but not present)

Major Edwin RUSHTON – Royal Fusilier garrisoned in the Tower
Mrs Margaret RUSHTON – his wife
Gwen – the Rushtons' housemaid
Sir Oswald CLYNE – good friend of the Rushtons
Sir Arthur RUSHTON – Major Rushton's father (mentioned but not present)
Adam HEDGECOE – Edwin's friend (deceased) (mentioned but not present)

1

The vestry door eased open a crack and one eye peeked through. As it spied on the seated congregation its gaze alighted on Mrs Fry and her husband. She stared back, fancying she saw it widen in alarm, and smiled to herself as it blinked rapidly and disappeared.

'Did you see that?' She nudged her husband until he glanced at her. 'That Reverend Weaver may be from Hampton Court Palace, but we have a perfectly good chaplain of our own.'

The Chapel Royal of St Peter ad Vincula within the Tower of London was full to bursting and Reverend Augustus Dench would normally have officiated, but this was no ordinary service. Two Yeoman Warders were to be honoured for their twenty-five years' service at the Tower, and to Mrs Fry's mind, Reverend Weaver was no more than an interloper who should not have been invited to lead the prestigious Holy Communion.

'Hmm?' said her husband, dressed in his uniform of a captain in the Royal Fusiliers, and he grunted as she elbowed him for attention.

'Remember me saying he helped unmask a murderer there?' she said. 'Barely a week ago, apparently, but why that gives them the right to afford him this honour is beyond me.'

'I – um . . .' Captain Fry looked distracted as the Governor of the Tower of London and his wife took their seats between two of the highest-ranking members of Tower staff, including Stuart Treadle, who held the coveted position of Chief Yeoman Warder.

Many other Yeoman Warders and officers from the Royal Fusiliers who guarded the Tower were also in attendance, some accompanied by their spouses, so Mrs Fry gave the governor's wife her best sugary smile. After all, there could be no harm in being pleasant and remaining in the good books of those with influence.

Mrs Fry did a double take when she caught sight of a middle-aged man lurking furtively by the wall near the front, wearing a dark-grey Ulster coat and carrying a black bowler hat. She supposed this was Detective Inspector Cole of Scotland Yard, the officer who had led the recent hunt for the Hampton Court murderer.

'Good grief,' she chuckled. 'They're letting them all in.'

A sudden unexpected bout of dizziness preceded a wave of nausea, leaving her with a headache and dry mouth, and she silently chided herself for having drunk two glasses of wine with her canapés before the service. She waved a hand at her face to cause a breeze. 'Do you think it's warm in here?'

'Hmm?' said Captain Fry.

Mrs Fry felt the increasing tug of a twitch at the corner of her mouth, becoming irritated when a new tic pulled at the corner of her eye on the opposite side. She glanced around to see if anyone had noticed, annoyed when she saw Dr Burford look away hurriedly.

A hush descended as Reverend Dench opened the vestry door and began the procession to the altar.

The first half of the service did not go smoothly for Reverend Weaver. Mrs Fry smiled as he caught his shoe in the hem of his cassock on the way to the high altar, and could not avoid grinning as he stuttered and stumbled over his words during the sermon and the celebration of the Yeoman Warders' achievements. His failure to remember all the correct words to the chosen hymns threatened to tip her over the edge into full laughter, but it was his loss of poise and grace as he slid down the tricky steps from the pulpit that had her stifling an outburst by coughing into her handkerchief.

By the time the most important religious ritual of the service arrived, for which Reverend Weaver again took the lead, the flush of his face and sheen of perspiration on his brow had alerted Mrs Fry to his soaring level of anxiety. *Reverend Dench would not have bumbled through in such a fashion*, she was about to whisper, but she refrained beneath her husband's steely glance.

Row by row, the congregation knelt at the chancel rail to receive Holy Communion, and Mrs Fry could not help tutting when she noted Inspector Cole kneeling with his head bowed and arms at his side, indicating he required nothing more than a blessing. Reverend Weaver obliged by laying a gentle hand on the top of the inspector's head and softly uttering a prayer.

As Inspector Cole left the chancel rail, Mrs Fry almost lost her composure once again as Reverend Weaver grimaced and used his cassock to wipe a sheen of hair cream from his fingers. Glancing at Cole as he retook his seat, her laughter threatened to bubble up as the policeman combed his hair back into place with a look of disgust.

Returning from her own turn at the rail, she gave Reverend Dench a stern glance and nudged her husband again. 'What's the point of me donating a chalice cloth if he doesn't use it?' she hissed through gritted teeth as her stomach cramped and her head pounded.

The whole inside of the chapel tilted and the face of her husband seemed to recede into the distance.

'I shall be glad when this is ...' She took a breath and closed her eyes.

After his calamities thus far, Reverend Weaver allowed himself to relax a little as the remaining congregants took the bread and wine, signifying the service was entering its closing stages. He then signalled for the organist to come forward as one of the final communicants, but before he could approach the chancel rail, one of the older ladies uttered a groan and gripped her stomach. Another staggered as she returned to her seat, supported by her neighbours as she reeled as though on the sloping deck of a listing ship. One of the Yeoman Warders clamped a hand over his mouth as he retched and rushed from the chapel, and the Fusilier major mopped trickling sweat from his brow, clearly in barely contained distress. Soon, almost everyone had been affected in some way, even Reverend Dench, whose wide-eyed, red-faced expression spoke volumes about his own condition.

A cry rose from the middle of a pew.

Gasps of horror echoed around the chapel as Mrs Fry slumped sideways in an apparent faint. Captain Fry held his wife as the nearby major shouted, 'Is the doctor present?'

'I am,' said Doctor William Burford, resident physician at the Tower of London, as he stood up unsteadily and pushed his way towards the commotion, clearly suffering himself.

Some of the wives seemed overcome by what they were witnessing, especially in a house of God, and grown men were pouting and jutting chins as though a stiff upper lip and bravado would stave off whatever ungodliness had taken hold. Reverend Weaver saw the governor and his wife being ushered from the chapel, while lesser mortals remained transfixed by the events unfolding around them.

Weaver realised Reverend Dench was leaning against him for support and helped him to a chair in the vestry. Returning to retrieve the blessed and precious items of the Eucharist, Weaver had a sinking feeling in his stomach that had nothing to do with whatever had afflicted everyone else, and wished he was back in his cosy lodgings at Hampton Court Palace where he always felt safe and in control.

Dr Burford stood to address the ailing congregation from the epicentre of former activity, bringing sudden silence and stillness to the chapel.

'I'm afraid she's dead.'

2

Reverend Weaver took a deep breath to stave off the dizziness threatening to overcome him. That someone should die during his Holy Communion service was horrific almost beyond his comprehension. Any dismay he might ordinarily have felt at anything untoward occurring at a time when he should be enjoying the limelight and the fruits of his endeavours paled into insignificance.

Captain Jeremiah Fry, still resplendent in his dress uniform but with his face crumpled in deep distress, stood helplessly nearby while others tended to his wife. Detective Inspector Cole seemed unaffected by whatever had struck down the congregation and introduced himself to Chief Yeoman Warder Treadle.

'I suggest you marshal your men into helping all those affected to leave the chapel and take in some fresh air, but do not let anyone leave the Tower just yet,' said Cole. He nodded to Captain Fry. 'Better take him with you, for his benefit and ours.'

Despite Captain Fry's ingrained military training and experience, at one moment he looked ready to lean forward in some misguided attempt to help and at another he shied away to stand stiff and formal as though he had no idea how one should react in such a situation.

The chief appeared about to contest Cole's orders, clearly

not used to a policeman taking charge while in his own domain, but he looked somewhat queasy himself.

Reverend Weaver's senses started to clear and he saw only three others, besides himself and Cole, remained in the chapel near the body of Mrs Fry.

Jasper Chant, the chapel's long-standing organist and a friend of Reverend Dench, appeared to have escaped the effects of whatever had taken hold of the congregation. Looking unruffled in his dark suit, white shirt and bow tie, he had taken charge of tidying the high altar and resetting cushions knocked over or aside during the hurried exodus. Weaver suspected Chant was much like his friend Dench and himself; someone who liked tradition, continuity and order.

Reverend Dench reappeared in the doorway of the vestry, still unsteady on his feet but seemingly recovered enough to take an interest in what was still unfolding in his chapel. His vestments were creased and askew, and his face had a sheen of perspiration.

Dr Burford busied himself examining Mrs Fry by loosening her high collar and checking her neck, looking into her lifeless eyes, and studying her wrists, hands, fingers, and finally her lips and mouth. He muttered, 'Curious,' from time to time but failed to explain. He flinched when something dangled close to his face and looked up to find Dench proffering the white chalice cloth. Burford looked at the wine stains but took it with a nod of thanks and laid it with respect over the face of Mrs Fry.

'The number of people who became ill at the same time is remarkable, wouldn't you say?' said Inspector Cole as he watched Dr Burford stand up with some effort, as though carrying a huge weight. 'Given the timing of the reception that preceded the service, I am inclined to point a finger at the canapés served in the officers' mess of the Royal Fusiliers building. What say you?'

'Now look here, army cooks, jolly damn good, loyal soldiers to boot,' said a voice with less conviction than the words suggested.

Heads turned towards the objector and Reverend Weaver realised Chief Yeoman Warder Treadle had re-entered the chapel unnoticed.

'I am merely speculating aloud,' said Cole. 'The simplest explanation is usually the right one, and that points to what just occurred being a case of food poisoning. No one's fault. Simple bad luck.'

'Death of Captain Fry's wife. Hardly "bad luck",' bristled the chief.

Reverend Weaver preferred full sentences for the sake of clarity and thought the staccato delivery of clipped phrases rather strange.

From the glance he gave the chief, Cole appeared to think so too. He looked back to the physician. 'Are you able to come to any initial conclusions, Doctor?'

Dr Burford mopped his forehead with a handkerchief and took a moment to catch his own laboured breath. 'I am concerned it may be more than common food poisoning because that usually takes a few hours to manifest and we've had, what, an hour and a half since the reception?'

'If it was particularly virulent, might it ...?' Inspector Cole's voice trailed off at the look from the doctor.

'I have seen similar symptoms before, during my time working at Guy's Hospital across the river, and I noticed Mrs Fry had some facial twitching as she entered the chapel. It remains to be established whether this was a tragic accident but, in all honesty, I cannot be certain.'

'Let me get this straight,' said Reverend Weaver, his face

having paled again. 'Are you suggesting the possibility this could have been deliberate?'

Dr Burford returned a single nod.

'Murder?' said Cole, frowning at the suggestion.

'Murder?' echoed the chief. 'Who—?'

'I didn't say that,' Burford interrupted. 'If it was a deliberate poisoning of the many that inadvertently led to the death of the one, I couldn't begin to understand why.'

'It's my job to find out,' said Cole. 'What do you think could have caused it?'

'We have to establish what *it* is first. Any uneaten canapés should be collected for analysis before they are thrown away,' said Burford.

'Can arrange,' said the chief.

'I still have old friends at Guy's Hospital from my time there. I'm confident any one of them will agree to arrange a fast toxicology test on Mrs Fry and the canapés. You'll need to call for a litter.'

'A litter? Trundled through the streets? Wife of a Royal Fusilier? Not on one of those three-wheeled contraptions,' said the chief, jutting his chin in indignation. 'A carriage. With my men.'

'As you wish,' said Inspector Cole, giving the chief a curious glance. 'I'll need to take some preliminary statements from Captain Fry and those who were in closest proximity to him and Mrs Fry. I'll also need to speak to all of you, and those who prepared and served the canapés.'

Reverend Weaver's heart sank at the thought of Detective Inspector Cole taking charge. Their paths had crossed on his most recent case and Weaver had suffered the ignominy of being accused of obstructing the murder investigation as he escorted him around Hampton Court Palace. His experience of the detective having been less than optimal,

Weaver suddenly longed to be far away, back in the safe haven of the palace.

'Forgetting where you are,' said the chief suddenly, drawing himself up to his full height. 'Military establishment. Heart of old London town. A City of London Police investigation. Or mine.'

Inspector Cole inclined his head to the side as a signal to the chief and the two men stepped away for privacy. Weaver wasn't about to let secrecy play a part and staggered towards a pew as near to the two men as he dared without raising suspicion. He put his head in his hands as though still suffering and listened intently to the conversation.

'It will take too much time for the City of London Police to dispatch a suitable officer, even if they have one to spare,' said Cole.

'My investigation then,' said the chief.

'But you are not a policeman.'

'Police and army. Civilian and military.' The chief smiled and produced a police whistle from a secret pocket near his left shoulder and a warrant card from his trouser pocket. Tower and its inhabitants. My domain. My forte.'

Inspector Cole held out his arms for emphasis. 'Which makes me impartial.'

'But not *au fait*. Military fortress. Certain sensitivities.'

Reverend Weaver thought he'd lost his hearing during the following silence and peeped through his fingers with one eye. He saw Cole gritting his teeth while the chief stared at him, unmoving. The detective relaxed slightly and glanced over his shoulder towards Dr Burford as though a decision had been made.

'How about a compromise?' said Cole. 'A joint investigation drawing on your knowledge and experience of the

Tower and its inhabitants and utilising my expertise and experience of investigating crimes and criminals.'

By the chief's narrowed eyes and slight frown lines on his forehead, Reverend Weaver could see him wrestling with his desire to retain overall authority and the need to clear up the incident that had occurred on his patch.

'Agreed,' said the chief, thrusting his hand forward.

Inspector Cole looked at it as though offered a piece of mouldy mutton left outside in the rain for three days, before accepting the gesture and shaking. 'Agreed. Quick arrest?' he whispered, with raised eyebrows and a knowing look. 'For appearances?'

'Arrest who?' said the chief, perplexed.

'Obvious, is it not?'

The chief's frown deepened. 'Not to me. Know something?'

Cole shrugged. 'No other choice.'

Reverend Weaver's heart thumped in his chest and he got unsteadily to his feet. Reverend Dench, still looking queasy, leant against a pillar and closed his eyes as he rested his forehead on the cold white stone. Weaver moved slowly across to him and touched his elbow.

'Augustus,' he whispered, waiting for Dench to open his eyes in acknowledgement. 'I require your assistance.' Dench glanced at Weaver's earnest face. 'I need you to send an urgent telegram on my behalf.'

'Of course, my friend,' said Dench. 'But why? Whatever is the matter?'

Weaver explained and had barely finished when a hand touched him lightly on the shoulder. He turned to see Inspector Cole with the chief at his shoulder, both of them with solemn expressions. His stomach turned to jelly and his bowels to water as Cole spoke.

'Reverend Thomas—'

'Weaver—' the chief interrupted.

'I know,' said Cole, irritably. 'Reverend Thomas Weaver, I am arresting you on suspicion of the murder of Mrs Catherine Fry.'

3

Mrs Bramble, Lady Housekeeper of the grace and favour apartments at Hampton Court Palace, sat at her breakfast table. Today, the occasional alternative of a soft-boiled egg with toast soldiers graced her plate instead of the usual two slices of toast with thick butter and a smear of marmalade. Fancy breakfasts came with fancy prices and she saw no need for either, unless for a special occasion.

Her jet-black cat, Dodger, emitted a questioning meow, his big green eyes seeming to luminesce like emeralds on black velvet.

Mrs Bramble chuckled. 'I know. I haven't forgotten your usual.' She took the thickly buttered remains of a toast soldier and placed it on the floor next to her chair. 'There you go.'

She watched his pink tongue licking the butter and gave thanks for his willing company, especially every evening. Named after a slippery character in *Oliver Twist*, her favourite novel by Mr Dickens, Dodger always waited patiently for the daily treat he earned through his mousing duties.

Turning her face to the window to gaze at the Outer Green Court, she sipped her cup of Earl Grey tea, subconsciously noting the usual to-ing and fro-ing across the bridge over the moat. This had formed a part of Mrs Bramble's early-morning routine since her first day in post five years ago, and she considered it an integral part of keeping the grace and favour residents safe and secure. She found it fortunate that her ground-floor apartment, on the south side of the turret forming the main entrance of the Great Gatehouse, was perfectly placed for such observations, and considered its suite of spacious and comfortable rooms, decorated with an understated elegance, a much-appreciated bonus.

Kitty, in her uniform of long-sleeved black dress, white apron and crocheted white cap, entered and propped a telegram against the marmalade pot. The young housemaid, employed by Mrs Bramble for the last three years and with whom a relationship of mutual trust and respect had grown, stood to one side. Mrs Bramble saw the concerned expression on Kitty's face and smiled wryly at the thought of what new gripe lay inside.

Some of the ladies resident in the grace and favour apartments were constantly dissatisfied with their allocations and wrote frequently to the Lord Chamberlain to complain about Mrs Bramble's unfairness and lack of consideration for their real and imagined plights. Invariably, the Lord Chamberlain's office wrote direct to Mrs Bramble and she could sense his waning patience at the current volume of correspondence. This was something over which she had no control, but she had great sympathy for his rising frustration.

Although many years a widow, she had been happily married to an infantryman in the British Army who had lost his life to cholera during a posting to Bengal. Serving herself as a military nurse, she left the profession a year after his death and used her experience dealing with the confused, wounded, self-important and irate to gain a foothold in the world of domestic service. Despite securing prestigious posts as housekeeper, she found the hierarchy in many hotels and private houses no less rigid than in the army, a situation she was eminently suited to cope with. Bombastic owners, colleagues and guests found themselves dealing with her on her terms, for she suffered no fools, gladly or otherwise.

Having had the good fortune to secure employment at Hampton Court Palace, such skills often came in useful in her current position.

Her attention returned to the telegram and she cleaned her butter knife before slitting open the envelope. She saw instantly it had come from her friend, Reverend Weaver, and recalled his delight at being rewarded for his part in catching a murderer by being asked to officiate at a special Holy Communion service at the Tower of London. Anxious on his behalf, she had hoped to discover how he had fared last night in the Chapel Royal of St Peter ad Vincula and was pleased he had sent a telegram.

Her face fell.

'Here we go again,' she said, as she read the telegram, drawing a surprised glance from Kitty. 'I'm afraid we'll be needing our travelling coats. It seems, inexplicably, that our good friend Reverend Weaver has been arrested for murder.'

4

'We are here to see Reverend Weaver,' said Mrs Bramble in the most pleasant manner she could muster.

The small one-storey building to which they had been directed stood near the main entrance for visitors to the Tower of London. The bespectacled official behind the counter of a tiny office within looked her up and down before checking a list attached to a clipboard.

'No Weaver here,' came the blunt reply.

'Detective Inspector Cole will do,' she said, her voice adopting a more authoritative tone, but his name didn't register either. 'Let us try either Reverend Augustus Dench' – the official looked up from his clipboard at the mention of the Tower's resident chaplain – 'or Chief Yeoman Warder Stuart Treadle.'

The invoking of the name of the Chief Yeoman Warder made the official's eyes narrow and he nodded to a lad standing nervously in the corner. The youngster hurried from the office and could be seen through the window, running towards the Tower itself.

'I'm afraid this office is a little cramped so please wait outside until the boy returns.'

'Gladly,' said Mrs Bramble with a glare, her hackles up because of the official's terse responses. 'But we shall leave our bags in your care until Chief Yeoman Warder Treadle sends to collect them.'

Mrs Bramble took a visitor's map from the counter and left the official to his silent seething. Outside, she studied the map with Kitty to familiarise herself. As far as she could see, the Tower of London fortifications differed from the rabbit warren of Hampton Court Palace by its relative simplicity of consisting of four main areas: the moat, the Outer Ward, Inner Ward and Innermost Ward.

The inner wall dotted with defensive towers enclosed the Inner Ward. This contained the largest and most important buildings, such as the Queen's House with its pristine lawn, guardhouse, Waterloo Barracks with its parade ground, the Royal Fusiliers officers' quarters next to the married men's quarters, the resident chaplain's house, and the Chapel Royal of St Peter ad Vincula. At its centre stood the familiar landmark of William the Conqueror's imposing White Tower with the area known as the Innermost Ward to its front.

The outer wall, also sporting a number of towers and strengthened with defensive casemates, formed the boundary of the low-lying Outer Ward. Many of the casemate chambers had long been converted to accommodation for the Yeoman Warder guard force and other occupants of the Tower.

The impressively wide moat, outside of which Mrs Bramble and Kitty currently stood, encircled the entire fortifications. A dry ditch since the Duke of Wellington ordered the fetid, disease-ridden waters to be drained, it still presented a formidable obstacle to anyone wishing to gain entry.

Mrs Bramble folded the map and looked up as a Yeoman Warder marched into view with the young lad trailing several paces behind. The Warder sported the red and dark blue 'undress' uniform used for daily duties, rather than the red-and-gold Tudor state dress uniform used on special occasions. Mrs Bramble could tell he was someone of importance by the gold crown sewn above four gold chevrons on his arm, and the gold edging to his uniform.

'Mrs Bramble?' he asked, as he approached.

'Yes, and this is my housemaid, Kitty,' said Mrs Bramble. 'And you are ...?'

'Stuart Treadle,' he said. 'Chief Yeoman Warder. Just Chief. Understand you had a telegram from Reverend Weaver?'

Mrs Bramble shook his proffered hand. 'Yes, I did. Is he well?'

'Accused. Arrested. Locked in the Tower.' The chief shrugged.

'Not the Bloody Tower, I hope.' She was only half-joking.

'The delicate reverend?' The chief chuckled and shook his head. 'Night under guard in the officers' quarters. Royal Fusiliers. Very cosy. Walk and talk?'

Mrs Bramble fell into step beside the chief, with the attentive Kitty two paces behind, and they passed through the gated archway beneath the entrance tower and crossed the moat over a stone bridge.

Mrs Bramble had been a little disconcerted at first by the chief's way of conversing and imparting information through the barest essential number of words. However, having seen and heard clipped orders barked by army officers during her time abroad as an army nurse, her ear soon tuned in to allow instant translation into standard English in her head.

'I'm afraid, doesn't look good for the reverend,' said the chief.

'On what evidence?' said Mrs Bramble.

He gave her a sideways glance. 'Detective now?'

'He is my friend, so you can't blame me for wanting to gauge the seriousness of his predicament. All I know is, he was arrested for murder and I should come quickly.'

The chief acknowledged a Yeoman Warder guarding the passage beneath the entrance tower and led them through to the Outer Ward.

He gave Mrs Bramble another glance and sighed. 'Very well. Congregation ill. Three unaffected. None a Tower resident. Mr Chant, the chapel organist? Known personally by the chaplain. Inspector Cole? A policeman, so beyond reproach. Witnesses from canapé reception and inside the chapel came forward. Only Reverend Weaver, also no illness, had direct contact with deceased. Briefly.'

'I'm not convinced anybody is ever fully above reproach, except maybe Reverend Weaver, but I take your point,' said Mrs Bramble. 'Have you recovered a murder weapon?'

The chief looked sheepish. 'Not yet. Congregation affected with vomiting, dizziness and diarrhoea. Suspect poison in the canapés but—'

'Then the deceased might not have been the intended victim?'

'True, but—'

'You have ruled out accidental food poisoning?'

'No, but again—'

'Then how can you even be sure a crime has been committed, let alone arrest a clergyman for it?'

The chief's face screwed up as though in mild pain. 'Dr Burford, resident Tower physician. The food and body of the deceased, sent to his colleagues in Guy's Hospital. Should be able to establish cause of death.'

'Does the deceased have a name?' continued Mrs Bramble.

'Mrs Catherine Fry.' He glanced at Mrs Bramble. 'Wife of Royal Fusilier garrisoned here. Captain Jeremiah Fry.'

He steered them to the left, through a passage beneath the Bloody Tower with its raised portcullis still in situ, and into the Inner Ward to pass the guardhouse. 'She had seen Reverend Weaver once before. Less than enamoured with his competence. Expressed concerns about ability. Found him "clumsy and bumbling".'

Mrs Bramble said nothing on the subject but privately conceded her friend's style might not be to everyone's taste. 'Is there anyone else who might be said to have an axe to grind with Mrs Fry?'

'Of course,' said the chief. 'Always petty squabbles when so many live in close proximity. Arise and dissipate very quickly, I can assure you.'

Not dissimilar to Hampton Court Palace, thought Mrs Bramble. 'How do you find Detective Inspector Cole?'

He pondered this for a moment, as though unsure whether to air any criticisms. 'Tell the truth, too officious. Tried to take charge of the investigation.' He shook his head. 'No authority here.'

'He is a Metropolitan Police officer from Scotland Yard, after all,' said Mrs Bramble, trying to give him the benefit of the doubt.

'Exactly,' said the chief. 'The Tower. Guarded by Yeoman Warders, manned by the Royal Fusiliers. Falls within the jurisdiction of the City of London Police.'

'I believe his recent high-profile success at Hampton Court Palace earned him his role as the Yard's representative at the special service. Are you saying that he didn't take kindly to being reminded of his place?'

'Acknowledged the sensitivities. Made a valid point. Time always of the essence in such investigations. Came to an arrangement.'

Mrs Bramble raised a questioning eyebrow. 'What arrangement?'

He hesitated, pausing their progress when they reached the top of a long flight of steps leading beside the magnificent White Tower after which the fortifications were named. 'Mrs Fry, married to an officer but effectively a civilian. Fusiliers not keen to become embroiled in an investigation. For the sake of expediency, governor agreed, joint investigation. Combine the inspector's experience and my local knowledge.'

Mrs Bramble failed to supress a laugh, drawing a look of rebuke from the chief.

'I am sorry, Chief, but I have some experience of Inspector Cole's technique. He is dogged and determined but never struck me as being one for collaboration.'

The chief shrugged. 'Given no choice. That or nothing.'

Mrs Bramble glanced back down the steps. 'I see the Tower is still open for visitors. Is that wise?'

The chief gave a facial shrug. 'Governor does not want to draw attention. Avoids panic. You understand?'

'And unwanted scrutiny from a higher authority.'

'Indeed. All inhabitants, confined to Tower. Until further notice.'

'I cannot bring myself to believe that Reverend Weaver is guilty,' said Mrs Bramble with a shake of her head. 'What's to stop the true murderer, if there is one, walking out with the day visitors?'

The chief's eyes narrowed. 'Guard doubled and on high alert. Visitors checked in and out.'

'Will that not arouse suspicion?'

'Special occasion next week. Convenient excuse.'

The chief motioned for them to continue and they turned right at the parade ground in front of the Waterloo Barracks.

A figure emerged from the building now directly in front of them that served as the headquarters of the Royal Fusiliers' garrison and contained the officers' quarters and mess. The way he descended the steps with his bowler-hatted head down and open Ulster coat flapping, Mrs Bramble could mistake him for none other than Detective Inspector Cole.

'Mrs Bramble,' Cole said, striding towards them. 'Thank God you're here. I was unhappy to hear that Reverend Dench had sent you a telegram on behalf of Reverend Weaver but now I'm relieved. Weaver is driving me insane with his incessant complaints and wittering.'

'And a good day to you too, Inspector,' said Mrs Bramble, having experienced Cole's bluntness before but still unaccustomed to such lack of polite niceties.

'What?' Cole looked confused for a moment. 'Oh. Yes, yes. Good morning and all that. As I was saying—'

'The reverend is rightly upset at being falsely arrested for murder. Am I correct?'

Cole's face clouded. 'You are further from your bailiwick than I am so I must warn you now, please do not interfere with our investigation.' He nodded to indicate the chief.

'As you stated, I am here at the request of my friend.' Mrs Bramble smiled, amused at having rattled the inspector so soon.

'I do not believe even you can help him now,' said Inspector Cole.

'As I understand from the chief, you have no direct witness to Reverend Weaver's involvement, no evidence that he had any hand in the death, no substantive motive as to why he would want to kill someone with whom he had minimal contact and no real quarrel, and you can't even agree on how the deceased died, or even if she was murdered at all!'

'That's not quite what—' The chief stopped open-mouthed as Mrs Bramble strode towards the officers' quarters and motioned to Kitty to follow, leaving him and Cole flat-footed.

'I will offer as much support to my friend as I am able,' she threw over her shoulder, as the two men hurried in her wake. 'In any way possible.'

5

Apart from the chapel, the impressive array of buildings and towers and walls that formed the fortifications of the Tower of London were of no import to Mrs Bramble at that precise moment. Her only concern was to speak to her friend, establish his side of the story, and persuade Inspector Cole and the chief they had the wrong man, if that was truly the case. Reverend Weaver had always been a humble man of integrity, good humour and, despite a propensity towards clumsiness, total professionalism. She could fathom no reason why someone of his ilk would suddenly turn to murder without preceding signs that something was amiss. Signs she hoped she would have recognised.

Forced to wait by a guard until the commanding officer had been informed, she stood with Kitty in the entrance hall of the headquarters building, remembering how different army quarters elsewhere had been in her day when compared to the less-than-salubrious billets of the enlisted rank and file. *Hardly the perfect way to encourage loyalty and obedience* she thought.

'Kitty,' said Mrs Bramble. 'After we've seen Reverend Weaver, I want you to find out anything you can from the workers who go unnoticed while others are about supposedly more important business. That includes Yeoman Warders, soldiers, maintenance men, and domestic servants if there are any.'

'Of course, Mrs B,' Kitty acknowledged, stepping back as Inspector Cole and the chief finally arrived.

'I need to hear the story from Reverend Weaver's own lips,' Mrs Bramble said to the chief.

'Unless he confesses, it will be a pack of lies,' said Cole.

Mrs Bramble scoffed. 'Please don't mistake him for a common criminal. You know as well as I what happens when something more intriguing and challenging arises.'

The familiar cloud covered Inspector Cole's face but any retort was forestalled by the appearance of an officer and a corporal sporting the red tunics and white accoutrements marking them as Royal Fusiliers. A wry smile crossed Mrs Bramble's lips when the officer barely noticed her but gave a lingering glance towards Kitty. Then he turned to Cole.

'I am Major Rushton, officer in charge,' the officer introduced himself. 'Mrs Fry, the wife of my second-in-command, Captain Fry, was technically a civilian so I am content with the governor's decision for you and the chief to take the lead on this one. All I ask is that you treat Captain Fry with sensitivity. We are taught to fight and cope with losing colleagues in wartime, but not to say goodbye to loved ones prematurely. You understand?'

Rushton asked them to follow upstairs and led them along a corridor, where several doors gave access to offices filled with men in the uniform of the Royal Fusiliers. At the far end, a guard came to attention outside a room before standing aside at Rushton's command.

'Take as long as you like,' Major Rushton said to the chief. 'If you need me further when you're done, the corporal will bring you to me, otherwise he'll escort you from the building.'

'Thank you, Major,' said Mrs Bramble, bringing a confused glance from Rushton. She watched him walk back along the corridor, leaving the corporal as their escort, and waited for the guard to open the door for them.

Inside, a dishevelled-looking Reverend Weaver sat slumped in a chair like a haphazardly draped coverlet. He still wore his dog-collar, and a jacket with more creases than a paper fan, but the usual sparkle had left his eyes. He barely acknowledged the door had even opened and seemed to look straight through Mrs Bramble. She ushered Kitty inside and firmly shut the door in the faces of Inspector Cole and the chief. She wanted his version of events untainted by having the two investigators hovering nearby.

Mrs Bramble drew up another chair and sat in front of Weaver, taking his left hand in her own to offer some human touch and comfort. He seemed to respond to the warmth of her fingers and laboriously hauled himself into a more upright position.

'I'm sorry you had to see me like this,' he said. 'I've been trying to understand why the good Lord would want to put me through this and all I can think of are the trials of Job.' He sniffed, holding back a sob. 'Despite my faith, that brings me little comfort.'

'This is not like you,' said Mrs Bramble, giving the back of his hand a gentle rub. 'You must regain your positivity if we are to get you out of this.'

Reverend Weaver scoffed. 'Inspector Cole has made up his mind. There is nothing to be done.'

'No, there is always something,' she said, the harder edge to her tone making Weaver look at her closely. 'They have nothing to say Mrs Fry was even murdered, let alone that you had a hand in the tragic events.'

His eyes seemed to regain their clarity at her encouraging words and she saw a glimmer of hope within.

'They gave me the impression they were dotting the i's

and crossing the t's before hauling me to Newgate Prison and throwing away the key,' he said.

'I don't think that is likely,' scoffed Mrs Bramble. 'They have no case whatsoever without solid evidence. Inspector Cole has allowed himself to be carried along by the drama of events and will come to his senses soon.'

'I do hope you are right,' said Reverend Weaver. 'I don't know how I'd break it to the bishop.'

'I need you to tell me everything. By that I mean any insignificant detail you can recall. From the beginning.'

'Oh,' he said, sitting up straighter. 'I-I ...' He cleared his throat. 'I arrived yesterday afternoon and Augustus – that's Revered Dench, the resident chaplain – showed me to my room on the first floor of his house next to the chapel. I unpacked, we talked about the service and my sermon, and went for a walk around the Tower. After dinner, we reminisced about old times and went to our beds.'

'Did you see anything unusual on your walk?' asked Mrs Bramble.

'No, nothing,' said Weaver. 'The last place on our tour was the chapel and Augustus took me inside to ensure everything was in place. He drew my attention to the history and points of interest around the nave and elsewhere inside. Did you know that three queens of England are buried there? Anne Boleyn, Catherine Howard and Lady Jane Grey. Anyway, he took me to the vestry to show me where everything was. He wanted me to enjoy the experience and honour of taking the service and even gave me his key to the cupboard where the sacramental wine is kept. He said I should take the lead as though I was the resident chaplain at the Tower, not he. I was flattered he thought so highly of me.'

'What did you do with the key,' said Mrs Bramble, thinking aloud.

'Kept it about my person at all times,' said Reverend Weaver.

'And yesterday morning?'

'We had an early breakfast before finalising plans for the service and preparing for the arrival of the congregation. There was a lot to do and think about. As soon as we were satisfied, we went to the mess hall downstairs, here in the headquarters of the Royal Fusiliers. As well as the special Holy Communion service, a reception with wine and canapés had been arranged in honour of the two long-serving Yeoman Warders.'

'Can you recall who you spoke to?' said Mrs Bramble.

The reverend frowned and pouted. 'Not really. Far too many to be honest, and I hadn't met anyone before, except Augustus and Inspector Cole. I do remember speaking to the governor, and Jasper Chant, the organist, of course. I passed a few moments with Chief Yeoman Warder Treadle and the two of his men being honoured, but everyone wanted to congratulate them so they were whisked away. Everyone else seems to merge into one person, I'm afraid.' He paused, looking up in thought as though seeking divine inspiration. 'Except the Fusilier major and captain, and their wives,' he said. 'I did chat to each couple on separate occasions. I say couple but each had a friend with them. Gentlemen. All part of London society, I suppose.'

Mrs Bramble frowned in thought. It didn't appear that Reverend Weaver had been afforded any opportunity to poison the food so she was perplexed as to why Inspector Cole and the chief might think so.

'Did you leave the reception at any time for any reason, Reverend?' asked Kitty, who had remained silent until then.

'Excellent question,' said Mrs Bramble, thinking the young woman had read her mind.

'Now you come to mention it, I did,' said Reverend Weaver.

Mrs Bramble's heart sank. Cole and the chief needed no ammunition in their pursuit of this case.

'I realised we had forgotten one thing and left quickly to return to the chapel,' Weaver continued. 'I know it's only a minor point, but I always like to prepare the wafers, water and wine in advance when taking a Holy Communion. It means I have one less thing to think about and can get on with everything else.'

'How long were you gone?'

'Five minutes, I suppose. Ten at a stretch. I returned to the vestry, unlocked the cupboard to retrieve the wine and wafers, placed them on the table with a carafe of water for diluting the wine, next to the Eucharist chalice and cloth already there, relocked the cupboard and returned to the reception.'

Mrs Bramble stood and went to the window. She estimated the distance from the headquarters to the chapel entrance as less than four hundred feet. Moving at his usual pace, and given the simple task he had performed, she agreed ten minutes to be the absolute maximum time he would have needed. Probably less.

'Did you see anyone else leave the reception?' asked Mrs Bramble.

'No, but I probably wouldn't have noticed, what with all the to-ing and fro-ing,' said Reverend Weaver. 'People were milling about and mingling, stewards were circulating with trays of food and white wine, and so on. Mrs Rushton did excuse herself from the mess hall for a few minutes as I returned to the reception but I noticed her shortly after, dabbing at splashes on her dress that I supposed were from spilled white wine.'

'What about in or around the chapel? Did you see anyone as you left, or before you returned.'

Weaver took more time over this, his eyes narrowed as he thought intently about his answer.

'Nobody specific, I would say,' he said. 'There were people outside; Yeoman Warders, soldiers, a few others going about their business. The Tower encompasses a community of people, after all.'

'Did anyone see you go to the chapel?'

'I suppose someone might have.'

Mrs Bramble sighed. 'This might prove more difficult than I first thought.' She looked at Kitty, whose expression confirmed her own fears. 'Inspector Cole and the chief will say you left the mess hall but went to the kitchen, not the chapel, with the sole intention of introducing some kind of poison to the food.'

'Why on earth would I do that?'

'Because you had an altercation with Mrs Fry, who did not like your – um – style of delivering a service and had tried to get you replaced.'

'She did what?' Weaver's face fell and his mouth dropped open.

'You didn't know?' said Mrs Bramble.

'I-I had no idea. Yes, she had told me to my face that she didn't much care for my flights of fancy but ...' His bottom lip quivered. 'Good Lord.'

'It doesn't explain why you'd want to poison everyone, including yourself,' said Kitty. 'People don't go around trying to kill themselves and everyone around them to get at someone they don't like or had a bit of a tiff with. Doesn't make sense.'

A sharp rap of knuckles sounded impatiently on the

door, which opened with a jerk. Inspector Cole's face appeared, bearing the hint of a smirk.

'Keep your chin up, Reverend,' said Mrs Bramble with a sympathetic look at her friend. 'Kitty and I will have our work cut out on this one but be patient. I have total faith that you had nothing to do with the death of Mrs Fry and we intend to prove it.'

'Good luck,' said Cole from the doorway. '

6

Having been deposited outside the entrance to the officers' quarters by the Royal Fusilier corporal, Mrs Bramble gave Inspector Cole and Chief Yeoman Warder Treadle her frostiest stare. Incarcerating anyone was not to be taken lightly but when the charge was spurious, the evidence circumstantial and the victim a member of the clergy being honoured for his good work in catching a murderer, it beggared belief that officers held in high regard by their respective organisations should jump to such a conclusion.

'Inspector Cole, given the manner in which our paths crossed not so long ago, I trust you have no objection to me staying around for a while?' she said.

Cole scoffed. 'I have every object—'

'After all, I fear there is much your superiors have not yet been made aware of regarding *our* most recent investigation into the murders at Hampton Court Palace.' Mrs Bramble gave Inspector Cole a sweet smile, watching his expression harden at her emphasis before she turned it on the chief. 'I do hope you will accede to my request that we ...' she indicated herself and Kitty '... the reverend's two friends, remain close by to offer him support should he need it.'

'Investigation in hand,' said the chief with a glance at Inspector Cole, whose face had gone puce with the effort of holding his tongue. 'Jurisdiction, and all that. Happy to accommodate, but within certain bounds. Leave to us. Agreed?'

Mrs Bramble gave a polite bow of her head. 'I take it we are free to wander, socialise and pass the time while we're here,' she said, seeking to set the parameters as wide as possible. 'Poor Kitty gets dreadfully bored and irritable in confinement.' She ignored Kitty's brief glance and raised eyebrows.

The chief smiled. 'Of course. Glad we understand each other.' He looked at Cole for support. 'Must get on. No?'

As the chief turned away, Inspector Cole donned his bowler hat and touched its brim at Mrs Bramble respectfully but leant in to whisper, 'I know what you're up to but I want to be clear: if you interfere with my investigation, I'll arrest you and have the chief lock you in the Bloody Tower with only bread and water for a week.'

'I wouldn't dream of it,' said Mrs Bramble with a straight face. 'What do you take me for?'

Before he could reply, she took Kitty by the arm and led her towards where the plaque in front of the Chapel Royal of St Peter ad Vincula marked the spot where Henry VIII's second wife, Anne Boleyn, had been executed.

Making a show of reading the inscription, Mrs Bramble spoke without looking up. 'Everyone is convinced Mrs Fry was murdered so we must believe so too while endeavouring to establish the true facts. See if you can find the housemaids of Reverend Dench and Mrs Fry. I'd like their perspectives on events leading up to the murder. Also, if you run into any ordinary soldiers and folk who can shed light on it, see if you can glean anything useful from them, but please do not put yourself in danger. We've only got the word of the inspector and chief that this was a personal matter.'

'Of course, Mrs B,' said Kitty. 'What are you going to do?'

'For a start, I'm going to have a closer look inside the chapel. It's not every day someone passes out and dies in front of an entire congregation afflicted by some mysterious agent.' She nodded to Kitty. 'Off you go, and good luck.'

Mrs Bramble watched her go and stood for a few moments longer until she was out of sight, contemplating what moves she might make next. Her priority was to clear her friend's name, and in so doing, nullify the threat of imprisonment in Newgate and a possible a trip to the gallows. That did not seem an easy task at present but could prove less difficult than what might follow. She knew she would be unable to rest if one assumed a real criminal remained at large to roam the walls and buildings of the Tower. Whatever his reason for poisoning the congregation, no one could be certain he would not strike again. The murderer had not revealed his intention nor claimed responsibility. The reason for the indiscriminate attack might still remain and therefore pose a risk of further criminal action, possibly leading to more deaths. The murder of Mrs Fry may have been deliberate and her death the culmination of a twisted plan. It may also have been an accident and her death, any death, considered collateral damage by the poisoner. She needed to know more, much more, and standing stock still in the middle of the Inner Ward wasn't adding to her knowledge.

Mrs Bramble made her move but had barely set one foot towards the chapel when a tall, thin, gangly man in a frock coat and top hat blundered into her, almost sending her flying. His bumbling apology, coupled with red-faced embarrassment compressed between his mutton-chop whiskers, stunned her into uncustomary silence.

'Are you all right? Not hurt, are you? I gave you quite a shove there.'

'I am all right, thank you,' said Mrs Bramble, watching as the handle of the man's small case came loose, causing it to drop to the ground and shed its contents across the cobbles. 'Do you need assistance?'

The man, now on his knees gathering medical paraphernalia back into the leather case, glanced up at her. 'I have everything in hand,' he said, displaying a handful of small pill bottles. 'Literally, it seems.' He chuckled at his own joke.

Mrs Bramble couldn't help a brief smile flitting across her lips. 'I take it you are a doctor of some kind?'

The man forced his case shut. 'I am.' He stood up with the case under his arm and thrust the offending handle into his pocket before holding out his hand. 'Doctor William Burford, at your service.' He indicated his bag. 'I won't bow, if you don't mind?'

She suppressed another smile and shook his hand. 'Mrs Lydia Bramble, Lady Housekeeper of Hampton Court Palace. At *your* service.'

'Bramble, Bramble.' Burford muttered with a frown. He opened his eyes wide in recognition. 'Reverend Weaver's friend?'

'Yes, I am,' she said. 'I hope you don't mind me asking, but are you any relation to Reverend Weaver?'

'Never heard of the fellow before yesterday. Handsome chap though, isn't he?' He chuckled again at his own joke.

'You look nothing like each other but your mannerisms ... They're uncannily similar.'

'Ah. You mean he's a clumsy old fool too?' said Dr Burford. 'There are a lot of us about, I'm afraid.'

'Maybe so, but he's very good at what he does,' said Mrs Bramble.

'As am I. At least, that's what they say.'

'In which case, you'll be able to tell me how Reverend Weaver managed to poison a whole congregation in front of everyone and murder a woman in the process.'

Dr Burford's mouth flapped open while emitting no sound.

'I have a theory,' he said eventually. 'But it's not one I'm ready to share as yet.'

'Can you not give me an inkling, Doctor? she said. 'I'm at a loss to explain why the personality of someone I know so well would suddenly change so drastically, turning him from a man of God, love and integrity into a brazen murderer.'

'I-I-I,' Burford stuttered, before clearing his throat and taking a deliberately long, steadying breath. 'I cannot speak about the state of Reverend Weaver's mind, or anyone else's if it comes to it. Not my area of expertise. All I can do is look at a body, do basic tests, arrange for more complex tests, and arrive at a diagnosis. Or at least come to a conclusion and make a referral to someone more qualified in a particular field.'

'An opinion or conclusion is all I am asking for, Doctor. However shaky and unsubstantiated it might be at this precise moment.'

Dr Burford nodded. 'In which case, in my professional opinion, the onset of symptoms was far too rapid for food poisoning.' He glanced around as though remembering something and searching for an escape route. 'I-I-Inspector Cole specifically requested – ordered, really – that I not speak to you.'

'Did he now?' said Mrs Bramble, her face hardening. 'In which case, perhaps you can help me by not answering my questions.'

'I beg your pardon?' Dr Burford looked perplexed at such a notion.

'I will make a statement. If, in your professional opinion, I am correct, you will do nothing. If I am wrong, you will give a small cough. In this way, you have not spoken to me or said anything at all.'

Burford looked dubious but Mrs Bramble saw in his eyes that this method of keeping everyone happy appealed to him. He nodded and Mrs Bramble smiled.

'My dear Doctor,' she began. 'Mrs Fry was poisoned.' Burford said nothing. 'And the whole congregation was affected by the same substance.' Again, no word from Burford. 'It was in the canapés.' Burford sighed. 'Ah, you're unsure. So, it could have been administered elsewhere.' Mrs Bramble frowned in thought. 'You know what the poison is.' Burford coughed. 'You don't know for certain, but you have a good idea.' Burford said nothing. 'It is an uncommon substance.' Burford coughed again. 'Hmm. It is a common substance, easily obtained.' Burford remained silent. 'Doesn't make it easy to narrow down, especially without the assistance of Inspector Cole and the chief. I know you await a response to your inquiries from your colleagues at Guy's Hospital. Will you let me know when it arrives and afford me the courtesy of another of these conversations?'

Dr Burford scanned the area around them again and nodded. 'I will,' he said.

'Thank you,' said Mrs Bramble. 'I'm so glad we didn't have this conversation.' She winked and saw Burford's cheeks take on a pink hue.

'I'm sorry, I must be going.' He touched the brim of his top hat, almost dropping his bag again. 'Good day, Mrs Bramble.'

'Good day,' she replied, watching with amusement as he bumped into passers-by and danced around others in his haste to retreat to the sanctuary of his house nearby.

Are you sure you're not related to Reverend Weaver? she thought.

Her attention returned to the chapel and she studied the outside for a moment. Despite having no more than a squat bell tower at the western end and containing no stained glass in its windows, it looked every inch a parish church. A doorway stood at the western end, which is how the congregation entered and departed, but Mrs Bramble suspected there would be others. Every church and chapel she had ever seen had at least two ways of getting in and out, often more, and she made a note to check the other side later.

Inspector Cole had been lax in securing the chapel as a potential crime scene, but he could be excused given the furore that must have followed Mrs Fry's demise and the almost spontaneous outbreak of sickness that had swept through the congregation. She also considered it within the bounds of possibility that Chief Yeoman Warder Treadle may have had something to do with it. After all, it was very much his jurisdiction and there had been a singular failure on his part to get to grips with both the initial uproar and panic, and to preserve what he should have recognised as a potential crime scene. Or maybe Reverend Dench was complicit. It was his chapel, his domain, and he had been right next to Reverend Weaver when the incident occurred. Inspector Cole, bless him, was outside his jurisdiction and dealing with very unusual and challenging circumstances. That did not stop the cogs in Mrs Bramble's suspicious and enquiring mind whirring and revolving.

Was it really possible the chief or Reverend Dench could have had a hand in Mrs Fry's death?

7

Glancing around nonchalantly to ensure no eyes of importance were watching, Mrs Bramble descended the short flight of steps to the chapel door and entered. The inside was pretty much as she had imagined. It looked like many other churches and chapels in the land, with rows of pews in the nave for the congregation, a chancel where Holy Communion took place, and the apse containing the High Altar. Being a chapel, not a church, there were no north and south transepts to form the traditional cross. Iron chandeliers hung from the wooden roof, constructed from Spanish chestnut so Henry VIII's first wife, Queen Katherine of Aragon, could worship God under the trees of her homeland.

A baptismal font stood to her right, and she assumed the two doors to her left led to the bell tower and crypt respectively. Memorials adorned the walls, a row of stone pillars supported arches dissecting the nave in two down the middle, and at the north-east corner stood the newly installed organ. Just beyond the organist's seat, another door led to the vestry. It is to this door that Mrs Bramble made her way, knocking gently and entering before anyone could reply. There was no one inside.

A small table at the centre caught her attention. An almost empty bottle of red wine stood between a gold chalice and dish of wafers; no doubt used for the previous day's Holy Communion service. A few wafers remained, slowly going stale. Next to these stood a small carafe with about an inch of water at the bottom. Mrs Bramble touched a water mark on the table with her fingers before holding up a wine-stained cloth that no doubt had wiped the rim of the chalice before each person had taken a sip.

As for the rest of the vestry, it looked like any other. Robes hung inside an unlocked cupboard, two more unlocked cupboards held ecclesiastical miscellanea, and she guessed a fourth cupboard – locked – held the wine and maybe the wafers used during Eucharist. If correct, this was the cupboard from which Reverend Weaver would have taken the sacramental wine prior to its dilution, confirming his statement that he had relocked it after use.

She turned to a second door, in the north wall. This looked to be in the right position to lead to the crypt, but she stopped when she heard a tinkle on the stone floor. A closer inspection revealed a shard of glass her boot must have kicked. She picked it up for safety's sake and took it over to a small metal bin that stood beside a third door, one she suspected accessed the outside through the east wall. The shard's presence in an otherwise tidy room gave her pause and she turned it in the light to reveal a tiny flower in relief. She wrapped it in her handkerchief but had no time to explore further as Reverend Dench entered the vestry from the nave.

'Oh!' he exclaimed. 'I wasn't expecting ...'

Mrs Bramble's heart leapt at the sudden intrusion, but she composed herself instantly. 'Reverend Dench, I'm glad I caught you. I wanted a word about yesterday's tragic event.'

His face fell. 'Ah, yes. Terrible business. Terrible.'

Realising she had brandished the wrapped shard at him,

she quickly thrust it into her pocket. 'What can you tell me about how it happened?'

'Shall I tell you what happened?' said Dench, earnestly.

'Um – yes.' She thought that was what she'd just asked. 'Please do.'

Dench shrugged. 'Not much, in fact. Thomas ...' He paused and peered at her. 'I do beg your pardon but who are you?'

'I'm a close friend of Reverend Weaver. He may have spoken about me. My name is Mrs Lydia Bramble, Lady Housekeeper of Hampton Court Palace.'

'Mrs Bramble, aren't you?' he exclaimed, grasping her hand to shake it vigorously. 'Thomas told me all about you. Couldn't stop, in fact.'

She smiled. 'Yes, he can be like that sometimes.'

'Can I help you?' said Reverend Dench, eyebrows raised questioningly.

'Possibly,' said Mrs Bramble, hoping they weren't about to go around in circles. 'I came to see where it all happened because I would like to help clear the name of my – *our* – friend.'

'Our friend,' repeated Dench, nodding. He looked intently at Mrs Bramble. 'How, exactly, do we do that?'

'I suppose we could start by you telling me everything you remember.'

'I'll tell you everything I remember but I'm not absolutely sure what happened,' said the reverend. 'The service hadn't gone as closely to plan as we'd hoped and rehearsed. You know what Thomas is like, sometimes as overenthusiastic as a Labrador puppy. He tripped over his own feet a couple of times, stuttered a bit when he became anxious, but apart from that I thought he was doing very well. Although I'm sure it wasn't his first important occasion, and the congregation was small by anyone's standards, this was an important one here in the Tower.'

'How small?' she asked.

'The chapel holds about a hundred and eighty people,' said Reverend Dench. 'Smaller than the average parish church. Although Thomas had negotiated a few tricky patches during the service, everything seemed to be back on an even keel as he led the Holy Communion. Most people had come up to the chancel rail to receive the bread and wine and everything appeared to be heading nicely towards a smooth finish. Until ...'

'Did you see what happened?' she pressed.

'I saw what happened,' said Reverend Dench with a nod. 'Mrs Fry fainted, or so we all thought, and then the whole congregation gradually seemed to become affected to various degrees. Even Chief Yeoman Treadle and myself experienced difficulties.'

'Difficulties?'

'Nausea, headache, shortness of breath, my eyes couldn't focus and I could barely stand. Some had these bizarre facial tics.'

'To what do you attribute these difficulties?'

'It wasn't divine intervention, if that's what you're thinking,' said the reverend. 'No, I suspect the canapés have a lot to answer for and I'm as certain as I can be that Thomas had nothing to do with it.'

Mrs Bramble nodded her agreement. 'Did you see anyone near Mrs Fry during the whole celebration?'

'Of course,' he said. 'The chapel was full and everyone inside had attended the reception.'

'I meant, anyone acting strangely?'

'This is the Tower of London, Mrs Bramble. It's full of Yeomen Warders in fancy uniforms performing centuries-old rituals, army men in other uniforms with their own modern but strange customs, myself and all that comes with the Anglican faith, and a wider community within these walls who are somewhat isolated and insulated from the world beyond.'

'Point taken, Reverend.' She sighed. 'If Mrs Fry could not have been murdered without those around seeing and no one was acting particularly out of character, this may not be murder after all. Unfortunately, from the viewpoint of the inspector and chief, Reverend Weaver is a suspect because he is only one of three who remained unaffected by the illness, and the only one of those three who spoke to Mrs Fry at the reception, someone with whom he had cross words earlier. He also left the reception for a short while, supposedly giving him the opportunity to foul the food.'

'Thomas left the reception for a while so it doesn't look good at all, does it?' It was Dench's turn to sigh. 'If it's any consolation, the words were not cross on his part. Mrs Fry was disgruntled he had been chosen to lead the service in preference to her own favoured clergyman and rather berated him for it. If you're looking for something, however insignificant, to prove a point, Mrs Fry had more reason to harm Thomas than he had to harm her. That said, I do not believe it of either of them. If, God forbid, someone intent on evil did employ this blanket approach deliberately, they cannot have known Mrs Fry would be the one to die, surely?'

Mrs Bramble found herself sharing the same opinion. Either someone had wanted to punish the whole congregation for an unknown reason, which seemed beyond belief, or the whole episode was indeed an accident originating in the kitchen of the Royal Fusiliers.

'I think I should finish what I came here to do and tidy

up,' said Reverend Dench, moving toward the table. 'I am hoping the inspector and chief allow me to reopen the chapel for tomorrow's service.'

'I don't think that is such a good idea,' said Mrs Bramble, steadying the carafe Dench had clumsily brushed with the sleeve of his cassock. She positioned herself between him and the table. 'They may consider Reverend Weaver as their prime suspect but they have yet to charge him.'

'Thomas has yet to be charged but—'

'If I were you, I wouldn't want to move any item or do anything that might be construed as suspicious, as aiding and abetting a criminal, or as tampering with evidence.'

'Are you trying to say you suspect me?'

'Of course not, Reverend,' she lied. 'I'm merely conscious that they are still investigating and will do so at least until Dr Burford receives the results of tests on the food and Mrs Fry.'

Reverend Dench looked concerned, his gaze darting around the vestry as though looking for incriminating evidence. 'Do you think *they* suspect *me*?'

Mrs Bramble relaxed, knowing she had got through to him. 'I'm sure that isn't the case but they, and we, can't be too careful until all the information is gathered and the true facts are known.'

'Can't be too careful.' Dench nodded in compliance. 'I think I shall continue to use the much smaller Chapel of St John the Evangelist in the White Tower for the time being.'

Mrs Bramble offered a silent prayer, hoping his propensity for repetition, as though the thoughts he regurgitated were his own, would not affect every future conversation.

'Can I ask you to think back one more time?' she pressed. 'Was there anything Reverend Weaver did that might shed light or doubt on his guilt or innocence? Did anyone look out of place or worried. Was anyone's behaviour suspicious or out of character? Any detail, however small, might make the difference.'

Reverend Dench's grimace of dismay as he thought for a moment turned to one of despair as he shook his head. Her heart sank a little. Even though Dench had to remain a suspect, how could she doubt a reverend when she did not doubt her friend? She still had many people to talk to and time was of the essence. If the test results came back before she finished her investigation, Inspector Cole might press ahead with charging Reverend Weaver regardless.

'Is there anyone new to the Tower that you know of?' she asked. 'Someone you are unable to vouch for?'

Dench shook his head. 'The only people who do not live in the Tower who were present yesterday are Inspector Cole, the organist Jasper Chant, a friend of the Fry family, and a friend of Major Rushton.'

Mrs Bramble's ears pricked up. 'Friends of the families? Are they still here?'

'I would imagine everyone is still here. The inspector and the chief haven't let anyone leave. Why, are they suspects too?'

'Do you remember their names, by any chance?'

'Do you know, I remember their names,' said Reverend Dench, perking up. 'Sir Stephen Lovell is staying as a guest of the Frys and Sir Oswald Clyne is a guest of the Rushtons. Both were allocated accommodation in the Royal Fusiliers' officers' quarters. Plenty of room in there since most of the regiment moved to a barracks in Hounslow ten years ago, I must say, I can't see this intelligence has any pertinence to the investigation. Although this is not their parish, they frequent the Tower often and I know both the gentlemen well enough to think them of good character.'

Mrs Bramble put a reassuring hand on the reverend's arm. 'I'm sure they are but they may have seen something important others missed, especially Sir Stephen.'

At that moment, the echoey sound of footsteps on stone came from within the chapel. Mrs Bramble moved to the vestry door and opened it enough to see the visitor stop. Inspector Cole had entered through the far door and was now standing stock still in the middle of the aisle, staring towards the altar. Not wishing to have another lengthy and difficult conversation with him just yet, Mrs Bramble moved towards the north door.

'It's the inspector,' she hissed. 'We should go.'

Reverend Dench shook his head. 'That way leads out through the crypt.' He stepped across to the east door. 'This way is quicker.'

Bowing to his superior knowledge, she hurried to his side as the footsteps resumed. He opened the door and they both exited with stealth, Dench easing the door closed behind them before leading the ascent of a short flight of six steps. Departing through a waist-high iron gate completed their escape and Dench turned to her with a look of satisfaction.

'Tragic circumstances, absolutely, but haven't had so much fun since I was in the seminary,' he said. 'Shouldn't admit to it in public, although God sees everything after all, but I've had cause to avoid a few parishioners in the past. Nothing compared to this, though. Fair got the old ticker going, as some say.'

Mrs Bramble looked hard at Reverend Dench. Given his calling, and accepting no man is without sin, why would a clergyman such as he wish to avoid any of his parishioners, never mind admit the practice? Humans were fallible, some more than others, and she and her husband had seen plenty of evidence of that with the army in Africa and India. The

Tower of London was an exciting place to visit for most people but perhaps some coped with the daily existence in such confines better than others. She resolved to keep an eye on him. Just in case.

After all, if Reverend Dench was willing to reveal such behaviour so casually to a stranger like herself, what else might he be capable of?

8

With a fresh offer of accommodation should she need it, Mrs Bramble parted ways with Reverend Dench and watched him disappear through the front door of his residence. Her mind still churned with the possibility of him being involved. After all, he may have been seen to fall ill too but that didn't mean he wasn't acting. The three who had not become unwell – Detective Inspector Cole, the organist Jasper Chant and Reverend Weaver – had not sought to conceal their good fortune as a would-be murderer might.

This was getting her nowhere. She needed to speak to Jasper Chant as soon as possible to shed light on the conundrum. A quick word with Sir Stephen Lovell and Sir Oswald Clyne wouldn't go amiss either. And she needed to find Kit—

'Mrs Bramble,' said Kitty, startling her employer. 'Sorry, Mrs B, but I managed a quick chat with Reverend Dench's chambermaid, Esther, after I saw him follow you into the chapel.'

'Well done,' said Mrs Bramble, hoping for a revelation. She looked around for eavesdroppers. 'Walk with me.' Kitty fell into step beside her. 'What did you discover?'

'Not much, I'm afraid. Reverend Weaver had dinner with Reverend Dench and stayed overnight. They breakfasted yesterday morning and left for the chapel to prepare for the service, coming back later to dress for the reception.

She said she heard the front door close, looked out of a bedroom window and saw them walking back across the parade ground past the barracks, but she only watched for a few seconds so couldn't confirm whether they deviated or went straight to the headquarters building.'

It wasn't as much information as Mrs Bramble had hoped for and a stab of frustration caused a frown. 'Did she see anything later, before the congregation evacuated the chapel?'

'As a matter of fact, she did,' said Kitty. 'She said she noticed someone entering the chapel through the main door but didn't know who it was until he came back out less than five minutes later and she recognised him.'

So, it was a him. 'Who was it?' said Mrs Bramble, eager for the answer but trying not to hurry Kitty.

'She said it was Reverend Weaver and she even watched him return to the reception.'

Mrs Bramble smiled with relief. The chambermaid witnessing Weaver entering the chapel, leaving shortly after and returning to the Fusiliers' building corroborated his account and explanation. Unless he had poisoned every tray of canapés before he left, without deviating to the kitchen where several cooks and stewards would have been hard at work, impossible by any stretch of the imagination, he could have had neither time nor opportunity to foul the food.

She stopped in front of the officers' quarters with her finger to her lips as though preventing her from uttering unnecessary speech as her mind worked quickly.

By the same yardstick, she thought, nobody else could have adulterated all the canapés, which would have been the only way to ensure the whole congregation fell ill.

'Kitty,' said Mrs Bramble at last, waving away the

concerned gaze of her housemaid. 'I think the testimony of Reverend Dench's chambermaid could get Reverend Weaver released.'

'How so?' said Kitty.

'Because unless everyone in the kitchen was in on it, the only logical explanation is accidental contamination leading to food poisoning.'

'That's great news,' said Kitty. 'Isn't it?' she added when she saw Mrs Bramble's solemn expression.

'Dr Burford is inclined to rule out accidental food poisoning because of the range of symptoms and their rapid onset throughout the congregation. He believes an unnatural substance contaminated the food.'

'What kind of unnatural substance?' said Kitty.

'He couldn't say, or wouldn't commit himself,' said Mrs Bramble. 'Did you manage to discover anything else?'

Kitty nodded. 'I have more but should we talk here, out in the open?'

Mrs Bramble saw Kitty's nervous looks over her shoulder and at passers-by and mentally ran through possible places to have a quiet talk. 'Follow me,' she said, knowing Kitty must have important news for her to be so concerned about eavesdroppers.

Having not yet settled on where to stay, the only place she could think of on the spur of the moment that might afford verifiable privacy was the walkway atop the battlements of the inner wall. Passing between the headquarters and the barracks, they pulled up their skirts and ascended the steps to the Martin Tower at the north-east corner, near where a long-demolished building had once housed the Crown Jewels. Emerging into the open, Mrs Bramble glanced down into the Outer Ward.

Chief Yeoman Warder Treadle strode into view with

Inspector Cole at his side and they hesitated momentarily at the door to one of the casemate apartments before it opened and they entered. This intrigued Mrs Bramble. Whom might they be visiting and why?

With this section of the walkway proving not as empty and private as she'd hoped, she beckoned Kitty to follow and they passed through the next two towers to halt before the Flint Tower. To the north, it overlooked the Outer Ward and further casemates. To the south, the rear of the large Waterloo Barracks obstructed the view. Although overlooked by many windows in the block, this section of wall was deserted and anyone approaching would be seen emerging from the towers at either end. Mrs Bramble stopped and turned to Kitty, raising her eyebrows in question.

Kitty seemed more relaxed but still leant in conspiratorially.

'As soon as I left you in front of the chapel, Mrs B, I decided to have a bit of a wander down there.' Kitty indicated the Outer Ward with a wave. 'I'd not long started my stroll when I met a housemaid who works for one of the officers. All maids talk, as you know, so what she told me wasn't a closely guarded secret among them. She said, Mrs Fry and the wife of one of the other officers had a long-standing feud over an incident that happened between their husbands during their time as students, before they joined the army.'

'Is that so?' said Mrs Bramble, intrigued. 'Did you find out what the feud was about?'

'She was reluctant to say but I assured her no one would know it was her who told me.' Kitty looked around, checking they were still alone. 'Jeremiah Fry, long before he joined the army and met the future Mrs Fry, was friends at Oxford University with Edwin Rushton, now the Fusilier major stationed here, and Rushton's best friend, a man called Hedgecoe. Something occurred between Mr Hedgecoe and Mr Fry and they had a bare-knuckle fight – not a duel with swords or pistols or anything – and it ended in tragedy when one of Fry's punches struck Hedgecoe to the ground and he hit his head, knocking him out cold. He died having never awoken.'

'That's awful,' said Mrs Bramble. 'But I've seen what so-called grown men can do to each other.'

'Captain Fry still maintains it was a fair fight, but Major Rushton has never seen it that way.'

'With such a tragedy in their past, there must have been much animosity between them, even hatred. I wonder by what logic the army decided to post the two men not only to the same regiment but also the same station?'

'Maybe they didn't know?' suggested Kitty.

'Something like that cannot be kept secret,' said Mrs Bramble with a shake of her head. 'Look how short a time it took you to discover it.'

'I think she wanted to tell me more but looked scared when one of the Yeoman Warders strode past. She clammed up afterwards and I hurried back to try to find you, arriving as Reverend Dench entered the chapel. That's when I took the chance of speaking to Esther, his chambermaid.'

They waited as two visitors emerged from the Flint Tower, passed them on the battlements and disappeared without stopping, into the next tower.

'Did you see the two officers or their visiting friends on your perambulation around the Tower?' asked Mrs Bramble.

Kitty shook her head. 'And I didn't think to ask Esther. The officers could be in the officers' quarters, but being married they most likely have accommodation in the building next to it, which provides the married men's quarters.'

'Hmm,' said Mrs Bramble. 'Only a small number of Fusiliers remained after the big relocation and most of the accommodation in the Waterloo Barracks has been converted into offices or storage. In my experience, married quarters aren't as spacious and luxurious as the name might suggest, and I believe their friends are staying in the officers' quarters, probably as a consequence.'

'Does it matter?' said Kitty with a shrug. 'The buildings are next to each other.'

'Probably not,' Mrs Bramble agreed. 'But we have no idea who poisoned the food, if anyone did, nor how or where it took place, so the geography of the Tower might prove important.' She shrugged. 'Or it might not.'

'What do we do now?' said Kitty.

Mrs Bramble was about to respond when she spotted a Fusilier striding behind the barracks in the direction of the chapel. Although the uniform was still unfamiliar, she recognised the insignia of a captain and indicated to Kitty to follow. They hurried through the Flint Tower and took a stairway down to the roof of what she thought must be the crypt behind the chapel. A further flight of stone steps led through an archway and down to the passage between the barracks and chapel where she and Reverend Dench had emerged earlier.

The captain had already crossed half the parade ground by the time Mrs Bramble and Kitty reached the corner of the chapel, where Inspector Cole halted them with an outstretched arm. Mrs Bramble feigned indignation, rather than the frustration she felt, but Cole didn't budge.

'Miss, um,' said Cole, looking at Kitty. 'Leave your mistress and me to speak in private, if you will.'

Kitty gave a little bob curtsey and hurried on to the parade ground.

'It is for me to dismiss my staff, Inspector,' said Mrs Bramble. 'I would not be so presumptuous as to instruct one of your constables.'

'We know that isn't true, now don't we?' said Cole, pressing his lips to a thin line.

'Have you got any further with our investigation?' she said, ignoring the reference to his case at Hampton Court in which she had intervened.

'It is not *our* investigation,' he said, exasperated. 'It is *mine*.'

'And the chief's.'

'What? Yes, mine and the chief's.'

'And mine.'

'And y—' He threw up his hands. 'No!'

'But you know I can be of assistance,' said Mrs Bramble, unwilling to concede so easily. 'I can find out things you cannot.'

'This is not your jurisdiction.'

'Nor is it yours. Yet here you are.'

She saw the familiar tic at the corner of Cole's eye and, knowing the tide was turning, decided to throw him a morsel in the hope of swaying his opinion.

'Did you know the chambermaid to Reverend Dench is a witness to Reverend Weaver's comings and goings before yesterday's service?' she said, almost nonchalantly.

Interest and anger fought for supremacy on Inspector Cole's face.

'That is unimportant,' said Mrs Bramble with a dismissive wave of her hand. 'The fact remains, she can corroborate his account of his movements when he left the reception briefly, and the timing thereof.'

Inspector Cole emitted a low growl. 'You're doing it again, Mrs Bramble, and I can't have it.'

'I'm glad you agree I'm making progress.'

'That's not what I meant.' He retrieved a handkerchief from his pocket and wiped it across his forehead. 'I will have you removed from the fortress if you persist in wheedling your way into my – into *the* investigation and interfering by speaking to potential witnesses.'

'Just the one. The reverend's chambermaid.'

'At least two,' said Cole. 'The chief and I spoke to a housemaid not half an hour ago and she said she'd already been approached by your own housemaid ... um ...'

'Kitty.'

'Yes. Kitty.' He looked serious as he stared into Mrs Bramble's eyes. 'You really shouldn't.'

Not one to be intimidated, Mrs Bramble returned an equally serious stare. 'Reverend Weaver is my friend, and he contacted me, requesting I come to his aid. How could I not answer his call? If this was one of your own, Inspector, I am sure you would do the same.'

Inspector Cole's expression softened, but he shook his head. 'You could prejudice the case.'

Realising she was near to victory, Mrs Bramble lowered her voice almost to a whisper. 'I have already discovered a witness who can help exonerate Reverend Weaver. Understanding the relationships between people who live in close proximity, almost confinement, with each other is my forte. It comes as part of my job, so let me see what I can do to bring you more intelligence.'

Cole rubbed his eyes with forefinger and thumb before reaching into his coat pocket and extracting a packet of cigarettes. 'This is not Hampton Court Palace, Mrs Bramble. You are out of your pond.'

'As are you, Inspector.' She ignored his sideways glance. 'I suspect you are here under sufferance, and under close scrutiny. I am a mere housekeeper with her housemaid in attendance, bringing comfort to a friend in need. No one is watching us, except you.'

As she watched the conflict playing out across his features, she could see he knew she was right, but his rising reputation was important to him. Despite the chief's cooperation, Inspector Cole was on his own in someone else's world and anything he did, or allowed someone else to do, would be investigated, analysed and judged.

His silence said it all.

Mrs Bramble caught distant sight of a red and dark blue uniform approaching from the direction of the Bloody Tower and recognised the gait of Chief Yeoman Warder Treadle. Although not intimidated – she had got off to a good start with him – she had no desire to afford the two men the opportunity of egging each other on.

'Here comes the chief, no doubt looking for you,' said Mrs Bramble. 'I'd better make myself scarce.'

Inspector Cole put a cigarette between his lips, scraped a match into life, drew smoke into his lungs and blew a cloud of white smoke into the air.

'Don't worry,' she said as she turned towards the married quarters, the direction in which Kitty had disappeared. 'I won't tell a soul.'

9

Mrs Bramble hoped she would find Kitty by the married men's quarters but only a few Yeoman Warders stood nearby, watching and marshalling the visitors who had come to see the historic fortress. She knew entry to the buildings housing the military quarters would be barred to her and Kitty but she had hoped to cross paths with those she wished to interview. The Tower was proving much harder to navigate, access-wise and socially, than Hampton Court Palace and Mrs Bramble knew time was ticking away. It would not be long before Inspector Cole and the chief decided enough was enough and Reverend Weaver would be charged and carted away to Newgate Prison.

Through his silence at the end of their conversation, Cole had given his tacit agreement for her to continue her investigation. Although pleased, she knew any mistake, however small, could be costly not only to Reverend Weaver's freedom, and life, but also her reputation and perhaps even her own freedom.

Movement to her right drew her attention to the unmistakable outline of the doctor lumbering uphill from the direction of the Yeoman Warders' Club.

'Dr Burford,' she called as he approached. 'Any news?'

Dr Burford stopped, short of breath, and touched the brim of his top hat. 'After plenty to drink, many of the unfortunates are recovering well and starting to nibble on a little ham, cheese and bread. A few of the weaker ones are accepting beef broth, so everyone's on the mend.'

'That's not what I meant but thank you for the report.' She cocked her head as a thought struck her. 'Were any of the other victims close to death at any time?'

'I think not.' Dr Burford shook his head. 'Everyone was affected to a greater or lesser degree – I myself felt unwell – but the men seem to have fared better than the women. Only to be expected, I suppose. Weaker sex and so on.'

Mrs Bramble frowned at him and he shrank from her.

'I think you'll find many of us are quite resilient, Doctor.'

'I-I-I didn't mean ...' Dr Burford's voice tailed off under her withering stare.

'Back to my original question,' she said. 'Have you any response from your colleagues in Guy's Hospital?'

'Ah, I misunderstood,' he said. 'I do apologise, Mrs Bramble, but I'm afraid there's no news at present. Bit too early to expect any, actually, but news could come at any time.'

'Of course,' she said. 'And how is Captain Fry bearing up?'

'He's as fit as a fiddle but hasn't eaten anything since yesterday. Nothing to do with the canapés, you understand? It's the grief at having his wife pass away in his arms.'

Mrs Bramble thought she understood the captain's pain, having witnessed more than her fair share of such tragedies while abroad. 'I don't suppose he has anyone to support him in his time of need?'

Dr Burford scoffed. 'He has his friend, but the army isn't renowned for its compassion. Death is its stock in trade, after all.'

Mrs Bramble knew that to be the truth from experience. When her husband had become ill with cholera while serving in Bengal, it was the doctors and nurses who had tried to keep him alive. The 'top brass' had turned their backs, more concerned with holding the line, the preservation of Britain's Empire and worldwide reputation, and the urgent call-up of reserves to fill the gaps left by the sick, wounded and dying.

'I would like to offer him my condolences,' said Mrs Bramble, knowing how indelicate her next question would seem. 'Have you just come from seeing him? I must speak to Major and Mrs Rushton as well.'

Dr Burford gave her a look that said *tread carefully*. 'I don't recall seeing the Rushtons in the last hour but I examined Captain Fry not twenty minutes ago, in there.' He nodded in the direction of the married men's quarters. 'He hurried me along, stating he had to go to the White Tower. The captain didn't venture an explanation but I can't imagine he is sightseeing, so I assume he's visiting the chapel to pray. St Peter's has been eschewed by churchgoers since yesterday, understandably. The inspector said he wanted to discourage worshippers, for a while anyway, so Reverend Dench said he will resume services from St John's.'

'Have you ever witnessed a certain chill in the relationship between the two officers?' said Mrs Bramble.

'What kind of chill?' said Burford, with a narrowing of his eyes.

'Any kind. I've been led to believe there may have been something in their past that causes some friction to this day.'

'Ah, you heard, did you? I don't know the details, but it was something at university. They get along now, professionally of course, because one is in command and the other is his deputy. Never seen them socialise in all my days here, although that may have more to do with their wives than the men themselves.'

Mrs Bramble's ears pricked up again. 'What do you mean, Doctor?'

'Ah.' A pained expression crossed Dr Burford's face as though he'd spoken out of turn. 'I'm not one for rumour and conjecture, I've always found no good can come from it, and I would only be repeating hearsay. I suggest you speak to Mrs Rushton herself. If she wishes to impart any information, that's up to her.' He dipped his head and touched the brim of his top hat. 'If you'll excuse me, Mrs Bramble.'

'Doctor,' she replied, and watched him lope towards the Waterloo Barracks.

The array of arms and armour on display inside the White Tower was designed to dazzle visitors and fill their minds with awe while leading them at a canter through the history of the nation. None of this was of any concern to Mrs Bramble, whose thoughts held a clock ticking towards the time when any influence she might have over the fate of Reverend Weaver would be lost.

She made her way through the slowly moving throng, climbed the stairs to the first floor and entered the medieval Chapel of St John the Evangelist through an archway. The white stone from which it had been constructed seemed to glow in the light from its windows. A gold cross and two candlesticks stood atop the stone altar in the apse at the eastern end, emphasising the plain simplicity of the interior when compared to the memorials adorning the Chapel of St Peter ad Vincula. A single span of rope enabled visitors to gawp but prevented them from encroaching too far.

Being the only worshipper to have breached the rope barrier, Captain Fry was easy to identify. Sitting in the front row of pews, his head remained bowed, no doubt in thought and prayer. Mrs Bramble felt a pressing need to join him and present her questions, but being compassionate and understanding about the loss a loved one could engender, she could not bring herself to be insensitive. In any case, she knew such an approach would get her nowhere.

Captain Fry must have been there for some time and had conveyed to the Almighty all he needed to because, head suddenly raised, he stood straight up, wheeled to his right and made to leave through the stone passageway at the rear of the chapel. Mrs Bramble did not intercept. Instead, she followed him at a discreet distance, descending through the levels of the White Tower until they emerged through the rear door, by the parade ground in front of the Waterloo Barracks. The captain stood looking up at the clear sky as though willing Godspeed to whatever thoughts and prayers he had offered in the chapel.

Mrs Bramble moved to his side and cleared her throat to alert him to her presence. Being considerably taller, he looked down at her, his expression confused as though a child had unexpectedly joined him on the battlefield.

'Can I help you?' he said. 'Are you lost?'

'I fear it is you who are lost,' said Mrs Bramble. 'My condolences about your wife.' The captain's expression morphed into a mixture of grief and anger. 'I should explain. My name is Mrs Lydia Bramble and I am assisting Detective Inspector Cole and Chief Yeoman Warder Treadle in the investigation of the tragic events of yesterday.'

'You have him, do you not?' snapped the captain. 'The murderer?'

'I'm afraid there is no evidence as yet to suggest it is murder, and a witness has corroborated Reverend Weaver's account of his movements before the service began.'

Captain Fry frowned. 'What are you saying? The murderer is still abroad?'

'It may yet prove to be a tragic accident but that is what I hope I can help establish. If indeed there is a murderer, we would wish the correct man arrested, would we not?' Mrs Bramble could see the conflict on his face but a man who attended church and prayed to God had to agree with her. 'I know the inspector and chief will have spoken to you but I would like to know whether you knew of anyone who would want to poison the whole congregation?'

'Don't be ridiculous,' he said. 'How should I know? It is an abomination beyond belief.'

She nodded her agreement. 'Is there anyone with whom you or your wife have been in dispute recently?'

He raised his chin to stretch his neck before looking back down at her. 'I suppose you must know about the situation existing between Major Rushton and myself.'

'I do.'

'Then you will know we have been completely professional since fate saw fit to bring us together in the same regiment and be given the same posting.'

'I know you were friends once, but you caused the accidental death of a mutual friend. Must be as difficult for you now as it was in university.'

'The death was ruled accidental, although I blame myself, of course.' Fry looked pained for a moment but his mask and stiff upper lip reset. 'Major Rushton did not consider the death an accident and we have never spoken as friends again. We seek not to be in each other's presence unnecessarily these days, preferring the company of others or to keep our own council.'

'Regrettable,' said Mrs Bramble. 'I suppose your wives stayed apart also?'

'Indeed.' Fry deliberately looked over her head, avoiding eye contact. 'No love was lost between them. Catherine supported me and Mrs Rushton was on the side of her husband.'

'Understandable under the circumstances.'

'I'm sorry, Mrs Bramble, but I have work to do and must get on.' He gave her a curt bow. 'If you'll excuse me?'

'Of course.'

She watched him stride towards the officers' quarters and take the steps two at a time until he disappeared through the front door.

The police might consider the lengthy dispute a suitable motive for murder but something bothered Mrs Bramble.

Every woman knew the widely held belief that men did not hit women to be no more than national delusion, touted mainly by men. Even so, a man could not behave in such a way and guarantee to keep his reputation. Above and beyond, a man could not expect to retain his liberty, no matter who he was or what the provocation may have been, had he taken a life.

Maybe Major Rushton wanted to take something from Captain Fry that he considered dear to him in the same way Fry had taken the life of his close friend. But why wait until now? Each officer must have had ample opportunity to get rid of the other surreptitiously in the heat, smoke and confusion of battle, but that was not the way of a true gentlemen and patriot.

In her experience, so-called gentlemen did not wait years for satisfaction. Reputation was everything, and although duelling became illegal seventy years ago, they still preferred to confront an issue head-on soon after it arose. There were exceptions that proved the rule, of course, but many who regarded themselves as gentlemen did not tend to sneak around in the shadows.

Would Major Rushton, who considered himself a gentleman, really have murdered Mrs Fry in such a public fashion but by such an underhand method? Could he have done so without revealing his identity, forgoing open satisfaction at the moment of revenge?

She pondered this for a moment and resolved to talk again with Reverend Weaver.

At present, Major Rushton could not be discounted as the murderer.

10

'I have no idea,' said Reverend Weaver in answer to a question from Mrs Bramble. 'I wasn't paying attention to anyone other than myself when I left the reception to go to the chapel.'

Mrs Bramble sat opposite Weaver in the room in which the chief still held him captive. The corporal on guard had recognised her from before and had instructions to allow her escorted access. She supposed she had Inspector Cole to thank.

'Reverend Dench's chambermaid saw you leave this building alone,' she said. 'She noticed no one else between then and the moment she saw you return and re-enter. Before I came to see you, I made a note of the time it took me to arrive at the front door from the chapel's main entrance. I walk as fast as you and it took a minute and a half. She reported you were in the chapel for perhaps five minutes. That means eight minutes in total, which is no time at all. She can't have been staring out the window all day so I'm sure that means someone present in the officers' mess during the reception, someone who perhaps was not in the company of others, left without being noticed.'

'Or they excused themselves from their conversation before popping out to do the deadly deed?' he suggested.

Mrs Bramble made a face suggesting improbability. 'Both methods are plausible for engineering an exit but what happened next? Are we to believe a guest at the reception waltzed past the stewards into the kitchens where, in front of all the cooks, they poisoned tray after tray of canapés?' She shook her head. 'It is as implausible for anyone else as it is for you.'

'It has to be one of the cooks,' said Reverend Weaver. 'What other explanation can there be? It must have been a simple accident,' he mused. 'A failure of hygiene. Someone forgot cleanliness is next to Godliness.' He seemed to perk up at the suggestion there may have been no murder and therefore no murderer stood to be apprehended.

Mrs Bramble felt it her duty to temper her friend's expectations, but at that moment they heard voices outside and the door opened without ceremony. Inspector Cole and Chief Yeoman Warder Treadle entered the room, the former looking a little sheepish and the latter tight-lipped. Reverend Weaver jumped to his feet, clasping his hands nervously.

'Inspector,' said Mrs Bramble, also standing to meet the delegation. 'To what do we owe the abruptness of this intrusion?'

Inspector Cole glanced at the chief and cleared his throat. 'I have checked the report stating a witness could corroborate Reverend Weaver's account of his absence from the reception held in the officers' mess.'

'You've spoken to Esther, Reverend Dench's maid?' said Mrs Bramble.

Cole ignored the question and looked at Weaver. 'It seems there is reasonable doubt to suppose you had the time—'

'And opportunity—' said the chief.

'I know,' said Cole, glaring at the chief. '*And* opportunity to adulterate the food,'

'As I said, yes?' Weaver blurted excitedly. 'As I said.'

'I have discussed the options with the chief and we have agreed to release you from this room with one proviso.'

'Anything, anything,' said Weaver.

'Released from room, yes,' said the chief, looking decidedly unhappy. 'From Tower of London, no. Woman dead. Deliberate or accident? No explanation. Have to get to the bottom of it. Investigation continues. Lots to do. Must get on.' He turned on his heels and the echoey sound of two sets of heavy footsteps receded along the corridor as the corporal followed him.

Inspector Cole barred the way to the open door and fixed Mrs Bramble with what she suspected he considered an intimidating stare. A smile played on her lips but she managed to stop it from becoming a smirk. She wished to continue her own investigation and that would prove impossible if she antagonised him.

'I seem to have made a habit out of telling you to mind your own business, Mrs Br—'

'Did you know that Captain Fry and Major Rushton have reason to dislike each other?' she interrupted. 'Hate, even?'

'Of course, a university incident.' Inspector Cole looked at her suspiciously. 'Wait, what? How did you kn—?'

'More than an incident, Inspector. Major Rushton's best friend died as a result of a punch from Captain Fry.'

'It was dealt with a long time ago. These are officers and gentlemen we're talking about.'

'Exactly,' said Mrs Bramble. 'The kind of people you have never looked up to, and whose word you usually take with a pinch of salt.'

The corner of Cole's mouth twitched. 'Meaning?'

'They've rubbed along through necessity up until now, having found themselves both posted here. Suppose something happened to fan the embers of animosity they felt towards each other all those years ago. Might that cause flames?'

'Very poetic, Mrs Bramble, but both officers were present at the reception the whole time. In fact, Reverend Weaver was the only person we know to have left the reception, and look how that's turned out.'

'Yes, you're back to square one.' Mrs Bramble could see the muscles of Inspector Cole's jaw tightening and relaxing. 'But I'm sure you'll have a breakthrough eventually.'

'Please do not patronise me, Mrs Bramble,' said Cole. 'It is my job to get a breakthrough, as you call it. To that end, the chief and I have spoken to those present in the chapel and at the reception, including the stewards and the cooks. We will speak to everyone again if need be but if I find you have been withholding evidence ...'

His meaning was clear but Mrs Bramble felt no threat. As long as she passed on all she knew, at the right time, the Inspector would have no leg to stand on if he tried to have her arrested for obstructing an investigation.

'I do beg your pardon,' said Reverend Weaver in a timid voice from over the shoulder of Mrs Bramble. 'Can I go now? My things are in the guest room of the chaplain's house and I'd dearly like to shave and change into some fresh clothes.'

'Of course, Reverend,' said the inspector. He glanced at Mrs Bramble. 'Please take heed of my warning. This may not be my jurisdiction, as people seem to enjoy pointing out, but the governor has put the chief and me in charge of this investigation, and investigate to the extreme of our limits we will do.'

11

Mrs Bramble escorted Reverend Weaver to the chaplain's house, where the housemaid let him in. Weaver retreated upstairs immediately, tripping up every other step as he went.

'I believe it was you who spoke to my housemaid, Kitty, earlier?' said Mrs Bramble.

'Yes, ma'am,' said the maid.

'I am not a ma'am. You may call me Mrs Bramble.'

'Yes, ma— Mrs Bramble.'

'Is Reverend Dench at home? May I speak with him?'

'He's in his garden, Mrs Bramble,' said the maid.

Mrs Bramble raised her eyebrows in surprise. She hadn't expected there to be a private garden in the Tower, at least not beyond the odd pot or two placed outside the casemate apartments down in the Outer Ward. She moved back on the flagstones as the housemaid stepped forward and pointed to a flight of steps further along the passage between the house and the western end of the chapel. They led up to an iron gate set in a stone arch but with no suggestion of foliage or flowers.

'He likes to go there for peace and quiet reflection,' said the housemaid. 'But he's with Dr Burford at present.'

Mrs Bramble thanked the young woman and walked to the base of the steps, passing the chapel door she had entered through before, and an open-doored but gated entrance to what appeared to be another part of the chapel. At the top of the steps, the gate swung on its hinges, only squeaking a warning once it reached its limit.

Two heads turned at once.

Laid out before her was a lead-covered flat roof around which had been set flowerpots and earthenware planters of all sizes. Each contained either shrubs of green foliage, bushes or plants displaying vibrant flowers, or stiff-stemmed standard roses. Steps up to the battlements on her left led her eye to a tower dominating the north-western corner of the inner wall, where doors afforded access for the current occupant, whoever that might be. A wooden bench on either side of the roof allowed one to sit and enjoy the sunshine and the flowers, although these stood unoccupied.

Reverend Dench and Dr Burford were on the far side of the garden, near a railing preventing visitors descending on their tour of the walls from encroaching on the private space. A few visitors ambled down at that moment but they were more interested in the view than anything a clergyman and his guests might be up to. Dench held a small can in his hand, of the type with a small nozzle and a hand pump to provide the necessary air pressure to power a spray. He had been directing it over a rose bush, no doubt to keep aphids at bay. Burford stood a pace or two away to prevent inhalation of the insecticide.

'Mrs Bramble, do join us,' said Reverend Dench. 'Any news?'

Dr Burford took another step away and knocked into a standard rose, dislodging his hat and almost tumbling backwards over the railing. Dench made a grab, but only succeeded in grasping the rosebush, yelping in pain and leaving the flailing doctor to his fate. Burford managed to grip the railing, employing bizarre contortions and the raising of his left leg as a counterweight, before he righted himself and assumed a pose suggesting nothing unusual had happened here, and if you thought it had then it was all an illusion.

The calamity amused Mrs Bramble but the smile she hid faded as she picked up the spray can the clergyman had dropped and held it out for him to reclaim. His hand displayed pinpricks of blood and a scratch caused by the rose thorns. 'You're hurt,' she said.

'I appear to have hurt myself.' Reverend Dench chuckled. 'A hazard of gardening, I'm afraid. I should have worn my new gloves.'

Dr Burford, brushing dust from his retrieved topper, leant in for a look. 'Nothing serious,' he declared. 'I've had worse paper cuts. Better give it a rinse under the tap, though, to wash out any dirt and insect spray.'

'In answer to your earlier query, Reverend,' said Mrs Bramble, wishing to get back on track, 'there is no news, not unless the test results have come back from Guy's Hospital?' She raised a questioning eyebrow at Dr Burford.

'I'm hoping for word quite soon but ...' The doctor shrugged. 'These things take time.'

'Time I'm not sure Reverend Weaver has,' she said.

'Are Inspector Cole and the chief still adamant?' said Reverend Dench.

Mrs Bramble chose to withhold news of her friend's conditional release for the moment. 'I understand the sacramental wine cupboard is kept locked but you gave Reverend Weaver a key?'

'I gave him the key to the wine cupboard,' Dench confirmed, placing the spray can on floor. 'It's a precious commodity for any church or chapel and I try to remember to keep it locked to hide temptation from the weak-willed, but it was to be Thomas's day and I wanted him to be in charge of everything. Everything I normally do, I mean.' I only have the one key, inherited from my predecessor. Which reminds me, I must have a spare made.'

'What about keys to the chapel as a whole?'

'I keep all the other keys in my study in the house but have no need of them. None of the gates or doors are ever locked.'

Mrs Bramble thought that odd. Even the Chapel Royal at Hampton Court was locked between the end of the last service of the evening and the first of the following morning.

'Are you not concerned about theft?' she said.

'This is a house of God inside a well-guarded fortification and there are sentries and guides during visiting hours, but we have no treasures to speak of,' said Dench. 'At any rate, none that could be smuggled away easily. The only thing someone might consider easy pickings would be the wine but they'd drink that. Also, the Lord's flock must have access to him at all times, and the crypt contains both Protestant and Catholic remains and memorials to which people must also have access to allow for the paying of their respects.'

An admirable policy, she thought. *But one open to abuse by the ungodly*. She wasn't sure where her mind was taking her with this train of thought, but the chapel appeared to be the only building neither constantly occupied nor guarded. Whether the fact would prove significant remained to be seen.

'How many ways in and out of the chapel are there?' she asked.

'There are several,' said Reverend Dench. He counted them on his fingers. 'The main entrance. One external gate to the crypt and one internal door from inside the chapel. A door to the bell tower. The vestry has three doors: one into the chapel, one out to the passage between the chapel and the Waterloo Barracks, and one giving access to an internal passage leading to the crypt.'

Mrs Bramble considered this a lot of doors to leave unlocked in any building but that was almost immaterial. Apart from providing a hiding place for someone awaiting their moment to sneak in elsewhere, and a sanctuary for them to escape to afterwards, none of it explained how the food could have been accessed and tampered with.

'Hello-oo,' called a sing-song voice from the archway as the freshly shaven face of Reverend Weaver appeared.

His arrival took Mrs Bramble by surprise. She had expected a decent period to speak to Reverend Dench alone, a condition already skewed by Dr Burford's presence.

'Thomas!' said Reverend Dench. 'You are free.'

'Alas, no—' said Reverend Weaver, as he tripped up the top step and stumbled forward to make his legs catch up with his body. He composed himself and approached. 'As I was saying. The inspector and the chief saw fit to release me under my own recognizance.'

'Can they do that?' said Dr Burford, with a frown.

'It appears so,' said Mrs Bramble. 'Although the decision should be taken by a court of law, it seems Inspector Cole and the chief have allowed Reverend Weaver the freedom to roam within these walls, but not to leave while the investigation progresses. If he absconds, it will be tantamount to an admission of guilt.'

'Exactly right,' said Weaver, his grin fading when the full realisation of his situation hit home. He looked at Mrs Bramble with pleading Labrador-puppy eyes. 'What do we do now?'

Mrs Bramble thought fast. 'I think we should allow

Reverend Dench to tend to his wounds, don't you? As an Anglican chaplain, having anything akin to Catholic stigmata on his hands could prove embarrassing.'

'Stigmata on my hands,' said Dench. 'Good Lord, I didn't think of that. Do excuse me.'

He grabbed the spray can before striding over to the archway and disappearing through the iron gate and down the steps, watched all the way by Mrs Bramble before she turned to Reverend Weaver.

'Feeling refreshed?' she asked.

'Much better,' said Weaver. 'What have I missed?'

'Doesn't matter. What's important is trying to find strong evidence to either exonerate you completely or prove someone else responsible.'

'Easier said than done,' he said, looking downcast.

Mrs Bramble had concerns about her friend's ability to cope with what was happening to him. Yes, his happily limited grasp of anything outside his own experiences meant a lack of full comprehension kept him jolly, but nothing focused the mind and brought one crashing down like being accused of murder. Under the circumstances, his mood swings were both typical and understandable, if unhelpful.

'I shouldn't worry, old chap,' said Dr Burford. 'The truth will out.'

The truth according to whom? thought Mrs Bramble. 'Did anyone complain about nausea and stomach cramps before the reception?' she said to the doctor.

Dr Burford's mouth turned down. 'Not at all. Apart from the usual management of specific conditions – gout and the like – I've had one sprained wrist and a fishbone stuck in a throat to contend with. The Tower inhabitants aren't always such a healthy bunch but it is not yet autumn. Once winter comes ...' He raised his eyebrows to indicate the wave of cold-weather ailments to come.

'I think we should vacate Reverend Dench's private garden,' said Reverend Weaver. 'Doesn't seem right us being here when he isn't present.' He swept his arm around to illustrate, knocking Dr Burford's top hat to the ground and sending it rolling towards the edge.

Weaver and Burford gave chase, each one tripping up the other and threatening to send the both of them sailing over the railing.

Weaver caught his shoe on the hem of his cassock and clung to Burford's frock coat, preventing the latter from reaching his topper.

Mrs Bramble strode forward and picked up the spinning hat, shaking her head in disbelief as the two men clawed at each other like two drunkards engaged in a street brawl outside an alehouse. 'When you have finished, gentlemen,' she said.

Dr Burford sheepishly accepted the offer of his hat from Mrs Bramble as Reverend Weaver smoothed back his hair and walked unsteadily to the archway. Upon descending to ground level without further incident, Dr Burford drew ahead.

'Extraordinary,' Weaver whispered. 'I have no idea how Dr Burford charts his way through life. Never have I seen such a clumsy fellow.' Mrs Bramble raised her eyebrows. 'What?' he said.

'Doctor,' Mrs Bramble called to get his attention. 'Before you go, are you not yet willing to reveal your suspicions as to the possible cause? If I knew what we were dealing with ...'

'I'm sorry, Mrs Bramble. I cannot speculate.' Dr Burford shook his head. 'It's more than my job's worth, as they say.'

He turned away but paused and looked back again. 'I can offer you tea in the Fusiliers' headquarters, though? I'm just off there myself. And if you need a place to stay tonight, I have room enough for yourself and your housemaid.'

Mrs Bramble inclined her head in thanks. 'I will forgo the tea, Doctor, but I'm sure Reverend Weaver would love some.' Weaver looked startled as her elbow nudged him forward. 'And I will let you know my decision about the latter.'

He nodded and touched the rim of his hat. 'Then I bid you good day.'

Reverend Weaver went to follow the doctor but hesitated when he saw Mrs Bramble looking at the goosebumps on the backs of her hands.

'Can't you feel it?' she said.

'Feel what, Mrs Bramble?' said the reverend.

She gazed at the receding form of Dr Burford.

'Murder in the air.'

12

Reverend Weaver caught up with Dr Burford and threw a nervous look over his shoulder at Mrs Bramble, who gave him an encouraging smile and a little wave of her fingers. He knew she wanted him to learn as much as he could from the doctor but he had never considered the ability to wheedle information from people to be among his sparse talents.

He turned back and bumped elbows with Dr Burford, sending both men weaving, stumbling and tripping over each other's feet, apologising to everyone they forced from their path like a bow wave.

Arriving at the steps, flustered but trying not to show it, Reverend Weaver fell up them almost in surprise that they were there at all. Dr Burford held out a supporting hand but seemed to forget he also needed steadying, and both men ended up sitting on the top step as though that had been their intention all along. The guard on the door of the Fusiliers' headquarters screwed up his face as though in pain and emitted a squeak through a cough.

Dr Burford and Reverend Weaver stood up and casually brushed dust from their trousers, glancing around as though contemplating the merits of going in versus going elsewhere. At last, Dr Burford stepped over to the door and spoke at length to the guard, whose red face suggested he might explode at any moment. Burford then turned, walked into the doorframe, and apologised to both the door and frame. Rubbing his nose, he ushered Reverend Weaver into the building. Behind them, the guard burst into a bout of uncontrollable laughter, which receded as first one set of doors closed and then another.

A white-coated steward appeared at their side as if conjured from thin air. 'Would you like tea, sir?' he said, eyeing Weaver.

'For two, if you will,' said Dr Burford. 'In the smoking room. And bring some of those delicious Shrewsbury biscuits, would you?'

'Yes, sir.' The steward shot Weaver a final glance before disappearing as mysteriously as he had arrived.

Dr Burford turned right at the corridor, bypassed the library and turned into the unoccupied smoking room at the far end.

'Should I be in here?' said Reverend Weaver, keeping his head bowed as though trying to make himself less visible.

'Of course,' said Burford. 'You are my guest. Please sit.'

Weaver selected a chair. 'Should *you* be in here?'

'I am considered an associate and too invaluable for them to refuse me. I tend to the medical requirements of everyone who lives in the Tower, including the governor, the Fusiliers and Yeoman Warders. I treat the sick and patch up the wounded. I dispense pills, potions and good medical advice to one and all. Not only am I frequently invited to dine here, I am also welcome in the Yeoman Warders' Club, unofficial as it may be, and not many outsiders can make such a claim.' Burford crossed one leg over the other for emphasis and succeeded in kicking the table over.

'Sounds not unlike myself at Hampton Court, actually,' said Reverend Weaver, helping to right and reposition the table. 'Although my realm is spiritual rather than temporal.'

'I must say – talking of your good self – you looked a little flustered out there,' said Dr Burford with a look of concern.

'Did I?' Weaver tried for nonchalance but only succeeded in sounding haunted. 'Oh, yes. I suppose I must have.'

'The inspector and chief still suspicious of you, even though you are free to roam within the Tower's walls?'

Reverend Weaver shrugged. 'It seems so, but it's not so much that. Mrs Bramble is desperate for news of the test results, as am I.'

'Ah.'

'Vital to her investigation, do you see?'

Dr Burford frowned. 'Mrs Bramble's investigation?'

'Not so much hers, more the inspector's,' said Weaver. 'And the chief's. But she is helping them.'

'From what I have seen of her, she is a formidable woman.'

Weaver smiled. 'As you might have already gathered, she tends to do things her way.'

'And this has ruffled feathers?'

'Only Inspector Cole's. And the chief's, to a lesser degree.'

Dr Burford chuckled. 'It seems to me the inspector is not only one of those people for whom that is an occupational hazard, but also one who permanently expects his feathers to be ruffled at any moment.'

The steward returned to deliver a pot of tea and plate of Shrewsbury biscuits. A buff envelope also lay on the small tray.

Burford raised his eyebrows at him.

'Darjeeling, Doctor. Your favourite. Shall I pour?'

'That won't be necessary, Thank you.'

The steward gave a polite bow. 'The letter arrived just after you, Doctor.' He withdrew, shutting the door as he left.

'Is that, um, word from your friends over the river?' Reverend Weaver hoped to feign disinterest but his darting gaze betrayed him, making him look like an anxious sparrow. 'At Guy's Hospital?'

Dr Burford leant forward to retrieve the envelope and glanced at the printed symbol on the front. 'As a matter of fact...' He extracted the contents and unfolded two sheets of paper.

Although Dr Burford's guest, Reverend Weaver elected to attend to the tea, for no other reason than to aid the containment of his enthusiasm and curiosity. He lifted the teapot lid, gave the contents a stir, held the silver strainer over Burford's cup to catch stray tea leaves, and poured a stream of golden liquid. Keeping an eye on the doctor's face, he then held the strainer over his own cup and mouthed a silent oath as steaming Darjeeling overshot into his saucer.

Crossing himself and apologising to the Lord, Reverend Weaver added the merest splash of milk to his own cup. Not knowing how the doctor took his tea, he left the second cup unadulterated, selected a biscuit and held it like a conductor's baton. 'And the results are...?'

'In-ter-est-ing,' said Dr Burford, thoughtfully.

'Interesting?' Reverend Weaver couldn't help but sit forward, intrigued. 'In so far as...?'

'The samples I took from the platters of canapés proved clear of any nasty substances.'

'Oh.'

'Oh, indeed,' said Burford. 'What is more intriguing are the results from Mrs Fry. It appears her body contained a large dose of nicotine. A fatal dose.'

Weaver almost crushed his biscuit. 'She died from nicotine?'

'Nicotine poisoning,' said Burford. 'Yes.'

This was important news and Reverend Weaver glanced at the door to ensure their continued privacy. Mrs Bramble would want more, so he waited for Burford to take greater care in the pouring of milk into his cup. 'Was she a heavy smoker?'

'She did not smoke at all,' said Dr Burford, plopping a sugar lump into his tea with silver tongs and tutting when tea splashed onto the tablecloth.

Weaver waved to decline the offer of sugar. 'Not even secretly, unbeknown to her husband?'

Dr Burford shook his head. 'We are sitting in the Fusiliers' smoking room, which no one could doubt from the smell lingering in the air as we entered. I never noticed cigarette smoke on Mrs Fry but sometimes detected the smell of cigar smoke, which was to be expected, given her husband smoked cheroots.'

'In which case ...' Reverend Weaver thought for a moment. 'How do you suppose Mrs Fry came to have taken such a large dose?'

'It's not something you take like normal medication,' said Burford. 'Some vegetables contain nicotine but you would have to eat a very large amount every day for it to have any effect at all. No, it arrives in the body through the consumption of cigarettes, cigars, pipe tobacco, snuff and chewing tobacco.'

Weaver considered this. Mrs Fry had not seemed the type to chew tobacco, although he admitted he had no real idea of the type of person who would, and if she did not smoke ... 'Could Mrs Fry have used snuff?'

Dr Burford shook his head incredulously 'My dear Reverend, you would have to smoke, sniff and chew an inordinate amount of tobacco. Even then, your body would get used to it over time and develop a certain amount of resistance.'

Burford sighed as the sodden half of his biscuit collapsed en route to his mouth and fell into his cup with a plop, spraying Darjeeling over the tablecloth and his trousers. He used his teaspoon to rescue the biscuit, which now resembled brown porridge, and carried on as though this was a natural and frequent occurrence, which Reverend Weaver suspected to be most likely.

'Then I am loath to say it but there can be only one solution,' said Weaver. 'Someone administered the nicotine to Mrs Fry.'

'Indeed,' Dr Burford agreed, selecting another biscuit. He held it poised over his cup to dip again but hesitated. 'But it also affected everyone present at the service that you led.'

Except Inspector Cole, Jasper Chant ... and me, thought Weaver.

Burford elected to eat this second biscuit dry and wash it down with a slurp of tea before continuing. 'As I too felt unwell, I took the precaution of sending a sample of my own blood for analysis.'

Weaver's ears pricked up. 'That was brave of you.'

'Hardly. A physician cannot afford to be afraid of needles these days. Anyway, my colleagues did detect nicotine in my blood but in a smaller concentration.'

'I don't understand.' Weaver's brow furrowed in concentration as his mind struggled to find possibilities. 'If everyone took the poison, how did Mrs Fry receive more than the others? There were some who were violently sick while others looked barely queasy. Did other victims have a larger dose but survive? How did everyone take it if there was none present in the canapés?'

'All valid questions to which I'm afraid I have no answers,' said Dr Burford, taking another biscuit and risking a dunk. 'Nicotine can affect people in different ways. As I say, some smokers may have built up limited tolerance. But as to how the poison was administered, your guess is as good as mine.'

Reverend Weaver stood up to leave, feeling the sudden urgent need to convey these latest revelations to Mrs Bramble.

'I'm sorry to have taken up your time, Doctor,' he said. 'I'm sure you have to speak to Inspector Cole and the chief, so I'll let you get on. Don't worry about Mrs Bramble. I'll let her know right away.'

Weaver made it as far as opening the door before he returned to the table, drained his cup and grabbed three biscuits from the plate as the astonished Burford was left to rue another lost half-biscuit as it fell into his lap with a wet flop.

13

'Mrs Bramble,' came a call, and she looked across to see Kitty hurrying towards her.

'Calm yourself,' said Mrs Bramble to her out-of-breath housemaid. 'What is it?'

'I managed to have a word with a couple of the Yeoman Warders and soldiers from the barracks,' said Kitty between deep breaths. 'The Warders don't like to air their views as much as the rank-and-file Fusiliers but everyone seems to be of the same opinion. There was no love lost between the wives of Major Rushton and Captain Fry.'

'Did anyone say how such dislike manifested itself?' said Mrs Bramble.

'Indeed, they did,' said Kitty, with a firm nod. 'Mrs Rushton bad-mouthed Mrs Fry at various events in an attempt to sully her reputation. Mrs Fry retaliated by conducting a campaign to have Mrs Rushton ostracised. I also managed to track down Mrs Fry's housemaid, Beth. She seemed nervous and wouldn't speak for long, but she did confirm the feud. In fact, it was the wives who seemed unable to let sleeping dogs lie.'

'Doesn't mean they wanted to murder each other,' said Mrs Bramble. 'And there's always the question of opportunity.'

'There's more, Mrs B,' said Kitty. 'It appears someone called Sir Stephen Lovell was a recurring visitor to the

Frys' home, and Sir Oswald Clyne frequented that of the Rushtons. They were both guests at the reception and the service, and ...' Kitty checked for anyone close enough to overhear. 'It is rumoured the animosity between the families rubbed off on their two friends.'

'In what way?' said Mrs Bramble.

'No one would say,' said Kitty. 'Or they didn't know. I suspect the latter because no one outside the two families had anything firm to tell me.'

Mrs Bramble frowned. If the effects of the fight at university had echoed down through the years, there was no telling how many people might be involved. She had seen petty squabbles lead to serious injuries during her career as an army nurse, even in one of the big houses where she had held employment as a rising housekeeper. Any dispute could spiral out of control but simmering feuds had the potential to be insidious, leading to deadly results months or years later.

'What're you thinking about, Mrs B?' asked Kitty.

'I'm thinking I need to speak to those two *sirs* urgently, before anyone else gets carted off to Guy's on a three-wheeled litter.' She looked towards the chaplain's house. 'In the meantime, I thank you for your intelligence-gathering but I'm afraid I must assign you a task that is somewhat mundane.'

Mrs Bramble dispatched Kitty to collect their bags from the official outside the main gate whose feathers they had ruffled earlier. She had anticipated the need to stay overnight because an arrest on suspicion of murder was not an easy circumstance to counteract. The issue of where she and Kitty might stay had not bothered her in the slightest. Something always turned up, and no doubt there were lodgings nearby they could have taken advantage of at a pinch. Although grateful for Dr Burford's offer of accommodation, she suspected his tall, thin house might prove a little cramped, with narrow stairs difficult to negotiate. Reverend Dench's more spacious abode offered a much better prospect.

Mrs Bramble notified Reverend Dench's housemaid of her decision and was shown to a guest bedroom. As a temporary measure, the facilities were adequate. Somewhere to perform her morning and evening ablutions and a bed to sleep in were all she required. She thanked the maid and they returned downstairs where a glance at a wall clock told Mrs Bramble that Reverend Weaver had been occupied for almost fifteen minutes.

Staying inside the chaplain's house would achieve nothing because all those she might wish to speak to were elsewhere. The Inner Ward afforded the best opportunity to bump into someone of interest, so she left the house and began an exploratory stroll. She gave a polite nod to the guard outside the Queen's House, who eyed her warily, and circled around the White Tower where her attention snapped into focus when she spotted Reverend Weaver emerging from the Fusiliers' headquarters.

Weaver skipped lightly down the steps without incident and scuttled away almost as though his legs were tethered at the knees. Mrs Bramble caught up with him halfway across the parade ground, much to the reverend's surprise, and he immediately began to relate his conversation with Dr Burford.

Mrs Bramble nodded her understanding as he spoke, and raised her eyebrows at the suggestion that nicotine poisoning had been the cause of all the illness and, ultimately, the death of Mrs Fry. The conundrum of how everyone was poisoned, Mrs Fry receiving twice the dose, puzzled her as much as it had Dr Burford and Reverend Weaver.

Always wary of eavesdroppers, Mrs Bramble glanced around before linking arms with the reverend. He seemed confused by the unusual gesture and she needed to steady his stumble as she steered him back towards the Fusiliers' building.

'The two gentlemen we need to interview are staying in the officers' quarters, but we have a problem,' said Mrs Bramble. 'I suspect you are considered *persona non grata* since your arrest and can only gain admittance on sufferance while in the company of a distinguished Tower resident. Inevitably, I am a woman to whom entry will be barred as a matter of course.'

'We mustn't do anything to antagonise the inspector or the chief,' said Reverend Weaver, his eyes widening plaintively. 'I-I don't want to give them a reason to lock me up again.'

'Nor do I,' said Mrs Bramble, truthfully, although she was not averse to crossing swords with anyone should circumstances demand, as they often did. 'We must devise some stratagem to either get us inside legitimately or bring our quarry out to us.'

'Excellent,' said Weaver, brightly. Then he frowned. 'How do we do that?'

Mrs Bramble pondered the problem as they sauntered towards the officers' quarters, where they stopped at the bottom of the steps.

'Do you have your small travel Bible about your person?' she asked.

'As always,' said Weaver. 'It's in my jacket pocket.'

'Then I think I know a way to get inside.'

She outlined her plan in a whisper before they ascended

the steps, only to be refused entry by the Fusilier guarding the front door.

'Officer,' Mrs Bramble addressed the soldier, although she could see by his uniform and insignia that he did not hold a commission. 'We request entry for the briefest of moments to retrieve an item of property.'

'I'm just a corporal, ma'am, and I'm afraid I can't let either of you pass.'

'And I am Mrs Bramble, Royal Housekeeper of Hampton Court Palace, here to chaperone Reverend Weaver, who was most recently here taking tea with Dr Burford, to the room in which he was held captive overnight.' Presenting herself as Royal Housekeeper instead of using her official title of Lady Housekeeper seemed as good a way as any of making a useful impression.

The guard looked unsure. 'I don't know what that means,' he said.

'It means I have access to areas within Royal Palaces to which most people do not.' She had put on her highest-quality cut-glass voice with its most officious tone. 'That said, I have no wish to be inside these quarters for any longer than is necessary to return the reverend's property to him.'

'Property, ma'am?'

'I-I fear I left my travel Bible in the room when I was released,' said Weaver, his face colouring at the deceit. 'It has great sentimental value, i-in addition to its religious worth, of course.'

'I'm sorry to hear that, Reverend,' said the guard. 'I still can't let you pass, not without an es—' He stopped as a short, slightly rotund steward with a neck like a tree-trunk, and the one chevron of a lance-corporal on his sleeve, passed behind him. 'Here, Bolter,' he said over his shoulder, never taking his eyes off Mrs Bramble and Reverend Weaver. 'You couldn't do us a favour and escort these two upstairs, could you?'

'Not my job, mate,' said Bolter.

'I know but the sergeant's swanned off and I can't leave my post, can I? Go on, it's only for two minutes. The rev's forgotten his Bible and Mrs What's-her-name's his chaperone.'

Mrs Bramble bristled at the dismissive term.

'*His* chaperone,' said Bolter. 'Good 'eavens, whatever next?'

'There's a pinch of baccy in it for you.'

Bolter hesitated. 'Make it two and you're on.'

The guard took a sharp intake of breath but nodded. 'Done.'

'Come on then, but we 'ave to be quick,' said Bolter. 'Can't be seen to let all and sundry come and go as they please.'

Reverend Weaver tripped over the threshold as Mrs Bramble hurried him through the door after the back of the retreating steward. They followed him along a corridor to a staircase leading to the first floor and Mrs Bramble could see the look of trepidation on her friend's face as he relived his journey to the site of his brief but traumatic incarceration. A moment later, the steward stopped outside Weaver's former prison.

'Be quick,' he hissed, opening the door enough for Weaver to squeeze through.

Mrs Bramble took her chance. 'I hear you have two knights of the realm staying here,' she said with an innocent smile. 'How exciting.'

'I wouldn't call it exciting, ma'am. A pain in the neck is what it is.'

'Oh? How so?'

'There's only a few of us Fusiliers left garrisoned here and a handful of stewards. It's bad enough when they hold a bit of a do in the officers' mess, like yesterday, but when they put people up at a moment's notice it makes even more work for the likes of yours truly. I'm already at the beck and call of officers and have my general steward's duties to perform so I don't take kindly to being run off my feet looking after a try-hard and a dandy into the bargain.'

Mrs Bramble nodded sympathetically. 'By whom you mean ...?'

'*Sir* Stephen Lovell and *Sir* Oswald Clyne, don't you know?' he said in a mocking high-class accent. 'Sir Oswald Tidy-beard is a slave to the latest fashions, but that curly-topped Sir Stephen hasn't enough class to compete.' He put his finger to his lips as though rebuked by the glare Mrs Bramble gave him. 'My apologies, ma'am. Don't mean to sound unkind.' He pointed back along the corridor. 'They have rooms opposite right there.' He indicated two doors facing each other. 'Kicked up a fuss, they did. Didn't want to be on the same floor, never mind the same corridor.'

'They know each other well?' said Mrs Bramble, intrigued.

'They seem to. No fisticuffs, just cold stares.' Bolter listened at the door. 'What's the reverend doing in there?' He opened the door and went in. 'Can I help you look?'

Mrs Bramble heard Reverend Weaver express his thanks as she moved along to the two facing doors and proceeded to knock on one. It remained firmly closed. Upon trying the other, it opened to reveal the face of a handsome gentleman. At least, Mrs Bramble thought so. The man wore a white shirt with winged collar displaying a large black bow tie. The ostentatious ruffles at his shirt cuffs and around the edge of the pocket square sprouting from the breast pocket of his jacket marked him as the dandy. His dark wavy hair covered the tops of his ears and curled out at his neck, and his close-cropped beard followed the outline of a firm jaw.

'Good afternoon,' he said, when he saw her standing there. 'Have you come to make up the room, or something?' He glanced over his shoulder into his room. 'I think it's already been done by one of the steward fellows.'

'I haven't come about the room,' she said, mildly amused. 'I should introduce myself. My name is Mrs Lydia Bramble.' She held out her hand.

'Sir Oswald Clyne,' he said with a smile, barely touching her hand before letting it slip away.

'I'm working with Detective Inspector Cole and Chief Yeoman Warder Treadle on the case of Mrs Fry.'

His face fell at the mention and he glanced along the corridor and at the door opposite to see if anyone had heard. 'In what capacity?' His eyes narrowed suspiciously. 'Why would they send a woman to investigate a sudden death?'

With those words, Mrs Bramble knew he would be amenable to talking. Had he been reluctant, he would have shut the door in her face, stating he had nothing to say to anyone but the chief and inspector.

'I have no official title,' she said, truthfully. 'My role is one of researcher, I suppose you could call it. Gathering background information on those who were present in the chapel when the unfortunate event occurred.'

'I had nothing to do with it.' He glanced along the corridor again towards where a commotion was coming from the next room along. 'I would ask you in but it's not the done thing to have a lady alone in one's room.'

'Not even with the door left open?' she said, fixing him

with the stare she often gave those whom she wished to influence.

Clyne looked pained but stepped aside to allow her entry. She had no intention of sitting, even when offered the solitary easy chair. The room was much like the one next door, in which Reverend Weaver had been held. It had a decent-sized bed, a single wardrobe, a large chest of drawers under the window, and the utilitarian feel of military accommodation, albeit more spacious and in better order than those of non-commissioned officers and ordinary fighting men. *Reverend Weaver should count himself fortunate to have been held in this building instead of the Yeoman Warders' guardhouse*, she thought.

'I am due in the officers' mess in five minutes,' he said. 'How can I help you?'

Clyne's head turned as a clunk came from the next room.

'I understand from Inspector Cole that you are a frequent visitor of Major and Mrs Rushton,' said Mrs Bramble.

Clyne's head turned back. 'I am. We are good friends.'

'Which explains why you were invited to the special service.' He didn't reply. 'How did you meet them?'

Clyne frowned. 'I do not see the relevance.'

It was Mrs Bramble's turn not to speak.

Clyne shrugged. 'I met Major Rushton when his father, Sir Arthur, sat for a portrait.' When Mrs Bramble still did not react, he continued. 'I am an artist, a member of the Royal Academy, and my work has appeared on several occasions in their summer exhibition.'

'Ah, a painter,' she said, and smiled inwardly as he winced.

'A little more than a mere painter, I hope, but I don't suppose you've seen any of my work.' It was more of a statement than a question. 'I mainly take commissions, these days. Her Majesty invested me with a knighthood for my work on royal portraits.'

'Then you have done very well indeed,' she said, watching his chest expand with pride. 'I believe such a path is not an easy one to tread.'

'I discovered I had a talent at an early age, but my father insisted I study engineering. Anything mechanical especially intrigued him and he loved building things. He became an engineer on the railways and would have been proud had I continued to follow in his footsteps.'

'What happened to change your mind?'

Clyne turned away and looked out of the window. Mrs Bramble took the opportunity to push the door to.

'I shied away from the manual labouring of my father when he lost his life in an accident while building a railway bridge,' said Clyne. 'In Chile, of all places. The company he worked for denied negligence and refused my mother any compensation. She never even received an apology.'

'I'm sorry,' she said.

He turned back to her, his face pale. 'I've always thought "I'm sorry" to be a strange sentiment to express. After all, you don't know my family and had no part in my father's death.'

'It denotes sympathy,' she explained. 'Empathy, sometimes.'

He nodded slowly and sighed. 'I chose an artistic life to escape his world of death and corruption, and to trade on skills I knew I had and thought I might make a living from.'

He preened his ruffles and fluffed his pocket square like a peacock getting ready to display its tail feathers, and Mrs Bramble suspected the artistic life had called him far earlier than he admitted.

'I suppose you must be aware of the friction, shall we

say, between Major Rushton, Captain Fry and their wives?' she said.

'Must I?'

'If you're as close as you say.'

He smiled. 'Yes, I know of their disagreements. The officers keep each other at arm's length, for reasons of professional discipline, but women tend not to let such courtesies get in the way of a good feud, I've found.'

Mrs Bramble ignored the generalisation. 'In what way?'

'Their wives tended to snipe at each other. Life at the Tower of London is sometimes not as glamorous as it might seem to those outside looking in. There is little to do by way of recreation if you are a wife. The Fusiliers have their mess rooms and the Yeomen have their club in which to socialise but the wives are rarely invited to either.'

'I believe very few women have the time or inclination to turn to gossip and conflict to fill their days.'

Clyne looked at her askance. 'I'm sure you're right, Mrs Bramble, but some get a bee in their bonnet, wouldn't you agree?'

Mrs Bramble thought about her experiences dealing with the grace and favour residents of Hampton Court Palace and found she could not disagree.

'I take it the disagreement between the two wives arose solely from the incident when the officers were at university?' she said.

'You know the details?' said Clyne, with raised eyebrows. 'Of course.' He gave her a wry smile. 'You wouldn't be here now, otherwise.' He thought for a moment. 'As I said, I met Edwin when I painted his father's portrait so what I know of the Frys I know through them. As I understand it, the two men were young when they joined the army and still full of animosity towards each other. When Edwin married,

Margaret naturally wanted to know everything there was to know about her husband. I suppose it must have been the same for the Frys. It can be frustrating, watching someone you love be unable to do anything about their situation. You want to help in whatever way you can, and I suppose the discord between the two wives existed solely because of their husbands' inability to act for themselves.'

Mrs Bramble's heart thumped. 'Are you trying to tell me Mrs Rushton killed Mrs Fry?'

'Good Lord, no!' said Clyne, his eyes wide with shock. 'It is well known Mrs Fry had a weak constitution. If food poisoning was to prove fatal to anyone, most people would have wagered good money on her. And don't suggest the captain had anything to do with it either. They may have had no time for each other but the Rushtons and Frys are not the killing kind.'

'Except on the battlefield.'

'I think you had better go.'

'Of course,' she said, opening the door. 'I wasn't casting aspersions, just trying to fill in the gaps for Inspector Cole.'

'Good day, Mrs Bramble.'

Clyne shut the door and she kicked herself for antagonising him so soon and with such apparent ease. A friend would naturally defend a friend but despite her probing, had he been a little too vociferous in that regard?

Was Sir Oswald Clyne the murderer?

14

Bolter and Reverend Weaver were not where she expected them to be, so she hastened downstairs hoping no alarm had been raised by her absence.

Her friend was in the corridor, remonstrating with the steward in a hissed-words and waving-arms way. *A friend defending a friend*, she mused. When Weaver fell silent, Bolter turned to find the cause and his face hardened when he saw Mrs Bramble descending towards them.

'Where did you get to?' he said in a stage whisper, using a pocket square to mop beads of perspiration from his thick neck.

'I do apologise,' she said, not sorry in the slightest. 'I needed the ladies' powder room.'

'We haven't got one,' said Bolter.

'I know, and it made the task all the more challenging.' She smiled sweetly. 'I had to make do.'

'Make do?' Bolter looked horrified. 'What do you me—?'

'Reverend, did you manage to retrieve your Bible?' she asked.

'I did, Mrs Bramble,' said Reverend Weaver, picking up on his cue and waving his Bible. 'With the kind assistance of Lance Corporal Bolter.'

Mrs Bramble went to shake the anxious steward's hand but was unceremoniously herded by him into the foyer with Reverend Weaver.

'Where in God's name have you been?' said the guard, looking even more agitated. 'I hoped you'd pop in and out and be gone in a flash. I didn't expect you to be in there so long you'd start paying rent.'

'Don't be so dramatic,' said Mrs Bramble, with a twinkle in her eye. 'No harm done.'

'You should never hurry a lady,' said Weaver, offering his arm to Mrs Bramble, who linked hers in his. 'Especially one with the title of Lady Housekeeper.'

'Here, I thought you said *Royal* Housekeeper,' said the guard as Reverend Weaver went to guide Mrs Bramble down the stone steps.

The roles reversed as Weaver almost rolled his ankle on reaching the level of the parade ground and Mrs Bramble held fast to halt his stumble. She looked back and saw the guard looking as stiff and efficient as ever, almost as though nothing had happened, but his stare was piercing.

'What now, Mrs Bramble?' Weaver rubbed his ankle. 'We're getting into the evening but no further forward.'

They sauntered towards the execution site in front of the chapel, Weaver with a slight limp but both he and Mrs Bramble exuding the air of being unconcerned by anything around them.

'Sir Oswald gave me the impression the feud between the Rushtons and Frys blew hot and cold,' she said. 'But he sounded convincing when he said they weren't the type to commit murder.'

'Is there a type?' said Reverend Weaver.

'Sir Stephen Lovell wasn't in his quarters when I knocked but we need to find and speak to him as a matter of urgency.' She glanced around at the few remaining visitors drifting towards the exit. 'Sir Oswald was expected in the officers' mess about now so I'm hoping Sir Stephen is too.'

'Drinks before dinner?' said a voice.

'Most likely,' she said.

'I beg your pardon?'

Mrs Bramble stopped and turned, experiencing a jolt at the sight of Reverend Dench standing nearby. *How long have you been there?* she wondered.

'Sorry, Reverend,' she said. 'I thought Reverend Weaver had spoken.'

'Ah,' said Dench. 'I don't suppose you'd both do me the honour of joining the doctor and Mr Chant for dinner at my residence? Shall we say, drinks in an hour?'

'I've not had much of an appetite since the congregation keeled over and I was arrested and hauled off,' said Reverend Weaver.

'We'd be delighted,' said Mrs Bramble, giving her friend a sly dig in the ribs. 'See you in an hour.'

'Splendid,' said Weaver, holding his side. 'I'm famished.'

They watched Reverend Dench walk in the direction of the chaplain's house and Mrs Bramble waited for him to be out of earshot.

'Where the devil did he come from?' she said.

'The White Tower, I expect,' said Reverend Weaver. 'Isn't he taking services there while St Peter's is out of bounds?'

Mrs Bramble wasn't so sure.

'Listen, Thomas. I'd like you to follow Reverend Dench back to the chaplain's house and keep an eye on him.'

Weaver looked taken aback. 'Whatever for? You don't suspect him of being involved, do you?'

'I always suspect everyone except you, me and Kitty to begin with,' she said. 'Although circumstances and evidence remove certain persons from the list one by one.'

'And Augustus is still on your list?'

'For the moment, but only for the sake of thoroughness.'

'I don't believe he's capable, Mrs Bramble,' he said, looking crestfallen at the prospect of his ecclesiastical friend being under suspicion. 'But if you think there's merit in my keeping his company ...'

'I do.' She gave him a reassuring nod and watched him walk away, amused by the increased severity of the limp he adopted.

As soon as she saw the door of the chaplain's house close behind her friend, she turned towards the chapel, opened the iron gate and descended the few steps to the vestry's east door. She tried the handle and found it locked. Frowning, she hurried back up the steps.

Walking round to the western end of the chapel, she entered the unlit nave through the main door. The columns, pews and memorials inside were just about visible in the gloom of fading light struggling to get over the Tower's battlements and through the windows. *Eerie but calm*, she thought, closing the door behind her.

Having crossed the nave to the vestry door, she found it unlocked and stepped inside.

A lamp, consisting of a single candle in a holder with a glass cover, shed enough light to see most of the vestry. A few shadows lurked in the corners, but no one occupied the room, so she made a quick circuit. Something at the back of her mind told her that Reverend Dench, who had appeared on their right side as they had walked from the officers' quarters towards the execution site, must have emerged from the Chapel of St Peter ad Vincula rather than the White Tower. She felt sure she would have noticed anyone coming from the left, having her head turned slightly in that direction when speaking to Reverend Weaver.

As far as she could tell from her previous visit in better

light, little had changed. A few papers had been tidied and a couple of books taken down from a shelf and laid on a table, but nothing else had moved. *Reverend Dench preparing for the next service, perhaps*, she supposed. The open bottle of sacramental wine, with its cork reversed and jammed into the top, still stood next to the almost empty carafe of holy water, the dish of wafers and the chalice with its cloth on the little table at the centre of the room. These remained untouched.

She stepped across to the far door, the one she had tried from the outside, raising her eyebrows in surprise when it opened a crack. She hadn't expected it to do that. Closing the door, she tried the handle of the third one in the room and found it too was unlocked.

She took the candle lamp through this door and entered the narrow passage, which took a turn to the left, leading past walls that held back the bones of centuries of burials. Hundreds of bodies mixed together in one giant tomb. Mrs Bramble was not afraid of the dead, or the dark on its own. These could not hurt you. Only the living were dangerous.

The short passage emerged into a larger chamber she knew to be the crypt. The flickering candle flame picked out small circular windows set into the ceiling. These were at the bottom of light wells, the glazed tops of which she had walked past when meeting Reverend Dench and Dr Burford on the roof garden earlier that day. There were no individual tombs here, no ghosts, only memorials to the departed. She often wondered if these were for the living rather than the dead. Surely her poor husband would have made his presence known to her if he could, if anything existed beyond the grave. The possibility of nothing brought a lump to her throat because she missed him and wanted so much to believe they would one day be reunited.

Dismissing such thoughts as idle fancy, Mrs Bramble passed the access door to the nave and reached the steps at the far end of the crypt. The heavy door was closed but unlocked and she ascended to the iron gate. This too remained unlocked, as Reverend Dench had said.

Her exploration through the vestry and crypt had shed less light on her investigation than the lamp she carried. Outside, the air had cooled and the light had bled away even more. She opened the main door to the chapel, blew out the lamp and set it inside before closing the door behind—

'What on earth!' Mrs Bramble cried as her heart missed a beat.

A pale apparition stood nearby and it took her eyes a few seconds to readjust from the brightness of the lamp, revealing her housemaid, Kitty.

'Ever so sorry, Mrs B,' said Kitty. 'I thought you heard me say your name.'

'I was deep in thought,' said Mrs Bramble, putting her hand over her heart to calm herself.

They moved into the open where the lamplighter could be seen doing the rounds of the Tower's many gas lamps, turning the twilight gloom into a pleasant evening scene. 'Must be magical here at Christmas,' said Mrs Bramble. 'Much like Hampton Court Palace.'

Kitty scoffed. 'And just as draughty?'

'Perhaps. And slippy in the snow. What have you found on your travels? Anything interesting other than daily castle gossip?'

'I think I have something.' Kitty pulled her coat more tightly around her neck against a slight but chill breeze coming off the River Thames. 'I managed to speak to another two housemaids and they both confirmed the bad blood between the Rushtons and the Frys. They never socialised unless the occasion demanded it, the major and captain hardly ever spoke to each other, even in mixed company, and the wives could not contain themselves from having sly digs at each other whenever opportunity presented itself.'

'Confirming what Sir Oswald Clyne said to me less than an hour ago,' said Mrs Bramble.

'Something else you ought to know,' said Kitty. 'Everyone says Mrs Fry was a delicate creature. Yes, she was outwardly hardy because being an army wife is no easy life, whether your husband's an officer or not, but she was considered weak in herself. I know that's a bit of a contradiction but it's what I've been told. Some say Mrs Fry had the strength to shift a barrel of beer if need be, but others say she swooned in the sun and often took to her bed.'

'Sir Oswald also said as much,' said Mrs Bramble. She shrugged. 'I suppose the world is made up of all sorts.'

She glanced across at the now-illuminated windows of the officers' quarters, and the married men's building next door where only one window showed the room was lit from within. The light went out and she had a thought.

'Kitty,' she said. 'I have no right to ask you this, and I will defend you to the hilt with Inspector Cole and the chief should you be caught, but I need you to do a little snooping.'

Kitty looked dubious. 'Over and above what I've done already?'

'Far and away.'

A smile slid onto Kitty's face. 'How exciting. What do you want me to do?'

'As we speak, the officers and their guests are gathering for drinks before dinner,' said Mrs Bramble. 'All of the off-duty soldiers should be dining also. Reverend Dench has invited Reverend Weaver and me to have dinner with himself, the organist Mr Chant and Dr Burford in his residence. The housemaids will be serving but as you too are a guest, I suspect you will take your dinner with them afterwards.'

'Nice to know where I am in the pecking order, Mrs B,' said Kitty, haughtily, but with a wink to show she was joking.

'Indeed,' said Mrs Bramble. 'And what this does is provide you with the perfect opportunity.'

'Perfect opportunity for what, exactly?' Kitty sported a suspicious frown as Mrs Bramble leant close to whisper in her ear.

'For breaking into the married men's quarters.'

15

Mrs Bramble conveyed her plan in great detail, hoping she'd thought of every circumstance: what Kitty should say if she were discovered, what she should do if she were pursued, what to do with anything interesting she found. Mrs Bramble assured her she would step forward and accept the blame should the mission fail. It being her idea and what could be argued as an unreasonable request to make of a domestic servant, Mrs Bramble also left the decision to assist or not entirely up to Kitty.

Kitty had accepted the challenge and promised to try. It would be easier to gain entry to an apartment than it would to get into the building in the first place, but Kitty said she might have an idea. It was Mrs Bramble's turn to feel reassured, knowing if it could be done then Kitty would do it. Hadn't her own foray into the officers' quarters been easier than expected? She watched as Kitty strolled towards the married men's quarters to begin her observations, hoping the effort would be worth the risk.

As Mrs Bramble went to turn away, she felt a flutter of disquiet in her chest. She had seen men walk into battle on the orders of officers they trusted, knowing the danger they faced. This was nothing nearly so perilous but still she almost recalled Kitty. It was one thing to put herself in harm's way when she felt the situation demanded but quite another to ask someone else to do so on her behalf.

Then she saw Kitty throw a brief wave that quelled her unease, but even this could not outweigh the one question playing on her mind.

Would there be anything of note to find?

Kitty sat on one of several wooden benches provided for the comfort of visitors and looked across to the brick edifice of the married men's quarters, pondering her predicament. She had promised Mrs B she would try to infiltrate the building, but sitting here alone made that a daunting prospect. She might be welcomed inside the single men's barracks if discovered there, or even in the officers' quarters, but wives would be on their guard here and their husbands on their best behaviour. At least, while observed.

Two lampposts shone their gaslight on the building in question and turned what in daylight was a rather nondescript frontage into something eerie and imposing. The chilly air made her nose tickle and she dabbed at it with a handkerchief, hesitating as she wondered if her part in the plan would work. It would hinge on whether her face was still unfamiliar and she could continue as an anonymous soul, someone who belonged and proceeded almost unnoticed. That remained to be seen.

Beside her on the bench sat a wicker basket containing a couple of scrubbing brushes, several cloths, a bottle of cleaning fluid and a jar of gloopy honey. These had been borrowed from the one of the housemaids she had spoken to that afternoon, with a promise to return them before the Ceremony of the Keys, which took place every evening at ten o'clock. Kitty prayed the plan would work, allowing the items to be back in the maid's possession well before. Laid across the cleaning items was her own over-apron for working, and she donned this now in readiness for what was to come.

Kitty had noticed a dim light earlier in one of the upper windows, and a shadow occasionally cast against the glass. At this time of the evening, it was more likely to be one of the Fusiliers or his wife in the room for that length of time, maybe both, but not a housemaid or steward.

She knew not how long she had sat there but the light being extinguished caught her attention and she stiffened. This was it.

She picked up the basket and moved with calm deliberation across to the steps leading up to the next level. She needed to look as though she belonged, and rushing might give the opposite impression. At the top of the steps, the front door gave access to the quarters within, but breaking in would be her method of last resort. Her intention was to be let in by someone for whom menial work was the realm of others like herself.

She made a show of examining her basket, taking out and replacing a cloth, then the bottle, and finally a scrubbing brush, as though checking the contents, and set it on the ground by the door. She then opened the jar of honey and anointed the bottom of the door and the step with it, creating a superficial but sticky mess. Finally, she adjusted her apron and laid a padded kneeling cloth on the ground, hoping all the time for someone, anyone, to leave or enter by the front door.

She had not long to wait.

The door opened and a Fusilier in a bright-red jacket halted with his foot hovering over where Kitty's scrubbing brush was poised.

'What the devil is going on here?' he demanded.

'Been a spillage, sir,' said Kitty.

She looked up with her best expression of innocence and sat back on her haunches to allow the officer to step over the offending liquid. He extended a hand back towards the doorway to assist a lady, one whom Kitty assumed was his wife, to follow him without soiling her dress. Kitty didn't look her in the eye but busied herself with selecting a cloth and folding it in a particular way until it formed a pad.

The officer almost closed the door but Kitty began to clean the threshold in short circular motions that suggested this might take some time to complete. The wife sighed theatrically and the officer's boots, currently on Kitty's eye level, shuffled as though they and not their wearer were caught in two minds.

'Take you long, will it?' said the officer.

'Best part of half an hour, sir, I shouldn't wonder,' said Kitty, looking intently at where the gloop was working into the woodwork. 'Someone's had a right upset and no mistake.'

'Well.' He cleared his throat as his wife huffed. 'Carry on but be quick about it.'

'Yessir,' said Kitty, without increasing her speed at all.

She cleaned the mess diligently while waiting for the couple to leave and made sure they were heading to the officers' mess before she stood up and checked that she remained otherwise unobserved. This was the chance she had been waiting for.

Wiping her hands on a cloth, she took the basket and stepped inside, closing the door behind her quietly. The entrance hall was dimly lit and no sound came from anywhere downstairs. She padded to the bottom of a staircase and ascended one step at a time, careful not to make any undue noise on an overly squeaky stair. A runner of thin carpet stretched the length of the first-floor landing, where doors led to various apartments. Silence reigned here too, much to her satisfaction, as she had no desire to be confronted by any indignant occupants.

Although chilly outside on the bench, here inside the air was warm, but the perspiration beading on her forehead was not due entirely to the temperature. One of Kitty's worries had been about how she might identify which room belonged to whom. Trying every apartment in the hope that fate might show mercy and indicate which belonged to the Rushtons and which to the Frys had seemed a risky strategy.

She wiped her upper lip, breathed a sigh of relief and smiled to herself when she noted a particular detail.

The names of the occupants had been engraved in fancy script on brass plaques screwed to each front door. Given what she already knew about the two couples, it came as no surprise to see their apartments set as far from each other as was possible, even in a building of this modest size.

She reached into her pocket and pulled out the cold piece of shaped metal Mrs B had slipped into her palm before they had parted ways. To a casual observer it was like any old key, but Kitty recognised this as a skeleton key, fashioned in a particular way to render it effective for opening many locks. She had heard of them but never even seen one before, never mind tried to use one. Every lock was different, so she had no idea how they worked but hoped they were as effective as their reputation suggested. Kitty listened again before inserting the key into the door of the Frys' apartment. It slipped in with ease and managed a quarter turn before meeting an obstruction. Mrs B had given her instructions for its use, but she almost gave up there and then.

Having willingly taken on this task, and not wishing to

disappoint her employer, Kitty persevered and gave it a wiggle back and forth. A weight lifted from her shoulders amid a mix of relief and satisfaction as the lock gave a soft click and the key performed a full turn.

She listened again, in case anyone asleep within had now awoken at the sound. All appeared well, so she pushed open the door, slid inside and quietly closed the door behind her. Realising she had been barely breathing, she took a few gasps of air, waiting until the light-headedness passed and her eyes adjusted to the light coming in from the gas lamps outside.

The room was much as she had expected. A sideboard stood against one wall, a drinks cabinet against another, both devoid of anything pertinent to the investigation. Two easy chairs faced a low table in the centre of the room, set upon a patterned carpet covering most of the wooden floor. A few paintings adorned the walls, not to Kitty's taste, and a mirror hung next to the door through which she had entered. She moved to the bedroom.

Another carpet lay on the floor but this time a double bed, made up and tidy, dominated the room. A small night-table stood on one side with a matching table the other side, and opposite was a chest of drawers on which stood a pitcher and bowl. A dressing table topped with a large oval mirror, in front of which a comb and brush set and a bottle of scent with a bulb for spraying had been neatly arranged, stood under the window. A double wardrobe filled one corner. Kitty checked every nook and cranny in pursuit of something to report back to Mrs B but could see nothing of interest. Except ...

Something had fallen behind one of the night-tables and, upon retrieval, it proved to be a small greetings card. Kitty did not recognise the reproduction of a religious painting on the front but an explanation on the back identified it as St Catherine fainting from her stigmata wounds, painted by Il Sodoma in 1526. This meant nothing to her, nor the spidery writing inside.

For today. Best wishes, M.

Kitty went to stand the card on the night-table but an extra-hard beat of her heart warned her to replace it where it had previously fallen on the floor behind. She checked she hadn't accidentally knocked anything askew, returned to the sitting room to do the same, and left quietly through the front door. The skeleton key did its job and the lock clicked shut.

Kitty felt as though she had been inside for an hour but common sense told her it was closer to fifteen minutes. She wanted to get out as soon as possible and dearly hoped the Rushtons' quarters would be as easily searched.

And, so it proved.

The skeleton key worked its magic again, with a little manipulation and patience, and gave access to an apartment not dissimilar to the one she had just vacated. Although the pieces of furniture were of different designs and sizes, and placed in different positions, their functions were the same as those in the Frys' apartment. The major difference was the absence of a fallen greetings card but the presence of a slightly fishy odour. Maybe the Rushtons had taken meals in their quarters; kedgeree for breakfast or smoked haddock for lunch, perhaps?

Kitty had always been taught not to meddle in a man's affairs nor to concern herself with the secrets of a lady, however trivial each might be. One should always stick to one's own private affairs because more often than not they were sufficient to take up one's time. Her discomfort at snooping through private belongings came to a head when she discovered a wooden box at the bottom of the wardrobe. Delicately decorated with lacquered flowers, it clearly belonged to Mrs Rushton. Dreading to think what might be hidden inside, she lifted the lid gingerly to reveal the contents, and smiled at her foolish fears. The box contained a small bundle of correspondence from Major Rushton, tied with a ribbon, several pieces of jewellery in a wooden tray, various other trinkets including a small string of beads with a cross, a small bottle of laudanum with maybe a teaspoon left at the bottom, an embroidered cloth with a small stain, and two empty tins of Skipper Navy Cut pipe tobacco. Major Rushton's perhaps. It seemed an eclectic collection of items for a lady to keep but Kitty could see nothing particularly unusual about them as such.

A creak.

Kitty froze, straining to hear any movement outside the door, unable to identify from where the creak had originated. Had it come from the landing? Had something been moved outside at the front of the building? Maybe the door to the main entrance had opened, although she couldn't recall it creaking when she had entered earlier. Had one of the officers or their wives returned early from their dinner? Her gaze went to the ceiling, as though staring at the white plaster would reveal the room upstairs, but no movement came from above either.

She relaxed, deciding it was one of those random noises old buildings often made at unexpected moments. As a child she had often been frightened by noises in the night, but her mother had soothed her, saying new buildings settled, old buildings groaned, and those in between breathed.

Kitty replaced every item back in its exact location, closed the wardrobe door, checked the rooms against her own clumsiness and left the way she had come. As she descended the stairs, ears pricked for any sound of activity, she hoped her lack of success in finding anything obviously incriminating would prove beneficial to Mrs B. After all, eliminating suspects was an important process in an investigation.

Closing the front door quietly behind her, Kitty noticed a movement to her left and dropped her padded cloth to the ground. She had barely knelt and selected a scrubbing brush in furtherance of the ruse when a cough came from her right. She jolted upright on her knees, ready to throw the brush at any attacker, but refrained when she saw the uniform of a Yeoman Warder.

'My apologies if I startled you, young lady, but I am the Yeoman Gaoler,' he said. 'May I ask what you're up to at this time of an evening?'

Kitty's heart raced at being questioned by the chief's second-in-command but she kept her breathing steady, relieved that the interruption did not mean she had been caught. 'A bit of a spillage earlier, sir,' she said, indicating the step and foot of the door. 'I need to get the stickiness off before they return from dinner.' She threw a worried glance towards the officers' quarters for emphasis, knowing he could not *see* stickiness and would probably take her word for it.

The Yeoman Gaoler followed her glance and nodded his understanding. 'All the same, I'd finish up quick smart if I were you,' he said. 'They released the visiting vicar earlier and you know what that means?' He raised his eyebrows knowingly.

Kitty shook her head. 'No, what?'

'It means you should keep your eyes peeled. If there's a murderer abroad and it's not him, it could be anyone.'

Kitty shuddered. *Even you*, she thought.

16

Mrs Bramble cut a slice of cheese and placed it on a water biscuit with some plum chutney. Having enjoyed a luscious rabbit stew with fluffy dumplings, she eschewed the sweet apple crumble for dessert, favouring the savoury option instead.

'You'll give yourself bad dreams,' said Jasper Chant, the chapel organist.

Mrs Bramble smiled. 'Rest assured; I've lived through worse times while awake than I could ever do while asleep.'

'Of course, you mentioned you were once an army wife. This must be familiar territory for you.'

'In some ways but it's certainly more comfortable than most of the postings my husband and I endured. Especially abroad. My apartment at Hampton Court Palace is luxurious in comparison to an army camp in India.'

Chant looked at Reverend Weaver. 'And are your lodgings at the palace comfortable, Reverend?'

'I should say so,' said Weaver. 'I occupy a large apartment in Seymour Gate near the western entrance.' He chuckled. 'Need to be in good condition to go up and down all the stairs, mind you.'

'I believe you mentioned you live in Farringdon, Mr Chant,' said Mrs Bramble. 'Is it a nice area?'

'Very pleasant, although there is a growing number of printing works springing up. The dust and noise of the works themselves and the deliveries that come and go make for an increasingly busy and correspondingly less serene environment. I find practising on the chapel's new organ a calming experience. The pipes are so resonant and the acoustics remarkable.'

Mrs Bramble had been waiting for a chance to turn the conversation. 'I'm aware we've avoided the subject of the investigation so far this evening but I cannot help wondering,' she said. 'You sit with your back to proceedings, Mr Chant, but do you have a mirror with which to see what is going on behind you? I know many do.'

'I do,' said Chant. 'Why do you ask?'

'I thought you might have noticed something before the first victim fell ill.'

'I've been over the very same question in my mind. From the moment I gave the organ keyboard the once over with a polishing cloth before the service, like I always do, to the moment the illness struck, I simply cannot say I saw anything at all.' Chant looked at his empty dish and shook his head. 'Are the inspector and chief any closer to solving the mystery of the ailing congregation?'

'Not as I understand it,' she said. 'I hear you were fortunate to escape the effects of whatever struck them down.'

'Most fortunate, I'd say.' Chant fidgeted on his chair. 'Has the cause been discovered?' He glanced at the doctor.

'I'm afraid not,' said Dr Burford. 'It remains to be seen where the finger can be pointed but I can confirm that tests absolved the canapés of any guilt.'

'Could there be another rational explanation, Doctor?' said Chant. 'A natural phenomenon to explain all this?'

Dr Burford gave him a facial shrug. 'There will always be a rational explanation, Mr Chant, but as to what that might be, I am not currently in a position to say.'

'Did you have cause to go into the vestry at any time before the service, Mr Chant?' asked Mrs Bramble.

Chant looked up at the ceiling, remembering. 'Only to check in with Reverend Dench and to wish Reverend Weaver good luck. I saw nothing out of place in the vestry and noticed no one in the chapel who I hadn't seen before at the reception.'

'It really is an extraordinary business,' said Reverend Dench. 'Tragic, but extraordinary.'

Dr Burford reached for his wine. 'Perhaps there is a—'

He stopped in horror as his hand knocked his glass flying. Reverend Weaver tried to save it but succeeded only in upsetting his own glass. Amid a jousting of glasses and apologies, Burford and Weaver tried to mop the stains with their napkins. The two men clumsily interlocking their efforts merely exacerbated the situation and the almost-empty carafe tumbled into the lap of Reverend Dench.

Mrs Bramble smiled in mild amusement at the developing chaos, wondering again whether the uncannily similar behaviour of Burford and Weaver proved some ancestral familial relationship. As the apologies and mopping continued, her thoughts returned to the vestry. Something about it – something obvious, perhaps – niggled her. She glanced at the carriage clock on the mantelshelf. An hour and a half since she had left Kitty. Plenty of time for her to complete her mission inside the married men's quarters, but still Mrs Bramble worried. What if she had been caught? What if Inspector Cole and the chief had her under arrest right at this moment?

'Are you all right, Mrs Bramble?' asked Reverend Dench.

'Pardon?' she replied.

'You look a little, um, distant. Is anything the matter?'

'Oh. No, no, Reverend,' said Mrs Bramble. 'Although I

fear I may have overindulged this evening and, as Mr Chant warned, eaten one cheesy water biscuit too many. A turn around the grounds should cure me, if you don't mind.' She stood and all the men followed suit out of courtesy. 'I'm sure I shall sleep well tonight but I feel a touch of fresh air will aid my digestion and clear my mind ready for me to climb the wooden hill to Bedfordshire.'

Dr Burford rubbed his chest. 'I also fear I've had a little too much chutney for my own good and have given myself heartburn.' He nodded at Reverend Dench. 'If you'll excuse me, I think I shall retire next door and take a powder.'

'I'd take a powder,' repeated Reverend Dench. 'If I were you. And I should get my trousers into soak before this wine stain takes hold. But first, may I thank you all for a most pleasant evening.'

After an affected exchange of felicitations, Weaver had almost retaken his seat when Mrs Bramble said, 'Reverend Weaver, would you care to join me?'

Weaver used his momentum to bounce straight back up again.

'It would be my pleasure,' he said.

Mrs Bramble stepped forward away from the doorway to accommodate the exit of Dr Burford and Reverend Weaver from the chaplain's house and to allow the maid to close the door. A short discussion ensued, mainly centred on how much chillier the evenings had become as the season progressed into autumn, and how the prospect of rain might further curtail outdoor activities. She had hoped Dr Burford would take the hint and retire to his house but it seemed he remained immune to suggestion. After a couple more minutes and another round of pleasantries, during which Burford and Weaver almost broke each other's fingers with an ill-executed handshake, the doctor finally excused himself and left them to their lamplit evening stroll.

After watching Dr Burford enter his home, Mrs Bramble took a deep lungful of night air, identifying the aromas of wood and coal smoke, fish, rotting waste and smelly Thames water. Cities, whether at home or abroad, were not her favourite places to be. Yes, everything one could wish for in terms of amenities were at your fingertips, but most, especially London, contained far too large a population for her liking and she much preferred the space and rural smells of the countryside

Looking out towards the parade ground, Reverend Weaver standing contemplatively on her right, a faint click sounded to her left. As she turned her head, a shadow appeared to move. She stared hard in the direction of the steps leading to Reverend Dench's roof garden, trying to see beyond the glare of the gas lamp affixed to the wall of the chaplain's house, took one step forward and stopped.

Seeing her move, Reverend Weaver made to follow, but her sudden halt surprised him and he tripped over his own feet. With a warning squeak from his throat, he barrelled into her back, knocking her forwards and alerting the shadow to their presence. Silencing her friend's apologies with a wave of her hand, she crept towards the steps and approached in time to see what she thought was the shadow of someone turning the corner at the bottom of the crypt steps. The gate and door stood open, not pulled to as they were earlier.

She signalled for Reverend Weaver to be quiet but follow, and descended swiftly, peeking round the corner of the wall. He slipped behind her again but caught himself before he tumbled. This still proved enough to startle the figure at the far end of the dark crypt. They turned, holding a candle lamp, maybe the one she had used herself earlier, but Mrs Bramble could not tell who it might be by the dim glow alone. As its carrier disappeared, heavy boots echoing in the chamber, the dull sound of an opening door came from up the steps and outside the crypt gate. Caught in two minds, she paused for no more than a second before deciding the pursuit of her quarry took precedence and whoever had entered upstairs could wait.

Her own light footsteps echoed as she hurried along in the dark, her hand following the line of the wall so she would not crash into unseen objects. As far as she could remember, the route was clear all the way to the junction. Muffled cries of distress came from behind as Reverend Weaver tried to keep up, but Mrs Bramble remained focused on negotiating the narrow passage leading to the vestry. The lamp glow at the far end pulled her towards it and she used its light to hasten her pursuit, while Weaver bounced off the walls like a ball in a bagatelle game.

Mrs Bramble reached the open vestry door at the end of the passage as someone entered via the door from the chapel. Her heart gave a jolt but settled quickly when she recognised Kitty. They glanced at each other for a split second before continuing their pursuit through the open door to the outside.

The gate at the top of the steps had been left open in haste as their prey fled, but the lamps on the chapel wall and corner of the Waterloo Barracks gave no indication of the direction of escape.

They listened intently.

No hurried footsteps breached the silence, so Mrs Bramble bade Kitty to stay put and waved Reverend Weaver towards the parade ground.

In turn, she hastened to the rear corner of the barracks,

checked no one had chosen to hide on the steps leading to the battlements and stepped into the wide passage between the inner wall and the rear of the building.

She spotted the outline of a Yeoman Warder within hailing distance on the wall above and knew an unseen sentry would be on guard outside the back door of the barracks, but she had heard neither issue a challenge.

Mrs Bramble glanced at an archway set into the inner wall to her left, the only viable escape route, and hurried towards it. She passed through and stood at one of the two unglazed openings, looking down at the Outer Ward.

No one moved below and she hesitated, feeling her neck prickle with apprehension.

Would an innocent man be skulking about the chapel? Would an innocent man run and hide in the shadows? Had she inadvertently disturbed the murderer returning to the scene of their crime? Her heart thumped at the sudden realisation of her position. Being shot by a guard was of far less concern than the fact that she was a woman alone and her prey might be hiding round any corner.

Waiting for her.

Mrs Bramble froze at the sound of a heavy clunk from inside the stairwell and she strained her ears to hear more. With seconds ticking away, she made a decision.

And stepped into the forbidding darkness.

17

After the light of the gas lamps, the darkness seemed even more intense.

Mrs Bramble kept her hand to the stone wall and felt for each step with her foot, edging her way down to the level of the Outer Ward. Expecting an attack at any moment, her heart thumped harder as her eyes struggled to become accustomed to the gloom.

Someone barged her from behind.

The force spun her round, knocking her to the ground.

She was back on her feet in seconds, head still spinning, and staggered into the open. All was still along the row of casemate apartments to her left, but the heavy footfall of boots echoed off the walls beyond the Flint Tower to her right. She hurried round the curved base but a figure had already reached the next tower further along. By the time she arrived there, she could do no more than watch as the figure rounded yet another tower and disappeared.

The chase had run its course and the murderer had escaped.

For now.

She tutted and—

'Halt! Who comes there?'

Heart still pumping from her recent encounter, the challenge startled Mrs Bramble and she turned to find a Fusilier pointing a rifle at her. She laughed at the absurdity of the situation and saw the soldier hesitate. In all her years as an army nurse she had never once had a rifle pointed at her. Not even by those considered the enemy. The soldier lowered his weapon.

'I know you,' he said. 'You're helping the chief and that detective.'

'Mrs Lydia Bramble at your service,' she replied with a bow of her head. 'Lady Housekeeper of Hampton Court Palace.'

The soldier glanced behind him and to either side. 'What're you doing out in the dark, Mrs Bramble?'

'Why, is it not safe?'

'It's usually the safest place on Earth but not at the moment, not when there's a murderer abroad in the night. Inside these walls, no less.'

Mrs Bramble thought hard about this, glancing around her to check they were alone.

'Am I the only person you've seen tonight?' she said.

'Yes, ma'am,' said the soldier. 'Although I came on duty not a minute before I saw you behind the barracks.'

'And what of the sentry you relieved?'

'He reported no activity since the gas lamps were lit, and stayed at the post to cover for me while I followed someone acting suspiciously. Of course, ma'am, I didn't know it was you until I could see your face.'

She frowned. If the Yeoman Warder on the wall had been distracted by the handover of guard duties, that would explain how her quarry had slipped by unnoticed.

'You shouldn't be down here,' said the soldier. 'I'm afraid I must escort you back up to your lodgings. I assume you're staying with the governor, ma'am?'

'I assure you I have no need of an escort, Fusilier. Reverend Weaver and my housemaid await me by the chapel and we have lodgings with Reverend Dench. You can witness my progress from the top of the steps, if you must, but I would not wish to keep you from your post any longer than necessary.'

The soldier looked dubious but nodded, and the two of them walked back to the Flint Tower. At the top of the steps, Mrs Bramble apologised for breaching any rules, bade him goodnight, and began the short walk between the barracks and chapel to the parade ground. Giving a wave to reassure him, she hastened towards the corner where Kitty and Reverend Weaver stood with their backs to her, looking out at the parade ground.'

'Jesus, Mary and Joseph,' cried Kitty, as Mrs Bramble put a hand on her shoulder. 'Gave me a start, and no mistake.'

Reverend Weaver succumbed to a sudden attack of the hiccups and covered his mouth with a pocket square to contain the intermittent noise.

'Did you catch him, Mrs B?' asked Kitty.

'Almost but he gave me the slip,' said Mrs Bramble. 'Nearly got shot by a jumpy Fusilier too, for my trouble.'

'Pardon?' said Kitty, wide-eyed.

Mrs Bramble waved away her concerns. 'I have no idea who we encountered but whoever it was, they went into the chapel for something and it wasn't to pray.'

Kitty thumped Reverend Weaver between the shoulder blades, forcing him to take a step forward.

'I say. That was rather violent,' he complained.

'Stopped your hiccups, though,' said Kitty, with a grin.

He took an uninterrupted breath and grinned back. 'Oh, yes.'

'Our mystery caller entered through the crypt and left through the vestry,' said Mrs Bramble, regaining their attention. 'There's nothing in the crypt so I think we should check the vestry to see if we can identify what they were after.'

'Could be anything,' said Kitty, frowning. 'And I haven't had my dinner yet.'

'It will take but a moment,' Mrs Bramble reassured her. Then she added with a wink, 'And I'll ensure Reverend Dench's cook knows to provide a larger portion.'

'Well, in that case ...' Kitty grinned.

Mrs Bramble smiled back and turned to Reverend Weaver. 'I'd be obliged if you could check anything ecclesiastical. Kitty and I will examine the tables and cupboards to ensure nothing has been dropped or knocked to the floor.'

'But what are we looking for,' asked Weaver.

'Anything out of the ordinary, that looks out of place or appears to be missing.'

'How will we know if it's missing.' He looked perplexed.

'Reverend,' said Mrs Bramble. 'Trust in God.'

Weaver gave her a wry smile.

Although Mrs Bramble knew the deadbolt had not been engaged in the east door, otherwise her prey could not have escaped, her previous look at the vestry had revealed the latch bolt could only be opened from the outside by a key, preventing them from entering that way. Instead, checking to ensure prying eyes were not on them, they returned via the west door near the chaplain's house and through the nave to the vestry where the mystery figure had abandoned the still-burning candle lamp. They lit another each and began their examination.

Despite there being little by way of clutter for them to rummage through, they made a thorough and diligent search of every nook and cranny. Mrs Bramble urged them on, convinced the figure had been heading for this room for some as-yet-undiscovered purpose and therefore something in here must be important. That said, the unlocked cupboards seemed undisturbed, the locked wine and bread cupboard remained secured, she had no reason to believe the few papers in a tray had been rifled through, and the religious clothing still hung on a rail in a wardrobe. With their limited knowledge of the vestry, nothing seemed out of place and she had to admit defeat, for now.

At that moment, Reverend Weaver backed into the central table and knocked it enough to topple the contents. Kitty made a grab for the carafe and chalice, Mrs Bramble managed to affect a rescue of the wine, and the dish of wafers skittered to the edge but was halted by the chalice cloth, avoiding it smashing on the stone floor.

'I do beg your pardon,' said Weaver, sheepishly.

'Not to worry, no harm done,' said Mrs Bramble. She gave one more glance around the room and patted the bundle in her pocket. 'There's nothing else here so we should leave back through the crypt to avoid risking any encounter with Inspector Cole or the chief. We wouldn't want them asking awkward questions about why we're in here, at night, especially without Reverend Dench.'

They extinguished two of the candle lamps and followed Mrs Bramble, who went ahead carrying the third. She took little care to be wary, knowing the figure wouldn't dare return again now their interest in the chapel had been discovered, and blew out her candle at the bottom of the steps. The trio ascended by the light of the gas lamp and once the door and gate had been pulled to behind them, Mrs Bramble turned to Kitty.

'Were you able to gain entry?' she said in a quiet voice.

Kitty nodded. 'It went like you said it would. An officer and his wife came out but saw me as a nuisance, nothing more.'

'Wait, what?' said Weaver.

'Don't worry, Kitty undertook a little task in the married men's quarters on our behalf while we were having dinner,' said Mrs Bramble.

'Right, good, right,' said Weaver, not looking at all convinced that something untoward hadn't happened while his back was turned.

'What about the rooms?' said Mrs Bramble to Kitty.

'They had brass name plates so I couldn't make a mistake,' said Kitty. 'The key worked like a charm.'

Mrs Bramble relaxed. If Kitty had been caught like a criminal or even suspected of subterfuge, she wouldn't be here now. It was a great relief to know that any danger she had put her trusted housemaid in had passed.

'And did you find anything of significance?' said Weaver, warily.

Kitty relayed the rest of her night's work, even down to the details of the card, the lingering reminder of a fishy meal and her encounter with the Yeoman Gaoler.

'You were fortunate, there,' said Weaver.

Kitty nodded. 'Don't I know it. And then I saw you two skulk off beside the chapel. You seemed to be following somebody into the crypt and there was no point in me tagging along for the sake of it. I knew you could take care of yourselves so I decided to go through the chapel instead. Perhaps to intercept whoever you were after.'

'It could have been dangerous.'

Kitty shrugged. 'I knew you'd be close by.'

Mrs Bramble pursed her lips and made a face to show her displeasure, but she was secretly proud of the young woman's courage. 'Did you see anyone approach the chapel before you saw us?'

'No.' Kitty shook her head. 'Everyone must still have

been at dinner.' She rubbed her stomach. 'And I still haven't had mine.'

'How did they get past us into the crypt, then?' said Weaver.

'They can't have come across the roof garden and down the steps because the gate squeaks and we would have heard it,' said Mrs Bramble. 'Which means they were already at the gate when we came out from dinner, or ...' She turned to look at the two doors in the chaplain's house wall facing the crypt entrance. 'Have you any idea where those two doors lead to?'

'As a guess, at least one must lead through to the scullery,' said Kitty.

'You're not thinking Augustus or Jasper have anything to do with this?' said Weaver, aghast.

'Apart from Inspector Cole and yourself, Reverend, Jasper Chant is the only other person unaffected by the poisoning,' said Mrs Bramble. She put her hand on the chapel wall. 'This is the domain of Reverend Dench and I can tell how proud he is to be resident Chaplain of the Chapel Royal. If someone threatened him or his position, might he defend himself?'

Reverend Weaver shook his head. 'I've known him a long time and cannot believe he would.'

Mrs Bramble sighed. 'Until we are completely sure how the congregation were poisoned, we cannot be sure of a motive. Until we are sure of a motive, we cannot be sure of the perpetrator.'

'And if we can't be sure of the perpetrator,' said Kitty, 'we can't be sure either is innocent.'

Weaver looked dismayed. 'And the inspector cannot be sure of me.'

18

Following a restful night's sleep in guest rooms provided by Reverend Dench, Mrs Bramble enjoyed a light breakfast that she was pleased to find included a soft-boiled egg with toast soldiers, as well as a pleasantly tart marmalade. Afterwards, she invited her fellow sleuths, Reverend Weaver and Kitty, to go for a stroll in the Tower grounds. The excuse given was the opportunity to take the morning air, despite the now-familiar smells emanating from the river and its environs. The real reason was to take stock of their situation out of range of pricked-up ears and plan what to do next.

'Has anyone seen the governor?' said Mrs Bramble, looking across to his black-and-white Tudor residence as they ambled alongside Tower Green towards the Bloody Tower.

'Not since I saw him and his wife ushered away from the service to safety,' said Reverend Weaver. 'I heard he agreed to Inspector Cole and the chief conducting a joint investigation, but beyond that I have no idea.'

'Hmm, he probably thinks it's best the chief keeps him informed while letting the investigation run its course. Talking of which, I must speak to Major Rushton and his wife today, and the Frys' friend Sir Stephen Lovell if possible.'

Mrs Bramble and Kitty wheeled to their left and descended a set of stone steps to the slope leading beside the guardhouse. Reverend Weaver followed suit a second later as though towed behind on a piece of rope.

'Reverend,' said Mrs Bramble. 'You cannot speak to the Rushtons, the Frys or their friends, not after the circumstances of your arrest.'

'I – well – no,' said Weaver. 'Of course not.'

'So, your job, if you will, is to keep an eye on Reverend Dench, Dr Burford and Mr Chant.'

They reached the arched passage beneath the Bloody Tower.

'Me—?' Weaver sidestepped at the last moment, avoiding a crunching encounter with the edge of one of the solid doors that stood open. 'Me?' he repeated.

Mrs Bramble turned sharp left with Kitty at Traitors' Gate and waited for Weaver to realise he'd turned the wrong way. 'I know it will be difficult,' said Mrs Bramble when he'd caught up. 'I think Mr Chant is the most intriguing, especially as he did not succumb to the poisoning, but please do keep a watchful eye all around. I leave it up to you to judge who might be acting more suspiciously than the others.'

'Right, good, right,' said Reverend Weaver, with a pained expression that suggested he was going to find the three-way surveillance quite a challenge.

'What about me, Mrs B?' said Kitty.

'The usual, I'm afraid, Kitty,' said Mrs Bramble, stopping after the next tower but before the out-of-bounds Yeoman Warders' Club.

She waited for a troop of Yeoman Warders carrying long-handled partisan spears to march beneath the arch, led by another carrying a long-handled battle-axe. Each wore the full red-and-gold tunics of state dress, sabre-hilted swords at their waists. On their heads they sported the familiar flat hats adorned with red, white and blue rosettes.

Mrs Bramble ignored Reverend Weaver's question of 'What's the occasion?' and turned to pass beneath the arched entrance back into the Inner Ward.

'I must know what the housemaids working for the Frys and Rushtons really think of their employers, and the feud,' she said. 'Servants are not shy about sharing their opinions with other servants, as you well know, and they may reveal some underlying animosity we have failed to uncover thus far.'

'It seems like you suspect everyone, Mrs B,' said Kitty.

'Yes, it does rather, doesn't it?' She smiled wryly. 'The chief let slip he is not enamoured by Inspector Cole's investigative style so you might want to look out for them too. Any chance to cause further chafing between them without attracting their ire towards us should be regarded as an opportunity for distraction.'

Continuing their circuit anti-clockwise past the stores block, Mrs Bramble halted outside the married men's quarters and looked first at Reverend Weaver and then Kitty to indicate the next instruction was for them both. 'If either man asks for me, tell them I am anywhere other than the Inner Ward. If you see me by the chapel, send them the opposite way. If you see me down here, send them up on the walls.'

Kitty peeled away to sit on her bench from the previous evening, Reverend Weaver almost cannoned into a Yeoman Warder but did a little dance around him on his way to look for his next quarry, and Mrs Bramble headed for the Waterloo Barracks. She had spotted Captain Fry outside the front entrance talking to a clean-shaven man with dark curly hair whom she recognised from his description as Sir Stephen Lovell.

As she approached, the captain wheeled away and strode

towards the officers' quarters without noticing her. Lovell turned the other way and she saw he was dressed in clothes similar to those worn by Clyne but without the frills, although his bow tie was a striking shade of royal blue. She supposed gentlemen of a certain type who moved in similar circles would naturally conform to the fashion of the day, and of their station.

He performed a polite touch of his top hat when he saw her advancing.

'Mrs Bramble, I presume.'

'Sir Stephen,' she replied. 'I'm glad I caught you.'

'I thought you might be.' He smiled at her slight frown. 'I have been made aware of your investigation, not least by Inspector Cole who seems to have a lesser opinion of you than most around here.'

'We crossed paths recently.' She smiled. 'The outcome, although highly satisfactory for both of us, did not endear him to me nor I to him.'

'But your quest and goal are the same, are they not?'

'They are.'

'But?' he said, with a raised eyebrow.

She paused to consider her words. 'The methods we use and the paths we follow to the truth are somewhat different. This often puts us at odds.'

'I can see it might.' Lovell chuckled. 'I wish you success in your endeavours.' He touched his hat again and went to leave but Mrs Bramble took a half-step sideways to block his departure.

'Oi,' he muttered in surprise.

'Forgive me,' she said, noting the lapse of decorum. 'Despite our differences, the Inspector asked me to fill in whatever background information I could gather, so if you could spare me some of your time?'

Lovell sniffed and hesitated. 'Of course,' he said, the mask of social respectability sliding back in place. Do you wish to walk or sit?'

'Here will do just fine, it will take but a moment.' She saw a look of suspicion flash in his eyes. 'Do tell me, Sir Stephen, how did you come by your knighthood?'

'Oh, that?' He seemed caught off-guard by the question. 'I was honoured for my work in the Intelligence Department of the War Office.'

'Intelligence? Intriguing,' said Mrs Bramble, hoping to boost the man's sense of self-importance. 'Are you a spy?' She smiled.

Lovell laughed. 'Nothing so glamorous, I'm afraid. Instead of intelligence, let's call it general information. We helped open up Africa through the drawing of a new map of the continent.'

Mrs Bramble put on her best *confused woman* expression. 'Surely the shape of a continent remains constant?'

Lovell smiled indulgently. 'The land mass, certainly, but our job was to make a visual record of the geographical reality to reflect the development, acquisitions and expansions of the British Empire.'

'Sounds grand.'

'Not at all. What little excitement came my way with the blokes in Africa and India was mixed with a lot of daily grind, although when one feels one is doing something for the good of the country one feels a sense of pride in one's work.

A lot of *ones*, thought Mrs Bramble. 'Is that how you met the Frys? I should imagine the army played a vital role in opening up Africa, as you put it.'

'Something like that.' Lovell sniffed. 'I became pals with Captain Fry's father, Lord Fry, whom I met during the interminable meetings held to discuss building railway lines abroad.'

Everyone seems to be in railways these days, she thought. 'Then you know them well?'

'I like to think so.' Lovell looked at her askance. 'Why do you ask?'

'I wonder if you could tell me – for background – the current nature of the relationship between the Frys and the Rushtons? I know about the incident in their past that soured their friendship.'

'Then you know all there is to know,' said Lovell, looking relieved. 'After university, they joined the army, found themselves in the same regiment and now with the same posting, but they are soldiers who do their duty. They keep their army lives professional, their daily interactions civil and their private lives entirely separate, unless these coincide at events held in the officers' mess.'

'Like the canapé reception?'

'Yes, but even then, they maintained a discreet distance between them.'

'And what of Sir Oswald Clyne?'

Lovell, who had been looking over Mrs Bramble's shoulder at nothing in particular, suddenly glanced down at her. 'What of 'im?' He rubbed his nose and sniffed.

'What is he like?' she asked, noticing Lovell's expression harden. 'What is your opinion of him?'

Lovell took a long breath before answering.

'I don't care for the bloke, if you want the honest truth. Major Rushton is a cold fish and Mrs Rushton is much the same. Their choice of Clyne as a friend is very much in keeping with their own personalities.'

'Really? I spoke to him earlier and he seemed pleasant enough.'

Lovell scoffed. '*Seemed* being the operative word. Instead of gathering the facts and coming to his own informed opinion, he is inclined to feed off the opinions of others; offering his – admittedly limited – support to the wrong sort while denigrating good people on a whim.'

'Do you consider the Frys the right sort?'

He smiled. 'As a matter of fact, I do.'

'Has their dispute ever manifested in other ways?' she probed. 'Through and between their wives, perhaps?'

'If nothing else, I'm sure your position at Hampton Court Palace has brought into focus for you the capacity of women to take umbrage and bear grudges. Nothing unusual in that, is there?' He rubbed his nose and sniffed again.

Mrs Bramble kept a neutral expression but bit her tongue so hard she thought she might draw blood. Why did most men consider all women no more than gossips and nags, easy to take offence and hard to appease? 'The bearing of grudges is not wholly the domain of women, Sir Stephen, as I'm sure *you* are aware, considering your vicarious dislike of Sir Oswald.'

Anger flashed in his eyes but faded in a second. 'I'm sure he has as little time for me as I have for him. We have nothing to say to each other and do not engage.'

'Then I take it Inspector Cole and Chief Yeoman Warder Treadle need have no fear of revenge being taken?'

Lovell laughed; a harsher, baser sound this time. 'Whatever people may think of us, first and foremost Sir Oswald and I are gentlemen and the major and captain fight only on the field of battle. In any case, for revenge to be taken, first there must be certainty about to whom it should be directed and it appears there is not. As much as I dislike the Rushtons, and as much as I would rejoice if blame were laid at their door, I cannot see Mrs Fry died of anything other than the same food poisoning that turned all our stomachs.'

'An accident then?' said Mrs Bramble.

'Unless you can prove otherwise.' He touched the brim of his top hat. 'Good day.'

She watched him start to walk away and wondered how much of what he had said was true. To her mind, Sir Stephen Lovell and Sir Oswald Clyne appeared similar in outlook, especially when it came to defending their friends. Not uncommon in any class of society, one might think, but neither was the kind of misguided loyalty that led to tragedy. She sincerely hoped Lovell would not take the law into his own hands, and Clyne would not rise to any challenge.

That hope seemed forlorn when he stopped after a few paces and turned, the light glinting on something nestled in the palm of his right hand.

'Of course, if you *can* prove otherwise,' he said, and touched the brim of his hat once again. 'Good day, Mrs Bramble.'

Her heart was still thumping in recognition of the small but deadly object she had seen before he hid it from sight.

A Webley British Bulldog pocket revolver.

19

After her escapade the night before, Kitty felt more than a little trepidation at the prospect of having to infiltrate the married men's quarters again, this time in daylight. Perched on the bench watching visitors amble past reminded her of sitting in the park at home, looking back at Hampton Court Palace. Except, she had never been called upon to stretch the bounds of the law there.

Given the probability of most if not all the officers being on duty, and the likelihood that Sir Oswald Clyne would not visit unannounced, Kitty suspected her only nemesis might come in the form of Mrs Rushton. If her absence could be ensured, getting access to her housemaid, and also the Frys', would be less fraught with danger.

Unfortunately, she spotted Inspector Cole and Chief Yeoman Warder Treadle approaching at the same second they spotted her, and her heart fell. No good would come from ignoring them or trying to run away so she stood up and prepared to lie.

'Miss Kitty,' said Cole, glancing around as though searching. 'Your mistress not with you today?'

Kitty mimicked his searching glances, looked at him in surprise and said, 'No, sir.'

She saw him go to say something, maybe sarcastic or a rebuke, but he thought better of it.

'Mrs Bramble. Nearby?' said Treadle in his usual staccato manner.

'I have no idea, sir,' said Kitty, truthfully. 'We went our separate ways a while back, and since I have no other duties in the Tower, I thought I'd take the opportunity to look around.'

Inspector Cole scoffed. 'By sitting on a bench?'

'Not reveal her intentions?' said the chief, ignoring Cole. 'Strange mistress.' He looked concerned. 'Treat you well?'

'I cannot believe for one moment that she is not off questioning someone inappropriately,' interrupted Cole, eyeing Kitty suspiciously. 'About the investigation, I mean.'

Kitty hesitated.

'Out with it, girl,' Cole said irritably. 'I should imagine even the likes of you would know it's better to help rather than hinder a police investigation.'

Kitty bristled at the put-down, especially as Cole knew the part she had played in helping Mrs Bramble, and him, with the investigation to catch the Hampton Court murderer.

'Joint,' said the chief, leaning forward with a crooked smile and a little wave. 'Point of order. Not your domain. Governor's dispensation. Nice to have help. Often goes awry. Last time, sixpenny piece for Christmas pudding, went missing. Kitchen in chaos. City of London superintendent, friend of the governor, arrested a cook. Accused of theft. Cook took umbrage. Covered superintendent in custard; skin and all. Upshot? Sixpence found on floor, cook absolved of theft.'

'That's good, surely?' said Cole, tentatively.

'Ah, not so. Cook? Arrested for assault. Superintendent? Demoted to inspector.'

Cole looked as though he didn't know whether to sit down, arrest the chief or explode.

'Miss Kitty,' the chief continued. 'Your mistress. Nearby, perhaps?'

Kitty glanced to her right, towards the archway which led to the Yeoman Warders' Club. 'I did hear Mrs Bramble say something to Reverend Weaver, about questioning one of the maids from a household in the Outer Ward.'

Cole threw his hands up in exasperation. 'I told her ... I told her.' He pointed a finger at Kitty. 'Where is the reverend?'

'With Mrs Bramble?' Kitty shrugged. 'Maybe?'

Cole showed his gritted teeth and shook his head before turning towards the path leading to the Outer Ward. 'Chief,' he called, without looking back or stopping.

The chief's eyes narrowed almost imperceptibly at being called to heel like a dog, but Kitty noticed this and the colouring in his cheeks a second before he followed Cole without another word.

Any relief and satisfaction at the success in diverting them away from Mrs Bramble was short-lived as her attention returned to the task in hand. She had no desire to wheedle her way back into the married men's quarters, so the only way forward she could see was to waylay the maids on their way to complete some errand. In itself, that posed a problem. A maid might ordinarily run errands beyond the walls of the Tower but the restrictions on movement imposed by Cole and the chief meant no one present on the day of Mrs Fry's death could leave. Kitty glanced around automatically, assessing the likelihood of there being somewhere a maid might go where she could follow and have a private conversation.

Everywhere she looked, Fusiliers and Yeoman Warders went about their duties, and visitors milled around with gazes upturned to take in the sights. She knew other residents such as wives and maids would be in the Outer Ward, busy with their daily tasks and chores. As the only non-resident well known to the residents, Mr Jasper Chant, the organist, could roam at will but the eyes of the Tower would be fixed on Mrs Bramble, Reverend Weaver and her. Privacy of any kind appeared elusive and her task seemed impossible.

Until she spotted Mrs Rushton at the far corner of the White Tower.

The major's wife appeared to be talking to someone and Kitty strolled up towards the officers' quarters to get a better look, knowing Mrs Bramble would want to know. Nervousness fluttered in her chest when she saw the Rushtons' housemaid listening and nodding as her mistress spoke, and they both turned their heads away from where Kitty stood as someone else approached.

Kitty noticed the housemaid take a discreet step backwards as Mrs Bramble came into view, and Mrs Rushton said something with a flap of her hand that was obviously a dismissal of some kind because the housemaid performed a bob curtsey and left the two women to it. Kitty saw her chance and slowly ambled into the path of the maid.

'Hello,' she said, bringing the maid to a halt. 'I'm Mrs Bramble's maid, Kitty.'

'Gwen,' said the maid, automatically, casting a look of suspicion and surprise.

Kitty nodded towards where their two mistresses stood in conversation. 'I've been sent away too.' That was sort of what had happened. Close enough for it not to be an outright lie. 'You work for Major and Mrs Rushton, I believe.'

The young woman gave her a sideways glance. 'What if I do?'

'When our mistresses started speaking, I thought I'd

ask you what someone at a loose end might do to entertain themselves.'

'A loose end?' Gwen frowned. 'You're lucky to be at a loose end. Why don't you take a turn around the Tower like most of us do if we get five minutes to ourselves?'

'And have you? Five minutes?'

'I ...'

'Have I said something wrong?' asked Kitty, curious as to why she had received such a frosty reception.

Gwen glanced over her shoulder, took Kitty's arm and guided her towards the married men's quarters. Kitty had no desire to risk crossing the path of Cole and the chief so soon after setting them on a wild goose chase so she reversed the hold to control the direction and steered Gwen towards St Martin's Tower at the north-east corner of the inner wall.

'I apologise,' breathed Gwen. 'Mrs Rushton told me not to talk to you or Mrs Bramble.'

'Why ever not?' said Kitty, intrigued.

'She said you were both casting aspersions to get your friend Reverend Weaver off the hook for Mrs Fry's murder.'

Kitty's heart gave a jolt. 'Murder. Who said it was murder?'

'The doctor said so.' Gwen shrugged. 'This is a small place full of rumours at the best of times but when strangers turn up, someone dies, and then we're all confined to the Tower ... Something must be up, mustn't it?'

'Something must be up,' echoed Kitty, who had intended a soft and slow approach but couldn't resist the opportunity to jump straight in, to see the woman's reaction if nothing else. 'Do you mean the feud?'

Gwen recoiled as though scalded. 'You know about that?'

Kitty gave ger a reassuring smile. 'Doesn't everyone?'

Gwen shrugged again. 'I thought not, but apparently I was misinformed.'

'By whom.'

'The master and mistress. She said it was no one else's business but theirs and people might get the wrong idea.'

'And have they?'

'Haven't you?'

'Not yet,' Kitty lied. 'I tend not to set too much store by gossip but I know about the incident at university. I know your mistress supports her husband, and I know Sir Oswald is as supportive of the Rushtons as Sir Stephen is of the Frys. Nothing wrong in that.'

Gwen stopped. 'So why are you interested?'

Kitty realised they had reached the stone steps leading up onto the wall, the way Mrs Bramble had taken her for their own private chat. She tightened her hold and urged Gwen to climb, stepping in unison. At the top, Kitty moved to the right, away from the steps and the direction most visitors took.

'If my mistress is happy and all is harmonious, I have an easier life,' Kitty admitted. 'At the moment she is worried about her friend, Reverend Weaver, which does not lend itself to a life free of strife.'

'With that I can entirely sympathise,' said Gwen.

'Thank you,' said Kitty, looking at the round tower to her right. 'This is a magnificent fortress but it is so cold and stark compared to the familiar surroundings of Hampton Court Palace.' She looked back at Gwen. 'All my friends are there, not here. It can be a lonely place if you know no one.'

Gwen pondered this. 'We could walk and talk another time, if you'd like.'

Kitty smiled. 'I would like that.'

They waited in silence as a group of visitors chattered, pointed and eventually moved on.

Gwen cleared her throat. 'If you know about the, um, what happened at university, you'll know Major Rushton has been at odds with Captain Fry ever since.'

'My mistress told me,' said Kitty.

Gwen went to speak but paused before fixing Kitty with a sideways look. 'I have witnessed the master and mistress have words about the past.'

Kitty's ears pricked up but she tried to keep her expression impassive. 'Words?'

Gwen sighed. 'Mrs Rushton would often bring up the dispute with her husband, especially whenever they were due to be in the same room with Captain and Mrs Fry. She said something ought to be done, even after all these years, but the major always said they should wait and bide their time because others would get their dues.'

'Do you know what he meant by that?'

Gwen glanced behind her as though someone might be right on her shoulder, listening. 'The Fusiliers' brigadier over at the Hounslow barracks has long made it known he thought it unnecessary to keep two officers with such experience at the Tower with so few men to command.'

'Even if they are of different ranks?' said Kitty.

'Rumour has it, he wanted to post one to either Poonah in India or Suez in Egypt.'

'How did Major Rushton take the news?' said Kitty, unsure where this was leading.

'Neither of the officers were pleased at the prospect of another long sea journey and spending years away from England, living in dust and heat, possibly fighting disease as much as fighting the locals.'

'But?' Kitty prompted.

'When the brigadier visited the Tower, he allowed them to make their case to stay here. I heard Major Rushton say he thought he'd gained the upper hand by stating Captain Fry had the greater experience in foreign parts and could be regarded as a steady hand in the command of reinforcements.'

'That's a good recommendation from someone who hates you,' said Kitty, frowning at Gwen's shake of her head. 'Isn't it?'

'As far as I know, it wasn't exactly true and I didn't know what to think, to be honest,' said Gwen. 'They were supposed to say why they should stay, not why the other should be sent abroad. My friend Beth, she's housemaid to the Frys, heard Mrs Fry say her husband had done enough for queen, country and empire at the expense of starting a family. She desperately wanted to stay in England so she had the captain say they were trying for a child. Who knows what was true?'

Now Kitty understood. 'Does trying for a child, an heir, trump military experience?' she said. She saw Gwen's eyebrows raise in affirmation. 'If you have two officers looking for a way out? Of course, I suppose it would,' she answered herself.

Would avoiding the prospect of an unwanted foreign posting be the catalyst for murder? she wondered. After all, the two men were professional soldiers with distinguished careers behind them and both had joined up voluntarily. That didn't smack of a reluctance to be in the thick of things, with the opportunities to bring more glory and battle honours back for the regiment. Mind you, if you were sick of battle and wanted to get rid of your rival ...

'You said you are friends with ... Beth, was it? Must be difficult, given the frostiness between your employers.'

Gwen cast a nervous glance around. 'All the maids are

friendly in some way or another and all the masters and mistresses know that. It must be the same at the palace as it is here, surely? I'm friends with Beth. She's friends with Esther, the chaplain's chambermaid. I'm sure the families disapprove but we don't do anything to give them cause to notice us. The likes of us are ignored unless we somehow get in the way.'

'Of course,' said Kitty with a nod of understanding.

'That's not all,' said Gwen, bringing Kitty's thoughts back to the present. 'Mrs Fry always had a go at Mrs Rushton behind her back.'

Kitty scoffed. 'I'd heard they were as bad as each other.'

Gwen frowned in annoyance. 'Yes – well – maybe so, but I imagine she started it long before I became Mrs Rushton's housemaid. She seemed the type, if you ask me. And as for Mrs Fry being unwell ... I doubt she's had even a headache in her whole life.'

'Is that not uncharitable?' said Kitty, feeling the conversation getting away from her.

'It's what Beth said. Well, not in so many words.' A pink glow had bloomed on her cheeks as though she realised she'd said too much. 'I-I'd better get back in case the mistress is looking for me.'

Unwilling to end the conversation yet, Kitty looked idly over the wall and down to the casemates in the Outer Ward below, realising her mistake as soon as her chest tightened in recognition of the men below. Chief Yeoman Warder Treadle happened to glance up at that precise moment. He waved a greeting, which drew the attention of Inspector Cole, who looked up with a grimace the very second that she politely waved back. He stood staring up with hands on hips for a few seconds before striding back the way he had come, pulling the chief along in his wake. She turned and saw with relief that Gwen's position by the inner railing meant she could not be seen from below. Even so, the inspector and chief would catch them together and ask awkward questions if they did not hurry.

'Perhaps I should leave you to your duties, but I'd like to speak again if I may?' said Kitty, taking Gwen's arm.

This drew a hesitant nod from Gwen as Kitty steered her down the stone steps and left her at the corner of the officers' quarters with promises to speak again. Kitty noted Mrs Bramble and Mrs Rushton had long since departed, but her attention became diverted as Mrs Fry's housemaid, Beth, hurried past, almost knocking her over. She needed to speak to her too, but the maid scurried away towards the rear of the Waterloo Barracks, oblivious to all those around her until she reached the back corner.

Kitty had almost caught up, despite having to weave through another cluster of visitors, when she saw Beth's face light up before she stepped out of sight. Although Inspector Cole and the chief might be approaching from behind at any moment, Kitty hesitated at going forward. As much as she wished to avoid being hauled over the coals again by the two investigators, she also had no desire to run headlong into Captain Fry and draw his ire.

She eased forward, promising herself she would flee at the first sign of impending conflict, and peered round the corner of the building. What she saw drew forth an audible gasp and she recoiled out of sight as though a tug-of-war team had yanked her back by a rope tied around her waist. That was the last thing she had expected to see.

She had witnessed a kiss delivered to the lips of Mrs Fry's housemaid ...

In broad daylight ...

By Jasper Chant.

20

Mrs Bramble watched Sir Stephen Lovell stride away, the sight of the pocket revolver in the palm of his hand imprinted on her mind.

She sincerely hoped his words would not prove hollow and he would continue to keep his distance from Sir Oswald Clyne. But if Clyne suspected Lovell's hand in the murder of Mrs Fry, would he do the same, or take direct action, forcing Lovell to make the ultimate defence?

The sight of Mrs Rushton ambling past the White Tower with her maid caught Mrs Bramble's eye and she moved to intercept them. There was no telling if or when those she needed to question would retreat into buildings where she was unable to follow, so she had to take advantage of catching them in the open, like a lioness with her prey. Despite Inspector Cole and the chief roaming the grounds like a pair of guard dogs, she desperately wanted to speak to Mrs Rushton and now seemed as good a time as any.

'Mrs Rushton,' said Mrs Bramble, displaying her best expression of concern. 'How are you bearing up?'

'I beg your pardon,' said Mrs Rushton, halting with an expression that questioned what business it was of anyone's.

'The tragic passing of Mrs Fry; it must be upsetting for everyone.'

'Yes, I suppose it must.'

'Although I hear you were not on the best of terms.'

'We were not on any terms,' said Mrs Rushton with a flap of her hand.

The housemaid took a step backwards and performed a bob curtsey before leaving them to speak privately.

'That implies you had no interest in each other at all.' Mrs Bramble raised her eyebrows as though perplexed. 'Which isn't true, from what I can gather.'

'How impertinent!' Mrs Rushton blinked rapidly. 'Why are you doing any *gathering* in the first place? This is none of your concern.'

'But I'm afraid it is,' said Mrs Bramble, noticing Kitty approach the housemaid. 'My friend has been accused of Mrs Fry's murder. Both Inspector Cole and the chief have entrusted me ...' she tapped her chest for emphasis '... with gathering information on their behalf.'

'Spying on us?'

A small laugh escaped from Mrs Bramble. 'Not at all. Speaking to people in the open can hardly be called spying.'

Mrs Rushton looked irritated 'We will have to agree to disagree.'

'And what of your dislike for Captain and Mrs Fry?' Mrs Bramble took two steps to the side, forcing Mrs Rushton to turn towards her and away from where Kitty was now leading the housemaid off. 'Do you disagree there was no love lost between you?'

Mrs Rushton scoffed, as though having to explain was beneath her, but another spate of rapid blinking betrayed her. 'Mrs Bramble, a person might meet hundreds if not thousands of people in their lifetime. One cannot hope to like them all, especially those one is forced to work with or live in close proximity to. Very few of those turn into true friends and, if you are lucky, even fewer become your enemies.'

'I agree, but talking of true friends, I was speaking to Sir Stephen Lovell a moment ago.' Mrs Bramble saw Mrs Rushton's face stiffen. 'Despite his loyalty to the Frys, he seems content, if content is the right word, that the death of Mrs Fry was not deliberate and nothing more than a tragic accident.'

'As do we all.'

'Not all, I'm afraid. Many are reserving judgement for the moment. At least, while the investigation is in progress. I strongly suspect even Sir Stephen would be swayed should any new evidence come to light.'

Mrs Bramble knew she had Mrs Rushton rattled as the woman's eyes bored into her during a second or two of silence.

'Then I wish you luck with your endeavours,' Mrs Rushton said eventually. 'Mrs Fry collapsed at the same time as the rest of the congregation fell ill and any of us could have suffered the same fate. It is only by the grace of God and good fortune that the poison did not prove fatal to many more. I hear Mr Chant and Reverend Weaver escaped the illness.'

Her meaning was clear and Mrs Bramble knew it had been delivered to irk her. To her annoyance, it had.

'As Inspector Cole also remained unaffected, are your suspicions to fall upon him also? A detective in the Metropolitan Police.' Mrs Bramble tilted her head questioningly.

A smug smile played around Mrs Rushton's mouth. 'I was merely stating a fact. Are you aware Mrs Fry had a weak constitution? Everyone else knew. It is a miracle she lasted as long as she did.'

Mrs Bramble could not recall meeting any woman quite so lofty and irritating, and she had met many in the army worthy of being placed in that category. Indeed, there were a few she could name at Hampton Court Palace.

'If I were to speak with Sir Oswald, would he bear the same ill will toward the Frys and Sir Stephen as they do to you?' she said.

The self-satisfied smile left Mrs Rushton's lips. 'Before you cast aspersions, Mrs Bramble, you have to remember, my husband and Captain Fry have served together for a number of years. During that time, Mrs Fry and I have fulfilled our duties as the wives of army officers. Not always an easy task. The army is not the place to open old wounds. Nor is it the place to settle old scores. Our friends might wish to defend our honour but would not act on our behalf without prior consultation.'

A jolt went through Mrs Bramble's chest.

Mrs Rushton flinched as she seemed to realise that she had spoken unwisely, and closed her eyes for a second against another onset of rapid blinking.

'How long have you known Sir Oswald,' said Mrs Bramble, but it was clear she would get no more information today as the woman backed away.

'I am disinclined to answer any more of your insolent questions, Mrs Bramble,' said Mrs Rushton. 'I have things to do and need to locate my housemaid, whom you seem to have scared off. Good day.'

Mrs Bramble watched her hurry away, her heavy-soled boots crunching and clumping on the parade, her head turning from side to side in apparent search of the elusive maid.

Had the woman unwittingly inferred that Sir Oswald Clyne had acted on her behalf? Or that of her husband? Was revenge truly why Sir Stephen Lovell carried a British Bulldog pocket pistol, or was it for self-defence? But how could Clyne have managed to kill Mrs Fry with nicotine poisoning? Had he taken a chance by poisoning the whole congregation, knowing she had a weak constitution? The whole scattergun premise seemed preposterous and she pushed it to the back of her mind.

Mrs Bramble needed to speak to Major Rushton and Sir Oswald Clyne to find out their stories. She also needed to find Reverend Weaver or Dr Burford to go over the results of the medical tests. And where exactly had Kitty taken Mrs Rushton's housemaid? What information might she have gleaned?

Her head throbbed and she decided to retreat to the chaplain's house for a nice sit down and a restorative cup of tea. She assured herself that no one could leave the Tower just yet so she could at least spare herself a rare five minutes.

Walking across the parade ground, she observed the many visitors idling by. Singles, couples and small groups surveyed the grandeur and history of the buildings surrounding them, oblivious to the unusual goings-on unfolding in their midst. She wasn't even sure she had a full grasp of events herself.

And that's when she saw Jasper Chant with the Frys' housemaid.

Standing in the middle of the passage between the chapel and the barracks, the couple seemed in deep conversation but were not arguing. While not exactly hiding in the shadows, their furtive looks at passers-by suggested a wariness of wagging tongues. Could they be sweethearts?

Mrs Bramble watched from her distant vantage point until Chant took the maid's hand, kissed it, and nodded towards the parade-ground end of the passage. He kept hold of her hand as she turned away, only letting go as she moved out of reach.

Chant watched as the maid walked towards the parade ground, turning away as she rounded the corner of the barracks and disappeared from his view. He then opened the waist-high iron gate and closed it behind him as he descended the steps to the vestry.

Mrs Bramble watched the maid hurry in the direction of the married men's quarters but decided not to pursue, preferring to leave her to Kitty. Instead, she turned her attention to Jasper Chant, curious to see if he would re-emerge. Reverend Dench had said services would be held in St John's Chapel in the White Tower while St Peter's was closed, so what could Chant be doing?

She waited for a moment, on the assumption he was still in the vestry, but her natural curiosity got the better of her. Chant's assignation with the maid had set hares running in her mind and she had to fight to rein in her thoughts, reminding herself that theories were all well and good but only facts mattered. To that end, but not wishing to be caught following people around the Tower, Mrs Bramble decided to enter the chapel via the main entrance at the western end. If questioned, she could always say she had sought a moment of quiet contemplation.

An instant later, she had reached the corner of the chapel when a figure she recognised as Jasper Chant crossed from the crypt's gate to a door at the far end of the chaplain's house, which she had noticed the night before. Chant entered quickly and shut the door behind him without a glance back.

Whatever he had been up to, he had not expected to be followed. Did this mean he felt safe and regarded the likelihood of being threatened as non-existent? If that was so, did it suggest he might be the murderer?

Mrs Bramble sighed and shook her head. She still needed to sit down with a cup of tea and take stock, but—

A hand on her shoulder almost made her scream.

21

Reverend Weaver had no clue how he would keep track of one person, never mind three.

Dr Burford could be on his rounds, dispensing remedies and medical advice to the ailing within the Tower. Reverend Dench could be on his own rounds to administer pastoral care to his parishioners, or attending to religious matters in the Chapel of St John the Evangelist in the White Tower. It was unlikely Jasper Chant was anywhere near his beloved chapel organ in St Peter's, but he could be in the company of Dench. Dench could be with Burford. Burford could be with Chant. They could all be together!

Weaver stood outside the officers' quarters, one hand on his forehead, the other on his hip, and his mind in a whirl. This was not his domain. Dealing with all these goings-on was not his forte. He was a simple man – a man of God – who thrived on certainty and routine. How on earth had he managed to become embroiled in a plot to murder the wife of an army captain, if murder it proved to be?

He ran his hands over his face and back through his hair, trying to marshal his thoughts.

He would not be welcome back inside the officers' quarters alone and would most likely be incarcerated again should he try. He could not enter the married men's quarters for fear of the same. The Waterloo Barracks, Yeoman Warders' guardhouse and governor's residence were definitely out of bounds, as was the Outer Ward where one would find the Yeoman Warders quartered in the casemates.

Entering St Peter's chapel alone would be foolhardy. Some might think he was returning to the scene of his crime. Although several of the smaller towers were privately occupied, many were open to him, as was the imposing White Tower, but to what avail? As for the open areas, only the Inner Ward and the walkway around the walls presented themselves, but he could see Mrs Bramble already engaged in conversation with Sir Stephen Lovell on the parade ground.

What a site this was. So many places where one could not go. So many places where one should not go. A dearth of places where one might escape the prying eyes and scrutiny of others. Three people to find and nowhere he could go to find them.

He longed for the sanctuary of the Chapel Royal at Hampton Court Palace and his apartment in Seymour Gate. He felt safe there – sure of his purpose in life. Leading the special service yesterday was meant to be a feather in his cap. Now it felt more like a punishment.

He shrugged to himself, aware of how bizarre that might have looked to casual observers, because it made him feel marginally better. Until …

He spotted Inspector Cole and Chief Yeoman Warder Treadle approaching Kitty with a look of purpose. Mrs Bramble had asked him to help Kitty distract and deflect the duo, but he knew she was a capable young woman, and the mere sight of the two men provoked an instant sense of panic. His head swivelled on his shoulders as he sought refuge, and his gaze alighted gratefully on Dr Burford. The doctor was standing, medical bag in hand, in the open door of the officers' quarters, conversing with the guard, but

Weaver's relief was short-lived. Burford looked ready to depart, leaving Weaver with no option but to intercept him while he still could, officers' quarters or not.

Reverend Weaver looked at Mrs Bramble still in conversation with Sir Stephen Lovell and at Kitty being confronted by Inspector Cole and the chief, and made his move. Despite trying to be as unobtrusive as possible, his natural clumsiness prevented smooth passage and he bounced and ricocheted from one visitor to another like a badly thrown skittles ball. Fortunately, only those in the immediate area seemed aware of the clergyman's bizarre progress to the foot of the building's steps. A few more chuckled in amusement as Weaver stubbed his toe, stumbled up the several steps and landed in the outstretched arms of the surprised doctor.

Reverend Weaver extricated himself from the impromptu embrace, muttering thanks and profuse apologies while trying to hide his glowing cheeks of embarrassment.

'My good fellow,' said Dr Burford. 'Are you quite all right?'

'Nearly took a tumble,' said Weaver, smoothing his coat. 'Par for the course, I'm afraid. Bane of my life.'

'Steps?' queried Burford with a puzzled tilt of his head.

'Steps,' said Weaver. 'Doorways. Pavements. People. Life in general, really.'

'Oh,' said Burford with a smile. 'I entirely sympathise but don't think I have a remedy for that.'

Weaver looked at him, realised he wasn't being serious and smiled back. 'No, I'm sure you haven't, more's the pity.'

'I saw you down there with your hands on your hip and forehead, looking for all intents and purposes like an abandoned teapot, and I wondered if you might be unwell.'

'I, erm ...' Reverend Weaver wasn't sure how to respond, having never been likened to a teapot before, abandoned or otherwise.

'I was on my way to, um ...' Dr Burford glanced around the Inner Ward. 'But I think your need is greater than theirs. Would you like to come in for a moment, so I can give you the once over?'

Although unsure what 'the once over' might entail, Weaver glanced towards Kitty, Inspector Cole and the chief, and nodded in feverish agreement.

The guard stepped aside to let the two men pass and Reverend Weaver almost flinched at being on the receiving end of his hard stare. Dr Burford led him through to the familiar smoking room, arranged two chairs and sat opposite Weaver as though in the consulting room of his surgery.

Reverend Weaver felt uncomfortable at the situation he found himself in but otherwise quite well, although self-doubt entered his head at the sight of the paraphernalia Dr Burford removed from his bag.

'Say "ah",' said Burford.

'Say wha-aaah—' Weaver almost gagged as Dr Burford surprised him by thrusting a tongue suppressor into his mouth.

'Good,' said the doctor, swapping to a light that he shone into the reverend's eyes.

Weaver felt tears springing forth at the sudden brightness, but in a second it was gone, leaving him with misty vision and small dark spots dancing in front of him. Unable to see clearly, he could not defend himself against having his ears inspected and the left cuffs of his jacket and shirt sleeve being forced up past his wrist. He winced as the doctor clamped his fingers over his pulse point and counted under his breath while studying the sweeping second hand of his pocket watch.

'I say—' Weaver then gasped as the doctor thrust the cold disc of a monaural stethoscope through a gap in his shirt.

Keen for the ordeal to be over, Reverend Weaver stayed quiet while Dr Burford placed his ear against the other end and listened intently, perturbed when the doctor tutted as though deeply concerned.

Burford returned all his instruments to his bag before putting his hands together dramatically as though about to pray. 'Your heartbeat is rapid and I fear your blood pressure is too high,' he said, solemnly. 'You should take steps to reduce your anxiety, starting by returning home and getting some bed rest.'

'I-I ... cannot,' said Weaver, looking at the doctor with a sense of helplessness.

Dr Burford looked at him as though he was a general whose order had been disobeyed, then he seemed to remember where he was, and the predicament they found themselves in.

'Of course, of course,' said Burford. 'The position is not ideal but do try to keep calm. It will do you the world of good. I'll not charge you for this consultation, of course. Common courtesy and all that.'

Revered Weaver thanked the doctor even though he had not requested an examination, and the thought of being charged had not even entered his thinking.

'Is there anything else?' said Dr Burford in puzzlement, as though Reverend Weaver had requested the consultation.

'Not on my account,' said Weaver, anxious not to initiate another examination. 'Although this business with Mrs Fry is a worry.'

'It is, indeed,' said Dr Burford, knocking over his medical bag.

Reverend Weaver made a grab but only succeeded in making matters worse, shedding the bag's contents across the room. Amid profuse apologies, he helped retrieve the medical paraphernalia, recoiling from a metal needle and syringe set, and assisted the doctor in snapping the clasp of the bag shut before any further mishaps.

As the two flustered men sat back, Weaver, tried to cover his embarrassment with questions.

'Have you thought any more about how Mrs Fry alone succumbed to the poison?' he said.

'That very question has plagued me ever since the report came back,' said Dr Burford. 'As I believe I said before, Mrs Fry had a level of nicotine far in excess of someone who did not partake of tobacco products.'

'Even so,' said Reverend Weaver with a tilt of his head. 'I have heard she was a delicate creature, prone to headaches and periods of general malaise. As such, would she not have been more susceptible?'

'Nonsense.' Burford laughed. 'You've been listening to too many rumours. It's a fallacy, no doubt the root cause of which can be traced back to Mrs Fry herself. She was as strong as you and I, and only acted otherwise to engender sympathy and favour. She had the constitution of an ox, could eat a horse in one sitting and drink the hardiest soldier under the table. It is sometimes advantageous to have others believe something about you that perhaps is not wholly correct, is it not?'

Annoyance pricked at Reverend Weaver for having been so easily duped. 'She was as fit as a fiddle?'

'Could outplay a whole orchestra, so to speak.'

'Then I must inform Mrs Bramble,' said Weaver, rising from his chair.

'And do tell the good lady to be careful,' said Dr Burford. 'Whoever administered the poison appears to have done so indiscriminately and may have no qualms in doing so again to prevent investigators from apprehending him.'

22

Kitty's mind whirled at the sight of Beth, the Frys' housemaid, kissing Jasper Chant.

As far as she was aware, Chant had mentioned nothing to Mrs Bramble about being sweet on Beth. And Gwen hadn't said anything either during their conversation a few minutes ago.

Was it such a scandal for an organist and a housemaid to step out together, forcing them to sneak around the back of the army barracks for a quick kiss? She wasn't sure what etiquette existed at the Tower, which possibly differed from London as a whole and certainly from any she had encountered in the countryside. Perhaps these things were frowned upon more than elsewhere, although Lord knows why.

With her back pressed to the cold stone, watching visitors stroll past without a care in the world, Kitty realised that keeping any assignations secret would be problematic. Even with its multiple towers and turrets, casemates, gateways and walkways, the Tower of London could not match the rabbit warren of rooms, passages, courtyards and stairwells of Hampton Court Palace. There were far fewer quiet corners where a couple might find a moment's privacy.

Even under the cover of darkness, the Tower was patrolled by the Fusiliers and Yeoman Warders, as she had witnessed with Mrs Bramble and Reverend Weaver the previous evening. Jasper Chant could take a walk at night with greater ease than Beth but would still face a challenge from sentries if he decided to stray from the central area of the Inner Ward. Beth would have the additional problem of explaining where she was going to her employers. If seen together, word would soon get back to the Frys.

Kitty peeked and pulled back. Chant and Beth had drawn apart but she was gazing lovingly into his eyes as they chatted. He too had the look of love in his eyes, which came as a strange relief to Kitty. She hated the idea of yet another housemaid being taken unfair advantage of, but the couple appeared equally smitten.

Given the obvious secrecy surrounding their affair, perhaps they thought meeting anywhere in the Tower during the day could be passed off as a chance encounter. But why take the risk of anyone seeing you kissing openly? It wasn't that Kitty hadn't witnessed such goings on between the domestic staff at Hampton Court Palace, but at least most employed some discretion. There had to be a good reason for snatching such an intimate moment in plain sight.

Kitty resolved to make it her mission to find out.

Fearing Inspector Cole and Chief Yeoman Warder Treadle turning the corner of the officers' quarters at any moment, she decided she had no choice but to disturb the loving couple. She stepped round the corner of the barracks block only to find that they had walked on.

By the time Kitty reached the rear entrance of the barracks, where a bored guard ignored her completely, they were nearly at the far end by the chapel. She hurried after the sweethearts, but they had disappeared by the time she reached the point where the Fusilier guard had left Mrs Bramble the previous night.

Kitty glanced around, relieved no one had followed her.

She knew wandering around the Tower all day without her employer would attract attention. As a visiting housemaid, everyone would expect her to remain by the side of her mistress and there were only so many excuses she could come up with before Inspector Cole and the chief would confine her to the chaplain's house. She also knew they would ask her what she had been speaking about with Gwen but the longer she could put that off, the better.

She decided to return to her room in the chaplain's house for a while. Not only would it be a nice rest, but she could mull over things and perhaps be afforded the chance to look at Reverend Weaver's room. Not that she expected to find anything incriminating. The absence of proof did not constitute an absence of guilt but at least it would be a step forward in her mind and Mrs Bramble's.

Kitty approached the far corner of the chapel and noticed the unmistakable figure of Mrs Bramble standing there. She appeared deep in thought, but Kitty had intelligence to impart and placed her hand on her shoulder.

'Good lord.' Mrs Bramble clutched her throat as though Kitty had attempted to strangle her. 'I thought the murderer had come for me.'

'Forgive me, Mrs B. I didn't think. I was anxious to tell you—'

'Jasper Chant and the Frys' housemaid are conducting a secret love affair?'

Kitty's mouth fell open. 'How did you ...?' She looked at Mrs Bramble with a mixture of admiration and confusion.

'I saw them talking by the chapel not a few moments ago,' explained Mrs Bramble. 'The way they looked at each other and he kissed her hand before parting company suggested something more than a chance meeting and a passing chat.'

'I saw them behind the barracks but they didn't see me. Mr Chant was kissing Beth – she gave as good as she got – but they weren't at it for long. Gave me the impression they wanted to keep it secret but couldn't stay apart.'

'That's always the way with true love,' said Mrs Bramble with an enigmatic smile.

'Do you think this has anything to do with the murder of Mrs Fry?' said Kitty

Mrs Bramble pouted. 'It's something I think we should get to the bottom of. I haven't heard a bad word said against Mr Chant, or Beth come to that, but it doesn't mean all was well between the two of them and the Rushtons. After all, Mrs Rushton would lose her trusted housemaid, and I have no idea whether a courtship with a domestic servant could affect Mr Chant's position.'

'Do you want me to find Beth and have another chinwag?' said Kitty, annoyed with herself for having lost sight of Mr Chant and Beth in the first place.

'Not for the moment. I think we've stirred a hornet's nest and need to let the angry insects calm themselves. It would do everyone a power of good if we were not seen flitting from person to person asking awkward questions. At least for half an hour.' She glanced at the door of the chaplain's house. 'Tea, I think, don't you?'

'Splendid!'

Kitty almost fell over at the sound of the man's voice behind them and Mrs Bramble rounded on him as though ready to do battle.

Weaver recoiled as though already struck and knocked his elbow on the lead downpipe at the corner of the chapel.

'Funny bone,' he groaned, rubbing his elbow furiously. 'Why is it always my funny bone?'

'Reverend Weaver,' said Mrs Bramble with an air of

exasperation. 'What on earth are you doing creeping up on people?'

'Well, I-I ...' said Weaver, stopping to take a breath. 'It didn't occur that approaching in broad daylight could be construed as creeping.'

'It does if you suddenly appear at one's shoulder.' She glanced at Kitty.

Weaver looked contrite. 'I do apologise, Mrs Bramble. I let my enthusiasm get the better of me. I have news to impart, don't you see?' He gave his elbow another rub and wiggled his fingers as though ensuring they still worked.

'As do we all,' said Mrs Bramble. 'Now, about that tea ...'

The housemaid let them in to the chaplain's house and explained that Reverend Dench was upstairs in his room, having popped back briefly to collect some papers. She seated them in the parlour with the promise of refreshment and gave Kitty a curious look before she departed, as though serving another maid was not the done thing. As the door clicked shut, they all talked at once but Mrs Bramble held up her hands and signalled for them to lower their voices.

'Why don't you go first, Reverend,' she said softly.

Weaver gave his elbow a final rub and related his conversation with Dr Burford.

'And you say she had the constitution of an ox,' said Mrs Bramble, her brow furrowed in thought.

'Those were the doctor's exact words,' said Weaver.

'Gwen told Beth pretty much the same thing,' said Kitty, explaining to Weaver who the two women were.

'Someone must have known Mrs Fry was as healthy as you or I to have given her a higher dose of nicotine.'

'Are we sure?' said Kitty. 'Others may have taken more accidentally and fared better.'

Kitty went on to reveal the rancour existing between the Frys, the Rushtons and their friends, and the various possible permutations therein.

'It is as we suspected,' said Mrs Bramble, having relayed her own information about Sir Oswald having a mind to take matters into his own hands, and the pistol witnessed in Sir Stephen's palm. 'It is difficult to establish who hates whom the most and whether that has any true bearing on this case. If everyone in dispute beyond the Tower's walls were to be considered guilty, all the prisons would be full and every street would seem empty.'

'Then what can we do, Mrs B?' said Kitty.

Pausing as the door opened, they waited for the maid to deliver their tea, biscuits and a carafe of diluted fruit cordial, and withdraw. Automatically, as befitted her station, Kitty stirred the pot and poured. Mrs Bramble saw a wry smile on her lips and realised only two cups and two glasses had been placed on the tray. Annoyed at the deliberate slight, she made a mental note to mention it to Reverend Dench.

Reverend Weaver noticed too and insisted Kitty take his tea, explaining he'd had his fill earlier.

Mrs Bramble continued. 'Identifying a few people who may have had a strong enough motive to kill Mrs Fry is all well and good, but we are still as far from discovering the method and moment of opportunity as we were at the beginning.'

'Not so,' said Weaver. 'What about Jasper Chant, the only one besides me and Inspector Cole who wasn't poisoned? He must be at the Tower all the time, to practise on the new organ and to play during services.' He looked from Mrs Bramble to Kitty and back. 'And you wouldn't poison yourself, would you?'

This was true on every count, but Mrs Bramble could not envisage how a chapel organist afforded limited contact with the congregation could have administered poison. 'I'm afraid that doesn't explain where he might have acquired the nicotine,' she said. 'Nor how he could have given some to everyone present at the reception.'

Far from looking crestfallen, Reverend Weaver looked at the two of them as though the answer was staring them in the face and he was waiting for them to see the solution too.

'Mrs Bramble,' he said. 'You've just stated that everyone was at the canapé reception.'

'Ye-es,' said Mrs Bramble.

'Where everyone ate and drank.'

'Ye-es.'

'Although they didn't, did they?'

Mrs Bramble frowned as she thought about this but could not fathom what her friend was getting at.

'Not everyone ate *and* drank,' said Weaver triumphantly. 'I didn't drink any of the white wine at the reception because I wanted to keep a clear head for the service and I didn't see Mr Chant take a glass either. Inspector Cole wouldn't have drunk anything other than water or a cup of tea because he was on duty. We thought someone put poison in the canapés but what if Mr Chant put it in the wine glasses?'

Mrs Bramble looked at Weaver and Kitty, struck dumb by this revelation and the possibilities it afforded. In the absence of any other rational explanation, this had to be the best and most logical solution. It remained to be seen whether they could find the evidence to prove it but at least they had something to pursue.

A series of alarming thuds came from the hall, which Reverend Dench's cook would later describe as a sack of potatoes tumbling down a coal chute. Only, it wasn't potatoes.

Mrs Bramble and the others rushed into the hall to discover the source of the commotion and witnessed a tableau frozen in the moment.

They saw the chambermaid sprawled and unmoving at the bottom of the staircase, the housemaid bending over her with a brass candlestick. The ashen-faced parlourmaid was standing in the open door of the dining room with the cook. A stern-looking Jasper Chant had stopped a few steps up from the bottom of the staircase, a gin bottle in his hand. Reverend Dench, open-mouthed and gripping a polished wooden altar cross, was peering over Chant's shoulder from two steps above.

With the three men seemingly rooted to the spot, Mrs Bramble's training sprung to the fore and she reacted in seconds, feeling for a pulse at the chambermaid's wrist and neck, despite the small puddle of blood under the woman's head signalling the inevitable outcome. A gash above the young woman's right ear seemed the obvious source of the blood and her neck appeared out of alignment, probably broken. Both these injuries could be explained by a fall down the stairs.

Mrs Bramble then retrieved her pristine white handkerchief from a hidden pocket and placed it over the young woman's face.

'I'm afraid she's dead,' she declared.

23

'Oh!' cried Kitty as she opened the front door to run for help, finding Inspector Cole already there with his fist raised ready to knock and Chief Yeoman Warder Treadle at his shoulder. Dr Burford, who happened to be returning to his home next door, diverted to investigate the commotion.

Shock and puzzlement registered on the faces of the three men as they took in the bizarre scene, but before anyone could speak, Dr Burford pushed to the front, drawing a frown from the inspector. He knelt by the young woman and lifted the handkerchief from her face before giving her a quick but professional examination. 'She's dead,' he confirmed.

Mrs Bramble took advantage of the momentary confusion to declare the hall too small to accommodate everyone. She told the housemaid to leave the candlestick on the bottom step and directed Kitty to shepherd the maids and cook back into the dining room, and to wait there with them. She then had Reverend Dench and Jasper Chant leave their cross and bottle respectively on the stairs and ushered them into the parlour with Reverend Weaver. No one complained about being ordered about by a visiting housekeeper and no one noticed when she remained in the hall.

'How did she die?' asked Inspector Cole, as the hall cleared and Dr Burford continued his examination.

'Hmm, well, she received a severe blow to the head and

broke her neck in the fall,' said Burford without looking up.

'Assuming she *did* fall,' said Cole.

'Beg pardon?' said the chief.

'The three people standing near the deceased when we arrived had potential weapons in their hands,' said Cole, reaching for the handle of the dining room door. 'They must all be treated as suspects until we can eliminate them from our inquiries.'

The same thought had crossed the mind of Mrs Bramble but she had seen something else on the woman's body and knew the doctor had too. She thought about keeping quiet, knowing any interruption would antagonise the inspector, but he seemed intent on missing vital information, again.

'Dr Burford, you cannot fail to have noticed those rashes on her wrists and neck?' she said. 'In your professional opinion, do they sit well with a blow from a cudgel or a mere trip and fall?'

'What rashes?' snapped Cole, turning back.

'These,' said Burford. The others drew closer to bear witness to the angry red rashes on the maid's wrists and neck. 'Curious, is it not?'

'Curious,' said the chief, cautiously. 'Um, why?'

'Because Mrs Fry had similar marks on her body,' said Burford.

'And she was poisoned, not bludgeoned, as the inspector is suggesting this poor woman has been,' said Mrs Bramble.

'Maid murdered thrice?' said the chief 'Struck, pushed and poisoned. That possible?'

'Don't be ridiculous,' said Inspector Cole, a frown springing to the chief's forehead at the rebuke. 'Doctor, how soon can you say for certain whether injury or poison killed her?'

'I don't think I can,' said Dr Burford, rising from his haunches with visible effort. 'This is another one for Guy's Hospital, I'm afraid.'

'More delays.' Cole shook his head and sighed. 'Right then, Doctor. If you press forward, the chief and I will conduct interviews. See if we can't get to the bottom of this.' He held up his hand and scoffed when Mrs Bramble made to follow. 'I was on my way here to tell you that when I agreed to you making your own inquiries, Mrs Bramble, I expected a little more discretion,' he said,' nodding to the chief and looking satisfied when he received a tentative nod back.

'I'm not sure what you mean,' said Mrs Bramble softly. 'I have been the soul of discretion.'

'I think not. Wherever we go, whomever we speak to, it appears you have always got there first. You are making us look like fools.'

The chief looked horrified, as though he had no wish to be lumped into the same category.

Mrs Bramble shrugged. 'I can no more be held responsible for the impressions others form of you than I can be held accountable for being quicker off the mark.' She smiled benevolently as the remark hit home.

Inspector Cole raised his chin and stretched his neck. 'You are undermining my authority by attempting to do my job.'

Mrs Bramble feigned surprise. 'As you said, Inspector, I had your permission. Not to mention, you are a detective from New Scotland Yard who had the head start of a day. Surely, I must be following in *your* footsteps?'

The wind seemed to leech from Cole's sails so she pressed home her advantage.

'I am sure you have already discovered no love is lost

between the Frys and Rushtons, not to mention their friends, Sir Stephen Lovell and Sir Oswald Clyne. I also suspect you know Sir Stephen carries a British Bulldog pocket pistol about his person.' She watched his face, satisfied when a tic at the corner of his eye showed he had not known. 'The doctor must have told you that Mrs Fry was poisoned by a fatal dose of nicotine but no such poison was found in the canapés, am I right?'

'Well ...' Cole rubbed his eye and visibly pulled himself together. 'It seems you are following in my footsteps after all.' He looked at the chief, who had a comical half-smile on his face. 'As long as you keep us informed of developments, I think we can leave it there. Don't you, Chief?'

The chief, clearly enjoying Cole's discomfort, followed him into the dining room and left the door open for Mrs Bramble to follow.

Kitty was standing by the parlourmaid, who was sitting on a dining chair dabbing her red and puffy eyes with her apron. Next to her sat the shaken housemaid and cook.

Mrs Bramble and Kitty withdrew to one side.

'Who can tell me what happened here?' said Inspector Cole in a stern voice.

Mrs Bramble thought a gentler approach would fare better but bit her tongue.

'The door was closed and we were in the kitchen so we didn't see anything,' said the cook, glancing at the parlourmaid.

'That's right,' said the parlourmaid. 'Not until we opened the door and—' A sob stopped her.

The housemaid took a steady breath. 'I was in here,' she said, patting the cook's hand and giving her a look that said all would be well. 'I was cleaning the brass candlesticks when I heard a terrible clattering from upstairs. I looked out just in time to see Esther ...' She caught her breath and shook her head. 'It was her birthday only yesterday.

'Noise heard,' said the chief. 'Maid fell. Saw nothing. That the gist?'

The cook and two maids nodded, all looking as though more tears would come any second. Inspector Cole appeared unconvinced and opened his mouth to continue, but the chief put a hand on his arm, suggesting that was enough. Mrs Bramble felt the same. No more would be gleaned from them for now.

This death was another tragedy for Inspector Cole to deal with on top of the first and he wasn't taking it very well. Mrs Bramble could sense his irritation by the set of his jaw and a flush on his ears, which did not bode well for any decisions he might make. Even so, his declared intention to search the bedrooms of the victim and suspects came as no surprise. After asking where their rooms were, he left the dining room with the chief and the housemaid.

While Cole stomped about upstairs, Mrs Bramble returned to the hall with Kitty, her mind cycling through the possibilities. None seemed to fit the facts or what little she knew about everyone. Dr Burford was oblivious to their presence, muttering under his breath and tutting as he continued his work. She was about to ask some more questions of him when Inspector Cole came stomping down the staircase in a huff and strode across the small hall, the chief in tow. Mrs Bramble nodded to Kitty for them to follow.

Inspector Cole burst into the parlour, making Reverend Weaver jump, and said, 'Right, I'm not having this. I need answers from all of you.'

Reverend Dench continued to stare out of the window with glazed eyes as though awaiting an important but overdue messenger, Weaver's arm around his shoulder. Jasper

Chant twitched in agitation, looking like he needed to pace up and down but the room was too small.

Mrs Bramble saw them all, wondering how on earth she could have let this happen, especially in such close proximity to where she had been sitting. Should she have known the killer would strike again, if he truly had? How had she not anticipated this? Or had a second murderer revealed themselves through their dastardly handiwork?

Jasper Chant looked at his pocket watch and compared the time to the clock on the mantelshelf.

'Somewhere to be, Mr Chant,' snapped Cole.

Mrs Bramble wondered whether Chant's concern for Beth could be the source of his agitation, for her safety or because of a missed assignation, perhaps. On the other hand, his position on the stairs showed he had descended before Reverend Dench, making him a firm suspect if it transpired the maid's death was unnatural.

Reverend Dench looked round at Cole with the kind of blank look one has when awoken suddenly from a deep sleep and unable yet to connect to the real world. But Mrs Bramble recalled him standing right behind Jasper Chant on the stairs. Her mind reeled. Either man could be a murderer. They could even be in it together, having conspired to kill Mrs Fry and now Esther, the chambermaid.

But to what end?

All eyes had turned on Inspector Cole and the chief, ignoring the presence of Mrs Bramble and Kitty, something they, as staff themselves, had long been used to.

'What news, Inspector?' said Chant, fidgeting with a ring on his finger.

'What news?' Cole snorted with derision.

'Did she trip?' said Chant. 'It's easily done.' He shrank back under Cole's scrutiny. 'Surely, a fall—'

'Would be the obvious conclusion,' Cole interrupted. 'It appears the chambermaid suffered a broken neck and a blow to the side of her head. If it wasn't for evidence of poisoning—'

'Poison?' cried Reverend Dench. 'Poor, poor Esther.' His face looked pale and drawn.

Inspector Cole glared at Dench and then Chant. 'Care to tell me which one killed her before the post-mortem confirms one way or the other?'

Jasper Chant dropped his left shoulder and leant towards Cole conspiratorially, even though everyone in the small parlour could hear.

'Inspector Cole, I have no idea what just happened.' He put both hands on his chest for emphasis. 'I was in my room, I admit for the purposes of taking a little livener of gin, when I heard a cry and rushed to discover the cause. That's when I saw the poor girl at the bottom of the stairs.'

'Had you seen her upstairs on the landing?' said Mrs Bramble, ignoring the sharp look directed her way by Inspector Cole.

Chant pulled back as though shocked at the suggestion. 'I did not.'

'What about you, Reverend?' said Cole.

'I-I was in here with Mrs Bramble and Kitty,' said Reverend Weaver, the haunted look Mrs Bramble had seen when she first arrived at the Tower fixed again on his face.

'Not you, buffoon,' Cole snapped. 'I meant Reverend Dench.'

'Me?' Dench croaked. He looked horrified, his mouth flapping open and shut for a moment until he found his voice. 'I too was in my room, trying to repair an altar cross that someone knocked over during that ill-fated service in the chapel. Like Mr Chant, I heard a noise and came out to investigate. There is no more to it than that.'

'And yet, here we are,' Inspector Cole sneered.

Mrs Bramble could tell from the detective's tight jaw and narrowed eyes how difficult he was finding it to keep calm, and probably to resist arresting both men to boot. The chief seemed to sense this too and stepped forward.

'Let the dust settle, shall we?' he said. 'Nothing to be gained. A time and a place. All will come to he who waits. And so on and so forth.'

Cole turned his glare on the chief. 'Can you not – just – speak – plainly?' he said, before turning on his heels and leaving the room.

The chief sighed and shook his head, went to speak, then appeared to decide better of it and followed the inspector. Mrs Bramble raised her eyebrows at Kitty as a signal she hoped would be understood as a request to keep everyone in the parlour, before she joined the men in the hall.

Dr Burford had commandeered a bedsheet and wrapped the body of Esther the chambermaid. He had the candlestick in his hand, peering at it intently.

'Gentlemen, and Mrs Bramble,' he said. 'I'll have to take a closer look later, but my initial impression is that none of these are a murder weapon.'

'Good God, man,' said Inspector Cole. 'Are you sure?'

'I am confident that even with the instruments in my surgery I will not find evidence of these items being used to bludgeon the chambermaid.' Dr Burford held up the candlestick and pointed to the gin bottle. 'These have round edges but the head wound is long and straight.'

'Like the edges of the cross?' said the chief.

'Exactly, but the cross has no hair, flesh or blood on it.

Neither can I see any indentation or other damage to the cross.'

'Then she was pushed,' said Inspector Cole. 'Doctor, I want confirmation of any evidence you find, or do not, as soon as possible.' He was already half out of the front door when he said, 'Either way, I aim to have one or both of those two suspects behind bars by the end of the day.'

The chief began remonstrating as he followed Cole outside, but his words were cut off by the door closing behind them.

Mrs Bramble's attention switched immediately to the staircase. Unwilling to let any evidence go undiscovered while it was still fresh, she ascended slowly, scrutinising the banister, skirting board and each step. Two-thirds of the way up, she found what she had suspected might be there and called for the doctor's attention.

'That would do it,' said Dr Burford, studying the sharp edge of the skirting board where the chambermaid had undoubtedly hit her head as she fell. 'But I cannot believe that either man would have the wherewithal to push the poor girl. In any case, she was suffering from a head cold and not sleeping well, making it more likely that she merely fainted.'

Her mind racing, Mrs Bramble quickly called Kitty and Reverend Weaver into the hall, whispered instructions, and hurried from the house. Inspector Cole and the chief were already passing the White Tower, having an animated discussion.

'Inspector,' she called as she hastened down the white stone steps. She didn't take kindly to calling and chasing across the grounds, but they either didn't hear or chose to ignore her.

When she caught up to them outside the Fusilier's

building, Inspector Cole's face was already clouding. 'What is it now?' he said irritably.

'The doctor found where the chambermaid hit her head on the stairs when she fell,' she said.

'Good for him,' said Cole, his voice laced with sarcasm. 'Does he know which one pushed her?'

'I have an idea that may carry the investigation forward in that regard,' said Mrs Bramble. 'We should speak to Captain Fry and Major Rushton, should we not?'

'What have they to do with the chambermaid's death?'

'Maybe nothing, or everything, but we still have Mrs Fry's murder to solve and finding the murder of one may lead to the other.'

'Spoke to both,' said the chief, looking serious. 'The Inspector and I. Nothing more to be gleaned. Am I correct?'

'I agree that they believe so,' said Mrs Bramble.

'You do?' Cole's eyebrows rose, emphasising his look of confusion. 'Then why should we speak to them again?'

Mrs Bramble turned her full gaze on Cole, deciding the time was right for the judicious use of an untruth. 'I believe it was you who once told me that asking the same question again at some later time, perhaps in a different way, might elicit new intelligence.'

'I did?' said Inspector Cole, dubiously.

'Jogs the memory, I think was the phrase you used. People might not realise they are in possession of important details, you said.'

'Quite right.' Cole nodded as though he did remember.

'Good point,' said the chief. 'One moment.' He held up a finger. 'Cannot oblige. The officers are rehearsing their men in the moat.'

'For what?' said Cole. 'We're not at war. At least, not today.'

'Bound to be – somewhere,' said Mrs Bramble, remembering the constant postings she and her husband had endured, and the many battles suffered around the British Empire.

'True, but ...' said the chief. 'Next week, foreign head of state visiting Queen Victoria. Yeomen? Red-and-gilt state dress abounds. Sabres, rosettes on flat hats and so on. Fusiliers? Dress uniform. Twenty-one-gun salute.'

'Explains the weapons I saw this morning,' said Mrs Bramble.

'Partisans,' the chief explained. 'Flat spearheads, long wooden shafts. Long-handled Dane axe? Carried by Yeoman Gaoler. Ceremonial.' He winked. 'Mostly.' He produced a pocket watch and flipped open the cover. 'Ah. All back soon.' He raised his eyebrows questioningly. 'Care to wait?'

Mrs Bramble had no need to answer as the rhythmic sound of boots on stone echoed from the direction of the Tower to the south. A troop of Fusiliers in red-and-white dress uniforms and carrying shouldered rifles, led by Captain Fry with a sword but no rifle, marched up the slope from the arched gateway. He ordered a halt and dismissed the men, who immediately headed for the barracks.

The chief approached and muttered something to the captain, who flicked a glance in the direction of Inspector Cole and Mrs Bramble. The captain rubbed his eyes with his thumb and forefinger, and nodded.

'Splendid,' said the chief to everyone. 'Officers' mess. That do you?'

It did Mrs Bramble very nicely indeed, and she was instantly impressed by what she considered a fine room.

A ruby-red carpet complemented the cream walls perfectly. Regimental and Queen's colours vied for supremacy with a number of paintings in gold frames. Three chandeliers lit the room, which was dominated by an enormous mahogany banqueting table surrounded by leather-padded dining chairs, suitable for seating forty guests comfortably.

Not as sumptuous as the Great Hall at Hampton Court Palace, she thought. *But still impressive.*

Captain Fry offered them refreshment but they declined for the sake of expediency, although they did all sit on the surprisingly comfortable high-backed chairs. To Mrs Bramble, their little cluster around one end made the table seem twice its true size.

'What can I do for you, gentlemen?' said Captain Fry. 'And Mrs Bramble,' he added.

Mrs Bramble allowed Inspector Cole to take the lead.

'What more can you tell us about this continuing feud you have with Major Rushton?' said Cole.

'That again?' said Fry, narrowing his eyes. 'Nothing more than I've told you already, Inspector.'

'Was your father, Lord Fry, ever involved?'

'No. Not that he hasn't had his own trials and tribulations.'

Mrs Bramble wanted to interject and ask why but held her tongue when she saw the chief raise his eyebrows at the captain.

Fry sighed resignedly. 'My father led a high life of wealth and privilege, investing heavily in a company building railways in Africa for the good of the Empire. It was successful and he eventually became its owner. Hard work and good sense always pay off, don't you think?'

Mrs Bramble nodded. 'He did well for himself.'

'At first, but it didn't last,' said Fry. 'My father's plans to build railways across the whole of Africa and India were stymied so he turned to building railways in South America.'

'Did he ever find out why his plans failed?'

'I'll come to that, Mrs Bramble.' He smiled ruefully. 'I loved my father, but even I have to admit he could be rude, arrogant, bombastic and highly demanding when it came to business. He believed himself to be better than he was and overstretched himself. He turned the company's attention to South America where the Spanish, French and Portuguese needed good railway engineers to open up the continent by building across difficult terrain. It was to be his downfall.'

'But an experienced man, no?' said the chief.

Captain Fry shrugged. 'Pioneers are noted for their heroic derring-do attitude but even they baulk when the tide turns against them. The company went bust when contracts to build a trans-Andean railway were cancelled. The Chileans couldn't stomach the persistently high number of deaths and injuries. Can't say I blame them.'

'Is that why you joined the army?' said Inspector Cole.

Fry chuckled. 'No, Inspector. Strangely enough, it seemed like a good idea at the time, in spite of the inevitability of more dead and wounded. Good career, nice uniform, three square meals. With hindsight, perhaps I should have gone for the easy life and joined the police.'

Inspector Cole's face hardened and Mrs Bramble could no longer restrain herself from stepping in.

'How did you meet Sir Stephen Lovell?' she asked. 'Was he at university? A friend of the family?'

'He was a friend of my father's originally,' said Fry. 'We became friends later. Their paths crossed in government circles when meetings were held about the African railways and contracts were awarded. Their relationship seemed friendly enough and mutually beneficial until certain contracts, those most lucrative, went elsewhere.'

'Lord Fry blamed Sir Stephen?' said Mrs Bramble.

Captain Fry nodded sadly. 'My father could not accept that a better company had won. Although they were supposed to be friends, Stephen's career was blighted thereafter by my father. He always believed Stephen had in some way exerted his influence and blocked his rail company's expansion in Africa and India, forcing him to turn to South America, which proved his downfall.'

'Sir Stephen; he knows?'

Fry shook his head. 'My father wanted to remain a person of influence in his career. Whenever Stephen became suspicious, my wife would mention Sir Arthur Rushton, insinuating it must have been he who took down the pair of them.'

'Why did you never tell him the truth yourself?'

'What good would it have done, Mrs Bramble? I am an army captain and in no position of influence to rectify past wrongs. My father had already chosen to isolate himself after the South American debacle and I would have lost one of my few friends.'

Mrs Bramble said nothing further to Captain Fry as the inspector and chief allowed him to return to his quarters, with assurances that they would leave no stone unturned to catch the killer no doubt still ringing in his ears.

She doubted he'd had a hand in his wife's death because she could see the sadness in his eyes and the slump in his shoulders. It had been some time before the sadness had left her own eyes and she'd felt able to square her own shoulders after her husband had died. She sensed this was a man not only forced to carry on in the face of overwhelming grief at the loss of his wife, but one whose pain extended far beyond her murder.

Did that mean she had ruled him out as a suspect? Yes,

she supposed she had. But it still left several possibilities, and it was high time they had another talk with Major Rushton.

24

Kitty watched through the window as Mrs Bramble caught up with the inspector and Chief Yeoman Warder, and she waited for Reverend Weaver to leave the chaplain's house before asking for water in the scullery. The housemaid who had stood over the body of the chambermaid gave her a searching look as she poured the drink in a glass without a word. Kitty thanked her and smiled wryly as she turned away. Often snootiness was not confined to those above stairs.

Kitty edged round where Dr Burford and an unfamiliar workman were manoeuvring the swaddled shape of the chambermaid through the front door and made a show of climbing the stairs to the room she had been given on the top floor at the back of the house. She deposited the glass and crept along to the bedroom she knew belonged to the chambermaid, having overheard the housemaid mention it to Inspector Cole.

Although furnished in similar fashion to her own room at Hampton Court, Esther's was a lot smaller, and Kitty performed a search in double-quick time. She found items of uniform and personal clothing, a comb, a hairbrush and a small hand mirror. She opened a tiny bottle labelled as lavender water and took a sniff, finding it contained a different but not unpleasant scent. Next to it stood a small jar of facial cleansing cold cream, and a small but empty buff packet with 'chloral hydrate sleeping tablets' scrawled in ink. The packet was dated and signed by Dr Burford. Taken separately or altogether, nothing appeared out of place or untoward.

Kitty crept back to the tight staircase, straining her ears for any sound emanating from the first floor where she knew Reverend Dench, Mrs Bramble, Reverend Weaver and Jasper Chant had their bedrooms. Mrs Bramble had asked her to conduct a search for any evidence that might help exonerate or incriminate, but the remaining presence of Dench and Chant in the parlour made Kitty a little jittery.

Either might come upstairs for any number of reasons. Perhaps to read, change clothes, ruminate on their predicament or even have a nap.

After all, Kitty thought Jasper Chant's illicit affair proved him underhanded, and perhaps not so bothered by accusations than the reverend. Nobody seeing the organist enter the chapel, emerging from the far end or entering the chaplain's house would suspect he had just come from a romantic liaison. If he subsequently left the house to take the air or stave off boredom while restricted to the confines of the Tower, surely no one would bat an eyelid.

Kitty listened for sounds originating from the first floor. When none came, eagerness finally got the better of her and she crept down the stairs. Her heart thumped in her ears. One of the maids might come up at any moment or a floorboard might creak, drawing attention to her illicit roaming.

She expected to find all the rooms locked but the first one was not, and she eased open the door, fearful of meeting someone lurking inside. The room was empty and she relaxed, scolding herself for being over-cautious.

From the painting of Jesus with fishermen on the Sea of

Galilee displayed on one wall, and a simple cross adorning the one opposite, Kitty realised immediately who the room belonged to: Reverend Dench. The detritus men accumulated almost by accident and seemed to regard as treasured possessions adorned every surface, and she felt uneasy. This was the private domain of a religious man and she almost backed out, but the opportunity seemed too good to pass up.

She entered but left the door open. If anyone caught her inside with the door closed, she would face all sorts of questions. By leaving it open she could claim she had mistaken it for Reverend Weaver's and was merely following her routine from the Palace by turning down the sheets and making sure everything was how he liked it. Even though she was Mrs Bramble's housemaid, not his, there was enough truth in there to form the basis of a believable lie.

A photograph of a man standing beside a seated woman, both in their Sunday best, he in a winged collared shirt and she wearing a hat adorned with a large feather, stood on a dressing table next to various small statuettes and trinkets. A mug containing several pencils, a pot plant in need of watering beside which lay the reverend's gardening gloves, and a small carriage clock huddled on the windowsill, and other bits and pieces similarly cluttered the surfaces of the chest of drawers, bedside table and the top of a large mahogany wardrobe. In a similar fashion to searching the rooms in the married men's quarters, Kitty went through everything methodically, unsure about what she thought she might discover, but found nothing incriminating. In fact, a square of glasspaper for rubbing down wood and a small bottle of polish suggested Reverend Dench's account of his activities to be truthful.

She returned to the landing and closed the door,

contemplating her next move. Sounds of activity floated up from the ground floor but the rest of the house was quiet.

Kitty tried the next room, also unlocked, finding it belonged to Jasper Chant. She left the door open again and went through everything with equal speed. The organist lived in a house in Farringdon and came into the Tower for services and events, and to practise on the newly installed organ. Not expecting to be trapped inside the Tower, he had brought no overnight things from his home and the room was virtually empty save for a dirty stained cloth, an old pair of what looked like gardening gloves, and two bottles of red wine. Only a folded nightshirt tucked under the edge of the pillow showed any occupancy at all, and Kitty suspected he had needed to borrow it from Reverend Dench. With nothing to search, she finished in no time.

But then ...

Kitty froze as a creak came from the direction of the staircase. She hadn't heard the parlour door open so it couldn't be Reverend Dench or Jasper Chant. It must be one of the maids coming up to check the rooms. She listened intently while pretending to attend to the bed, intending to slip straight into her pretence if the maid came in.

Her chest ached after a few seconds and she realised how shallow her breathing had become. A creak from the room above allowed her the luxury of a quiet sigh of relief but she wasn't out of the woods yet. A few more creaks sounded as the maid walked around the room and it eventually fell silent. What was the maid doing now?

Kitty tensed again, nervous perspiration forming on her brow and upper lip in fear that the maid would not return straight to the ground floor.

Seconds ticked past.

The staircase creaked as footsteps descended and Kitty

exhaled, taking a few lungfuls of air to clear the red hue from her vision and light-headedness from her brain. That had been close and she knew she had to work more quickly to avoid detection.

Recognising Mrs Bramble's things in the next room, Kitty deduced that the last one on the landing nearest the stairs had to be Reverend Weaver's. She tried the door, not now expecting to find it locked, and it opened with ease. She got to work going through all his travelling possessions and the room's furniture with a fine-tooth comb.

The reverend travelled light. One change of clothes lay folded in a drawer, a nightshirt had been stuffed under his pillow, his accoutrements of religious ritual were folded on the chest of drawers, and the usual items for abluting such as a hairbrush, washcloth, soap, razor and a toothbrush were next to a pitcher and ewer on the dressing table. A carpet bag, in which he had undoubtedly brought these things from his apartment at Hampton Court Palace, contained what appeared to be another change of clothes. Worn.

It seemed odd and unsettling to go through a man's things, especially in such an underhand and furtive manner, but she found the failure to discover anything untoward most encouraging. Nothing in the men's rooms had caused her to believe them guilty but that did not mean evidence didn't exist elsewhere. Any poison could have been discarded in a bin, disposed of down a sink, dropped over the walls into the Outer Ward or moat, or even sunk to the bottom of the water at Traitors' Gate.

It was all right thinking Reverend Weaver, Reverend Dench and Jasper Chant might be innocent, but the conundrum of who the murderer might be remained.

With no more she could do in the chaplain's house, she had no intention of sitting around idle and descended to the ground floor. If residents in the Tower wanted to look down on her for striding about as if she owned the place, so be it. She needed to leave now, find Mrs Bramble and add her latest news to the puzzle.

But the housemaid's hand on her arm stopped her in her tracks.

A feeling of smug satisfaction settled across Reverend Weaver's shoulders. He had unearthed information useful to Mrs Bramble's investigation and had gained one up on Inspector Cole, albeit for the shortest of times. But that didn't matter. The mere fact of being ahead of anyone for once instead of trailing like a bouncing rowing boat towed erratically behind a yacht had given him a sense of euphoria. No doubt the good Lord would frown upon such conceit but he fully intended to enjoy it while it lasted and would say a few prayers of contrition tonight.

He stood looking across the green towards the governor's residence, where a guard in a red tunic marched slowly up and down as though at quarter speed. It wasn't the tempo that fascinated him so much as the way the guard looked as though he was stamping his feet at each turn while placing them gently to make no noise.

'That's to—'

Reverend Weaver flinched and raised his arm as though defending against some impending blow from a walking cane.

Dr Burford mirrored the action, and the two men looked at each other sheepishly.

'My apologies,' said Burford. 'I did not mean to startle you.'

'Good Lord,' said Weaver, now recognising the physician.

'I'm afraid I did not see your approach.' He smoothed his jacket. 'No harm done.'

'My fault entirely. It's these new shoes, you see. Mr Chant wears the same kind and recommended them to me. They make not one sound unless I'm marching across gravel.'

'Oh. Do you do that often?'

'What? No, no. You misunderstand.' Dr Burford shook his head as though to clear it. 'As I was saying about why the sentry doesn't stamp his feet; it's to ensure the governor and his wife remain undisturbed inside their residence.'

'Perhaps he should wear your shoes.'

Burford chuckled. 'Perhaps he should.'

'Actually, I'm glad you caught me,' said Reverend Weaver, looking around in case Inspector Cole or some other eavesdropper was in earshot. 'Have you concluded your work regarding ...?'

'Regarding?' Dr Burford looked blank. 'Oh!' you mean th-the ...' He cleared his throat as though a piece of his latest repast had become lodged there. 'I have, and now her body awaits transportation over to Guy's Hospital.'

'Right, good, right,' said Weaver. 'Well, not good in one way but you know what I mean.' He glanced nervously at the doctor. 'I actually wanted another word with you about the canapé reception.'

'Oh, yes?' Burford looked interested.

Reverend Weaver experienced a wave of apprehension and looked around again, just in case. 'Is there somewhere private we can go for a quick chat?'

'In the Tower of London?' Dr Burford laughed. 'The only really private place is one's bedroom, or a water closet, and I would suggest neither of those are appropriate. He nodded in the direction of his house. 'I had to abandon my morning rounds because of, um … and was on my way to the Yeoman Warders' Club for a pot of tea and some lunch when I saw you.' Burford swept his arm in the general direction of the club. 'Would you care to join me?'

Reverend Weaver thought he'd had too much tea today and his waterworks might not take the strain. But he needed to question Dr Burford, and if there was no other opportunity …

'I'd be delighted,' he said.

Moments later, they sat in the farthest corner of the club room, being eyed from behind the counter by the Yeoman Warder whose turn it was to man the bar. Reverend Weaver had begun to think Dr Burford must exist on tea and biscuits but it transpired that his idea of a pot of tea and lunch was to down a glass of gin and smoke a pipe of aromatic tobacco. Weaver declined both gracefully and opted to wait for real tea and a cold mutton sandwich.

He was taken aback by the barman's glare and liberal helping of sarcasm until Dr Burford explained this was due entirely to Reverend Weaver's request for refreshments. Ale and spirits were in plentiful supply, but the barman would need to call for his wife to rush out a sandwich, all because Weaver was a man of the cloth. The rooms had been designed to store goods, and then converted to house Yeoman Warders, not to accommodate a hostelry. Providing food for visiting clergymen and resident physicians had certainly never been on the minds of those whose idea it had been to replace the three public houses of the Tower, lost after an edict from the Duke of Wellington, with a new, if unofficial, pub.

The Yeoman Warders' Club was perhaps a grand name for a couple of spartan rooms containing a motley collection of chairs, benches and a few tables, with a makeshift bar to one side. Provided almost entirely for the Yeoman Warders — the Fusiliers had their own mess halls and canteens to drink in — others could drink there by invitation only. Reverend Weaver suspected Dr Burford had stretched the bounds of his own invitation by bringing him, a stranger, into the club.

The thought made him uncomfortable and wary, especially given his own predicament, and he wished he'd asked for nothing more than a small glass of ale.

He cleared his throat and took the plunge.

'Subsequent to our earlier chat, Doctor, I met with Mrs Bramble and her maid to discuss general progress on the case and I suddenly had a strange notion.'

'Ah,' said Dr Burford. 'They can be dangerous things, notions.'

'Indeed, but I think this one might not be. You see, nicotine was found in the body of Mrs Fry and in your own blood sample but not in the food. Now it appears the chambermaid may have been poisoned too.'

'Correct.' Burford sat forward. 'All most odd. I have seen accidental mass nicotine poisoning before but only in agricultural and horticultural workers using large quantities of nicotine-based insecticides.'

'Are such insecticides used on the vegetable gardens here in the Tower's moat?' asked Weaver.

'Probably but none of the gardeners have reported being ill. In any case, the whole congregation would have needed to traipse through the gardens repeatedly at the moment of spraying to get it on their skin and inhale enough to generate the effect we saw in the chapel.'

'Which brings me to my notion.' Reverend Weaver glanced at the barman, who was giving them a sideways look while polishing the same glass he'd had in his hands when they had first entered. 'I thought perhaps the poison could have been in the white wine.' He looked back at Burford. 'Do you see?'

'Hmm.' Dr Burford frowned as he thought. 'It's a possibility. Although, are we not left with the same problem of how the poison got into everyone's drink?'

A gentleman in a dark suit entered and spoke to the barman, and Weaver lowered his voice further, causing Burford to lean even closer.

'At first, I thought the poison could have been added to the clean glasses before the drink was poured, or to the wine after pouring,' said Weaver.

Dr Burford shook his head. 'Any liquid concentrate in a glass before pouring the wine would be visible, and allowing it to evaporate to leave a dangerous residue would not work either because that takes time and any steward worth his salt would see it as dirty and wash it. Surely there were too many glasses to poison each one?'

Although not a man of science, Reverend Weaver had considered this, and another illicit twinge of self-satisfaction gripped him. 'That was my feeling too, leaving only one way. The nicotine must have been added to the wine bottles before pouring, which would explain the poisoning of the chambermaid, if she drank from an opened bottle given to her. Staff everywhere have been known to benefit from leftovers.'

Dr Burford took a sip of his gin before responding. 'Each bottle would have needed to be uncorked and adulterated without anyone else noticing.'

'It's not impossible.'

Burford shrugged. 'Improbable but not impossible if more than one person is involved.'

'Then I have a plan,' said Reverend Weaver, making sure

the barman and the gentleman were still in conversation and had not turned their attention to the doctor and himself. 'Can you find a sample of the wine used at the reception and have it tested?'

'I can try but it may prove difficult,' said Burford. 'No one thought to check the glasses because all eyes were on the food, and I'll wager they'll have been washed and put away.'

'All you can do is try your best, Doctor. I'll make discreet inquiries among the stewards to find out how the wine was prepared and by whom. I hope my release from captivity will convince them I am no threat and only trying to help.'

'I too hope that is the case,' said Dr Burford, looking dubious. 'But they are still military men and not used to being questioned by civilians.'

'I shall cross my fingers,' said Reverend Weaver. 'If this goes well, we may yet prove my innocence and uncover the real murderer. If not, I fear Inspector Cole and the chief still have me in their sights.'

25

Major Rushton, the last suspect yet to be questioned by Mrs Bramble, proved a harder man to track down. The trio of investigators eventually caught up with him at the Tower standing next to the infamous Bloody Tower, after the final call on his rounds.

'Wakefield Tower, Crown Jewels displayed in iron cages,' said the chief, matter-of-factly. 'First floor. Constant stream of visitors. Daily inspections.'

Much to Mrs Bramble's relief and satisfaction, Major Rushton emerged from the Tower exactly nine minutes later and strode up the slope towards them. He took the steps two at a time and had almost reached the trio when Inspector Cole sidestepped to block his path.

Major Rushton halted and looked up, a shadow of mild annoyance passing across his face. His eyebrows, although dark and bushy enough to lend themselves to black moods and brooding, seemed permanently raised aloft as though signalling a perpetual state of bafflement and surprise.

'Major Rushton,' said Inspector Cole. 'I thought we'd find you here.'

Mrs Bramble and the chief exchanged a look that Cole either missed or ignored.

Cole indicated the others. 'We wondered if you could spare us a few minutes to answer some questions?'

'What kind of questions?' said Rushton, his face now displaying a complete lack of interest.

'Background, mainly. About your family's dealings with the Frys over the years.'

Major Rushton's expression morphed into one of boredom, despite his fixed eyebrows. 'But you already know of the feud between myself and Captain Fry, and that we remain cordial but distant.'

'*Professional* but distant, I would say,' said Mrs Bramble, ignoring a sharp look from Cole. 'I get the impression cordiality has been absent for many years.'

Major Rushton shrugged. 'I agree that may be a more accurate assessment and I dare say I employ a little sugar-coating for onlookers, but my point remains.' He looked towards the officers' quarters building. 'I have no wish to be rude, but do you mind if we conduct this exchange elsewhere? It is almost past lunchtime and many hours since breakfast. Somewhere a little more private would not go amiss too.'

Mrs Bramble took the major's hint and suggested the officers' quarters, expecting to be led through to the mess again. Her eyebrows mirrored his when he diverted their group to a small room on the left of the entrance hall. A door leading through to the officers' mess remained firmly closed as the major motioned for them to select their preferred chairs.

The pale walls displaying paintings of battles, fortifications and other military subjects contrasted with the deep red of the carpet. Various cabinets stood around the room, including one occupying an alcove to the right of a fireplace, which contained various trophies. Above the mantelshelf, a large mirror reflected light back into the room.

A white-jacketed steward appeared and Major Rushton

despatched him to the kitchen to fetch tea and sandwiches for four, a not unwelcome consideration on Mrs Bramble's part. Their pointless hike around the Tower had made her peckish.

Rushton sat stiffly on a high-backed chair as they clustered around a small table to await the refreshments. Mrs Bramble eyed him curiously and could not restrain herself.

'Major, may I ask why you did not take us through to the officers' mess?'

'Simply because you are a woman,' he replied. 'And I mean no offence. I appreciate you visited Reverend Weaver when he was held in a room upstairs but that was in contravention of the rules under exceptional circumstances. Protocol dictates women are not allowed elsewhere in this building other than in this room, unless it is to attend a formal dinner in the mess to which they have been invited and are accompanied. We have a snooker room, a library, and a smoking room, all of which can be used by officers and their gentlemen guests to relax during the day. This room is reserved for officers who wish to entertain ladies.'

Mrs Bramble seethed inside but kept her expression impassive. Yes, this was a military building but, having been married to a soldier, she was well aware of the number of women who travelled with the army as domestic servants and, like herself, spouses and nurses. In her opinion, this was no more than another of those so-called gentlemen's clubs, which excluded women to ensure the men were able to avoid growing up and evade a large proportion of their adult responsibilities.

She was about to ask her first real question when the chief cut in, giving her a sympathetic glance.

'The feud,' he said. 'Captain Fry gave an account. Your perspective?'

Major Rushton gave their faces careful scrutiny before answering.

'Captain Fry had a trifling disagreement with our friend, Adam Hedgecoe, while at university,' he said. 'A fist fight ensued, during which Adam lost his life. Although essentially an accident, the trivial cause should not have led to blows in the first place. Thereafter, I found I could not forgive Fry and our friendship soured.'

The chief sat forward. 'Lingering resentment? Just cause to take revenge, perhaps?'

Major Rushton looked at the chief with eyelids drooping sadly but incongruous eyebrows still floating above. 'After all this time? No. We dislike each other but have to work together. It's as simple as that. There have been many opportunities for me to get shot of him, if I'd wanted him dead. But I am a professional soldier, not a murderer.'

Inspector Cole cleared his throat for attention. 'Your father, Sir Arthur Rushton, was the Head of the Foreign Scrutiny Department—'

'At the British Admiralty,' interrupted the chief.

'I was about to say that,' Cole hissed.

'Yes, a position he secured because of his baronetcy,' said the major. 'His full title is Baronet Rushton of Old Soar.'

'Did his position cause him to have any dealings with Lord Fry?' said Cole.

'It did, as a matter of fact.' Major Rushton nodded. 'Lord Fry had a substantial interest in a company building railways across Africa. Their paths crossed on several committees.'

'So I understand, but did Lord Fry and Sir Arthur get along or did your feud with Lord Fry's son colour their relationship?'

Rushton scoffed. 'Such matters would have been

unimportant to them. Business is business. Money is money. Respect is everything. Love and friendship are irrelevant. It can be beneficial for such men to get along but it is in no way essential.'

'Sir Stephen Lovell, friend of the Frys,' said the chief, 'Lord Fry get on all right?'

'You'll have to ask them,' said Rushton with a shrug. 'All I can say, based on rumour and conjecture, is that the friendship seemed strained.'

'Because Lord Fry thought Sir Stephen had adversely affected his planned expansion in Africa?' said Mrs Bramble, her curiosity overriding any attempt to keep quiet.

'I cannot be expected to know the minds of other men, madam.' The major's voice carried a hint of frost.

'Just Mrs Bramble, please,' she said, ignoring the now-familiar glare from Inspector Cole. If looks could kill, she suspected she would have shattered like a cracked pot in a kiln. 'It seems Lord Fry brought his influence to bear, causing Sir Stephen's career to stagnate.'

Major Rushton's eyebrows forced themselves a little higher. 'Maybe so, but I can tell you it wasn't Sir Stephen who stood in the way of Lord Fry,' he said.

The conversation paused as the steward returned with their refreshments and left a large silver pot of tea and a tray containing tea-strainer, cups, saucers, teaspoons, a milk jug and a bowl of sugar lumps. Departing briefly, he returned with four plates and napkins, and a four-tier stand displaying dainty sandwiches and cakes.

Mrs Bramble cooed appreciatively and accepted the men's offer to have first pick, choosing a ham and mustard sandwich and a delicate butterfly cake. As an afterthought, she selected an additional sandwich of cheese and cucumber. That was more than enough for a light lunch and she was amazed when the major, the inspector and the chief descended on the fare like biblical locusts, leaving nothing but crumbs and fresh air on the stand.

Finishing a mouthful, as one should before speaking, Mrs Bramble picked up the thread of their interrupted conversation.

'You were saying, Major. If it wasn't Sir Stephen who stood in the way of Lord Fry, who did?'

Inspector Cole almost choked on his second butterfly cake and coughed until his eyes watered.

'My father,' said Major Rushton. 'It was he who persuaded senior government officials to withdraw their support for Lord Fry's company in Africa, then South America. As I said, the strained relationship between myself and Captain Fry was unimportant to them. My father simply considered Lord Fry a particularly bad businessman who should not be given important government contracts. I suspect you are aware of his exploits in South America. A case in point, wouldn't you say?'

'And what of your friendship with Sir Oswald Clyne?' said Mrs Bramble.

This seemed to catch Rushton unawares.

'What of it?' he said. 'It's as healthy as it has always been.'

'Sir Oswald and Sir Stephen,' said Mrs Bramble. 'Do they get on?'

'They take their lead from myself and Captain Fry. It's what friends do, Mrs Bramble. Offer support. Take your side.'

'Support extending to murder?'

'Preposterous!' Major Rushton's expression hardened. 'I cannot begin to imagine what has been said or what evidence you have to back up your assertion.' He glanced at Inspector Cole.

If he expected any support from that quarter, he remained disappointed because Cole was still fighting to regain control of his breathing after his coughing fit.

'It was not an assertion, I assure you,' said Mrs Bramble calmly. 'Merely speculation.'

Major Rushton shook his head. 'As much as I dislike Captain Fry, I can assure you neither he nor I, nor any of our family and friends, are in the habit of killing on a whim.' He looked at the inspector and chief. 'We are *gentlemen*.'

'Maybe so, but *I* can assure *you* that murder is not confined to the lower classes,' croaked Inspector Cole. 'The rich and titled and powerful may think they can get away with committing the ultimate crime, but Scotland Yard does its best to bring all murderers to justice.'

That seemed the final irritation for Major Rushton who stood up to leave.

'In that endeavour, I wish you well, Inspector.' Rushton wiped his fingers on a napkin and drained his teacup. 'Now, if you'll excuse me, I have further duties to perform this afternoon. The steward will show you out.'

'As guilty as sin,' said Cole after Rushton had left the room, but his words carried little real conviction.

'Rushton and Fry, nothing to gain,' said the chief. 'Kept the peace for years. Murderers? Unlikely. Code of honour, do you see?'

'Ha,' Cole scoffed. 'Heard that before.'

Mrs Bramble drained her own teacup and set it on its saucer with a clink. She had guessed there was more to the animosity between the Frys, Rushtons, Sir Stephen and Sir Oswald, and now she knew why. She sighed, sensing not all cats had been let out of the bag and more revelations were yet to come. Whoever poisoned Mrs Fry, Esther and the whole congregation was still free to roam, albeit inside the Tower walls.

The trouble was, a caged tiger was just as dangerous a killer as one that remained at large.

26

Kitty looked down at the hand on her arm and up at the face of the housemaid who had given her the glass of water and hard stare. The maid looked apprehensive, as though stopping her leaving was as bad a thing as it was good, and Kitty couldn't help but be intrigued.

'What is it?' she asked, expecting some kind of rebuke for having searched the bedrooms. She supposed a creaking stair or floorboard had betrayed her, although she had purposely listened out for such a giveaway noise.

'You, Mrs Bramble and Reverend Weaver are helping the police,' said the maid.

It was a statement rather than a question but Kitty nodded anyway.

The housemaid looked at the door as though someone dangerous standing on the other side might come through at any moment, then indicated the dining room with a tilt of her head.

'We don't want to get in trouble with Reverend Dench but we have something you might want to hear,' she said.

This intrigued Kitty even more, so she allowed herself to be guided away from the front door, through the dining room and into the kitchen, where the parlourmaid closed the door behind them. The cook entered from the scullery. In any other situation like this she would have felt intimidated, maybe even frightened, but maids and cooks were her people and she sensed they were taking a risk even talking to her.

'You've got to be careful round here,' said the housemaid. 'All the domestics talk among themselves – you'd expect that, wouldn't you? – but not everyone can be trusted.'

'In what way, not trusted?' said Kitty.

'Most are friendly enough but there are others who report everything back to their masters and mistresses, like the little snitches they are,' said the parlourmaid. 'Causes no end of trouble. Is it not the same at Hampton Court?'

'It is,' said Kitty, accepting that hierarchies, friendships and feuds existed below stairs as much as upstairs, in any establishment or household.

'We wanted to help your mistress catch the murderer before he tries again because next time it could be any one of us, but we thought it best to speak to you,' said the housemaid. 'It's not our place to be telling tales to Reverend Dench, the inspector or the chief.'

'Tales?' said Kitty, looking at each of them in turn. 'What tales?'

The parlourmaid moved across to the window and peered through it for a few seconds before giving a thumbs-up.

'We see things,' said the cook. 'Notice people as we go about our dailies. They're not mean but they don't notice us because we're there all the time. We're so familiar we've become unseen and unheard and they either trust us to be discreet or forget we're even there.'

'And what is it you've noticed?' Kitty coaxed.

The parlourmaid hesitated as she went to speak but the cook winked encouragement.

'I saw the organist sneak out the other day,' she said. 'Mr Chant.'

'What do you mean, sneak out?' said Kitty, her curiosity

well and truly piqued. 'I thought he could come and go as he pleased while lodging here.'

'He can but he didn't leave by the front door. He went out through there.' She pointed through the far door leading to the scullery, where Kitty could see another door. 'Through that door is the courtyard where I hang the washing on fine days, and a back door that comes out opposite the crypt gate.'

'When was this?' asked Kitty, her mind sifting through the possibilities.

'Last night at the end of dinner,' said the parlourmaid. 'Mrs Bramble had not long left through the front door with Reverend Weaver and Dr Burford for an evening's stroll when Mr Chant came through here. He had his finger up to his lips to shush us before he disappeared out the back.'

'He was very quiet,' said the cook. Never even heard the back door open or close so I had a quick peek, fearful of what he might be up to.'

'Had he left?' said Kitty.

'He'd gone all right, but the odd thing was, he came back not fifteen minutes later. Through the same doors.'

'Why odd?'

'Because he usually left by the front door every other evening and returned the same way at least half an hour later,' said the parlourmaid. 'Something must have happened.'

Kitty knew exactly what had happened. Mrs Bramble and Reverend Weaver had chased someone through the crypt. But surely it would have taken more than fifteen minutes for Jasper Chant to return, if indeed it was he whom Mrs B had chased into the Outer Ward. He wouldn't have risked returning any earlier for risk of discovery.

'Do you think Mr Chant is ...? You know?' said the

parlourmaid, with frightened eyes looking up from her bowed head.

Kitty couldn't imagine Mrs B and Reverend Weaver had made a mistake, but this new information seemed contradictory and confusing. Was it possible that more than one person had been abroad last night in the same place and at the same time as they?

'I should be grateful if you would refrain from telling anyone else about this,' said Kitty. 'I don't know if it means anything and it might turn out to be quite innocent, but you were right to tell me. I'll let Mrs Bramble know and she can come find you if she has any questions.'

Kitty thought she ought to leave, but when the threesome made no move, she sensed they had more to tell.

'What is it?' she said, looking at the parlourmaid.

The parlourmaid looked at the housemaid.

'I saw something else,' said the housemaid. 'Two gentlemen having a disagreement.'

'In this house?' said Kitty. 'With Mr Chant?'

'No, no,' said the housemaid, holding her hand up to stop any thoughts along those lines. 'It was two days ago, a couple of hours after the service. I'd been to the casemates to see one of my friends and borrow some clothing starch because we can't leave the Tower to buy anything. I was on my way back when I saw them. I'd got to the top of the Flint Tower steps when I happened to look left, along the wall behind the barracks. They must've only been seven or eight yards away.'

'Were they shouting?' said Kitty. 'Coming to blows?'

'No, nothing like that. They seemed gentlemanly about it but were obviously upset because of the way they waved their arms and looked at each other. Stern-faced, frowning and the like.'

'Could you hear what they were arguing about?'

The housemaid frowned and looked up in thought. 'I only caught a bit. The one with dark curly hair and a blue bow tie seemed the most annoyed. He kept saying, "We agreed, we had a deal," while jabbing his finger and pointing.'

Sounds like Sir Stephen Lovell, thought Kitty.

'The other one with dark wavy hair and beard kept protesting that he'd kept his word and done nothing wrong.'

And that sounds like Sir Oswald Clyne, thought Kitty. 'Did they see you?'

The housemaid shrugged. 'They might've done but they had no interest in me.'

'Do you think any of them had anything to do with it?' said the cook. 'You know, with Mrs Fry and poor Esther?'

'Mrs Bramble, the inspector and the chief have questioned everyone once already and we're working with the doctor to get to the bottom of it,' said Kitty, avoiding the question. She had no idea how or if the two sirs and Jasper Chant were involved but her confidence in Inspector Cole, the chief and even Reverend Weaver had wavered. That didn't matter; she knew Mrs Bramble was up to the job.

'I wouldn't worry about it,' Kitty emphasised, wondering whether there was still anything to be worried about. The secret squabble between the two sirs was of concern, but having seen Jasper Chant with Beth the housemaid, both of them looking smitten with each other, she hadn't considered him a potential murderer.

Until now.

Dr Burford drained the dregs of his third gin and tonic, which he insisted was for the medicinal purpose of ingesting quinine to keep malarial mosquitoes at bay. Having never encountered such dangers in the British climate, Reverend Weaver had stuck to tea to wash down his mutton sandwich. A spiced tomato chutney had made a most pleasant accompaniment (although he had dolloped a large spoonful into his lap), and brought back fond memories of his time in a little country parish in Kent.

The two men left the Yeoman Warders' Club – Reverend Weaver leaving a coin for the barman to get himself a drink to assuage his sheepish feeling – with a firm agreement to pursue the agreed line of inquiry. Weaver's chest held a tingle of anxiety. He wasn't sure how he was going to make any progress without crossing the paths of the inspector and chief.

Of the two, the chief was perhaps of least concern but the more he was in their minds the less chance he had of staying out of prison. Weaver remained convinced that Inspector Cole believed him to have been involved in Mrs Fry's murder, and now Esther's, as either the poisoner or his accomplice, and needed to persuade him otherwise. He had pinned all his hopes on the wit and guile of Mrs Bramble, so whatever he could do by way of assisting her must be done.

Parting company with Dr Burford as they passed the White Tower, Reverend Weaver paused for a moment to take stock. The doctor could waltz in through the main entrance of the Fusiliers' building and request to be shown the kitchen in the furtherance of the investigation, but he could not. The situation called for another strategy, perhaps employing cunning. There was only one problem. He had never considered himself a sly man, nor one to tell untruths, but that was mainly because he frequently forgot what he had said, to whom he had said it, and when.

He was beginning to worry that standing stock still while

visitors flowed around him like water around a mooring post would attract adverse attention. He had already heard the Lord's name taken in vain, directed at him because of his inaction, but he needed a way to execute his half of the plan. One particular passing visitor bumped him a quarter-turn and he found himself staring into the alleyway between the married men's quarters and the officers' building.

A lightbulb flickered on.

Those whom he wished to evade would undoubtedly use the front door, leaving the rear delivery entrance open for exploitation. Of course, he might encounter security, apathy or hostility but he could always say he'd been following Dr Burford and taken a wrong turn. The excuse was as thin as the wash used by the ladies back at Hampton Court Palace in their watercolour paintings but that couldn't be helped. *As they say, needs must when the devil drives*, he thought.

With little more ado than a glance to left and right, Reverend Weaver ducked into the alleyway and slipped into the shadows between the rear of the building and the inner curtain wall. At moments like these he often recited the Lord's prayer automatically and silently, and he found his lips forming the words right now as he edged along the wall past overflowing bins towards the rear door. A previous unsavoury encounter with rubbish at Hampton Court Palace came to mind, one where Mrs Bramble's request had him delving inside bins for evidence during the inspector's previous murder case.

A clink of glass and the clanking of pots drew him closer until he recoiled back in alarm as a man in a singlet emptied a bowlful of water by throwing it onto the ground in front of him.

'Oh, sorry ...' The man squinted. 'Reverend, isn't it?'

'It is,' said Reverend Weaver.

The man chuckled. 'You've strayed off the beaten track here, Reverend. Where are you supposed to be?'

'Right here. I'm supposed to be here.'

'This ain't the place to be saving souls. What's your business? Can I help?'

Reverend Weaver almost turned and fled but dredged up the courage from somewhere to remain.

'I-I'm helping Inspector Cole and the chief with their in-inquiry,' he stammered. 'I'd hoped to speak to someone who either prepared or served the white wine at the reception the other night.'

'Aye, a rum do and no mistake,' said the man, performing the sign of the cross. 'I can't help you, I'm afraid, 'cause I was on washing-up duties, but I know a man who can.'

'Thank you.' Weaver managed a crooked smile of encouragement and the man disappeared into the bowels of the Fusiliers' building.

Moments later, the man reappeared and introduced another. The new man wore blue trousers with a vertical red stripe on the outside of each leg, and a white jacket buttoned up to the neck. Weaver recognised the steward as the one who had earlier served him and Dr Burford with tea in the smoking room.

'Ah, I, um, wondered if you could tell me who prepared the white wine for the reception?' said Weaver.

'That'd be me and my mate,' said the steward.

'And how did you do that? Exactly?'

'What? Like anyone would, I suppose. We uncorked the bottles, poured equal measures into each glass and took them out to the guests as soon as they started arriving.'

Reverend Weaver frowned. 'Uncork, pour, serve.'

'You've got it,' said the steward.

'You didn't let the wine breathe after uncorking?'

'We weren't allowed to open the bottles too early for fear of someone taking an early tipple, and we were watched closely. Weren't allowed to finish any leftovers either but some of it got spirited away.' The steward winked. 'We all had some while the officers and bigwigs were in the chapel.'

'Did anyone unauthorised enter the kitchen?' asked Weaver.

'Not that I saw and no one mentioned anything.'

Reverend Weaver scratched his ear in thought. 'May I ask, were you or any of the stewards ill on that day?'

The steward gave him a shrug and shook his head. 'Not that I know of, Reverend, although we were a bit worried when you lot keeled over, I can tell you.'

'Oh,' said Weaver.

'You sound disappointed we weren't ill, Reverend. That's not very charitable.'

'What?' Weaver's mind was racing. 'No, no, of course not. I'm most glad you escaped the carnage. It's just, I had a theory you may have blown out of the water.'

'I'm sorry. Is there anything else I can help you with, Reverend?'

'No, thank you. You've been most helpful.'

Reverend Weaver made the sign of the cross as though offering the steward a blessing but he did so because he had no idea what to say or do next as he turned away.

It would still prove prudent for Dr Burford to test the wine, if he could find any. However, from what he'd learnt, the chances of Guy's Hospital finding anything nasty in it were fading fast. What on earth had happened? How had someone poisoned the guests en masse without also poisoning the cooks and stewards?

As he hurried from the alleyway, Reverend Weaver worried for his own safety and that of Mrs Bramble and

Kitty. Inspector Cole and Chief Yeoman Warder Treadle may be the official investigators but the three amateur sleuths had been delving into things they should perhaps have left alone. He feared retribution, because as they discarded theories, they perhaps got closer to the truth.

The killer of Mrs Fry and Esther wouldn't wait to be discovered; he would come for them!

27

Satiated after her lunch in the so-called ladies' room, Mrs Bramble marvelled at how moneyed families managed to take breakfast, morning tea, lunch, afternoon tea, high tea, dinner and supper without bursting at the seams. She left the Fusiliers' building in search of Kitty and Reverend Weaver, with Inspector Cole's insistent words still ringing in her ears. His reiteration that she should come to him with any information was entirely pointless, as she had no intention of doing so unless absolutely necessary.

A large group of visitors had congregated on the parade ground at the western end of the Waterloo Barracks, which forced her to circle clockwise around them. It was chance, therefore, that the bobbing head of Kitty caught Mrs Bramble's attention as she cast a casual glance at the group. Hurrying after the maid and catching up with her by the corner of the White Tower, Mrs Bramble led Kitty to one of the benches strategically placed there for weary visitors to take a moment's respite from traipsing around the fortress.

'I'm glad I ran into you,' said Mrs Bramble, ensuring they sat apart enough so no one else could join them and overhear their conversation. 'I've not long enjoyed luncheon with the inspector, the chief and Major Rushton.'

'It's all right for some,' said Kitty.

Mrs Bramble chuckled. 'It was all in a good cause, I assure you. We met Captain Fry earlier as well and the pair of them corroborated everything we'd learnt about their feud.'

She gave Kitty a quick summary of the conversations.

Kitty shifted on the bench to face Mrs Bramble. 'Revenge may give Sir Stephen a motive for wanting Lord Fry dead but not Mrs Fry, surely? She can't have had any influence.'

'Maybe not, but Captain Fry might have,' said Mrs Bramble. 'Let's say he knew of his father's interference in his best friend's career and didn't tell him. If Sir Stephen discovered this, he might have seen it as a serious betrayal, giving him a motive to take revenge on the family. Perhaps he saw Mrs Fry as the easiest option, killing her to cause pain to all of them.'

'That would be an exceptionally wicked and cowardly thing for him to do,' said Kitty.

Mrs Bramble could not disagree and listened intently as Kitty recounted her own morning's achievements and discoveries.

'If what the staff said is true, that would seem to rule Mr Chant out as the person I chased,' said Mrs Bramble when Kitty had finished. 'But that doesn't preclude him from being the murderer or having an accomplice.'

'Why would he kill Esther?' said Kitty. 'Why would anyone?'

'I can only think she found out something damning that made her dangerous to him. Perhaps about his affair with Beth.'

'Room for a little one?' said Reverend Weaver, surprising Mrs Bramble with his unusually stealthy approach.

She and Kitty slid further apart to allow him to sit in between.

'You look buoyant, Reverend,' said Mrs Bramble, noticing a twinkle in his eye that had not been there since she saw him leaving Hampton Court for the Tower.

'I am, rather,' said Weaver with a smile. 'I've eliminated the possibility that the wine was poisoned before it was sent out.' He proceeded to tell them about his conversation with Dr Burford and the steward.

'Interesting,' said Mrs Bramble. 'Perhaps it wasn't something they ate or drank after all. Maybe it was something they touched instead, absorbing concentrated nicotine through their skin.'

'We've got two problems, though,' said Kitty. 'How did the murderer manage to get everyone to touch it on the same day at the same time? The kitchen staff, Inspector Cole, Mr Chant and our own Reverend Weaver – they can't have touched it, can they? Of all the people at the service, only Mrs Fry had a rash. Esther had a rash, but domestic staff didn't attend.'

Reverend Weaver threw up his hands. 'I'm at a loss to know what to think or do next. It's one step forward, two steps back. I just want to go home to my nice apartment at Hampton Court Palace.'

'Don't we all,' said Mrs Bramble, hoping her friend wasn't about to lose his grip on reality.

That would really put the cat among the pigeons and might give Inspector Cole a way of wrapping up the case. If he could show Reverend Weaver was losing his mind, her friend could end up in an asylum with virtually no chance of ever getting out. His buoyancy on arrival, so at odds with his previous mood and demeanour, had now dissipated. She had thought to spare him a full account of what had happened throughout the day but now decided it was best to fill him in. By demonstrating they were making progress after all, perhaps Weaver would take heart and keep his head above water.

Mrs Bramble told him everything, reiterating the most

salient points of their investigation and calling on Kitty to fill in any gaps. By the time they'd finished, Weaver looked a little brighter and she had renewed hope he would get through this.

'This looks a jolly gathering,' said Reverend Dench suddenly, making them all jump. 'All you need is a picnic.'

Mrs Bramble marvelled at the ability of so many people to creep up on her at the Tower. She found it unnerving, especially considering she knew most of the footfalls of her grace and favour ladies at Hampton Court.

'Merely taking a moment to reflect, Reverend,' she said with as much cheer as she could muster.

'Quite right,' said Dench. 'Leave all that investigating to the professionals, eh? Do what we're good at.'

He waved a spray can in the air that Mrs Bramble hadn't noticed him carrying before and she heard liquid slosh about inside. A faintly fishy smell wafted her way and she wrinkled her nose.

'More spraying, Reverend?' she said.

'Those little blighters love the taste of my flowers,' said Dench. 'Got to keep up with them.'

'Why are you carrying it around with you? Are they after you as well?'

Reverend Dench laughed. 'I've been to the vegetable gardens in the moat. I can always persuade the gardening folk there to give me a little of their insecticide.'

He waved the can again and a waft of fish accompanied the sloshing sound.

'Why does it smell like that?' asked Kitty, waving her hand in front of her nose. 'It smells like a trawler at the seaside.'

'My apologies,' said Dench, putting the can behind his back. 'I'm afraid I got to chatting for longer than I'd intended and left the can in the full glare of the sun. When it gets warm it gives off a slightly fishy aroma. I've become used to it since I started spraying my flowers with the preparation but I suppose it can seem a little pungent to the uninitiated.'

'It's not that it's strong,' said Kitty, 'but it does come as a bit of a surprise in the middle of a fortress, even if we are right by the Thames.'

'Yes, I suppose it must,' said Reverend Dench with a nod. 'Anyway, I must get on so I'll let you return to your moment of reflection.' He went to turn away but hesitated. 'I know it's closed for services until Inspector Cole and the chief say so but you could always have a quiet moment in the chapel.'

He smiled and headed for his garden.

Mrs Bramble couldn't help smiling too as Reverend Dench ambled away. He seemed so content with his lot at the Tower, as much as she and Reverend Weaver were at the palace.

Her face fell.

Something Reverend Dench had said chimed with conversations she'd had elsewhere, and with what they had been discussing moments before he'd arrived. She looked at Reverend Weaver and Kitty, who had fallen silent at her change of mood and saw their looks of concern.

'Are you well, Mrs Bramble?' said the reverend.

'I am,' she said. 'Because I believe I know how Mrs Fry was murdered.'

28

Reverend Weaver and Kitty had been sitting in the front pew before the high altar inside the Chapel of St Peter ad Vincula for the last four minutes. After the departure of Reverend Dench, Mrs Bramble had led them there without further explanation other than to tell them she needed a moment to gather her thoughts.

As Mrs Bramble paced up and down the aisle, she feared making the kind of mistake that might cause Inspector Cole to throw her out of the Tower of London. She thought she had finally found the solution but something appeared to be missing still. Talking through a problem had always served her well in the past so she stopped in front of the frowning Kitty and wide-eyed Weaver like a schoolteacher about to deliver a lesson.

'Reverend, your discovery about the unlikelihood of the wine having been poisoned is an intriguing one,' said Mrs Bramble. 'It would do no harm for us to await Dr Burford's report once his samples have been tested.'

'If he can find any left,' said Reverend Weaver.

'If he can find any left,' echoed Mrs Bramble. 'And that got me thinking. Where else did everyone partake of wine?'

Weaver and Kitty exchanged a glance but came up with no answer.

'In here,' said Mrs Bramble with a sweep of her arm to indicate the chapel.

Weaver looked around as though something present would provide more explanation.

'You mean the communion wine?' said Kitty, looking sceptical.

'Exactly,' said Mrs Bramble. 'If the poison wasn't in the food and the tests confirm it wasn't in the white wine served at the reception, it must have been administered here during the Eucharist. After all, I've been told everyone succumbed to its effects at pretty much the same time, with greater or lesser effect depending on the constitution of each person.'

'True,' said Reverend Weaver, his brow creased with puzzlement. 'But I don't see how the bottle could have been adulterated. It was locked in a cupboard to which only Reverend Dench held a key until he gave it to me the day before the service.' He looked up at Mrs Bramble in despair. 'If Inspector Cole hears of this, he'll lock me up again.'

'I don't wish to cast aspersions on a man of the cloth but all avenues must be explored. If Reverend Dench gave you the key, might he not have already tampered with the wine? If he has a spare key, could he not have gone to the cupboard himself at any time, thus framing you? Perhaps he had become jealous of your recent lauding and wanted to sully your reputation at the very least. Maybe his long-standing organist, Jasper Chant, agreed to become his accomplice but Esther overheard their plotting, forcing him to silence her.'

'I-I can't believe a man of faith would do such a thing,' said Reverend Weaver, almost in tears at the suggestion. 'I-it's all conjecture.'

Mrs Bramble did not disagree but still she scoffed. Although she envied anyone who believed in a higher being and the certainty and peace that brought them, she had witnessed many a conflict based on religion, blind faith and fanaticism.

'Don't forget his spray can,' she said. 'Not only is Reverend Dench in charge of the communion wine but he also has ready access to insecticide.'

'If he'd put some in the wine, wouldn't people have complained about the fishy smell?' said Kitty. 'If it tastes fishy too, surely they'd have mentioned it?'

Mrs Bramble looked at Reverend Weaver. 'Did they?'

Reverend Weaver shook his head. 'No one complained and I certainly didn't smell anything.'

'Hmm,' she said, remembering Dench's words. 'Reverend Dench did say it whiffed when heated. The communion wine will have been served cool.' She turned towards the vestry. 'Come with me.'

'We're not supposed to be in here,' reminded Kitty as they trooped into the vestry and looked at the wine bottle still standing on the table between the dish of stale wafers and water carafe.

Mrs Bramble fluttered her hand. 'I understand it's been like Piccadilly Circus in here since before we arrived so I'm sure even Inspector Cole couldn't make a case against us for that.' She looked in a cupboard and found a small glass, which she took back to the table. 'I think it would be prudent for us to ask the good doctor to have this tested at the same time, wouldn't you?' She poured a small measure of red wine.

'What if there's nothing in it?' said Kitty. 'What do we do then? We know Reverend Weaver isn't a murderer but what if Reverend Dench and Mr Chant aren't either?'

'One thing at a time,' said Mrs Bramble, a niggling image worming its way into her thoughts.

She glanced around the room as though the answer might lie somewhere within. As her gaze alighted on the small metal bin by the door that led outside the chapel, she remembered the shard of glass still wrapped in her pocket handkerchief.

'What happens to the water, Reverend?' said Mrs Bramble. 'During a service.'

'Water?' said Reverend Weaver, looking surprised at the question. 'Um, prior to a service, the vicar or chaplain cleanses his hands. Fresh water is used to dilute the wine immediately before Holy Communion where it receives a blessing. After the last person has taken the bread and wine, the vicar or chaplain uses the last of the water to rinse out the dregs of wine from the chalice, which he drinks.'

'It is all used up, usually?'

'Always.'

Mrs Bramble looked inside the chalice. 'There is red wine remaining in this chalice and some water in the carafe.'

Reverend Weaver nodded. 'That is because circumstances prevented me from completing the ritual. Only two people had still to take Holy Communion: Mr Chant and myself.'

This took Mrs Bramble by surprise. The answer was one she had not expected. 'Not Reverend Dench?' she asked.

'He was the first to whom I administered the bread and wine,' said Weaver, looking a little sheepish. 'But I became concerned that I had not prepared enough wine for the number of people in the congregation so I decided to defer my own communion until the end. Just in case.'

That made sense but posed another question. Had everyone partaken or had someone avoided their own poison, merely pretending to be ill?

'Did anyone abstain from Holy Communion?' asked Mrs Bramble.

Weaver looked up at the flat wooden beams of the Romanesque roof, thinking. 'There was one. Inspector Cole knelt at the chancel rail but received only a blessing.'

'So, the only three not to be taken ill – Inspector Cole, Jasper Chant and yourself – were the only three not to take the bread and wine.'

'Correct.'

Mrs Bramble tapped the table. 'Which definitely points the finger at the contents on this table, don't you think?' She weighed the parcel in her hand. 'Did you or Reverend Dench suffer the misfortune of breaking something during your preparations for the service?'

'Breaking something?' echoed Weaver, his eyebrows forming a shallow V. 'Such as?'

'Oh, I don't know. A glass or bottle. A vial perhaps? Maybe even a glass bowl or dish?'

'I think not, I would remember doing so. Although I cannot vouch for Reverend Dench, I don't recall seeing or hearing him break anything. Nor did he make mention.'

'I thought as much.'

'Whatever are you thinking, Mrs B?' said Kitty.

Mrs Bramble indicated the contents of the table. 'The wine, water and wafers are the only substances ingested by virtually the whole congregation, beyond the refreshments provided at the reception. Inspector Cole, Mr Chant and Reverend Weaver are the only three we know of who did not partake. Therefore, we must come to the inevitable conclusion that the poison is contained in one or all of these three items.

'Do you have a pocket square, Reverend?' said Mrs Bramble. 'To keep a few of these wafers safe? I don't want to use the chalice cloth.' She took two more glasses from the cupboard and poured some of the chalice wine into one and some of the water into the other.

'As it happens ...' Reverend Weaver produced a piece of folded white cotton and proceeded to wrap half a dozen wafers. 'Funnily enough, that is not the usual chalice cloth. Augustus told me just before the service that he thought he'd fetched the one Mrs Fry had donated, which she had hand-embroidered herself. I did remember seeing it and felt embarrassed that I had mislaid it. We had to use that one and he was most concerned that Mrs Fry would voice her displeasure.'

'Really?' Mrs Bramble frowned, then turned her attention to the handkerchief in her hand. 'I have a shard of glass I need to get to Dr Burford along with these three glasses of liquid and those wafers. We'd better hurry before he leaves for Guy's Hospital with the other samples.'

'Good Lord,' Weaver exclaimed as Reverend Dench hurried in through the door from the nave.

'Whatever is the matter?' said Mrs Bramble, Dench's presence alarming enough but his look of concern causing her heart to thump in her chest.

'I saw you enter earlier and thought I might find you still here,' Dench said in a stage whisper as he glanced nervously over his shoulder. 'I spotted Inspector Cole and the chief striding this way and thought you might wish to avoid awkward questions, seeing as this chapel is supposed to be closed.'

Mrs Bramble looked at him curiously. Why was he, a suspect, warning them? 'Thank you, Reverend.' She turned to Kitty and Reverend Weaver. 'Please ensure these samples reach Dr Burford before he sends the others with Esther's body for testing. We need to know if they contain nicotine poison.'

Reverend Dench looked astounded and started to speak but Mrs Bramble ignored his stuttering question. She opened the door to the outside and shooed her friends through, quietly closing the door behind them. She watched their legs through the window, disappearing upwards as they ascended the stone steps, before joining Dench at the door to the nave.

He opened it a crack before declaring it all clear.

By the time Mrs Bramble heard footsteps as the two men entered the chapel through the main door, she was sitting in the front pew facing the altar and Reverend Dench was kneeling at the chancel rail, praying.

'Inspector, Chief, what can I do for you?' she said without looking round at them.

'How did you kn—?' Inspector Cole stopped and took a breath. 'What are you doing in here?' he said, a note of suspicion in his tone.

'I would have thought that was obvious,' said Dench, getting to his feet. 'Communing with God, as is natural.'

'What is your excuse?' said Mrs Bramble, knowing the question would irk the inspector, thus disrupting his train of thought.

'I don't need an excuse,' snapped Cole.

'A reason then?'

'To find out what you are doing, as you damn well know!' Immediately, Inspector Cole put up a hand defensively. 'I do apologise. I did not mean to speak so harshly, especially to a woman. And in a house of God.'

'Apology accepted, Inspector,' said Mrs Bramble.

Reverend Dench looked at Cole and put his hands together as though in prayer.

'Tempers frayed, understandable,' said the chief. 'Murderer at large. Progress slow. Help each other, yes?'

On the verge of asking to speak to the inspector and chief alone, Mrs Bramble hesitated. Reverend Dench's willingness to warn of the inspector's approach with the chief, thus letting them get the samples away to Dr Burford, swayed her towards thinking him innocent rather than involved in murder.

Decision made, she said, 'To answer your question: I have been engaged in nothing more than the objective I stated upon my arrival.'

'You were to keep me informed,' said Inspector Cole, the red of his cheeks still betraying a simmering irritation. 'We agreed.'

'*Us* informed,' said the chief, sharply.

'I assure you I have tried to be as forthcoming as possible.' She ignored Cole's scoff. 'Since your last rebuke about my inquiries we have unearthed a little more information.'

'Go on then.' Inspector Cole sat in the pew opposite, bowler hat in hand. 'Let's hear it.'

'You were fixated on Reverend Weaver being Mrs Fry's murderer but still I can find no evidence for it,' said Mrs Bramble. 'Nor do we have any one individual in mind.'

'Not an auspicious start,' muttered Cole.

Mrs Bramble sniffed at the interruption. 'We had begun to exclude the organist, Mr Jasper Chant, but not only was he first on the stairs immediately after the chambermaid, Esther, was found, but I have since learnt he was abroad around the Tower on the night I chased someone through the chapel and lost them in the Outer Ward.'

'You chased . . .' Inspector Cole threw his arms up as if to say, what next?

Mrs Bramble ignored his gesticulation, and astonished glances from both Reverend Dench and the chief. 'One explanation for his nocturnal movements may be his clandestine courtship of Beth, the Frys' housemaid.'

'Beth?' said Reverend Dench, aghast. 'Jasper? How? When? He shook his head. 'How did I not notice?'

'They were observed stealing a kiss behind the Waterloo Barracks not far from where Sir Stephen Lovell and Sir Oswald Clyne were seen conducting an argument.'

Inspector Cole's ears pricked up and he sat straighter. 'How do you know all this?' He held up his hands. 'No, don't tell me now. My heart won't take the strain.'

Mrs Bramble suppressed a smile – she was getting rather good at doing that in Cole's presence – and told them everything she had discovered.

'How many times must I ask you to bring evidence to me, or better still, leave it alone?' said Inspector Cole.

The chief tutted. 'What is done is done. Narrows the suspects, no? Bread, wine, water. Who had the opportunity?' He looked at Reverend Dench suspiciously.

'I believe whomever I chased through the crypt last night had returned to the chapel to retrieve the damning evidence,' said Mrs Bramble. 'They knew it was only a matter of time before we worked it out.'

'But you chased them off,' said Inspector Cole.

'Exactly. Which means unless they are close enough to us three standing here to be aware we have already taken samples, they may return for another try tonight.'

'Then we must be waiting,' said Inspector Cole with a defiant lift of his chin.

Mrs Bramble looked at Reverend Dench. 'When we spoke earlier you said you had filled your garden spray can with insecticide obtained from one of the men tending the vegetables in the south moat.'

'That is correct,' said Dench.

'Do you know if it contains nicotine?'

'I have absolutely no idea, I'm afraid'

'That question,' said the chief. 'Ask the gardeners. Lovely fellows. Sure to help.'

'The answer could point the finger at me,' said Dench with a quiver in his voice.

'I think not,' said Mrs Bramble, ignoring the inspector's raised eyebrows. 'Anyone could have stolen some. In any case, you were ill yourself, I understand.'

Reverend Dench put his hand to his throat as though reliving the experience. 'I was.' He coughed weakly for effect. 'I was.'

Inspector Cole stood. 'I would argue that the two reverends and the organist must remain our main persons of interest.' Dench looked horrified. 'However, I think it would be prudent to question the two sirs again, and the sooner the better. Chief, can you post one of your men on guard in the vestry until we return this evening?'

'Vestry? Man inside?' said the chief. 'Highly irregular.'

'Maybe so but I would prefer no one else walked through willy-nilly.

'Chap in mind. Just outside chapel.' The chief raised his eyebrows at Cole.

The two men began to leave but Inspector Cole halted halfway to the door and looked at Mrs Bramble who was following two paces behind. 'What are you doing?'

Mrs Bramble fixed him with her best no-nonsense stare. 'If you think you can exclude me when I have volunteered all my information to you, you've got another think coming.'

'We are going to speak to Lovell and Clyne, that is all.'

'And I am coming with you.'

'You have spoken to them before.'

'As have you, but circumstances change,' said Mrs Bramble. 'Information comes to light and is discarded. Theories are born, adapted and allowed to run their course or wither and die.'

She saw Inspector Cole's face harden in annoyance, his cheeks redden with irritation, and then his features soften as he became resigned to the fact that she would never take no for an answer. She enjoyed playing on his fear of her going off half-cocked or at a tangent, and she could sense his mind working behind his eyes as he tried to reconcile his police procedural training with her propensity for playing the unrestrained sleuth.

'I—'

'Inspector,' she interrupted. 'We may be near to confirming how Mrs Fry's murder was committed but not the chambermaid's, and we are no closer to finding out who or establishing why. We are surrounded by sundry people holding grudges, two knights of the realm squabbling like schoolboys, a housemaid acting above her station with a man who should know better, and a multitude of military men toting firearms because they fear what they cannot see. The murderer, or murderers, will know we are making slow progress, but any progress is progress nonetheless. They will fear discovery so we need to be prepared in the vestry tonight.

'Until we have them behind bars, I fear we are all still in mortal danger.'

29

As Reverend Weaver and Kitty made as much haste away from the vestry's eastern door as they could without spilling the precious samples, Kitty glanced over her shoulder to ensure no one was in pursuit. She saw the face of Dr Burford through an open window on the first floor of the resident surgeon's house and called a halt to their flight.

'What is it?' said Weaver nervously. 'Are we discovered?'

'It's the doctor,' said Kitty, nodding towards the tall, narrow dwelling squeezed into the gap between the Beauchamp Tower and the chaplain's house. 'He can't have left yet.'

'Right, good, right,' said Weaver. 'Actually, he can't leave at all, can he? Inspector Cole and the chief ordered everyone to remain inside the Tower's walls.'

'Are we too late? Has someone been sent to Guy's?'

'Only one way to find out,' said Reverend Weaver, licking his lips but making no move.

Kitty sighed. It looked like this was up to her. 'So, let's find out,' she said.

She hurried to the surgeon's house with the reverend scurrying behind her, all the time expecting the inspector and chief to catch them in the act in the open.

Kitty's heart pounded as they waited for a veritable lifetime for the door to be opened by the housemaid. In response to their entreaties, they were let in to the parlour and Kitty heard the footfalls and creaking stairs as the maid went upstairs to announce their arrival to the doctor.

Moments later, the face of the doctor, framed by his mutton-chop whiskers, appeared in the doorway as though he were checking their presence was real. His body followed and he stood wide-eyed before them.

'Whatever can I do for you?' he said. 'Is someone ill? Is Mrs Bramble well?'

'I-I ...' Reverend Weaver began.

'Begging your pardon, Doctor, but Mrs Bramble sent us with these.' Kitty held up the two glasses.'

'I don't understand.' Dr Burford looked perplexed, one questioning eyebrow raised. 'I have my own refreshment, should I need any.'

'No-no.' Weaver chuckled.

'They're samples for testing,' Kitty explained. 'One is from the bottle of wine used during the Holy Communion service where Mrs Fry died. This one is from the carafe of holy water used to add to the wine.' She held that one higher. 'And the reverend's holding the diluted mixture given to the congregation from the gold chalice.'

'Oh,' said Dr Burford. 'Come in, come in.'

'Did you manage to find any leftover wine as we discussed earlier?' said Reverend Weaver, discovering his voice at last as they stood in the parlour.

'As a matter of fact ...' Dr Burford disappeared for a moment and returned, tripping over his own feet but recovering in a split second to avoid cannoning into his guests. Apologising profusely for his clumsiness, he held a canvas bag by its strap and withdrew an almost-empty bottle of white wine. 'It was the last one left and I'm assured the contents were served at the reception.'

'Then you must add these to your collection as a matter

of urgency,' said Kitty, thrusting her glasses forward insistently. 'Before the chief and the inspector catch us with them.'

Dr Burford danced from foot to foot as though picking his way over hot coals before he disappeared and Kitty heard footsteps descending creaky stairs to the basement. She cast a worried glance at Weaver, who merely shrugged, almost spilling his wine. The muffled rattle and clink of glass percolated up through the rug-covered floorboards as Kitty glanced nervously out of the parlour's window. She had expected to see the looming body of the policeman and chief approaching but almost gasped in relief when she saw Mrs Bramble walking with the two men past the surgeon's house, away from the chapel towards the governor's residence.

She jumped as Dr Burford suddenly reappeared, a lopsided grin on his face and brandishing three, small, cork-stoppered glass flasks.

'These will do,' he announced. 'These will do nicely.' He placed them on a small occasional table beside a padded chair and began uncorking them. 'We must make haste. A Yeoman Warder will be here any moment to take my bag over to Guy's Hospital with the body of the unfortunate maid and no doubt any delay will make him suspicious.'

'Will he not be suspicious anyway?' said Weaver. 'After all, he will be expecting one wine bottle, will he not?'

'Not at all, not at all,' said Dr Burford, taking a glass.

He decanted its contents into the first flask, his hands shaking so much with the effort of directing the small stream into the neck of the bottle that Kitty thought it remarkable any liquid survived the transfer at all.

'I merely requested the services of a fellow to convey my bag with the maid's body to Guy's,' said Burford. 'I don't want to keep him waiting.' He poured the other two glasses into the remaining flasks, replaced the corks, and went across to a small bureau.

'We have a few communion wafers and a shard of glass for you to test too,' said Kitty, gesturing for Reverend Weaver to hand them over. 'The shard *must* be returned.'

Reverend Weaver put the two small packages on the table. 'Everything is to be tested for nicotine,' he said. 'Mrs Bramble is convinced this is the way everyone was poisoned.'

'Good heavens,' muttered Burford. 'Who'd have thought it?' He returned with three labels identifying *wine*, *water* and *diluted* in pencil, and tied them to the necks of the three flasks with string. These he placed with exaggerated care into the bag alongside the wine bottle, and followed this up with the two wrapped packages and a note Kitty suspected set out his requirements for the tests.

Reverend Weaver almost slid off his chair and one of Dr Burford's knees jerked upwards in fright from a heavy rap on the front door.

Kitty peered through the window and saw a Yeoman Warder in his undress uniform of dark blue with red features standing back from the door. As a muffled exchange ensued, the Warder stepped forward, took the bag from Dr Burford and turned on his heels. She felt a weight lift from her shoulders as the man marched away and she noticed the reverend visibly relax, his body almost moulding to the shape of the chair as he slumped back into it.

Dr Burford reappeared and Reverend Weaver sat bolt upright.

'All done,' said Burford. 'All we can do now is wait.' He smiled at them. 'You're perfectly welcome to sit here and take tea, if you wish?' The upward inflection at the end made it a question.

Kitty declined politely on their behalf, declaring she fancied a stroll in the fresh air after the recent excitement. Reverend Weaver agreed, patting his chest rapidly as though his heart was going ten to the dozen.

Dr Burford saw them to the front door and as it closed behind them Kitty said, 'You do realise, if the hospital tests prove those samples to have been poisoned, Inspector Cole might be inclined to jump to more conclusions.'

'It is his nature,' said Reverend Weaver with a dismissive wave of his hand. 'And his job. He is a naturally suspicious man.'

'You miss my meaning, Reverend,' she said, not wishing to scare him but wanting him to face reality. 'You had access to everything in the vestry. The wine, the water, the wafers. You had the key. Reverend Dench was poisoned but you were not, even though you should have taken Holy Communion with him first, at the same time. Regardless of what anyone close to you might think or believe, it will look suspicious to outsiders.'

Reverend Weaver's sudden change of expression gave him the look a haunted man.

'You have to be careful and on your best behaviour,' Kitty continued. 'Otherwise, Mrs Bramble won't be able to help you, and Inspector Cole will have no other option but to arrest you again. For murder.'

30

Chief Yeoman Warder Treadle stopped in front of the Beauchamp Tower and indicated the governor's residence further along with a flick of his thumb.

'Must leave you here, I'm afraid. Just remembered. Governor needs informing. Progress on the case and whatnot. Immediately after, Tower Green, behind me. Swearing in a new Yeoman Warder.'

'But what about Lovell and Clyne?' said Inspector Cole, looking unsure of himself. 'We need to question them urgently.'

'Carry on,' said the chief, looking as though he had not one care in the world. 'Perfectly fine. Every faith in you. Mrs Bramble, an able colleague. No?'

Mrs Bramble saw Cole's mouth form the word 'No' but no sound emerged.

'After the ceremony, toasts in the club. Do come.' He looked at Mrs Bramble. 'Not you, Mrs Bramble. Not the done thing, but the inspector, very welcome.' He tapped the side of his nose and winked. 'Beefeater gin, all round.'

Mrs Bramble smiled and watched as the chief turned on his heels and marched towards the governor's residence.

'He has no idea, has he?' said Inspector Cole with a wry smile.

'None at all,' said Mrs Bramble. 'He is correct, though. I am most able, and also at this current moment, impatient to have another talk with Sir Oswald and Sir Stephen.' She held out her hand in the direction of the officers' quarters. 'Shall we?'

The walk across the parade ground to the Fusiliers' building was conducted in silence. Mrs Bramble knew Cole was seething inside at having her as a companion instead of the chief. For her part, she was busy trying to rearrange what little she knew into some semblance of order before confronting the two knights again. Something was niggling at her thoughts and every remembrance of the British Bulldog pocket pistol made her shudder.

She had been around guns of every size during her many years as an army nurse and had become used to their shapes, noises and smells. What she had never managed to get used to was their ability to shatter whatever their projectiles came into contact with, whether that be countryside, masonry or flesh, nor a particular type of man who wielded them. Some did so under orders, some out of necessity, but an unfortunate number revelled in their cold, utilitarian abilities and efficiencies. It was the latter man she feared the most and she hoped Sir Stephen Lovell, with his quick temper, could restrain himself from doing something drastic, foolish and fatal.

The guard on the door of the Fusiliers' building called for a steward and directed him to take them straight to Sir Stephen Lovell. The steward beckoned for them to follow and led the way along the corridor to a room with a snooker table at its centre. Lovell looked up from potting random balls as they entered.

'Do you play, Inspector?' said Lovell, recovering snooker balls from the pockets at the corners and along the sides.

'I have been known to,' said Inspector Cole. 'But I don't think—'

'A sixpenny piece up for grabs.' Lovell took a wooden triangle and racked the red balls.

'I haven't the time, sir.'

'Of course, you have.' Lovell winked at Mrs Bramble and began placing the other coloured balls on the spots marking their starting positions. 'I take it you're here to ask more questions. You can do so as we play.'

Mrs Bramble thought Inspector Cole to be a man who could never resist a challenge, but it was clear the wager was putting him off. Lovell must have thought so too.

'I tell you what, let's make it a penny.' Lovell smiled at Cole. 'Just so there is a wager on the table but losing won't break the bank.'

'Well,' said Cole, placing his bowler hat on a chair and removing his coat. 'I do like the odd game here and there.' He took a cue, looked along its length and inspected the tip before placing a silver threepenny coin on the side of the table. 'Let us split the difference, to make it interesting.'

Lovell grinned. 'You're on.' He placed his own coin alongside Cole's.

Mrs Bramble rolled her eyes and prepared to sit on the sidelines while the two stags locked antlers over the green baize. A tossed coin gave Inspector Cole the break and Lovell stood back. Cole struck the cue ball, which gently broke the tight triangle of reds and came to rest in a favourable position.

'Bravo,' said Lovell. 'Good shot.' He lined up to take his turn.

'When we spoke earlier, you said you became friends with Lord Fry while developing the railway service in Africa,' said Mrs Bramble, eager to progress the interview.

Lovell managed to hit but not pot a red ball. 'And India,

yes. I had a healthy respect for the man. The businessman. It grew into a friendship.'

'Has this friendship ever been tested?'

Lovell moved out of the way for Cole. 'I'm not sure what you mean.'

'Every relationship has its ups and downs,' said Mrs Bramble. 'Don't you agree?'

'I do agree, but civilised gentlemen resolve their differences respectfully over brandy and cigars.'

'On the other hand, you hold no respect whatsoever for Sir Oswald Clyne. A cold fish, I think you likened him to.'

'What of it?' said Lovell.

Mrs Bramble shrugged. 'You left me with the distinct impression that you think little of his intellect. That he deals in second-hand opinions.'

Having pocketed a red, Inspector Cole took the black and another red.

'You have an admirable talent for recall, Mrs Bramble,' said Lovell.

'Are you still of a mind to seek redress for the passing of Mrs Fry?' she said.

'Are you saying Clyne was involved?'

Mrs Bramble kept quiet and returned a neutral expression. She was suggesting nothing of the sort but if her silence sowed any kind of doubt about who Lovell could trust, perhaps he might say something unplanned but useful.

Lovell's response was guarded. 'If a culprit could be identified, I would surely support the maximum penalty. But as I'm sure you remember, it is my belief that food poisoning caused her tragic and untimely end.'

'I'm led to believe you harbour a grudge against Major Rushton's father, Sir Arthur,' said Mrs Bramble.

'Grudge is perhaps too strong a word, although I do hold him responsible for the lack of advancement in my career.'

'How so?'

'Excellent shot, Inspector,' said Lovell, tapping his cue on the floor in salute as Cole's fourth black took his break to thirty-two points.

'How so?' Mrs Bramble asked again, trying to keep Lovell's attention on her questions.

Lovell gave her a sideways glance. 'He knew of my close friendship with Lord Fry and because of this I believe he considered my position far too influential for his liking. He wanted to exert a measure of control and used his connections to place obstacles in my way. Mrs Fry told me as much. Surviving in this world is challenge enough without others actively working against you, hoping to see you fail.'

It was becoming clear to Mrs Bramble that Lovell knew next to nothing about the true nature of the machinations that had been going on in the background. That might yet prove to be to her advantage in the wheedling of information from him.

'You have strong beliefs but are you secure enough in your knowledge?' she said, watching his face closely.

'What do you mean?' Lovell half frowned. 'Do you know something I don't?'

'I have it on unimpeachable authority that it was not Sir Arthur who stood in your way.'

Lovell scoffed but gave her a curious glance. 'If not he, who?'

Mrs Bramble paused for effect, as though reluctant to let the cat out of the bag.

A clatter of balls from the table followed Inspector Cole's aggressive potting of his eighth black, taking his break to sixty-four. He had taken no part in the conversation and appeared to have no interest in it at all. Lovell was momentarily distracted as he congratulated the inspector, but his attention soon returned to Mrs Bramble.

'Lord Fry,' said Mrs Bramble.

'Don't be ridiculous,' hissed Lovell. 'What possible reason could he have? He is my friend.'

She shook her head. 'It appears you are not as close as you believe.'

'Mrs Fry was adamant.'

'Mrs Fry was mistaken.'

She did not wish to say Mrs Fry had lied because she needed him to feel his friend's wife had been egregiously wronged. If he suspected Mrs Fry had had a guiding hand in the deception, his opinion of her might change, causing him to become tight-lipped. He stared at her as though searching her features for untruths but she remained impassive. Iron-voiced sergeant-majors had shouted at her in the past and come unstuck, so she had nothing here to fear on that score.

'Sir Arthur Rushton thought Lord Fry's expansion plans in Africa too big an investment risk for the government to support his company,' said Mrs Bramble. 'It was Sir Arthur who became instrumental in persuading influential people to place their trust elsewhere. That is why the big contracts were lost. However, Lord Fry holds the mistaken belief it is you who was in some way culpable for the failure of his business ventures.'

Shock registered on Lovell's face in his wide eyes and open mouth. He tilted his head a few degrees like a dog cocking its ear, unsure of the sound it was hearing. 'Lord Fry thinks *I'm* to blame? Why would he even entertain such a notion when I am a long-standing friend of the family?'

Inspector Cole slid his marker on the scoreboard up to 104. 'You need snookers, *old chap*,' he said.

Lovell scoffed, and the policeman re-chalked his cue before bending for another shot.

'Why?' Lovell asked her again.

Mrs Bramble held his gaze. 'Simply because of your increasing reputation and influence in that area, and no doubt your intimate knowledge of his business. Lord Fry could not accept a better company had beaten his. He sought any other reason, any excuse, and unfortunately settled on you as one who had the power to do him damage. I suspect the notion was not discouraged by Sir Arthur but we can never know whether he sowed the original seed of discontent.'

The pain of betrayal lined Lovell's face as he took in this new revelation, and his lips moved as though his heart wanted to talk but his head wouldn't release the words. Mrs Bramble watched the conflict play out across his features and waited patiently for him to come to a decision. She knew there was more to come, although not what that might be, but she could not pursue it. She had to wait for him to volunteer the information.

Mrs Bramble saw his eyes glisten with gathering tears and suddenly felt great sympathy. Here was a man whose supposed friends had mistrusted and lied to him. No doubt he had a larger circle with whom to console himself, but he could not get away from those in the Tower while confined within its walls and was destined to be in their company until the case was solved.

Lovell sniffed and wiped away a tear with the back of his hand.

'I have something to confess,' Lovell said, turning to face Mrs Bramble. 'Not to Mrs Fry's murder, I should add.' He sniffed again, solemn-faced. 'Mrs Fry summoned me one evening several weeks ago. She said she had a delicate matter to discuss and a task only I could be trusted to perform. She spoke about the feud from university, which I had known about for years, and fed me example after example of how insidiously evil Sir Arthur and all the Rushtons were. She spoke at length, getting my dander up, and I never once challenged the truth of it, nor why she should be telling all this to me now.' He took a deep breath and let it out slowly. 'The meeting culminated in a request for me to kill Major Rushton, to take from Sir Arthur something he loved more than money.'

It was Mrs Bramble's turn to be taken aback. 'Did you consider it?' she said, trying to keep her voice steady and matter-of-fact.

Lovell gave a half-hearted shrug. 'I must admit I was angry enough to comply there and then, had the major been in front of me at that moment. I left her company and thought about what she had said for several days. As my anger and fervour dissipated, rational thought replaced it. I avoided being alone with her to prevent any further discussion. I came to brooding alone for many hours, not visiting the Tower or attending functions where I feared the captain and Mrs Fry would be.'

Inspector Cole adjusted his scoreboard marker to 120. 'Only the colours left, Sir Stephen,' he smirked.

Lovell seemed unable to raise a smile this time as the inspector positioned himself to take a shot on the yellow ball into the top-right pocket.

Lovell looked back to Mrs Bramble. 'Unfortunately, such evasion could not last. When I told her I understood and respected her passion but I was a peaceful man who could not go through with it, she raged at me for a full five minutes. Having called my class into question, and after the storm had blown itself out, she said in as calm a manner as I'd ever seen her use that she would have to take matters into her own hands.'

Mrs Bramble's heart missed a beat. 'Did she explain what she meant?'

'She did.' Lovell nodded. 'She knew I carried a pocket pistol, the one you saw, and demanded I hand it over. I refused and we did not discuss the matter further. She never asked again and acted rather distant thereafter.'

'Did Captain Fry not suspect anything?'

'Nothing at all. He was far too busy with his duties here in the Tower.'

Mrs Bramble's mind was racing. How did all this fit with what they knew about Mrs Fry's murder? Lovell had been wronged, but the man in front of her appeared innocent. Lord Fry had reason to harbour hatred towards Sir Arthur but would Sir Arthur have arranged for Mrs Fry's demise? It all seemed far too fanciful. There had to be something missing.

'Do you think Major Rushton could have found out about Mrs Fry's intentions and decided to remove her as a threat?' said Mrs Bramble.

'Mrs Fry could be quite vociferous on occasion but she was more inclined to keep her own counsel,' said Lovell, sounding rather deflated. 'I truly believe she told no one else.'

'One four seven!' cried the inspector, startling the others. 'Maximum break.' He snatched up the two silver threepenny pieces and slipped them into his pocket. 'Thanks for the game,' he said, taking Lovell's hand and giving it a pumping shake. 'Sorry you didn't come to the table more than once but that's the nature of competition sometimes.'

'My pleasure, Inspector,' said Lovell, somewhat bemused. 'Only glad I could offer you some sport.'

Inspector Cole donned his coat and retrieved his bowler hat. 'I do love a game. Been playing since I was a nipper.' He gave Lovell a friendly pat on his back and turned to Mrs Bramble. 'Shall we toddle off and leave this gentleman in peace?'

With Cole obviously eager to leave, Mrs Bramble said goodbye and left the Fusiliers' building with him.

Once outside, Inspector Cole said, 'I must say, that was an interesting conversation.'

Mrs Bramble scoffed. 'The one you took no part in while busy with your snooker?'

'The one you had fully under your control while I scored a maximum break, like I sometimes achieve against my fellow officers. Lovell was on a hiding to nothing, to be honest.'

'You could have helped.'

'I had no reason to intervene while you were doing such a sterling job. I may have acted disinterested while potting balls but I heard every word. You did very well, Mrs Bramble, and I think it's high time we had a talk with Sir Oswald Clyne. If he somehow got wind of Mrs Fry's intentions, perhaps he decided to take direct action himself. If true, he could strike again.'

31

Although all visiting members of the public had left for the day, a gathering of people attracted the attention of Mrs Bramble as she left the Fusiliers' building with Inspector Cole.

It appeared some kind of ceremony was about to take place and she remembered Chief Yeoman Warder Treadle had a new member of his unit to swear in. They walked across to Tower Green to take in the proceedings along with a few residents from the Tower and discovered Reverend Weaver and Kitty already there.

'I hope you two have been behaving yourselves while we've been busy,' said Inspector Cole.

Kitty looked a picture of innocence but Mrs Bramble caught the faintest flush on Weaver's cheeks.

'Let's just enjoy the ceremony for a while, shall we?' said Mrs Bramble.

Cole held her gaze for a few seconds before he harrumphed like some old colonel and turned his attention to where the chief stood in a scarlet overcoat. Nineteen other Yeoman Warders in their blue-and-red undress uniforms stood with him in a horseshoe shape facing a table, behind which stood the governor and his lieutenant in their ceremonial hats displaying sprays of white feathers.

The chief stood proud and upright, taking his role and duties seriously. Mrs Bramble approved. Pomp and ceremony, displays of magnificence and elegance, centuries-old tradition. It might look silly or outdated to some or unnecessary to others, but the costumes and symbolism all meant something and therefore had worth. It spoke of unity and solidarity. It represented a shared continuity that reassured and comforted. There was a lot to be said for it.

Drawing Reverend Weaver and Kitty away from Inspector Cole and bringing them in close, Mrs Bramble relayed the essence of their meeting with Sir Stephen Lovell as succinctly as she could without alerting the smattering of people around them. Weaver's face was blank with shock but Kitty merely shrugged with resignation as though it was nothing less than she expected of such people.

Out of the corner of her eye, Mrs Bramble noticed Lovell had joined the gathering of spectators and was about to bring this to the attention of the others when she saw Sir Oswald Clyne on the other side of the throng. She had no wish to confront him in front of other people but fully intended to intercept him afterwards. She thought it would be interesting to discover whether he knew of any plot to murder Major Rushton. That would take careful questioning on her part.

These men of the Tower and their friends were used to keeping military and business affairs secret. Talking about such things to strangers was not a natural state for them. Adding personal matters, affairs of the heart, grudges and feuds into one mixing bowl perhaps made it surprising that explosions did not happen more frequently.

Mrs Bramble's attention turned back to the ceremony as a hush descended and the governor addressed the probationer standing before him and the lieutenant. After brief introductory words, they reached the most important section where the Warder-to-be repeated the oath of allegiance, ending with:

'I will keep the Queen's peace myself in the Tower and all other places, as much as in me lyeth, and shall cause all others to do the same, to the utmost of my power. All these things I will faithfully and truly perform, so help me God.'

The governor declared him sworn in as a member of the Body of Yeoman Warders of Her Majesty's Tower of London and a cheer arose from colleagues and spectators alike.

With the official ceremony finished and the grinning man swamped by a tidal wave of congratulations, Mrs Bramble searched the small pack of spectators for Sir Oswald Clyne but he was no longer among them. As some of the Yeoman Warders not returning to their duties began drifting towards their club, Mrs Bramble felt a tap on her arm and looked down to see Reverend Weaver's hand at her elbow. She glanced at him questioningly and followed his gaze and that of Kitty to see Clyne walking and chatting with Major Rushton.

Mrs Bramble brought this to Inspector Cole's attention and they all fell in beside the group flowing towards the passage under the Bloody Tower. Sir Stephen Lovell was nowhere to be seen, but given the direction Clyne and Rushton were taking, it seemed logical to assume they would be joining the Yeoman Warders in the club. She was under no illusions that she and Kitty would be refused entry to witness the toasting of the new Yeoman Warder, but she hoped the chief would allow the inspector and reverend to do so. If Clyne could get in, so could they.

Mrs Bramble made eyes at Kitty to walk alongside Inspector Cole as a distraction and waited for her to move into position. She then held Reverend Weaver back a couple of paces. The look of confusion on his face might have seemed comical in any other circumstance, especially when he stumbled down the first few steps near the Bloody Tower, but now was not the time for levity. If he could insert himself into the Yeoman Warders' Club, he could ensure he put the right questions to Sir Oswald Clyne even if the inspector did not.

'Reverend,' whispered Mrs Bramble to focus his attention. 'I need you to ask Sir Oswald a few questions if you are allowed inside.'

'Oh dear,' said Weaver with a wide-eyed look of alarm. 'What I mean to say is ...' he swallowed '... anything you say, Mrs Bramble.'

'Excellent. Now remember what I told you before about Sir Stephen. I need you to find out whether Sir Oswald or the Rushtons knew of Mrs Fry's intentions. If any of them did, it will place a whole different complexion on the matter because Major Rushton or Sir Oswald may have sought the ultimate redress.'

As they approached the club building, Mrs Bramble felt rising trepidation that all would not go well without her there to direct the conversation. With a look she hoped conveyed the importance of the reverend's mission, she issued one more vital instruction.

'Whatever you do, Reverend, do not let Inspector Cole or the chief push you to the side or exclude you from the conversation. I need to know what is said in there and I need you to ask vital questions on my behalf. There is no telling when or if we will get to speak to Sir Oswald again.'

'I will do my very best, Mrs Bramble. I can assure you,' said Weaver.

Of that, she had no doubt, but the reverend's very best sometimes matched other people's average. He was her friend and a trusted ally, alongside Kitty, but he rarely functioned to his best advantage outside his familiar territory of the Chapel Royal of Hampton Court Palace. He had found his forte, his niche, his calling and his whole life had been devoted to little else.

Mrs Bramble wanted desperately to get inside the club, if only to be a fly on the wall, and it irked her to be excluded. On any other occasion she might have talked her way inside, if only for a moment, but this was a men's club full of proud men witnessing a men's ritual. She was but a housekeeper, albeit at the top of her profession, and not even part of the Tower of London's community.

She crossed her fingers as the Yeoman Warders stepped forward to enter, Inspector Cole and Reverend Weaver joining the queue to get in. Chief Yeoman Warder Treadle spotted them and called them forward, holding back a surge as he hustled them inside. Sir Oswald Clyne and Major Rushton stood on the far side awaiting their turn, but of Sir Stephen Lovell and Captain Fry there was no sign. *Perhaps that is a good thing*, she thought. Having Rushton, Fry, Lovell and Clyne together in the tight confines of the club at the same time might have caused no end of trouble.

Even within the restriction of the wider Tower, Mrs Bramble found it surprising that their close proximity to each other had not created a spark to set the whole tinderbox alight.

It still might.

32

As Mrs Bramble and Kitty strolled back along the Outer Ward, they stopped by the gated entrance once called the Water Gate because it used to afford access from the River Thames. Known for centuries as Traitors' Gate, it had become a lasting symbol of all those who had been deemed to have committed the ultimate betrayal of treason or some other serious crime. Through here many a prisoner would have been brought, perhaps never to see the outside world again. Perversely, a murderer, or maybe two, now resided on this side of the gate, temporarily at least. It seemed highly likely Mrs Fry and Esther had known their respective killers, perhaps very well, surely the essence of betrayal.

'A penny for your thoughts, Mrs B,' said Kitty.

'Hm? Oh.' Mrs Bramble gave her a wry smile. 'Merely mulling things over as usual. Given the recent horror, I think I should talk to Beth about her assignation with Jasper Chant. I should imagine Captain Fry's absence from the swearing-in ceremony and the Yeoman Warders' Club means he is on duty elsewhere in the Tower. That should leave the way clear for us to speak freely, if we can find her without too much trouble.'

'We can ask Gwen if she's seen her,' said Kitty, pointing to where the Rushtons' housemaid approached from the direction of the visitors' entrance.

Too impatient to wait for the slow-moving young woman

to reach them, Mrs Bramble closed the distance in a few strides. Gwen went to manoeuvre around her with the basket she carried but stopped when she saw who had blocked her path.'

'Gwen,' said Mrs Bramble. 'I'm glad we caught you.'

'Caught me?' said Gwen, looking briefly like a startled deer.

A look of guilt replaced the one of surprise but Mrs Bramble took no notice of either expression. In her experience, members of the lower classes always attracted suspicion whether warranted or not and frequently looked guilty when confronted by someone of a higher class or in a position of authority. That did not mean they were guilty any more than someone seen laughing was happy on the inside.

'I have it in mind to speak to Captain Fry's housemaid, Beth, and wondered whether you'd seen her,' said Mrs Bramble. 'Is she in the captain's quarters, by any chance?'

'I saw her not ten minutes ago, back there at the main entrance, ma'am,' said Gwen. 'We've got to get others to deliver our goods while we're stuck in here and have to collect them from the main gate because they won't bring them in. It's such a nuisance. Do you know how much longer we'll have to endure?'

'I'm sure Mrs Fry would love to be alive to endure such a nuisance,' said Mrs Bramble, watching the rebuke hit home in the form of the young woman's flushed cheek.

'Sorry, ma'am,' said Gwen. 'What I meant was—'

'It doesn't matter.' Mrs Bramble waved away any excuse for insensitivity. 'Do you know if Beth is stepping out with anyone?'

The question seemed to take Gwen by surprise. 'I-I don't know if I should tell tales, ma'am.'

'It is not telling tales when you are assisting with an official investigation.'

'But that knowledge is private.'

'Is it, if myself and Kitty already know of it?' She indicated Kitty, who nodded.

This made Gwen pause to think. 'Perhaps not so private as they'd like, it seems.' She bit her lip. 'Beth has been meeting with someone but from what she said, he's a cut above her position as a housemaid and they've tried to keep it quiet to avoid scandal.'

'You mean he's tried to keep it quiet.'

'Not at all, ma'am. Beth knows it'll cause a right old stir and they could both end up losing their positions if it gets out. Not that they're doing anything wrong, mind, but you must know what employers are like. Seems like they have no fun themselves and don't want anyone else to neither.'

On any other occasion, Mrs Bramble might have chuckled at such a cynical view but she understood why Gwen felt that way, given what she knew about the Rushtons and Frys.

'Do you know his name, by any chance?' she asked, knowing the answer but wanting to establish how widely known the affair had become.

Gwen shrugged. 'That's the thing, I don't rightly know. She said he's not a toff or a soldier, or one of the Beefeaters, so I haven't a clue.'

That was the first time Mrs Bramble had heard the term *Beefeater* used since her arrival. She knew the Yeoman Warders weren't fond of the medieval nickname so had shied away from using it herself, especially in front of the chief.

'You must have seen something,' urged Mrs Bramble.

'Domestics don't have much time to themselves so we

tend to do what we need to get done for ourselves when we have a spare moment. That's not to say we don't get together now and then but Beth wouldn't be seen dead bringing her fella along.'

'Especially if he's above her station?'

Gwen looked sheepish. 'You'd be best off asking Beth, ma'am.'

Mrs Bramble thanked Gwen for her time and let her go on her way, not wanting to show her hand by revealing how much she knew.

The building that formed the main entrance for visitors lay back the way Gwen had come so Mrs Bramble and Kitty wandered that way. They spotted Beth at almost the same time as Beth spotted them. The young woman glanced about, looking in vain for an escape route, and her expression changed to one of resignation as they approached. She carried a wicker basket with its contents covered with a cloth. That was nothing unusual. There was no telling what might be in the air to contaminate fresh food, whether intended for boiling or not.

'Beth,' said Mrs Bramble as they met in the middle of the bridge over the moat. 'Can you spare me a moment? I have something I wish to discuss with you.'

Beth looked from Mrs Bramble to Kitty and back again, several times, as though weighing up what to say. Mrs Bramble had not the patience at present to wait too long for an answer and decided to force the issue.

'I am reliably informed that you and Mr Jasper Chant are courting, although not openly. Is that true?'

Beth's eyes opened so wide that Mrs Bramble feared they might drop out of the woman's head of their own accord.

'Not true,' squeaked Beth, with a shake of her head. 'Who said it was?'

'I did,' said Kitty. 'And no use denying it. I saw you both behind the barracks.'

Beth gasped and held her mouth with her free hand. 'I'm done for, I'm done for, I'm done for,' she repeated.

'Don't be ridiculous,' said Mrs Bramble, putting a comforting hand on the woman's arm. 'We only want to ask you about your courtship—'

'He didn't do it,' Beth blurted out.

Mrs Bramble was taken aback.

Beth's head swivelled from side to side and her gaze flicked here and there.

'Not out in the open,' she said. 'The captain's on duty for at least another hour so you'd better come back with me to his quarters.'

Mrs Bramble was left open-mouthed and about to speak as Beth pushed between her and Kitty and set off at such a pace they almost had to trot to keep up.

Mrs Bramble was a little out of breath by the time they climbed the steps for Beth to open the door to the married men's quarters. But more steps followed as Beth led them upstairs and unlocked Captain Fry's front door. She ushered them inside and heaved a sigh of relief. It was the first time Mrs Bramble had seen the woman relax since they had spotted each other.

'Jasper – Mr Chant – didn't kill Esther like they're saying,' said Beth.

'Like who is saying?' said Mrs Bramble.

'Everyone. Word gets around quickly in a place like this. I'm sorry, ma'am,' she said. 'I'm forgetting my manners. Can I get you anything?'

'A cup of tea would soothe all our nerves, I think,' said Mrs Bramble. 'Earl Grey with a splash of milk, if you have it, but it doesn't matter if you haven't either.'

'Nothing for me,' said Kitty.

'Of course.' Beth did a little bob curtsey and disappeared into another small room.

Mrs Bramble smiled in amusement at the unnecessary gesture and turned to Kitty. 'Greetings card,' she mouthed, pointing to the floor to ask, *here?*

Kitty flicked a glance towards a door on the opposite side of the room.

Mrs Bramble returned a single nod with her eyebrows raised, a gesture Kitty appeared to understand because she turned and disappeared through the door. Something had churned away in the background of her thoughts ever since Kitty reported seeing that card.

'We shan't keep you long, dear,' Mrs Bramble called through, in the most soothing voice she could muster. 'And rest assured you are not in any trouble.' She sat in one of the two easy chairs.

'I will be if the captain finds out,' came Beth's voice from the other room. 'He's always been all right with me but usually went along with what his wife wanted. Mrs Fry was a bit of a terror.'

Kitty reappeared with the card and handed it over.

'Really? How so?' Mrs Bramble studied the painting of the fainting St Catherine and quickly read the explanation on the back. The spidery inscription, *For today. Best Wishes, M*, had been the specific detail niggling her. Unless it was a middle initial or from a nickname, Margaret Rushton was the only person she could think of with the initial M. If true, the card seemed an odd thing to have sent to a rival as an olive branch.

She handed it back to Kitty.

'You said you wanted to know about me and Jasper,'

said Beth, the tinkling of a spoon on a cup filtering through the open door.

Kitty hurried away to replace the card.

'I'm not sure it's relevant to Chief Yeoman Warder Treadle's investigation but Inspector Cole seems interested,' said Mrs Bramble, crossing her fingers to nullify the lie. 'He's a funny sort of man so it's probably nothing.'

'Mr Chant and I have been courting for many months,' said Beth. 'We are in love.'

'Of course you are, dear.' Mrs Bramble didn't doubt it.

Kitty reappeared seconds before Beth brought in the tea and set it on an occasional table.

'It's the truth, we are,' said Beth. 'The problem is, Mrs Fry didn't like the idea of me running off to get shackled, as she put it, and leaving her employment.'

'Mrs Fry knew of your affair?'

'Only in the last two weeks. Up until then, we had been discreet and careful. You see, Jasper was saving up for us to get married and didn't want to make things awkward for me. For her part, I think Mrs Fry was afraid of the risk of scandal.'

'How so?' said Mrs Bramble, keen to know whether something lay deeper.

'She was a stickler for appearances and how things looked, even if that hid the truth,' said Beth. 'She considered someone like me, a lowly housemaid, cavorting with someone above my class like a chapel organist, went against decency. Even sullied the British Empire. That it was a sin against God. I don't know why Mrs Fry thought it so wrong. Love is love, isn't it?' She looked towards Mrs Bramble and Kitty as though seeking reassurance. 'Anyway, we kept it as secret as we could for as long as we could because anyone of influence knowing would have given Mrs Fry apoplexy.'

'How did Mr Chant take all this?' said Mrs Bramble.

Beth frowned. 'He did get angry recently, especially each time I told him Mrs Fry had had another go at me, which she did almost every day.' She smiled. 'He wanted to ride to my rescue like some knight in shining armour, but I wouldn't let him.'

'Did Esther know?' said Kitty.

'I think most of the domestics thought they knew something, some more than others, but no one else until Mrs Fry found out. Jasper always said she couldn't keep us apart but I persuaded him we should bide our time until we had enough to get married. We wouldn't have to wait long, maybe a few months more.'

'And he was content to wait?'

'Of course. He was impatient but understood.'

'You're telling us that you and Mr Chant had no reason to want Mrs Fry or Esther dead,' said Mrs Bramble.

'Good heavens, no!' Beth stepped back, horrified. 'Mrs Fry couldn't hurt us because we were almost ready to leave together, and Esther was a good friend to me and Gwen. I even gave her some perfume yesterday for her birthday.'

'If you had kept the secret for so long and then abided by Mrs Fry's wishes, albeit as a means to an end, why did you now let yourselves be seen together?' asked Kitty. 'I saw you kissing behind the barracks block but in view of many visitors to the Tower. What had changed?'

'The passing of Mrs Fry,' said Beth. 'As I said, it was always Mrs Fry who was the stickler. Jasper and I thought a quick peck couldn't do us any harm now.'

'I would have thought it still posed a risk, what with

Mrs Fry having died only two days ago,' said Mrs Bramble, rising from the easy chair in preparation to leave.

'Captain Fry doesn't care about us, as long as his domestic needs are met. And I'm a very good housemaid.'

Mrs Bramble stopped at the apartment door and scratched the end of her nose in thought. 'Was Mrs Fry a Catholic, do you know?'

'Oh.' Beth looked surprised. 'No, she was Anglican, like her husband.' She looked from Mrs Bramble to Kitty. 'Is that important?'

'Probably not,' said Mrs Bramble. 'Don't worry, we'll see ourselves out.'

'But your tea ...'

A few minutes later, standing outside with the White Tower looming above them, Kitty said, 'What was all that about, Mrs B? Does it matter what religion she was?'

Mrs Bramble shrugged. 'I'm not sure but until we get closer to the truth any detail might prove important. For example, who sent her the card and why? Does the painting on the front mean anything? Was there more to Mrs Fry's objection to Beth and Chant's courtship?'

'What do we do now?' said Kitty. 'We've spoken to everyone, I've searched several rooms, and Dr Burford is having samples tested as we speak.'

'There is only one thing we can do,' said Mrs Bramble. She looked around in the hope of spotting her prey.

'Another talk with Jasper Chant?' said Kitty, dubiously.

Mrs Bramble pouted. 'Confront him, more like, about his intentions. Even if what Beth says is true, and I cannot see why he would want Esther dead, if Mrs Fry still represented the one big obstacle standing in the way of their happiness ...'

Kitty shuddered. 'How far would he go to remove her?'

33

Although the building housing the unofficial Yeoman Warders' Club was long and thin, it was also spacious enough. Usually.

At this time of the swearing in of a new colleague, many Warders had crammed in. Some wore the familiar daily undress uniforms of blue and red, having been part of the ceremony on Tower Green, while all the others wore their Sunday-best civilian clothes.

Reverend Weaver stood at the back of the gathering, feeling uncomfortable in the white dog collar of his profession. Beside him stood Inspector Cole and Sir Oswald Clyne, looking smart and respectful, and Major Rushton in his striking scarlet tunic.

For their part, the Yeoman Warders took no notice. They had their attention fully focused on the new chap as two of their number paraded a large pewter bowl into the centre of the club and set it on a table. The popping corks of bottles of port being opened then preceded the glug of the contents being poured into the bowl.

Each Yeoman Warder collected a silver tankard with his name engraved on the side and filed past the bowl to dip it into the port. Once he had collected his share ready for the toast, he gathered with his colleagues around the bowl alongside which the new recruit had taken up position.

At a signal from Chief Yeoman Warder Treadle, one

Warder detached himself from the group with a tray on which sat four small glasses and a bottle of port. With a nod, he bade Weaver and the others take a glass each and then filled them from the bottle. They thanked him but he disappeared just as silently. *Obviously not enamoured by our presence*, thought Weaver.

The chief raised his tankard to toast the newly sworn-in member with the cry, 'May you never die a Yeoman Warder!'

The others present followed suit and repeated the toast, each taking a good swallow from their tankards. A great cheer went up amid enthusiastic backslapping, filling the room with noise.

Reverend Weaver sipped his drink and hoped the chief might join them but he was clearly enjoying himself in the company of his fellow Yeoman Warders.

'That was a privilege to witness,' said Inspector Cole, in a tone suggesting the ceremony had stirred him, someone who was rarely impressed.

'Indeed,' said Major Rushton, sounding more bored than anything else.

Sir Oswald Clyne's enthusiasm shone through and it was obvious the glass of port had gone down well, although he became a little miffed when his gestures for a refill were ignored. He waggled his glass at the Warder who had served them but the man looked him up and down and turned back to the celebrations, clearly not amused by Clyne's dandy fashion and haughty expression.

Reverend Weaver went to say something to Inspector Cole, for conversation's sake, but the policeman turned away to speak with the major. Although a wave of trepidation shuddered through him at the thought that Cole harboured such a dislike for him that he still considered him guilty, Weaver saw this as an opportunity to complete the mission Mrs Bramble had set him.

'Sir Oswald,' he said, distracting the man from his quest for more alcohol. 'Have you painted much recently?'

'I beg your pardon?' said Clyne with a momentary look of confusion. 'Oh, of course. I do so whenever I have the time, especially when I have a commission and am getting paid.'

'You painted the major's father, I understand.'

'Sir Arthur. Yes, I did.'

'Was he a good subject?'

Clyne gave a shrug. 'A little fidgety, perhaps, but most people are, to tell you the truth.'

'I was sorry to hear your own father died abroad.' All the moisture suddenly leached from Reverend Weaver's mouth at the unfamiliar foray into interrogation. 'Chile, wasn't it?' he croaked, his eyes watering as he desperately tried to avoid a coughing fit. 'Such a tragedy.' He took a gulp of port that made his eyes water even more.

'An avoidable one,' said Clyne, giving Weaver a curious look. 'It is no secret that Lord Fry's company was negligent. They compromised on safety for the sake of expediency and profit.'

'Oh. Lord Fry's company, was it?' Weaver said, hoping he looked the picture of innocence.

'Indisputably,' said Clyne. 'Mrs Rushton discovered Lord Fry was the majority shareholder so the onus fell to him.'

'What a coincidence.'

'A coincidence my family could have done without.'

'Of course, of course,' said Weaver. 'That must have made you angry. Eager for revenge, even?' He mentally kicked himself for being heavy-handed but Clyne appeared not to have noticed.

'I must admit, at one time I could have been moved to kill Lord Fry for depriving me of my father, but as you must know from your profession, Reverend, such feelings generated by painful loss do subside and rational thought returns.'

'That is a good thing,' said Reverend Weaver. 'If Sir Stephen Lovell hadn't baulked at a similar thought of taking a life, he might very well have carried out Mrs Fry's instructions.' *Still as heavy-handed as a lump hammer*, he thought, *but I'm in at the deep end now*.

'What instructions?' said Clyne with a frown, placing his empty glass on a nearby table. 'What are you talking about?'

'Oh, I thought you knew,' said Weaver, hoping Clyne would keep his temper. 'Mrs Fry asked Sir Stephen to kill Major Rushton on her behalf. To settle old scores. He refused, of course.' Unable to meet Clyne's stare, Weaver fixed his gaze on the man's neat beard instead. 'I thought you might have received a similar request. From Mrs Rushton.'

Clyne looked aghast and Weaver thought he might strike out or storm off at any moment. Then the look in the man's eyes seemed to signal a decision made.

'I did, I'm sad to say,' said Clyne. 'Mrs Rushton must have reached the same point of impasse as Mrs Fry because she came right out with it one day and insisted I kill Captain Fry.' He flicked a glance at Inspector Cole, who was deep in conversation, and held up his hands. 'I know what you're going to ask, Reverend. Did I kill his wife instead?' He scoffed. 'No, is my resounding answer. I was angry enough at the time to do so but, in essence, I am not a violent man. Morally, spiritually, legally, I could not go through with it. And before you ask, I had no reason to wish harm to Reverend Dench's chambermaid.'

'Did Sir Stephen know about Mrs Rushton's intentions?' said Reverend Weaver, trying to keep pace with the change in tone of the conversation.

Clyne paused again, perhaps searching his conscience, and Weaver had to remember to breathe.

'He did,' said Clyne, eventually. Another decision made. 'I broached the subject with him, to warn about the parlous state of affairs between the two families. What with a posting abroad in the offing for one or other of the two men, the growing animosity between their wives and all that had gone before, it seemed like everything was coming to a head.'

'What did he say, exactly?' said Weaver, knowing Mrs Bramble would want details.

'Like myself, Lovell is not a man inclined to violence, which is why I thought I could reason with him. We talked and discovered Mrs Fry had made the same demand of him as Mrs Rushton had of myself; and that he swear an oath to keep the request far from the ear of her husband. Between us, Lovell and I agreed to do nothing illegal on behalf of Mrs Fry or Mrs Rushton and to keep their murderous requests to ourselves. We weren't convinced they were serious in any case but one can never be sure.'

'You do know Sir Stephen has a pocket pistol about his person?'

'A British Bulldog, yes.' Clyne chuckled; a sound that struck Weaver as incongruous with his recent demeanour. 'I wouldn't worry about it. He carries it for show and is too frightened to load it.' He chuckled again. 'As far as I know, he's not once had his pocket picked, never mind been confronted by a robber, so he's never even drawn it.'

'But you were seen arguing with him behind the Waterloo Barracks,' said Reverend Weaver, watching for signs of lying but unsure what form such signs usually took. 'Did you two have a falling out?'

'Not as such,' said Clyne, but the smile faded from his face. 'We've never really seen eye to eye, but we did on this matter.'

'So why the cross words?' said Weaver. In trying to remember all this, he gesticulated with his glass and splashed ruby red port on a rug. No one but Clyne seemed to notice so he surreptitiously worked it into the rug with the sole of his shoe, unwittingly making it look like he was trying to dance on the spot, or needed the water closet.

'He accused me of reneging on our agreement,' said Clyne. 'Lovell thought I'd murdered Mrs Fry in contravention of everything we'd spoken about.'

'Had you?'

'I've already said I did not.'

'What did he say?'

Clyne shrugged. 'He took some convincing but eventually believed me. We decided to keep a low profile and say nothing about the intentions of the wives. We saw no point in mentioning it because neither of us heeded their instructions. I must apologise for your incarceration, Reverend. Not for one moment did we believe you capable of murder and we thought the lack of evidence would result in your early release. We hoped Inspector Cole would find the real culprit quickly. Then Mrs Bramble turned up.'

'She has a habit of doing that.' Reverend Weaver nodded. 'And she certainly gets stuck in. At her request, Dr Burford is having samples of the wine tested for poison.'

Clyne raised an eyebrow. 'I thought it was in the food.'

'As did we all but it appears not.' Weaver felt a stab of alarm. Had he said too much? After all, Clyne could turn out to be the murderer. 'I-I'd better go.'

Clyne looked partially deflated, like a slowly collapsing hot-air balloon. 'What are you going to do now, tell the inspector?'

Reverend Weaver shook his head and glanced at Inspector Cole. 'If I've learnt anything from Mrs Bramble it's not to tell the inspector anything he doesn't yet need to know. If at all. I believe Mrs Bramble might be getting an inkling about who might have killed Mrs Fry and why, and I for one can't wait for the unmasking.'

Raucous laughter filled the room again as though some hilarious tale had concluded, but none of the Warders had yet drifted towards the door.

'The party shows no signs of breaking up but I should make my excuses,' said Weaver, anxious to escape. He hoped he had done as well as could be expected but knew he had an unfortunate habit of upsetting situations and had no desire to put his foot in it and blot his copybook.

'Off to report to Mrs Bramble?' said Clyne with a smile.

Weaver looked sheepish and felt his cheeks burn. 'If anyone can solve this case, Sir Oswald, I'd wager my last farthing on her.'

He turned on his heels for dramatic effect but cannoned into Inspector Cole who had somehow managed to manoeuvre into position directly behind him. In turn, Cole fell into Major Rushton who fell into the chief who fell into the Yeoman Gaoler. Weaver could not have upset four more important men of the moment if he'd carefully planned over several months to do so. The timing and effect were perfect, not unlike a line of dominoes falling or a house of cards collapsing at the first sign of a tremor.

With the four men still seeking to regain their equilibrium and composure, Reverend Weaver left the chaos and confusion behind in the building and made a beeline for the chaplain's house. *Sanctuary*, he thought to himself. *I need sanctuary*.

34

Mrs Bramble had not been inside the confines of the Tower of London for long but the constant wanderings in such a limited area had taken their toll. She'd found the walls, towers, greens, passageways and steps becoming familiar enough for them merge into one and fade into the background. She had experienced this rarely at Hampton Court Palace because of its intricate layout, variety of architecture and extensive grounds. The Tower was altogether more utilitarian and functional.

Although Mrs Bramble feared every moment wasted encouraged the killer to strike again, she was tired of chasing suspects from curtain wall to curtain wall, and sometimes atop the walls. From what she knew about Inspector Cole, his patience could snap at any moment, resulting in Reverend Weaver once again becoming the erroneous victim of his urge to wrap up the case. Even so, she decided it might be prudent for her and Kitty to find a suitable vantage point from which to watch and wait. She couldn't remember a year since leaving nursing when she'd spent so much time on her feet, either standing around or walking, even including her daily rounds back at Hampton Court Palace.

'Let us sit here for a while,' said Mrs Bramble, selecting the same bench they had occupied previously. 'If we continue to chase around like stray leaves on the surface of a stirred cup of tea, our paths may never intercept with

Jasper Chant. If we remain in one place, I am confident he will pass us in one direction or another, sooner or later.'

She was content to sit there for a while if need be but Kitty appeared decidedly uncomfortable at the prospect.

'Is there anything the matter, Kitty?' asked Mrs Bramble.

'I feel as though everyone is watching us, Mrs B,' said Kitty, her gaze darting as people passed in all directions.

'Maybe because many are. I have presented myself to the Tower residents as some kind of consulting assistant to Inspector Cole so I would be surprised if they did not view us both as akin to the police.'

'And we've rubbed a few people up the wrong way.'

Mrs Bramble nodded. 'Indeed,' she agreed.

They continued their discussion for a while, going over events since the fateful telegram had arrived at Mrs Bramble's breakfast table, and watched the occasional Tower worker idle by. All the singles, couples, families, children and tour groups they had seen during the visiting day had gone and none could have had the slightest inkling that a drama as strange as any witnessed at the Tower had been playing around them. A killer lurked among them; a fact that would surely have terrified them.

Mrs Bramble had started to fidget, finding it increasingly uncomfortable sitting on the hard bench, when Jasper Chant came into view. Kitty nudged her elbow but she had spotted him the moment he rounded the corner of the White Tower. He tried to hide his alarm and began to veer away at his first sight of them, but Mrs Bramble was having none of that.

'Mr Chant,' she called.

Chant made a show of looking over with feigned surprise, altered his course towards the bench and greeted them with a touch of his forefinger to the brim of his hat. 'Mrs Bramble, Miss Kitty, we meet once again.'

'When you are forced to remain inside its walls, the Tower of London does not seem such a big place after all,' said Mrs Bramble with a smile. 'One has only to wait long enough and those with whom you wish to converse must surely pass you by.'

Chant smiled back. 'And I suppose you wish to converse with me.' He winked.

Mrs Bramble patted the empty space next to her and Chant took the hint, sitting, or rather flopping onto the bench.

'Tell me, Mrs Bramble, what is it about me that intrigues you enough to summon me to your side?'

Mrs Bramble chuckled. 'Hardly summon, Mr Chant, but everyone is intriguing under the circumstances, are they not?'

'Depends on which side of the fence you sit,' said Chant, picking an imaginary hair from his trousers before glancing at Kitty. 'Or which end of the bench.'

Mrs Bramble turned her head to watch him out of the corner of her eye. She wanted to gauge any reaction he might have to what she was about to ask.

'Mr Chant, if I may ask you a question, what are your intentions towards Captain Fry's housemaid, Beth?'

She stifled a laugh as Chant's face assumed the spit and image of a cod fish out of water gasping for oxygen. He then suffered a series of hiccups, burps and coughs, so much so that she thought she might need to send for Dr Burford.

When Chant had regained his composure, Mrs Bramble pressed him.

'My Kitty here stumbled upon an intimate moment between yourself and Beth earlier today and I assume you sneak the odd nocturnal liaison into your schedule too.' She knew Chant understood as his gaze flicked towards the Waterloo Barracks and his face went another shade of pale. 'Normally, that would be of no concern to me whatsoever but, under the circumstances, I feel a little explanation might be in everyone's best interests.'

'What do you mean, Mrs Bramble?' said Chant, running his finger around the inside of his collar.

'I mean, you have been carrying on with a lowly housemaid' – she ignored Kitty's flinch – 'in the employ of Captain and Mrs Fry.' Mrs Bramble offered what she hoped was a disarming smile to lull him into a false sense of security.

'I cannot deny it, but I don't see the relevance to anything.'

'The relevance. Hm. We have learnt that Mrs Fry discovered your liaisons quite recently and she fiercely disapproved. Considering this presented a formidable barrier to the continuation of your affair, the death of Mrs Fry can be seen perhaps in a different light. Maybe Reverend Dench's chambermaid was the one who told Mrs Fry and that got her killed.'

'I-I ...' The cod fish impression returned. 'I can see how it looks but I can assure you I had no need to murder anyone. I have been saving every farthing in order to take Beth away from all this, working night and day, taking jobs a chapel organist shouldn't have to ...'

Mrs Bramble saw him take a half-breath and glance over his shoulder as though he'd let the cat out of the bag. He chewed his lip and leant in closer.

'I can tell you're a woman of the world, Mrs Bramble,' he said with a nod and a wink. 'I make a decent living from music generally and by being a chapel organist, enough for us to live on comfortably, but I needed a bit extra to set us up.'

'And how did you come by this *extra*?' said Mrs Bramble, dreading the answer.

'I'm not sure I should tell you all my business secrets,' he said, clearly nervous behind his smile.

'Should Inspector Cole be concerned?'

Chant's face dropped. 'No, no, no.' He waved his hand as if to brush away the notion. 'Let's just say I put buyers and sellers in touch. For a small fee. And all with a means to an end.'

'Is it your defence that Beth was about to leave her employ, get married and set up home with you?' said Mrs Bramble, seeing Chant rattled.

A little colour returned to Chant's cheeks. 'I refrained from going down on one knee because that would have involved a ring and we had no desire to antagonise Mrs Fry. But yes, we wish to marry very soon.'

'Why should we believe you?' said Mrs Bramble, aware that this corroborated Beth's account but not unfamiliar with empty promises made in the hope of gaining advantages.

Chant delved into his pocket and produced a small cube-like box. 'I have taken to carrying this with me since Mrs Fry passed away.' He opened the box to reveal a gold band inset with what looked like small diamonds.

'Looks expensive,' said Kitty, clearly impressed by the sparkles.

'Especially for a musician saving for a home,' said Mrs Bramble, also impressed by the piece as a whole but instantly suspicious.

'Looks is the operative word.' Chant smiled. 'Those are not the kind of diamonds, real diamonds, the likes of you and I can never hope to afford. No, the ring belonged to my mother and the jewels are made of paste.'

'As long as it looks the part, Beth will be overjoyed, I'm sure,' said Mrs Bramble.

'I do hope so.' Chant closed the box and replaced it in his pocket. 'I should return it to a place of safe keeping for now. I know it could be construed as insensitive but I was trying to find the right time to propose without upsetting anyone. I'd like to do it sooner rather than later, but given all that's been going on I think we should wait until this tragic business is over.'

Mrs Bramble gave him a knowing smile. 'I think that would be for the best and I'm sure Captain Fry would appreciate his housemaid remaining with him for now, while he comes to terms with his awful loss.'

Chant nodded. 'Beth will understand. She will wait.'

Chant got up from the bench and smoothed his trousers, looking about him as though surveying the scene of a great battle. Mrs Bramble thought he looked a little melancholy but that was understandable. A few days ago, he would have been on the verge of proposing to his sweetheart, safe in the knowledge she would say yes and confident no one could legally or religiously stand in their way.

'I should warn you – nothing stays secret for long in here,' said Chant. 'The fact that the wine is being tested for poison is common knowledge and the gossips have been in fine voice this afternoon.'

'Perhaps inevitable,' said Mrs Bramble with a shrug. 'It is in people's nature to be wary and suspicious to a degree.'

'Maybe so but speculation is rife. Some believe Major Rushton is to blame because of the vitriol between his wife and Mrs Fry. Others are convinced Captain Fry killed his own wife but offer no rationale. Dr Burford himself has come under scrutiny from chinwags. He knows about poisons and was on hand to give medical assistance, or, as some believe, withhold it. I know myself and everyone in the chaplain's house are now under suspicion too because of poor Esther.'

'Nothing the inspector and chief haven't considered,' said Mrs Bramble, mentally crossing her fingers because those thoughts had crossed her own mind in the course of her investigation.

'Maybe so,' Chant continued. 'But some even say Reverend Weaver killed Mrs Fry in revenge for her opposition to his taking of the service, even though she attended after all. Others say Reverend Dench was jealous of Reverend Weaver's accolades and sought to frame him for the murder.'

'Both notions we know to be ridiculous,' said Kitty.

Well, at least one of those, thought Mrs Bramble.

'Beth's name has not been mentioned so far, at least not within my hearing, but that will change soon enough,' said Chant. 'The longer the case drags on, the more those who have no direct connection will be swept up as suspects by the swirling rumours.'

'Then I shall have to ensure a swift conclusion is achieved and the murderer is brought to book,' said Mrs Bramble.

'Good day, Mrs Bramble, Kitty.' Chant tried to wink but it just looked like a half-blink. Instead, he dipped his head and touched the brim of his hat. 'Believe me when I say I wish you every success.'

They watched him stroll towards the chaplain's house until he disappeared through the front door.

'What did you make of that?' said Mrs Bramble.

'As he said, why would he or Beth need to kill Mrs Fry?'

said Kitty. 'He obviously has the means to keep her, even if some of his dealings have been shady; and she is smitten with him.'

'He did come across as sincere, I admit.' Mrs Bramble looked at her left hand where her own wedding ring still resided. She didn't begrudge anyone their own slice of happiness and often wondered what might have been had her husband not passed away far too young. 'I'm inclined to believe him, for now, but he did have access to the vestry and was first on the stair above Esther's lifeless body.'

'It can't be good, Mrs B, everyone knowing our business,' said Kitty.

With a slight tilt of her head, Mrs Bramble shrugged one shoulder. 'Normally, I would agree with you, Kitty, but that might work in our favour. Everyone knows the wine served at the reception is being tested but only the murderer knows what the outcome will be.'

'How does that help us?'

'Earlier today ...' Mrs Bramble lowered her voice as two of the Tower's handymen hurried past. 'Earlier today, while you and Reverend Weaver took the glass shard and samples of communion red wine, wafers and water to Dr Burford, I suggested to the inspector and chief that whoever I chased last night could have been after those items. They agreed and posted a guard discreetly in the vestry. This leaves us in an intriguing situation. As long as we do not show our full hand, the murderer cannot know what has been sent for testing so they could risk returning for a second time to remove the evidence. I'm sure Inspector Cole will not want us there, but prudence dictates we should all watch the chapel.'

'And what if the killer becomes desperate and violent?'

said Kitty, her face pinched with worry.

'Then we must trust that the inspector and chief are the kind of men they purport to be.'

35

Stumbling along, occasionally tripping, much like an autumn acorn hits branches on its tumble to the ground, Reverend Weaver made slow and erratic progress towards the chaplain's house. He hoped to find Mrs Bramble there, taking respite from all the scurrying and madness. In truth, the effect of the port wine he had drunk at the ceremony – was it one or two glasses? – had gone to his head and the fresh air had done him no favours in this regard. He had to admit, some kind of respite for himself would not go amiss.

'I do beg your pardon,' he said, stopping at the sound of a commotion behind him.

Concerned someone might be finding his unpredictable progression difficult to bypass, he turned to apologise again and came face to face with a group of the Tower's most important residents: three giant ravens with shiny black feathers. Unsure whether their ire was directed towards him or to each other, he stepped backwards and they hopped forward, keeping their dark eyes on him.

With rising panic, Reverend Weaver turned and scurried round the corner, and having no comprehension of how it could have happened, suddenly realised he had stumbled up the stairs leading into the White Tower.

He found this somewhat disorientating and disconcerting, having never been inside this building before and having never harboured any desire to do so. Although the existence of the medieval Chapel of St John the Evangelist intrigued him, all that his usual haunt of Hampton Court Palace represented and contained was history enough for him.

He skittered back down the steps and professed his undying thanks to a Yeoman Warder whose firm hand stopped him from tumbling to the ground. All this combined with his recent intake of alcohol to make Reverend Weaver feel giddy.

He took a few deep breaths, waited for the nausea to recede and his equilibrium return, and said a silent prayer in thanks for his safe deliverance. At that moment, someone jostled him from behind and he turned in surprise to find Reverend Dench apologising profusely.

'My fault, Thomas, my fault,' said Dench. 'I had no idea it was you I had bumped into. Not that it would have made a difference had it not been you. I don't make a habit of going around bumping people for the fun of it.'

'Right, good, right,' said Reverend Weaver, recovering his composure. 'I'm sure you don't. Accidents will happen.'

'Accidents will happen.' Dench nodded sagely, then looked up brightly. 'Actually, it's fortunate I did bump into you, literally and metaphorically, because I have a snippet of news for you. Ah, not news, exactly. More a piece of information, to fill in a gap.'

'Oh,' said Reverend Weaver, suddenly alert. 'Which gap would that be?'

'I've not long returned from an errand to the south moat—'

'Is that the gap?'

'What?' said Reverend Dench, momentarily confused.

'The moat,' said Weaver, feeling the conversation slipping away from him.

'No, no. The gap is in your knowledge. The information I possess will fill it.' He looked triumphant. 'Nicotine!'

'Nicotine?' It was Reverend Weaver's turn to look perplexed.

'Sorry?' Reverend Dench frowned. 'Oh, I don't mean fill the gap with nicotine. What I meant to say was, Mrs Bramble asked if the insecticide I use on my garden contains any nicotine. I spoke to the gardener who supplies it to me and I can now report that it does. If you could pass that on to the good lady, I should be most grateful.'

'Of course, I shall.'

'Must dash but we'll speak later and maybe have a cup of tea to calm the old nerves.'

Reverend Weaver was about to say his nerves were far too shredded for tea to work its magic, but Reverend Dench had already turned away.

Mrs Bramble caught sight of Reverend Weaver on the parade ground between the White Tower and the barracks and Kitty called out, waving her arms to attract his attention. He looked like a piece of driftwood caught in the eddy of a stream as he appeared to hear his name called at last and spun on the spot as though trying to detect the source. It still took him a few more seconds of looking this way and that before he saw them and came over.

'Just the people I needed to see,' he said, scuttling over to the bench where they were sitting. 'I'm having quite the afternoon.' He sat heavily on the seat next to Mrs Bramble.

'In a good way or bad?' asked Kitty.

'A bit of both,' he admitted. 'I had a tot of port wine, to be sociable and take part in the toast. It was stronger than I'm used to and went straight to my head.'

'Oh dear,' said Mrs Bramble. 'Are you recovered?'

Reverend Weaver held out his hand and wobbled it from side to side to indicate his uncertainty about the outcome. 'I'll live, God willing.'

'You've not long missed Mr Chant,' she said, and proceeded to give him a brief summary of their conversation.

'Well, I never,' said Weaver when she'd finished. 'That puts a different complexion on things, I shouldn't wonder.' He looked at Mrs Bramble and Kitty in excitement. 'But I too have news.'

'You managed to question Sir Oswald?' said Mrs Bramble, hopefully.

'I completed a successful mission.' Weaver gave her a little smug smile and leant in conspiratorially to give her his report.

'Good work, Reverend,' said Mrs Bramble at his conclusion. 'Most interesting.'

She thought about all this for a moment, a strange sensation in the pit of her stomach. Her conversations with Major and Mrs Rushton, and Sir Stephen Lovell, had left her with the impression, through omission, that they and Lord Fry had never met Sir Oswald Clyne in a business sense. Under the circumstances, she thought they would have mentioned any past dispute over the death in service of Sir Oswald's father, surely?

'Are you all right, Mrs B?' said Kitty, looking concerned.

'Just taking it all in,' said Mrs Bramble. 'Sir Oswald believes his father worked for Lord Fry's company, as does Mrs Rushton, apparently. During all our questioning, not one other person has mentioned this.'

'Why would they?' said Kitty.

'Because if the accidental death of a school friend can cause a lifelong feud, wouldn't you expect the death of a parent to do the same? Yet Lovell and the Frys have said nothing about the Clyne family.'

'Maybe they don't want to stir things up,' suggested Kitty.

'That did occur to me,' said Mrs Bramble, 'but another reason has entered my mind. What if there is nothing for them to stir up?'

'I don't—'

Mrs Bramble was already on her feet casting her gaze about for Inspector Cole. With a trap to be set in the chapel for tonight and Dr Burford's results due back later, she needed Cole to verify an important piece of information. She had a feeling one of the suspects had employed deceit in an effort to get their own way and this was an important cog in the wheel that had turned the dial to murder.

'Why is it, the inspector and chief are never to be seen when one wants them?' said Mrs Bramble. 'They seem to have a knack for being in the wrong place at the wrong time and it's becoming tiresome.'

'They may not have emerged from the Yeoman Warders' Club,' suggested Reverend Weaver.

'Then it's about time they got back to work, don't you think?' said Mrs Bramble. 'If they are destined not to come to us, we had better go to them.'

She set off to circle round the White Tower for what felt like the umpteenth time and strode down the slope towards the club. As they walked, she issued instructions.

'It is imperative we ask the inspector to find out who owned the railway construction company operating in Chile,' she said.

'I-I would much prefer to stay away from the inspector for a while,' said Reverend Weaver, performing a half-walk, half-trot beside her. 'I seem to antagonise him the moment he sets eyes on me and my preference is not to give him cause to keep me in his thoughts.'

Mrs Bramble stopped walking and looked on in mild amusement as Kitty followed suit but Weaver did not. He only realised he was alone after taking several more steps, and looked around in panic until his eyes focused on Mrs Bramble.

She sympathised with her friend and had found Inspector Cole akin to a dog with a bone at times, often when the bone was the wrong one for him to gnaw on. 'Perhaps you would be better employed keeping an eye on Dr Burford,' she said. 'I'm anxious to find out when he expects the results of the latest tests to be delivered because they could be crucial for what may come this evening. Also, could you inform him that Inspector Cole and the chief will require his presence in the Fusiliers' mess hall after the Ceremony of the Keys has taken place and the trap has been sprung. I shouldn't imagine it'll be much after ten o'clock.'

'Can I reveal why?'

'You may but do ask him to keep it under his hat.'

'As you wish, Mrs Bramble,' said Reverend Weaver, his eyelids fluttering in a sign of relief. 'Dr Burford is an altogether more amenable fellow.'

Mrs Bramble left Weaver and continued with Kitty until they reached the Yeoman Warders' Club.

'Kitty,' she said. 'With hindsight, I should be grateful if you could find Gwen and ask her whether she ever overheard anything said about doing harm to the Frys.'

'Of course, Mrs B,' said Kitty.

'Even if she believes it was said in jest, the most offhand comment could be important.'

Kitty frowned. 'What're you thinking, Mrs B? That Major Rushton could have done it after all?'

Mrs Bramble shrugged. 'Mrs Rushton and Mrs Fry wanted each other's husbands killed. When Sir Stephen and Sir Oswald refused to get involved, who's to say the housemaids Beth and Gwen were not recruited to step into the breach? Perhaps they tried to get Esther involved, which somehow led to her death.'

'I cannot believe it of Beth,' said Kitty, shaking her head.

'And of Gwen?'

There was no time for Kitty to answer as Yeoman Warders streamed from the open doorway of their club. Soon Major Rushton emerged followed by Inspector Cole, and finally Chief Yeoman Warder Treadle. All seemed in good spirits but none nearly as worse for wear as Reverend Weaver had been.

At a touch on her elbow, Mrs Bramble half turned to see Kitty walking away along the Outer Ward between the two sets of walls, no doubt to intercept Gwen the housemaid whom she could see walking in their direction.

'Mrs Bramble, what brings you here at this time?'

She turned back to see Inspector Cole looking unimpressed by her presence. 'A distinct lack of policemen going about their job,' she said frostily. 'We have a trap to set for tonight, but the outcome relies on whether the samples have been tested so, on your behalf, I've asked Dr Burford to expedite matters and join us in the Fusiliers' mess hall later.'

'You did wh—' With a half-step backwards, Inspector Cole thew his hands in the air but then took a deep breath to calm himself. 'Reverend Weaver not with you?' he said.

'Not at present,' said Mrs Bramble, ignoring what she saw as Cole's theatrics. 'He is another who moves in different circles. We do not live in each other's pockets.'

'Hm,' said Cole, eventually breaking away from Mrs

Bramble's defiant gaze. 'I've been thinking. If it transpires the communion wine or wafers were poisoned, Reverend Weaver was still the only one with the opportunity, method and motive to kill Mrs Fry, who had lobbied to get the special service taken from him.'

Mrs Bramble scoffed. 'In which case, why not accuse Reverend Dench? He uses a nicotine-based insecticide. Perhaps he was jealous of Reverend Weaver's success?'

Inspector Cole's eyes widened. 'You think Dench tried to kill Weaver but got Mrs Fry by accident? Now, there's a th—'

'Or there's Jasper Chant and his sweetheart Beth,' interrupted Mrs Bramble. 'The Frys disapproved of their courtship and wanted to keep them apart.'

'You think I should arrest them all?' said Inspector Cole, rubbing his hands together.

Mrs Bramble almost sighed in exasperation. 'I think we should keep an open mind. Do you know, perhaps you should check the ownership of the company Sir Oswald's father was working for when he died.' She gave Cole the kind of curious look that suggested this had occurred to her that second.

'Do not presume to tell me how to do my job, Mrs Bramble.'

'As if I would, Inspector,' she said as innocently as she could manage, believing it essential for her to do so on occasion. Ignoring his scowl, she proceeded to bring him up to date on everything else they had learnt recently.

Inspector Cole cleared his throat. 'Is it any wonder my investigations falter when you're around—'

'A telephone,' the chief interjected, almost as though surprised that such a thought had entered his head. 'A great privilege.'

'What?' said Cole, frowning. 'What has that to do with anything?'

'In the Byward Tower. My office.'

'*You* have a telephone?'

The chief became solemn. 'Don't get many calls. Don't make many. Difficult to hear. Like talking through a waterfall.'

'Have you ever even seen a waterfall?' said Inspector Cole.

'No. You?'

Cole shook his head as though clearing it of clutter. 'Please can I use your telephone, chief? To call—'

'Scotland Yard on official business,' the chief interrupted with a smile. 'Of course. Thought you were never going to ask.'

'Why does everyone inter—'

'I'm sorry to break up your conversation, fascinating though it is,' said Mrs Bramble. 'May I remind you that the reputation of my friend is at stake, and his life, and I would very much like to solve this case before the pair of you arrest the wrong man for murder. Again!'

36

Reverend Weaver found Dr Burford in the sitting room of his home at the surgeon's house, massaging his toes through his socks. The doctor looked up with a guilty expression as Weaver espied him from the open doorway. His discarded shoes lay nearby and he had been making ooh and aah sounds prior to Weaver's sudden appearance.

'M-my apologies, Doctor,' said Weaver, his cheeks colouring as though he'd burst in at an intimate moment.

'Bad circulation,' Burford explained, recovering his shoes and slipping them on. 'My toes get terribly cold even on the hottest summer day. What can I do for you?' He gestured to an easy chair, almost knocking a vase and its posy to the floor.

'Um, I-I come hot-footed from Mrs Bramble.' Reverend Weaver sat. 'She, Inspector Cole and the chief hope to bring this case to a conclusion tonight but they are waiting on important news.'

Dr Burford nodded thoughtfully, then shot a curious look at Weaver. 'What news is that?'

'What n—?' Weaver stopped. Had he got this wrong? Was he asking the right question? He took a second to compose himself. 'The tests you are having performed over at Guy's Hospital are vital to the solving of this mystery.'

'Oh, yes. I don't doubt they are.' Burford scratched his head. 'Sorry, I've been all over the place today. What with cuts, bruises, the common cold, chilblains, bunions and so on and so forth, not to mention this poisoning lark, I've had more than my usual burden to contend with.'

'Some days can test a man, that's for certain,' Weaver agreed. 'But I must ask, are you able to estimate the time you might expect the results to arrive?'

'Results?' Dr Burford's blank face suddenly lit up. 'Oh, the results! Of the tests. Yes, yes. My colleagues in Guy's Hospital are very busy and I knew they would tell me it might take days for them to test the canapés. Given the nature of the situation, I included a note emphasising the urgency of my request to assure it would take priority. And it did.'

'Not the ca—' Reverend Weaver stopped in mid-correction as Burford held up his hand.

'Tell Mrs Bramble not to worry, Reverend,' said Dr Burford. 'I was going to say I had the presence of mind to include a similar note with the latest package to ensure it was treated with the same care and expediency as the first. I asked for the results, however preliminary, to be delivered as soon as possible and by this evening at the latest.'

'Excellent, excellent,' said Reverend Weaver, although it fell short of excellence. As good to hear as it was, this news failed to allow Weaver to relax. Depending on your purpose and perspective, the interpretation of evening could range from five o'clock until midnight. 'Can't narrow it down, no?'

'I'm afraid not. Although I did ask them to be aware of poor Esther's head cold. It would have made it more difficult for her body to fight off other infections. Or poison.'

Dr Burford's attempt to get his shoes back on threatened the posy vase once again.

Reverend Weaver sighed heavily but it bypassed Burford,

who was preoccupied with a knotted shoelace. 'I have another request to deliver, Doctor. Mrs Bramble would be obliged if you, and I, could remain available to present ourselves to the officers' mess in the Fusiliers' building later this evening. After the Ceremony of the Keys, in fact.'

'In the mess, you say?' Dr Burford looked up. 'Whatever for?'

'I understand that she, Inspector Cole and the chief are out to trap a murderer. Should all go to plan, they will require God-fearing people to be on hand as witnesses, especially one such as you with knowledge of medical science. But you must keep this arrangement under your hat until we are summoned.'

Dr Burford finished tying his shoes and moved the posy vase from its precarious position at the edge of the table back to the centre. 'In which case, I shall ensure my hat is in sight at all times.' He smiled and scratched his mutton-chop whiskers.

A tremor of nervousness passed across Reverend Weaver's chest. He considered Dr Burford a clumsy fellow at the best of times who often seemed less than with it. Anything beyond the realm of medicine seemed beyond the bounds of his abilities.

Weaver went to stand, intending to leave, but Burford waved him back.

'Dinner is at eight, but my cook has made some delicious shortbread fingers and it would be churlish of me not to share them with you, Reverend. And a pot of tea would wash a couple down very nicely.'

Here at the Tower, refreshments seemed to be the order of the day, at any time of the day. Dr Burford appeared to possess the ability to inhale victuals on multiple occasions with no discernible effect, but Reverend Weaver was feeling satiated. Dinner lay in little over an hour but he did concede the port wine so recently imbibed needed sopping up. He had always been partial to a shortbread biscuit and one wouldn't hurt. Relaxing in the doctor's sitting room would also keep him out of Inspector Cole's line of sight. And had Mrs Bramble not asked him to keep a close eye on the doctor so she could be informed the moment the test results arrived?

That settled it.

'I'd be delighted,' said Weaver.

Gwen hesitated at Kitty's approach and attempted to conceal herself round the curve of a tower. This fooled no one, least of all Kitty.

'Hiding from anyone in particular, Gwen?' said Kitty.

Gwen's head appeared, followed by the rest of her. 'Wanted to be on my own, is all. The chief and that inspector keep going on and on, not to mention your mistress.'

'Mrs Bramble is trying to get to the bottom of this quickly so you can all get back to normal and we can go home to Hampton Court Palace.'

'I suppose she sent you, did she?' Gwen cuddled a package closer to her chest.

'She did,' said Kitty, noticing the housemaid looking past her towards the Yeoman Warders' Club. 'I'll walk with you if I may. We can go round by the other path, if you'd like?'

Gwen looked relieved as they detoured away from the club.

'What's in the package?' asked Kitty as they took a slow walk towards a flight of steps at the end of the path.

'Just some glassware,' said Gwen. 'Mrs Rushton sent out for a new piece and had it delivered to the main gate because none of us can leave the Tower.'

'Is that where you've been? To collect it?' asked Kitty.

Gwen nodded and looked at her suspiciously. 'Why are you here?'

Kitty ignored the question. 'Did Major and Mrs Rushton have words with each other recently, or someone else, perhaps?'

Gwen shook her head. 'I didn't hear anything. Why do you ask?'

Kitty tilted her head and made a face that suggested Gwen might be missing the obvious.

'Oh, of course, Mrs Bramble wants to know.' Gwen gave her a wry smile. 'I've only ever heard the master and mistress argue once and they've never done it again, not within my earshot anyway. Mrs Rushton wouldn't allow it 'cause she'd die of embarrassment.'

They ascended the steps and hurried up the slope towards the married men's quarters.

'I take it you've never heard them have cross words with the Frys?' said Kitty. 'Anything that might suggest they wished them harm?'

Gwen scoffed. 'Course not. As I said before, they all kept at arm's length, but Mrs Rushton was one for casting aspersions, often saying "Holy Mary mother of God" and "God will smite them down" after every slight, as if that justified it. Never had a good word for them, did the mistress.'

At the front of the married men's building, Gwen opened the door. Kitty was about to thank her and leave when they both spotted Captain Fry's housemaid, Beth, leaning heavily against the hallway wall.

'What is it, Beth?' said Kitty, her forehead lined with concern. 'You look pale.'

Beth shook her head. 'I'm not feeling myself this afternoon. A bit dizzy and queasy, if you must know.'

Kitty moved closer and put the back of her hand to Beth's forehead. It felt hot under her touch and she noticed the young woman's eyes struggling to focus on her.

'You do feel a little warm.' Kitty sniffed. 'Is that perfume you're wearing?' She recognised the scent from the tiny bottle in Esther's room.

Beth's eyes widened in alarm, her gaze darting back and forth between Kitty and Gwen. 'It is, but please don't tell the master. It's Mrs Fry's brand-new one from France, and I only sprayed a tiny bit on my wrists while I put the washing out. I've never had expensive perfume and I only wanted to try it. To feel like a lady for once, if only for five minutes while the master is out.'

'Don't worry. It's not at all strong so if you go straight upstairs and wash it off with carbolic soap, Captain Fry will never know.' Kitty smiled reassuringly. 'I'm sure Gwen won't say anything.'

Gwen shook her head in agreement. 'Course not. I did it once a year back but scared myself silly at the thought of getting caught.'

'Come on, let's get you upstairs,' said Kitty.

She held Beth's arm as she stumbled up the stairs and took the young woman into the Frys' apartment, allowing Gwen to carry on to the Rushtons' apartment with her package.

Kitty put the kettle on to boil and took Beth to the sink to wash her wrists, which she appeared to have scratched red raw. A few moments later, they sat sipping hot sweet tea in Beth's room, all trace of the perfume erased.

'Have you had other dizzy spells recently?' asked Kitty, wondering if her affair with Jasper Chant had advanced more than stated.

'None at all,' said Beth. 'I'm usually as right as rain.'

Maybe not pregnant then, thought Kitty. 'What do you think upset you? Was it something you ate, perhaps?'

'Don't know,' said Beth. 'The captain's been in good health, but he doesn't like bread and dripping and I do.'

'You think it was beef dripping?'

Beth shook her head, then nodded and shrugged. 'I don't know. Could be. It's a few days old. I'll throw the rest away to be on the safe side.'

'Good idea,' said Kitty. 'I must say, you're looking a bit better with a drop of tea inside you. A lot more colour in your cheeks. Have a bit of bread and cheese to settle your stomach and don't worry about the captain. He's got his own worries on his plate.'

Beth gave her a wan smile. 'I know he has but for a while there I thought the poisoner had got me too.'

Something pricked at Kitty's thoughts.

'You didn't give any of that scent to Esther, by any chance?' she said.

'Actually, I did,' said Beth. 'Just the tiniest of bottles. It was her birthday yesterday and she said she'd never had a birthday present before.'

37

Chief Yeoman Warder Treadle opened the door to his office in the Byward Tower and let Mrs Bramble and Inspector Cole enter first. Mrs Bramble wasn't sure what the room had been designed for or who it had once accommodated but three people represented one more than she deemed comfortable. It wasn't that the office lacked roominess but it had become well filled.

A series of bookshelves dominated one wall while almost every other square foot of wall space was occupied by framed photographs and small paintings. A walnut writing bureau and leather-topped oak desk, both with matching chairs, a mahogany grandfather clock and two worn easy chairs stood in positions around the room. A hardy carpet on the floor muffled their footsteps. Every other available surface including the mantelshelf over the fireplace held piles of papers, vases, statuettes, ornaments and knick-knacks, and a carved stone bust of someone Mrs Bramble didn't recognise.

As far as offices went, Mrs Bramble had to admit she had seen some containing far more clutter in her time but she guessed by Inspector Cole's slightly open mouth that his office at Scotland Yard must be a good deal more spartan. She accepted the offer of an easy chair while Cole was installed at the desk in front of which a telephone was affixed to the wall. The polished wooden box sported a mouthpiece, two bells and an earpiece attached by a wire.

The chief showed Cole how to operate the telephone and sat back in the other easy chair.

Inspector Cole's raised voice relayed his request for information into the mouthpiece but it became clear that whoever had answered at the other end in Scotland Yard was having trouble identifying the most appropriate person to talk to him.

'Not him,' said Cole. *'Get the sergeant.'*

'This is cosy,' said Mrs Bramble to the chief.

'Not him either,' said Cole, irritably. *'He's a buffoon.'*

'Share with Yeoman Gaoler,' said the chief. 'Rarely here together.'

'Ah, Simmonds.' Cole sounded relieved. *'As a matter of extreme urgency, I want you to find out which railway company the father of one Sir Oswald Clyne was working for in Chile when he was killed.'*

'I have a little more space at Hampton Court.' She smiled.

'Not chilly as in cold,' said Cole. *'Chile – the country.'*

'Bit cluttered,' said the chief.

'Not skilled – killed!' snapped Cole.

'British Empire? Tower of London?' said the chief. 'Run on protocols, procedure, paperwork.'

'I don't know, that's why I'm asking you.' Cole turned to them with an expression that conveyed a mix of incredulity, exasperation and vexation. He shook his head and shrugged.

Mrs Bramble chuckled. 'And royal palaces.'

'Thank you,' said Cole. *'Call me here at the Chief Yeoman Warder's office at the Tower of London.'* He finished with the number and hung up. 'Blithering idiots.'

The chief smiled at Inspector Cole. 'Business concluded? Good.'

'God knows what they think I've requested,' said Cole, still staring at the telephone. 'I'm not even sure I could've had a decent conversation with the fellow if we'd been in the same room together.'

'This evening's entertainment. Discuss?' said the chief, with eyebrows raised.

'Perfect,' said Mrs Bramble. 'I've been giving that some thought.'

'I bet you have,' said Inspector Cole, still frowning.

She ignored him as though he hadn't spoken. 'There are three ways into the chapel from the outside; through the main door, the crypt entrance and the vestry. There are three ways into the nave itself: directly through the main door, of course, via the crypt and from the vestry. That is how the intruder got away last time I chased him. We just didn't realise how many ways in and out there were.'

'Easily covered, I should think,' said Inspector Cole.

'Easily,' the chief agreed.

'Thinking about the wine,' said Mrs Bramble. 'Everyone knows the doctor has sent samples from the reception for testing but I think we three know the results will be clear.'

'Do we?' said Inspector Cole.

'As we discussed this afternoon, the murderer will know that too but I hope he'll attempt to recover the bottle of communion wine before it too is tested.'

'It *is* being tested,' said Cole, irritation returning to his features.

'But the murderer won't know that.' It was Mrs Bramble's turn to feel irritated. 'Do keep up, Inspector. We're in the company of a professional.'

Inspector Cole's face clouded at the rebuke and Mrs Bramble experienced a twinge of guilt at her implication that he was not the professional detective in the room. She began to outline her ideas about how the trap should be sprung.

'Men outside, follow in?' said the chief at the end.

'Exactly,' said Mrs Bramble.

'Yeoman Gaoler. Good man in a tight spot. Inform governor and lieutenant?'

She considered four men outside the chapel to be ample, as long as she could hide inside herself; and the fewer people who knew about it the better.

'I'd prefer you refrained from telling anyone else, Chief. If only a select few know what we are planning, there can be no mistakes when the trap is sprung. I think Captain Fry, Major Rushton, Inspector Cole and you will be able to manage perfectly well.'

The chief looked apologetic. '*Must* tell governor and lieutenant in the Queen's House, I'm afraid.'

Mrs Bramble suppressed a sigh of disappointment. 'If you must,' she said. 'Without giving too much of the game away, if you please.' She hoped the chief understood her reluctance to inform anyone of the finer details.

'What if it's one of us?' said Inspector Cole. He looked suddenly horrified. 'I mean one of them, of course. The major or captain?'

'It's not beyond the bounds of possibility but I'm starting to formulate a picture of the kind of person who would be likely to poison a congregation. If I'm wrong and it is one of them, I'm sure you'll cope,' said Mrs Bramble with what she hoped was an encouraging smile. 'In any case, there will be Yeoman Warders and Fusiliers guarding the Tower as usual, all within hailing distance.

'And where do *you* intend to wait with your cronies while we put ourselves in the line of fire?' said Cole.

'Oh, I'll be nearby, don't you worry, Inspector,' she said angelically.

'Why does that not fill me with confidence?'

Mrs Bramble laughed. 'Because you are a naturally cautious man, Inspector. Generally, that would be an admirable quality but for a Scotland Yard detective investigating a poisoning and perhaps about to apprehend the murderer ...' she shrugged '... perhaps not as much.'

Inspector Cole's mouth twitched.

'May I make a suggestion, Chief?' said Mrs Bramble.

'By all means,' said the chief, gazing at her with interest.

'Of the several suspects we have been investigating, we hope one will incriminate themselves by putting in an appearance tonight. That said, we cannot rule out the possibility that someone else may visit the chapel for legitimate reasons. After all, it is not locked and several people have already waltzed through in spite of what took place there. If the inspector and yourself are fortunate enough to apprehend someone, an immediate search of their accommodation should follow. Apartments in the Tower are quite small and it should be easy to eliminate the innocent and make discoveries that incriminate the guilty.'

'I was about to suggest the very same thing,' said Inspector Cole, raising his chin defiantly. 'It is standard police procedure.'

Mrs Bramble gave a nod of acknowledgement, although her encounters with him made her doubt he ever followed any procedure rigidly.

'We should implement this plan as soon as possible,' said Cole. 'Can't see anyone trying their luck before dinner, though.'

'You and I are in agreement for once,' said Mrs Bramble. 'Before dinner is too soon and it will still be light. During dinner is no good because, if I'm correct, the poisoner will be having their own dinner too. Probably in company.'

'After dinner, good idea,' said the chief. 'After Ceremony of the Keys, better idea.'

'What the devil is that?' said Inspector Cole. 'Whoever heard of a ceremony for keys? Nothing but pomp. Stuff and nonsense.'

Mrs Bramble almost laughed at Cole's insensitivity, and at the chief as he bristled with indignation.

'Locking the gates to the Tower of London,' said the chief. 'Bit of pomp? Certainly. Keep the Crown Jewels safe? Necessary.'

'My apologies, Chief,' said Inspector Cole, holding his hands up in a placating gesture. 'I've never seen the point in all that parading and peacocking myself, although the Metropolitan Police is as guilty as any for making a show of itself.'

Coming from Hampton Court Palace where ostentatious display was sometimes the order of the day, Mrs Bramble was not averse to a little colour and tradition. It represented continuity and sometimes everyone needed a little of that. As an ex-army nurse, she would have appreciated watching the ritual, but the Ceremony of the Keys was a serious business not generally witnessed by anyone other than the Fusiliers and Yeoman Warders.

'Conclusion of ceremony, five minutes past ten o'clock,' said the chief.

'Then we should move into position immediately after,' said Cole, firmly.

'Very well,' said the chief. He glanced at a carriage clock on a nearby shelf and got up from his easy chair. 'Will seek permission for searches.' He tapped the side of his nose. 'Mum's the word.'

'I shall inform Major Rushton and Captain Fry of our intentions and their required role in proceedings,' said Inspector Cole, moving to leave with the chief.

'Perhaps warn them about the guard posted in the vestry, too,' said Mrs Bramble. 'Although he'll be withdrawn when you're in position, we don't want anyone trying to gain access before we are ready to pounce.'

'Aha!' said Cole, a look of smug satisfaction settling on his face. 'I knew it.' He jabbed a finger in her direction. 'You have no better idea than I about who could have killed Mrs Fry.'

Mrs Bramble watched in amusement when his smile dissipated as he appeared to realise his admission and sought to cover his mistake.

Cole coughed. 'What I meant to say was, this is a shot in the dark for you.'

'On the contrary,' said Mrs Bramble. 'I don't know if you play cards as well as snooker, Inspector, but it never pays to show one's hand. I sincerely believe the culprit will make an appearance tonight in order to recover evidence that will identify and convict them.'

'As long as you remember who is a policeman and who is a housekeeper we should get on like a house on fire. I don't want to see you, your housemaid or that vicar of yours anywhere near the chapel until we've caught the devil.'

'Of course not,' said Mrs Bramble angelically. But please do emphasise the need for total secrecy when you speak to the major and captain. We don't want one of their friends or anyone in their households getting wind of our intention.'

Cole threw up his hands in exasperation and ducked out through the door. The chief allowed Mrs Bramble to go next, and by the time he had joined her Cole was nowhere to be seen.

As they walked back along the Outer Ward, Mrs Bramble touched the chief's arm to get his attention and lowered her voice.

'Chief, I learnt at a tender age that most men – present company excepted – need more help than they are often willing to accept, whatever their station in life. When I first met the inspector, I quickly realised he needed mine more than most.'

She did not consider the chief exempt from her assessment but had no wish to sour their relationship, because she needed him too.

'Funny fellow,' said the chief, thoughtfully. 'In here, fish out of water.'

'As am I,' said Mrs Bramble. 'It won't surprise you to hear that I will not be standing by idly while you and the inspector are taking care of business.'

'But Inspector Cole . . .'

'Need not know I shall be hiding behind the door to the bell tower.'

38

As the sun disappeared over the western horizon shedding orange and pink on its journey, the Tower's lamplighter lit the last of the gas lamps and Reverend Dench's housemaid closed the curtains of the chaplain's house. Mrs Bramble, Reverend Weaver and Jasper Chant had joined Dench for dinner again and had just put down their knives and forks after finishing the minced mutton pie that had followed a tasty pottage. Whatever else detracted from their time at the Tower, the quality and quantity of the food did not.

It had been a subdued affair, with the conversation stilted and the atmosphere markedly different to that of the previous evening. Mrs Bramble could see Weaver struggling throughout the meal to keep quiet about the trap and she was glad when Dench and Chant excused themselves to go to their respective rooms.

The others retired to the parlour, where Kitty was already waiting, the first chance they'd had in over three hours to be alone together and bring each other up to date with the latest information. Closing the door to ensure privacy, Mrs Bramble invited Reverend Weaver to speak first.

'We expect Dr Burford's test results from Guy's Hospital to be here any time now,' he said. 'He thought they might be preliminary rather than comprehensive but I didn't think you'd mind.'

'That is good news,' said Mrs Bramble. 'I'm relying on it

to support my theory.' This was true but she didn't want to worry them by admitting the wrong result would throw the entire investigation into disarray. 'What about you, Kitty?'

Mrs Bramble listened as Kitty recounted her time with Gwen and Beth, her mind trying to fit this new information into the bigger jigsaw puzzle. When her maid had finished, Mrs Bramble relayed the results of her own discussions with Inspector Cole and the chief.

'Interestingly,' Mrs Bramble continued, 'Inspector Cole's colleague at Scotland Yard replied to his request for information in double-quick time. The inspector relayed the message to me in a note before dinner. It transpires the company Sir Oswald Clyne's father was working for when he was killed did not belong to Captain Fry's father, Lord Fry.'

'Good grief,' said Reverend Weaver. 'Does that mean Mrs Rushton was mistaken?'

Mrs Bramble chose her words carefully. 'It means Sir Oswald was led to believe something that could have resulted in him taking matters into his own hands and seeking revenge. He did not, which I think is testament to his own courage and self-restraint.'

'Good for him,' said Weaver. 'Knew the fellow had something morally trustworthy under the surface.'

Mrs Bramble smiled. Not even she had known whether the man was any different beneath the veneer.

She glanced at the clock. A quarter to ten. The Ceremony of the Keys would be about to commence and she needed everyone to be ready to get to their positions, including herself.

A knock came from the front door, then the parlour door and Dr Burford was let into the room.

'Dr Burford,' said Mrs Bramble. 'We've been waiting for you.'

'I'm sure you have,' said Burford. 'As I have been waiting anxiously for this.' He waved a buff envelope in the air before extracting about half a dozen sheets of paper and the returned shard of glass. He handed them to Mrs Bramble. 'I think you'll be interested in the top sheet, which tells you all you need to know.'

Mrs Bramble read the top sheet carefully, twice, which encapsulated all that the other pages held. She still skimmed through the others but those went into scientific detail she had no time to study.

'What does it say, Mrs Bramble?' said Reverend Weaver, an uncharacteristic note of impatience in his tone.

'It confirms the blood samples taken from Dr Burford and others all contained nicotine, but Mrs Fry received a dose high enough to cause her death,' she said at last. 'Esther's dose, although high, shouldn't have killed her, but she was in a weakened state after suffering from a head cold. All the food and wine used for the reception was clear, the communion wafers were clean and the bottle held nothing but red wine. However, the residue of wine in the communal chalice contained a high level of nicotine and the water used to dilute it immediately prior to Holy Communion held a high concentration. High enough, in fact, to have caused irritation of the mouth if drunk neat.'

'Good Lord,' said Reverend Weaver, a quiver in his voice and his face suddenly pale. 'I did poison everyone and kill Mrs Fry after all.'

'Nonsense,' said Mrs Bramble, looking up at the doctor. 'Why did no one taste or smell the poison?'

'Because of the wine,' said Dr Burford. 'It would have masked the slightly bitter taste, and nicotine gives off a slightly fishy odour only when heated.'

'Hmm,' said Mrs Bramble. 'The scientific facts may be

irrefutable, but they do not offer a rational explanation at all. If Mrs Fry and Esther received doses so much higher than everyone else, how did they come by it, Reverend?' She raised her eyebrows at him. 'Esther wasn't at the service and Mrs Fry couldn't have taken more than a mouthful from the chalice in the chapel because you, Reverend Dench or someone else would have noticed and made comment. Neither could Mrs Fry have been given it over a period of days like some poisoners are known to have used arsenic. She would have become ill long before the service. It doesn't make sense.'

'It does to me,' said Dr Burford. 'There can be only one explanation for why these results and those from the other samples do not fully explain the outcome of Mrs Fry's post-mortem.' He cleared his throat. 'Shortly before she entered the chapel on the day she died, Mrs Fry had already been given another dose of nicotine.'

39

Mrs Bramble looked out of her open bedroom window at the multitude of gas lamps lighting the Inner Ward of the medieval fortress. To her left stood the Chapel Royal of St Peter ad Vincula. Beyond, the Waterloo Barracks faced the magnificent White Tower across the parade ground. To her right lay Tower Green, with the guardhouse, Bloody Tower, and the Wakefield Tower housing the Crown Jewels beyond. Staying in yet another famous royal residence steeped in history should have been a pleasure, but the circumstances of her visit had dulled its lustre.

Nothing and no one moved within her sight and silence reigned until she heard the muted sound of boots marching in the Outer Ward. She glanced at the wall clock showing a few minutes before ten o'clock.

The Ceremony of the Keys.

'Halt! Who comes there?' The challenge was barely audible beyond the inner curtain wall.

The marching stopped. 'The keys,' answered another.

'Whose keys?'

'Queen Victoria's keys.'

'Pass, Queen Victoria's keys. All is well.'

The marching resumed and got louder as the military escort emerged from beneath the Bloody Tower. Then it stopped.

Mrs Bramble could not see the ritual, even from her

vantage point, but knew the keys and their escort now stood in front of the guardhouse.

'God preserve Queen Victoria.'

'Amen!'

Ten o'clock chimed and the Last Post from a lone bugler by the guardhouse echoed throughout the fortress. The ceremony completed, a shouted command dismissed the Fusiliers and Yeoman Warders, who returned to their various quarters.

Time for Mrs Bramble to move.

She shrugged into her coat and descended to the ground floor, quietly opening the front door to slip outside. The chief already stood at the corner of the chapel and he beckoned her forward. She nodded but said nothing as she passed him and entered the chapel by the front door. The dim light of two candles shed enough light to see where to go but cast deep shadows into every corner and between the pews. She assumed the chief had provided these deliberately and thanked his foresight.

She hadn't spotted Major Rushton or Captain Fry getting into their positions outside either end of the chapel, but then again, she hadn't expected to. On the other hand, Inspector Cole would enter the chapel at any second on his way to his hiding place in the vestry and she did not want him preventing her from taking part. Nor did she wish to be caught by the Yeoman Warder posted inside the vestry earlier by the chief.

She tested the door to the bell tower, not expecting it to be locked, but it did not budge. With a huff of annoyance, she grasped an iron ring and tugged, which proved the door unlocked as it came unstuck with a crack. Wincing at the loud echo bouncing around the empty nave, she stepped through the door and pulled it silently closed behind her as far as she dared, ensuring it would open at her merest touch.

Her ears pricked up at the sound of another opening door but for a moment she couldn't work out whether the sound had come from the main door or elsewhere. Was it Inspector Cole arriving or the poisoner putting in an early appearance? Then she heard the sound of slow bootsteps on flagstones as they came closer and realised she had alerted the sentry in the vestry to the presence of someone in the nave. She wished she had checked the bell-tower door an hour or so ago. She hadn't even considered it might be stuck, creaky or even still locked, and mentally kicked herself for her carelessness.

The scrape of boots stopping nearby made her heart thump so hard in her chest that she feared the sentry would hear it even through the door. His pause seemed interminable and she expected the door to be yanked open at any moment and for her to be marched across to the guardhouse to keep her out of the way while all the excitement took place without her.

Then the main door opened and she recognised Inspector Cole's voice as he entered the nave.

'Ah, good man,' said Cole. 'All is in order, I take it?'

'Yes, sir,' said the Yeoman Warder. 'No one in or out all evening.'

'Good, good. The chief's outside and I'm here to guard the vestry so you can go and get some dinner now. I expect you're famished.'

Mrs Bramble heard a grunt of acknowledgement from the other man and his bootsteps recede as he left the chapel. Inspector Cole's footsteps, much lighter in his shoes than the sentry's military boots, receded in the opposite direction and she heard the vestry door open and close before silence descended again.

She knew the chief, once he had dismissed the sentry, would take up a similar position behind the back door leading to the yard of the chaplain's house, hopefully with less noise. His observation post would be like hers: more of a listening post to begin with until they both considered it safe enough to emerge and follow whoever had passed by.

Of course, their plan could go awry if someone innocent happened to enter the chapel. Although, who on earth would be completely innocent if they were abroad after the Ceremony of the Keys and choosing to enter the darkened chapel?

Or no one might come.

Their whole strategy relied on the assumption that the poisoner would want to recover any remaining incriminating evidence before the police or Dr Burford found them out. It had crossed her mind more than once that this plan might fail if the murderer simply chose to put themselves in the hands of fate. After all, the growing weight of circumstantial evidence still failed to tip the scales towards any one individual. Mrs Bramble had her own theory and prime suspect but that wasn't the same as knowing for sure and being able to prove it beyond any reasonable doubt.

She felt a wave of nervousness for the first time since her arrival at the Tower, not because of what might be about to happen, but about what the consequences might be if nothing happened at all.

As Mrs Bramble waited in the cold darkness of the bell tower, time started to drag and minutes seemingly elongated. Through her nervous expectation, boredom was quick to set in, but she had experienced this before, waiting in the pre-dawn darkness before a battle as her husband prepared to fight. In those far-off days, with the sounds of cannon and rifle fire booming and crackling sharp above the cries of the wounded and dying, she and the other nurses and doctors would wait with rising anxiety to see who and how many would be brought on stretchers into the hospital tents.

She thought of her black cat, Dodger, waiting not so patiently for her to return to her Lady Housekeeper's apartment in Hampton Court Palace. If it hadn't been for her friend, Reverend Weaver, being falsely accused of murder by the less-than-thorough Inspector Cole she would be at home in her comfortable bed right at this moment – the exact moment someone entered the crypt from outside.

Mrs Bramble strained her hearing and heard them pause by the door between the crypt and the nave before moving. As the vestry door clicked, she had a mind to leave her position to investigate ... just as someone else joined them in the chapel, neglecting to close the main door fully.

From the sound of the footsteps, they were made by another pair of shoes, the kind a man would wear, but this person walked slowly and softly to avoid unnecessary noise. As the vestry door clicked, Mrs Bramble prepared to leave her hidey-hole but froze as yet another person stepped into the chapel. They too appeared to be attempting stealth but failing in this regard. She now had no idea what was going on in the nave but suspected the first person had fully entered the vestry and would be apprehended by Inspector Cole at any moment. The chief would prevent any escape by the mysterious second person, but curiosity forced her to take the risk of leaving her surveillance post.

The bell-tower door eased open a fraction at a time, thankfully without the accompanying cacophony of before, and Mrs Bramble slid into the dimly lit nave. A moving shadow paused by the vestry and she thought she had disturbed its owner, but it appeared to listen at the door. She moved closer, placing each foot with care to avoid any noise, and had reached the relative safety of the last stone pillar as the shadow opened the door and slipped into the vestry ...

At the same time as two others entered the chapel, the first via the crypt and the other through the main door.

In any other circumstance, Mrs Bramble might have laughed, but as things stood, this was no laughing matter. Including herself, Inspector Cole and whoever had entered the crypt, vestry and nave, seven people now stood somewhere in the chapel. Rather crowded and not what she had expected at all.

At least she recognised the reassuring form of the chief as he approached her down the aisle. She put her finger to her lips for silence and he diverted to light a hurricane lamp from one of the candles. She had no idea what would happen if anyone else turned up. Things were complicated enough, thank you very much.

Mrs Bramble stood by the vestry door with the chief, listening to a whispered conversation being conducted inside between two male voices. Then the click of a latch and the squeak of a hinge preceded the voice of a young woman whispering, 'Jasper? Jasper?' before another female voice said, 'Beth?'

This sent Mrs Bramble's mind reeling.

While accepting an innocent party might be caught up in the trap, she had hoped the poisoner alone would make their move. The ruse had failed and stealth no longer mattered.

Mrs Bramble burst in through the vestry door to find Inspector Cole frozen like a sculpture in the British Museum, in front of the open cupboard from which he had undoubtedly just emerged, his hands out as though undecided who to catch first. Jasper Chant and Beth were embracing like escaped criminals run to ground by a search party. Reverend Dench was standing in the corner, scratching his head like he had been given a taxing conundrum to solve. Wide-eyed Gwen had her finger poised amid a jab towards Beth.

Mrs Bramble and the chief exchanged a puzzled glance, just as Mrs Rushton's clumpy heavy boots announced her entrance from the crypt. She halted as she took in the crowded scene and squealed as the pursuing Captain Fry almost bowled her over.

'What the—' began Cole, but the appearance of Major Rushton framed in the east door stopped him.

'Margaret, why are you here?' said Major Rushton, his eyebrows emphasising the question.

'I could ask you the same thing,' said Mrs Rushton.

'But you're with Fry.'

'I am not.'

'She is not,' confirmed Captain Fry, stiff with indignation.

'Did you follow me?' Jasper Chant snapped at Reverend Dench.

'Well, I-I-I ...' Dench stuttered.

Beth threw a glance at Gwen. 'And you too?'

The room descended into chaos as everyone accused and questioned everyone else at the same time, the volume getting louder as fingers wagged, chests puffed out and chins jutted.

'Why are you here, Inspector,' said Beth amid the melee, holding Chant even tighter.

'Quiet!' shouted Cole to get attention. 'Never mind me.' He growled, glaring at everyone accusingly. 'What in God's name are the lot of you doing here?'

40

Several minutes later, everyone from the chapel had been shepherded across to the officers' quarters mess hall and seated around the long dining table. Major Rushton had at first complained about such a violation of the Fusiliers' building but Inspector Cole and the chief had pointed out that they could hardly put questions and carry out their investigation while people sat on the pews of the Chapel Royal.

'For God's sake,' Inspector Cole had said. 'It's not the Middle Ages, after all.' Then he'd apologised to Reverend Dench for taking the Lord's name in vain twice in as many minutes, all while standing in the chapel.

Others had joined them in the mess hall moments after their arrival, with Sir Stephen Lovell the first to enter and taking a seat next to Captain Fry. He was followed shortly after by Kitty, Reverend Weaver and Dr Burford, much to the obvious annoyance of Inspector Cole, who grimaced and scowled like a contestant in a gurning competition. Sir Oswald Clyne became the last to arrive as Cole looked to be losing patience with so many new arrivals.

The almost palpable sense of seething resentment emanating from those in the mess hall formed an atmosphere thick enough for Mrs Bramble to slice with a butter knife. The captain looked at the major with contempt. The major held a steady accusatory stare at his wife sitting next to him. Mrs

Rushton avoided his gaze and gave a curious look sideways towards her housemaid, Gwen. Gwen gave a disappointed shake of her head as she looked at Beth sitting opposite. Beth didn't notice because her pleading eyes had their gaze fixed on Jasper Chant, whose arm she held tightly. Chant's intense glare was set at Reverend Dench sitting across from him. Dench was oblivious. His unfocused eyes exposed befuddlement at what had begun with a night-time invasion of his beloved Chapel Royal.

Mrs Bramble took in all these visible emotions and started to doubt her assumptions. Of course, she knew why each of these people might harbour grudges against each other, several of whom had also borne ill-will towards Mrs Fry. It irked her that the trap had not gone entirely to plan, although she had no doubt the murderer was among those now sitting around the dining table, and was confident she knew who that was. She set the evidence brought with her from the vestry down on the table and took a step back. Work still needed to be done but Inspector Cole's face had already adopted the dark and ominous qualities of a thundercloud.

She knew she had to take him and the chief in hand, quickly. Without her to steady the ship and guide them through the next hour, she suspected the pair of them would go off at a tangent, arrest the wrong person again and cause untold mayhem in the process. She whispered instructions to Kitty and prepared to grasp the nettle.

'Is this you about to interfere again?' said Inspector Cole, as she approached him.

'Not at all,' said Mrs Bramble, smiling sweetly. 'I thought you might need reminding, that's all.'

'Reminding?' Cole frowned. 'About what?'

'About what we agreed. A search should be carried out

of the quarters of anyone making an appearance in the chapel tonight.'

'*We* agreed?' said Cole.

'Of course.' Mrs Bramble ignored his sneer. 'Is it not standard police work to investigate any person coming to the attention of a constable of the law during his inquiries into a felony?'

'Do not presume to tell me my job, Mrs Bramble,' said Cole.

'As if I would do such a thing.' Mrs Bramble feigned contrition, knowing the seed had been sown and all she needed to do was watch it germinate. She had less than a minute to wait.

'Major Rushton,' Inspector Cole called the Fusilier to his side. 'I would be obliged if you could keep everyone confined to this mess hall until the chief and I return. We have important tasks to perform before we can start to make sense of the events that have taken place tonight.'

'Tasks?' said Major Rushton. 'What tasks? How long will they take? I can't keep everyone cooped up for long.'

The inspector held up placating hands. 'We need to conduct a search and I assure you it will be expedited.'

'What do you hope to find?'

'Anything suggestive of a method or motive.'

'For whom?'

Inspector Cole wasn't listening. He was already at the door with the chief in tow and Mrs Bramble at his heels with the two housemaids, Beth and Gwen. Cole hesitated and Mrs Bramble thought he might be about to debar her from participating but she gave him her sternest look that said, 'You really shouldn't bother arguing,' and saw him wither beneath it.

*

Their first port of call was Captain Fry's quarters in the married men's block. Beth let them in with her key and stood in the corridor outside with Gwen, the two housemaids not speaking.

'A comprehensive search, if you will, Chief,' said Inspector Cole.

'Is there any other?' said the chief, looking miffed at the suggestion that he would be less than thorough.

Mrs Bramble thought she knew what to look for while Cole and the chief blundered their way through the rooms, prodding and poking around like housewives selecting vegetables at the market. Nothing escaped her attention in the apartment and she retrieved the small greetings card with the picture of St Catherine.

Then, as she dodged around the two fumbling men, a small bottle of perfume on an occasional table caught her eye. Unfamiliar with continental perfumes, Mrs Bramble gave it a tentative sniff. It held a faint scent she considered pleasant enough but would not have paid good money for, although she suspected it cost more than her daily wage. As she went to place it back on the table, she wondered if this was the one from France that Beth had given a sample of to Esther before trying it herself. Inspector Cole glanced her way and gave her a quizzical look. She held up the card and bottle for him to see and shrugged. He scoffed and went back to his ferreting, so she pocketed them.

Next came Major Rushton's quarters.

'The housemaid, Gwen, needs to get on top of her housework, if you ask me,' said Cole. 'Last Friday's fish supper is still making its presence known.'

The chief sniffed the air and gave a facial shrug.

Mrs Bramble agreed that frying fish in such a small apartment was bound to leave its mark for a while, although she could tell scented furniture polish had been deployed to mask the smell.

She soon found what she was looking for and drew the attention of the inspector and chief to a small wooden box decorated with lacquered flowers. The chief shrugged and Inspector Cole seemed less than enamoured with its contents of jewellery, trinkets, beads, embroidered cloth, empty tobacco tins and bundle of letters. Only the small glass laudanum bottle interested him and he took this from her. She shook her head and kept the whole box.

Mrs Bramble wandered into the small kitchen, which had been overlooked by the men, and noticed the brand-new item of glassware Kitty had mentioned.

Inspector Cole ordered Beth and Gwen be taken back to the mess hall and he marched across to the chaplain's house with the chief and Mrs Bramble. The chief's face didn't seem to know whether to express dismay, puzzlement, joy or irritation at Cole taking charge of the situation so publicly. He had gone along with the detective so far but Mrs Bramble could see the usurping of his authority had worn the Chief Yeoman Warder's patience to an almost transparent veneer.

Reverend Dench's housemaid let them into the hallway and led them up the stairs to the master and guest bedrooms. Inspector Cole seemed intent on finding something, anything, with which to beat Reverend Weaver, and Mrs Bramble was annoyed by the overzealous thoroughness with which he insisted on searching her friend's room.

He found nothing.

The search of Jasper Chant's room threw up an eclectic mix of a pair of old and threadbare gardening gloves giving off a faint aroma of fish, a dirty cloth with a reddish stain that looked like a chalice cloth but smelled of wood polish, the two bottles of red wine Kitty had mentioned and a carafe with purple residue at the bottom. Mrs Bramble suspected it had held wine but upon giving it a quick sniff discovered it had probably held the fruit cordial from earlier.

The search of Reverend Dench's things passed without incident and the rooms of Mrs Bramble and Kitty were spared the ignominy of being ransacked due to their arrival after the murder had been committed. Inspector Cole seemed increasingly exasperated by what he called a dearth of solid evidence.

'Inspector,' said Mrs Bramble. 'Could you indulge me for a moment and allow me a peek in the chambermaid's room?'

'Be quick,' said the chief as Inspector Cole opened his mouth to answer.

Mrs Bramble was already moving to the room with an affirmative wave as the chief spoke, not wanting to leave any opportunity for him to change his mind. She trusted Kitty to have made a thorough search of the room and went straight to the table to retrieve the tiny lavender water bottle. She was back in a moment, to raised eyebrows from the chief and a scowl from Cole.

'All we have is an empty bottle of laudanum and that wasn't even the substance administered to the congregation,' Inspector Cole grumbled to no one in particular as they returned downstairs. 'Lord knows why you're carrying around an armful of meaningless detritus,' he scoffed at Mrs Bramble.

She chose to say nothing because biding her time was the best policy. Whatever she said now or however she tried to explain, he would dismiss it out of hand. But she thought she'd worked out who the poisoner was and how they might have committed murder. With just a little more time to get everything straight in her mind, she could bring the killer to justice. The last thing she needed was Inspector Cole blithering and blustering and accusing the wrong people, and he certainly had a track record in that regard.

'Come!' snapped Inspector Cole from the open front door, and he left.

The chief's face hardened as he stared after Cole but Mrs Bramble pouted at him and shook her head to forestall any response. An altercation on the parade ground in full view of the Tower guards would be less than constructive and she had an armful of evidence to get safely to the mess hall.

The chief asked to take some of her burden, an offer she graciously accepted, although she only relinquished possession of the least delicate items. That way it would be her own stupid fault and she would have only herself to rail at if she tripped and broke something important.

When they walked into the Fusiliers' mess hall, Inspector Cole's scowl deepened at the sight of Reverend Weaver and Kitty, but Mrs Bramble set about organising proceedings, seating them the furthest from her position at the head of the table. She ignored the dismayed glances thrown her way by the two soldiers in the room as she placed her collection of items directly on the highly polished surface of the table next to those retrieved from the vestry. At this late hour, everyone was tired and anxious and sitting in the presence of a killer. Now was not the time to stand on ceremony.

Inspector Cole stood on one side of her and the chief on the other.

'Is this you again, is it?' growled Cole. 'Doing your thing?'

She gave him a disarming smile. '*Our* thing, Inspector. You have solved the case again.'

'I-I have?' He looked suddenly bemused, wrong-footed. 'Then you know who did it?'

'*We* do.' She indicated the items on the table. 'And how.'

41

The three pockets of conversation that had sprung up around the table – among the Frys, the Rushtons and the rest – stopped abruptly when Inspector Cole rapped his knuckles on the table.

'Quiet, if you please,' he said. 'As you know, the chief and I have been investigating the events that took place a couple of days ago in the Chapel Royal of St Peter ad Vincula. Most of you were present when Mrs Fry tragically collapsed and died during Holy Communion.' He puffed his chest out. 'There is no doubt in my mind that one of you sat around this here table had a hand in her death and we, together with Mrs Bramble ...' he nodded at her for emphasis '... hope to demonstrate who that was, how they pulled it off and why.'

Mrs Bramble couldn't resist narrowing her eyes as Inspector Cole introduced her as one of his assistants (even though she had played on the role herself) and took a half-step sideways away from her.

She took a breath, cleared her throat and began.

'Reverend Weaver is a good friend of mine; someone I've known through our work at Hampton Court Palace over the last few years. I know he was thrilled to receive the invitation to lead the special service here at the Tower of London and he accepted readily. He is a fine man, a good Christian, and I would trust him with my life.'

'I wouldn't, he's the inspector's primary suspect,' said Mrs Rushton, looking around the table and garnering nods of agreement.'

'Was,' clarified Mrs Bramble. She knew such interruptions would come but they irritated her nonetheless. 'As you know, he was detained and then released through lack of, or should I say *no*, evidence.' She looked at Reverend Weaver. 'When I received the telegram informing me of his arrest, I knew it could be little more than a simple mistake in need of rectifying. Inspector Cole and I worked together before on a murder case at Hampton Court Palace and his policeman's instinct is to make a swift arrest based on the facts in front of him. However, not every fact is always visible immediately. Every place and situation has its own quirks and foibles, and this fortress is no different. The challenge was to unravel the mystery before the letter of the law forced Inspector Cole to charge Reverend Weaver and throw him into Newgate Prison.'

'Where, I have little doubt, he should be,' said Captain Fry, pointedly avoiding Weaver's glance of alarm.

'Let us examine the facts and see if we can change your mind, Captain.' She pointed to a key obtained from Reverend Dench earlier. 'When Reverend Weaver arrived at the Tower, Reverend Dench instructed him in his way of doing things, showing him where pertinent items were kept and giving him this key to the cupboard where the sacramental wine and wafers were stored. It would be the responsibility of both clergymen to bless the wine, the water and the wafers prior to commencing the Eucharist.'

'Is this relevant?' said Major Rushton.

'It is if you want to understand the complexities, Major.' Mrs Bramble gave him a withering look that challenged whether he was capable of such understanding. When he looked away, she continued. 'I have learnt from many witnesses that all went well for the first three-quarters of an hour until the taking of bread and wine for Holy Communion had all but concluded. At that time, and almost in unison, virtually everyone in the chapel became ill and Mrs Fry collapsed and died. Only Inspector Cole, the organist Jasper Chant and Reverend Weaver suffered no ill effects. Dr Burford suspected mass food poisoning.'

Captain Fry scoffed. 'But still Inspector Cole arrested the reverend. Surely that tells you something?'

'And I can see why you would think that,' said Mrs Bramble, holding up her hand against whatever interjection Inspector Cole was about to make. 'Everyone attended the reception before the service so it was reasonable to assume any accidental food poisoning might have occurred in this very room or in the kitchen of this building. Until it could be confirmed or discounted, perhaps it was logical for Inspector Cole to arrest the man who was leading the service when the illness struck but remained unaffected. Only two others had escaped the illness. Mr Chant was still at his seat at the organ and had yet to take the bread and wine. The inspector, having never undergone confirmation into the Anglican church, bowed his head to receive no more than a blessing.' She nodded to Dr Burford, inviting him to speak. 'Doctor?'

Dr Burford stood as if about to address a seminar of his peers, hit his thigh on the table and reeled back into his chair, knocking it to the floor with a clatter. 'Sorry,' he appeared to apologise to the chair as he righted it. He turned to the gathering and apologised again. 'Sorry, completely my fault, sorry.' He composed himself and cleared his throat. 'Ahem. A post-mortem on Mrs Fry's body at Guy's Hospital plus a subsequent series of tests have ruled categorically that she died of nicotine poisoning, not food poisoning.'

A buzz of disbelief filled the room and Inspector Cole raised his hands for quiet.

Dr Burford continued. 'Nothing dangerous was found by my colleagues in either the food or the white wine served at the reception. Furthermore, I have received confirmation that other blood samples I sent for testing, including my own, proved positive for abnormal levels of nicotine. Those of Inspector Cole and Mr Chant were normal for a smoker. Reverend Weaver's was negative.'

Dr Burford went to retake his seat, hesitated as he checked his chair was still in position, and sat down gingerly.

'Thank you,' said Mrs Bramble. 'The doctor's information reinforced Inspector Cole's belief and mine that the fatal dose had to have been administered in front of everyone during the sacrament. But let us leave that for a moment and turn to the households of the Frys and Rushtons.'

'Why us?' said Major Rushton, stiffening on his seat.'

'For the sake of completeness, Major,' said Mrs Bramble, securing a nod of support from the chief. 'Many in the congregation knew Mrs Fry was against Reverend Weaver taking the service because she had advocated for another chaplain to be given the honour. Although having met Reverend Weaver only once before, she had labelled the delivery of his sermons as clumsy and bumbling, and she had petitioned the bishop to honour her friend instead. Earlier that day, Reverend Weaver had a direct run-in with Mrs Fry over his invitation. He was later heard to say her behaviour "would try the patience of a saint" and "I'm only human". These statements, although not damning, were circumstantial and gave rise to suspicion. Could the reverend have sought the ultimate revenge for Mrs Fry's attempts to sully his name and reputation?'

Captain Fry took his turn at directing glares, first at the terrified Reverend Weaver and then at Reverend Dench, being the only two clergymen in the room.

'Another thing I have learnt: there are many around this table who might have wished ill to Mrs Fry,' said Mrs Bramble. 'Years before the captain and major joined the army, a long-standing family feud had begun as the result of a student incident at Oxford University. Mr Fry, as he was then, accidentally killed Mr Rushton's best friend in what he saw as a fair fist fight, but Mr Rushton could never accept that. The two men joined the army, rising to captain and major respectively, but, being in the same regiment, I suppose it was only a matter of time before they received the same posting.'

'Are you now backtracking, suggesting Major Rushton killed Captain Fry's wife because of something that happened so long ago?' said Inspector Cole.

'The major's prior friendship with the captain might have accounted for them having kept the peace for so long because they always behaved professionally in each other's company, never arguing or being confrontational,' said Mrs Bramble. 'However, they never spent any more time together than absolutely necessary. This was in stark contrast to their wives. We discovered Mrs Rushton had begun to bad-mouth Mrs Fry at every opportunity in an attempt to sully her reputation.'

'I object, Chief.' The major leapt to his feet. 'Are we to be subject to such slander without intervention?'

'In time, all revealed,' said the chief. 'Please sit. The truth will out.'

Major Rushton sat. His cheeks had coloured while his wife's had paled.

'Thank you, Chief,' said Mrs Bramble. 'As I was going

to say, Mrs Fry was not one to take such personal attacks lightly and she retaliated by initiating a campaign to have Mrs Rushton ostracised.'

Major Rushton suddenly looked defensive. 'You would expect wives to support their husbands, would you not?'

'Of course, but there is a lot more to this family feud when you scratch beneath the surface. Sir Stephen Lovell' – she gestured towards him – 'is a good friend of Captain Fry's father, Lord Fry, whom he met during meetings to build railway lines in Africa and India, and is a staunch supporter of the family. He was knighted for his work in the Intelligence Department of the War Office where he helped open up and shed light on the Dark Continent of Africa through the creation of a new map. This map incorporated all the recent developments, acquisitions and expansions of the British Empire.'

'Is there any need for such digressions, Mrs Bramble?' whispered Inspector Cole out of the side of his mouth.

Mrs Bramble chose to ignore him, as usual. 'Lord Fry led a high life of wealth and privilege, investing heavily in a company building railways in Africa, eventually becoming its owner, but his African plans were stymied, so he turned to building railways in South America. Unfortunately, he overstretched himself and his company went bust when contracts to build a trans-Andean railway were cancelled due to the high number of deaths and injuries. Soon after, Sir Stephen found his career progression being blighted in some way but did not know why. That was until Mrs Fry told him Sir Arthur Rushton had used his connections to continually block his advancement because of his close connection with Lord Fry.'

'That is preposterous,' snapped Major Rushton. 'Why would my father do such a thing?'

'He didn't,' said Mrs Bramble. 'Mrs Fry lied.'

Captain Fry banged the table with his fist. 'Now hold on a minute. You can't sully my wife's memory.'

'Captain, calm yourself, sir,' said the chief, giving Fry a look that defied any challenge. 'Explanation soon.'

Inspector Cole turned to Mrs Bramble with a hopeful look. 'I take it you can explain yourself?'

Mrs Bramble nodded, noticing a mixture of anger and disappointment on Lovell's face. 'Through her own connections Mrs Fry discovered it was Sir Arthur, in his role as Head of the Foreign Scrutiny Department of the British Admiralty, who had eventually persuaded senior government officials to withdraw their support for Lord Fry's company in Africa, then South America. Sir Arthur had no interest in Sir Stephen and no impact on his career at all, but Mrs Fry knew who had.

'Even considering their professional rivalry, Lord Fry could never believe a respected businessman like Sir Arthur would deliberately seek to undermine another man's company. It had to be someone else and, despite their supposed friendship, Lord Fry became convinced Sir Stephen had in some way exerted his influence and blocked his rail company's expansion in Africa, forcing him to turn to South America, which proved his downfall. Lord Fry blocked Sir Stephen's path out of bitter spite, but neither Captain Fry nor Major Rushton knew anything of this.'

'What does all this matter, Mrs Bramble?' said Inspector Cole. 'This is all to do with business.'

'I'll come to that in a minute, Inspector,' said Mrs Bramble. She was beginning to tire of Cole's interruptions and lack of understanding but that was exactly why she had to carry on. 'But first, let us look at Sir Oswald Clyne, as close a friend to the Rushton family as Sir Stephen is to the

Frys. Knighted for his work on royal portraits, he is an artist whose work has appeared in the Royal Academy's Summer Exhibition. He met Major Rushton when the major's father, Sir Arthur, sat for a portrait. During questioning, Sir Oswald revealed that his choice of an artistic life offered escape from a lifetime of manual labouring. That had been the lot of his father, a railway engineer who lost his life in an accident while building a railway bridge in Chile. The company had denied negligence and refused compensation.'

'But why does he have a hatred for the Frys?' said Inspector Cole, suspiciously.

'Simply because Mrs Rushton told Sir Oswald that Lord Fry was the owner of the company his father was working for on the day he died.'

'Now look here—' began the major.

'Slanderous,' his wife spat.

The outbreak of accusation, counter-accusation and arguing was perhaps inevitable and Mrs Bramble was certainly grateful for the expanse of dining table separating the two feuding parties. This was a necessary part of the chain of events for her to tell because unless they let her do so, there could be no comprehension of why Mrs Fry and Esther had lost their lives.

The chief and inspector exerted their authority and brought the verbal melee to an uneasy conclusion. The chief gave Mrs Bramble a friendly wink and said, 'Speed things along, no? Atmosphere's fraught. Tension's high.'

'Ladies and gentlemen,' said Mrs Bramble, thinking these people were as argumentative and irritating as some of the ladies back at the palace. 'If I could continue with fewer interruptions, all will be explained in detail.' She waited for some acknowledgement but received barely two nods and a few grimaces in reply.

She cleared her throat for emphasis.

'These were not the only conflicts within these walls,' she said. 'The family housemaids, Beth and Gwen, were forbidden to speak to each other because of the feud but had become friends despite this.' She noted Mrs Rushton's disapproving glance at Gwen, who had her gaze cast down. 'That is how Gwen discovered the clandestine courtship between Beth and Mr Chant.' Captain Fry pointedly avoided looking at the pair, who held each other's arms more tightly. 'Their stations in life are different and Mrs Fry forbade Beth to have any contact with him. But there is no accounting for love and there never will be. They found ways to be together and steal the odd kiss.'

'I mean, really,' Captain Fry exclaimed, as Beth's cheeks reddened.

Jasper Chant banged his fist on the table. 'There is nothing sordid or tawdry going on here.' He met Fry's angry glare with his own. 'My intention is for us to marry.'

'But—'

'Gentlemen,' said Mrs Bramble, raising her voice for the first time. Just a notch. Inspector Cole and the chief looked at her in surprise but she remained unmoved. There were far too many stags with oversized antlers in the room for her liking and they needed to realise she was in control. She waited until Jasper Chant and Captain Fry turned their attention back to her before continuing.

'Unable to be open about their affair and perhaps fearful of being forced into a workhouse if she lost her job, maybe that could have been enough of a motive for Beth to kill her mistress. After all, if Captain Fry ever found himself suddenly alone, he would need to keep her employed as a housekeeper. Mr Chant insisted he would never stand by and see his sweetheart turfed out onto the streets, giving him a motive to do all he could to help the woman he loved.

'Are you saying they *were* involved in the murder?' said Inspector Cole, looking perplexed. He looked at the chief, who merely shrugged.

Mrs Bramble shook her head at the outburst and continued. 'Despite Mrs Fry's threats, of which I'm sure the captain was unaware, Mr Chant stated his and Beth's intention to marry. He has saved long and hard and accrued enough money to allow them to buy a home, with the intention of living off his talents in music. Although true—'

'Mrs Bramble ...' said Chant, imploringly, as he held Beth closer.

'Please trust me,' said Mrs Bramble with a reassuring nod towards them. 'Mr Chant could not hope to accrue enough to set up home with Beth without additional income, so he turned to buying and selling anything people would sell and buy.' She pointed to the table. 'During a search of his room, we found these tatty gardening gloves, which smell a little fishy, this dirtied and stained chalice cloth smelling of wood polish, along with this empty carafe that had held fruit cordial. I also found these two bottles of sacramental red wine, no doubt taken from the cupboard in the vestry, which I suspect he intended to sell.'

Mrs Bramble held up her hand to forestall any interjections. 'Reverend Dench's staff had already witnessed his late-night clandestine comings and goings. Could Esther have discovered one or both of Mr Chant's secrets and threatened to expose him and Beth to Inspector Cole and the chief, ruining any plans they had of a happy life?'

'Jasper Chant,' said Inspector Cole, stepping forward and pointing. 'I am arrest—

'Not yet, Inspector,' said Mrs Bramble, resting her hand on the confused Cole's outstretched arm.

'How in God's name can you think we had anything to do with killing Esther and Mrs Fry?' said Beth, hand at her throat, looking open-mouthed and teary-eyed at those around the table. 'We just want to be left alone.'

'I don't,' said Mrs Bramble. 'I did think these gloves incriminating because of the smell, until I remembered that Mr Chant polishes the organ keyboard before every service. Reverend Dench has new gardening gloves and a fresh chalice cloth so Mr Chant must use his old pair and the old cloth to clean with.'

'That only leaves Reverend Dench for you to accuse,' said Inspector Cole, looking at Mrs Bramble as though she might have lost her mind.

'Dr Burford?' offered the chief, looking sheepish when Mrs Bramble turned a look of pity on him and Cole.

Reverend Dench and Dr Burford looked greatly unimpressed by being scooped up in the round.

'Each man had the opportunity and a motive of sorts,' Mrs Bramble admitted. 'The reverend does use a nicotine-based insecticide, hence the fishy gloves—'

'What have fishy gloves got to do with it?' Cole snapped.

Mrs Bramble ignored the outburst. 'And no doubt the doctor has access to nicotine-based medications. But are these men the killing kind?'

42

'God help us,' said Reverend Dench, his palms up as though appealing direct to the Almighty. 'Does this mean we're no closer to unmasking the real poisoner?'

'On the contrary,' said Mrs Bramble. 'Let me explain the events in the chapel. Major Rushton, Captain Fry, Inspector Cole, the chief and I set a trap for the poisoner tonight and took up secret positions. I had already worked out how the poisoning in the chapel took place but needed to confirm the identity of the murderer in front of witnesses. I had expected, hoped, for one visitor alone. I was wrong.'

'That makes a change,' muttered Inspector Cole.

'No one is infallible,' said Mrs Bramble, giving Cole a knowing look. 'Jasper Chant arrived first, entering through the main door and heading straight to the vestry to let in Beth by opening the outer door so they could avoid arriving together. Gwen followed Beth because she knew of her courtship and was concerned for her safety.'

'That's right,' said Beth. 'Especially after Esther's murder.'

Mrs Bramble acknowledged this with a single nod. 'The night before last, I was outside the chaplain's house when I saw someone acting suspiciously. I followed them through the chapel, thinking it may have been Mr Chant attempting to remove damning evidence, but he wears the same kind of shoes as Reverend Dench, not the clumpy boots I heard as I chased the figure down into the Outer Ward before losing them. Reverend Dench's staff told us later that Mr Chant often went out late in the evening and on this occasion had left through the scullery and side door. We now know these excursions were to meet Beth but this time, unusually, he returned only fifteen minutes later and I saw no sign of Beth, perhaps because my pursuit of the true murderer had interrupted and scared them.'

Jasper Chant and Beth nodded in unison. Mrs Bramble continued.

'Whenever Mr Chant stayed at the chaplain's house, Reverend Dench had also noticed he often went to the chapel late at night. Undoubtedly, the reverend had become curious about such behaviour and discovered Mr Chant's liaisons with Beth. Sympathetic to their situation, I suspect the reverend gave Mr Chant the bottles of sacramental wine to sell. Am I right?'

With a look of guilt and avoiding her gaze, Reverend Dench nodded.

Mrs Bramble continued. 'Recent events had unnerved Reverend Dench, so he followed Mr Chant tonight. Other than those I've mentioned, almost everyone else in this room was going about their legitimate business elsewhere in the Tower until we met here in the mess hall.

'Are you ever going to get to the point and expose the murderer?' said Inspector Cole, his patience clearly hanging by a thread.' It seems you eliminate people the moment you point the finger at them.'

Mrs Bramble returned a wry smile. That was exactly what Inspector Cole did, invariably getting the wrong end of the stick, but at least she didn't demand an arrest before all the facts had been gathered and verified.

'Mr Chant, Inspector Cole and Reverend Weaver were

the only three who did not fall ill during Holy Communion but this can be explained,' she said. 'Mr Chant had yet to leave his seat at the organ, Inspector Cole had a blessing only, and people fell ill before Reverend Weaver could complete the ritual by taking the bread and wine himself and drinking the wine remaining in the chalice. Therefore, the items used during the Eucharist must have been to blame. Dr Burford's colleagues over at Guy's Hospital established and confirmed that the water used to dilute the communion wine, not the wine itself, held enough liquid nicotine poison to make you all ill.'

Mrs Rushton put her hand to her throat. 'And poor Mrs Fry died because of her weak constitution.'

'Ah,' said Mrs Bramble. 'Again, no, but more on that later.'

Mrs Rushton went to speak but the words seemed stuck in her throat and she coughed.

'For the love of all that's holy.' Inspector Cole's shoulders sagged. 'Sorry, Reverends.' He glared at Mrs Bramble. 'What next?'

'I'm afraid we need to return to our esteemed knights of the realm,' said Mrs Bramble. 'For this is where it gets interesting.'

'Ha!' scoffed Cole.

'After a conversation with Sir Stephen, I had an inkling something was awry and suggested to Inspector Cole that he look into the death of Sir Oswald's father.' She looked at Cole. 'Inspector?'

'What?' said Inspector Cole. 'Oh, yes. My colleagues at Scotland Yard confirmed Lord Fry owned an entirely different company from the one Sir Oswald Clyne's father worked for, proving Mrs Rushton had lied.'

It was the turn of Clyne's face to display pain and anger

as Mrs Rushton went to protest, though a glare from the chief left her open-mouthed but silent. The major stared at her as though unable to recognise her as his wife.

Mrs Bramble hurried on. 'To such loyal friends and staunch supporters of the Frys and Rushtons as Sir Stephen and Sir Oswald, almost any request to hit back at the rival family would have been considered. Except one.' She saw a flash of fear in Mrs Rushton's eyes. 'Mrs Rushton had become so incensed by the simmering feud and by Mrs Fry's attempts to besmirch their good name that she put the most serious of requests to Sir Oswald.'

'There's more?' said Major Rushton, looking at Inspector Cole and the chief in dismay.

'I'm afraid so,' said Cole, and he motioned for Mrs Bramble to continue.

Mrs Bramble acknowledged the nod with one of her own. 'It was well known that Mrs Fry harboured the same feelings towards Mrs Rushton and, unbeknown to her and Sir Oswald, Mrs Fry had posed exactly the same question to Sir Stephen Lovell.'

Mrs Rushton glared at Lovell but he ignored her and flicked a glance at Clyne, who was staring glassy-eyed at a point on the far wall.

'As I said,' Mrs Bramble continued. 'A most serious question, the ultimate question, had been asked of the family friends by the two feuding wives.' She paused to ensure everyone was listening. 'Will you kill her husband for me?'

43

Gasps burst from almost everyone seated at the table and Captain Fry jabbed a finger towards the Rushtons but seemed unable to speak. Mrs Rushton had her hand on her husband's arm but he pulled away as he looked about to leap across the table to confront Lovell and Fry.

Inspector Cole pointed accusingly again, trying to arrest Sir Oswald Clyne, but Mrs Bramble held up her hands, calling for calm until the hubbub died down.

'Sir Stephen and Sir Oswald were filled with anger on behalf of their friends,' she said. 'In fact, both men told me they had been angry enough at first to comply with the requests, but they are essentially good and moral men and neither found themselves able to go through with it.'

'But my wife is dead!' Captain Fry snapped.

'Not by their hands.'

'How do you know this?' said Dr Burford. 'We've been here for years. You've been here a matter of days.'

'Because I saw the British Bulldog pocket pistol Sir Stephen carried with him as a deterrent against robbers.' She noted the major's wary glance at Lovell. 'He and Sir Oswald were seen arguing by my maid, Kitty, and when questioned it transpired the pistol never contains bullets. Too scared to load it, he carries it for show, just in case.' Lovell looked crestfallen, as though his manhood had been inspected and found wanting. Mrs Bramble smiled and nodded encouragement at him. 'The argument was about what they should do in light of the requests from the wives of their good friends. In the end, they agreed to do nothing.'

'Beg pardon,' said the chief. 'Nothing?'

'A decision you would expect good men to come to.' Mrs Bramble raised her eyebrows questioningly. 'As a digression: Mrs Rushton, are you or have you ever been a Catholic?'

Mrs Rushton looked suddenly guarded. 'Y-yes, I have. I converted to Protestantism to marry my husband.'

'Ah, that explains the rosary beads we found in your quarters this evening.' Mrs Bramble selected them from the table and held them up. 'A search of Captain Fry's quarters also revealed this card.' She held it up with her other hand. 'In case you're wondering, it says on the back, *Il Sodoma's 1526 paining of St Catherine fainting from the stigmata*.'

'If you say so,' said Mrs Rushton. 'I'm not familiar with it, I'm afraid.'

'Oh, I think you are, Mrs Rushton, although that doesn't matter. It's the imagery that's important. The stigmata is a Catholic belief, and inside is written: *For today. Best wishes, M*. Did you send Mrs Fry this card? M for Margaret?'

'I-I ...'

'A quick handwriting test would prove you did.'

Mrs Rushton hesitated, then relaxed, seemingly having made a decision. 'I admit, I did send her the card.'

'What?' said the major, looking at his wife with incredulity. 'Why?'

'As a threat?' suggested Mrs Bramble, putting the items back on the table.

Mrs Rushton scoffed. 'A threat about what? It was an olive branch. I was trying to make amends with her.'

'By sending a Catholic card to an Anglican, even though

you've converted?' Mrs Bramble shook her head. 'When I showed the inspector, he thought the subject of a person's wounds, especially related to anyone nailed to a cross and left to die, was a veiled warning.'

'No!'

'Did you send it with a gift?'

'A-a what?' Mrs Rushton's eyes widened and she looked imploringly at her husband.

'Chief, are you content to let accusations be bandied about willy-nilly?' said Major Rushton, throwing a challenging glare at Inspector Cole when the chief turned to him for help. 'Inspector, I haven't seen or heard any substantial evidence for or against anyone in this room so far. Are we all to be tarnished by a housekeeper's speculation and gossip. And Reverend Weaver is keeping unnaturally quiet, if you ask me.'

'Now who's speculating and accusing?' said Reverend Weaver in a small but defiant voice.

'Returning to the Eucharist,' said Mrs Bramble, hoping to keep the gathering civil for a while longer. 'Holy water is always mixed with red wine and the special service was no different. Reverend Weaver and Reverend Dench prepared the sacramental wine in full view of everyone, using wine retrieved from the cupboard by Reverend Weaver and water taken from a carafe provided by Reverend Dench.'

Mrs Bramble took the glass shard between thumb and forefinger and turned it in the light to show the motif of the tiny flower.

'I found this in the vestry and for a long time I couldn't work out why it was there. Everywhere else was so clean and tidy.'

'I don't understand what that has to do with my wife,' said Major Rushton.

'Major, do you smoke pipe tobacco?' she asked.

'No. Cheroots, actually. They're more convenient and I prefer the taste.'

'These are not yours?' Mrs Bramble swapped the shard for the tobacco tins. 'They appear newly purchased.'

'Certainly not.'

'They were found in your wife's box, along with the rosary beads, embroidered cloth and laudanum bottle.' Mrs Bramble returned the tins to the table and removed the cork stopper from the bottle. She gave it a tentative sniff before offering it to Inspector Cole, the chief and Dr Burford to do the same.

'This isn't laudanum,' said Dr Burford. 'It should be reddish-brown and sweet-smelling.'

'Inspector Cole, would you mind striking a match and holding it under the base of the bottle for a moment.'

'Whatever for?' said Cole, but he did as she asked.

Mrs Bramble held out the bottle. 'Please take a very small and careful sniff of the fumes, if you will.'

They did so.

'Fish oil,' said Inspector Cole, recoiling.

'I agree,' said the chief.

'Wrong,' said Mrs Bramble. 'Dr Burford, do you think you could explain?'

'Er, well, yes. Pure nicotine, which is a clear fluid, is pretty undetectable until it warms up. Then it smells faintly of fish.'

'Which is why the gardening gloves smell fishy and it proves this bottle contains the residue of nicotine poison,' said Mrs Bramble.

Everyone, especially Captain Fry, was staring at Mrs Rushton in disbelief. Major Rushton had edged away as far as his chair would allow.

'I suggest you steeped the tobacco from these tins in hot water and boiled the liquid until it became highly concentrated, hence the fishy smell Inspector Cole, the chief and I noticed in Mrs Rushton's room.' She omitted Kitty's part in the previous search. 'But how did the nicotine get into the wine?'

The major looked suddenly hopeful. 'Yes. How could my wife have poisoned a bottle of wine locked in a cupboard in the chapel's vestry?'

'A fair question,' said Mrs Bramble. 'Reverend Weaver admitted he left the reception and returned to the chapel briefly because he didn't want any rush before the service. He took the wine and wafers from the locked cupboard, filled the carafe with water and placed these on the table with the chalice and an embroidered cloth. He then returned to the reception. From an upstairs bedroom in the chaplain's house, Reverend Dench's chambermaid, Esther, witnessed Reverend Weaver entering and leaving the chapel, confirming the time and duration of his visit. Unfortunately, his little ritual meant everything was left on the table where anyone could have tampered with them.'

'Anyone other than my wife,' said the major. 'She was with me.'

'I surmise that as the guests enjoyed their canapés, the poisoner excused themselves,' Mrs Bramble continued, without looking at the major. 'With only a few minutes available, they quickly sneaked across to the vestry, unseen by Esther who had most likely moved to another room. Finding the bottle of communion wine on the table had yet to be uncorked, they thought quickly and turned to the carafe, deciding to add the nicotine to the water. Unfortunately for them, they knocked over and smashed the carafe before they could do so. They cleared up the debris but not well enough, leaving behind this one stray shard.'

'It still could have been anyone,' said Mrs Rushton, her cheeks and throat a dark shade of pink.

'I have to agree,' said Inspector Cole, 'but—'

'I was told by a witness that you, Mrs Rushton, had left the reception,' Mrs Bramble interrupted. 'Returning later with splashes on your dress, you explained truthfully that you spilt water over your gown.'

'If she broke the carafe and the wine had yet to be opened, how did the poison get in?' challenged the major.

'Another excellent question,' said Mrs Bramble. 'The carafe needed to be replaced quickly for her plan to work so she cleared up the glass and returned with the broken pieces to your quarters, Major. Reverend Dench told me he had to use a plain chalice cloth because an embroidered one donated by Mrs Fry had gone missing. This embroidered chalice cloth, still with tiny flecks of glass caught in its weave.' She held up the cloth from Mrs Rushton's box.

'Ah, yes,' said Captain Fry. 'I remember my wife noticed its absence from the Eucharist. She commented on it just before she fell ill.'

Mrs Bramble replaced the cloth. 'Mrs Rushton then grabbed a carafe from their quarters, took it to the vestry and poured almost the whole bottle of nicotine into fresh water.'

'Shard of glass, missed?' said the chief.

Mrs Bramble indicated three carafes on the table. 'This is the poisoned carafe from the vestry and this is the one Gwen was sent to collect from the main gate after Mrs Rushton ordered a new one. My maid, Kitty, saw and spoke to Gwen. As you can see, the designs match and probably came from the same shop nearby. The third, belonging to

Reverend Dench, which I know to have held fruit cordial, I took from Jasper Chant's room during the searches. It is smaller but, as you can see, it also has a tiny embellishment of a flower, much like the one Reverend Weaver said they'd taken from the chaplain's house to use for the service.' She looked at the doctor. 'Dr Burford?'

'Um, oh yes,' said Burford. 'Most people became ill because the dose people received from the diluted wine was insufficient to be fatal.'

'Except poor Mrs Fry,' said Mrs Rushton. 'You accuse me, but Reverend Weaver knew she had a weak stomach.'

'How could he have known?' said Reverend Dench. 'He had never been to the Tower nor met Mrs Fry before.'

'Nonsense anyway, I'm afraid,' said Dr Burford. 'As Mrs Bramble alluded to earlier, many knew Mrs Fry had the constitution of an ox and would have survived the dose we all received. In fact, she merely played on the assumption she was weak-stomached.'

'How do you explain her death then?' Mrs Rushton lifted her chin defiantly.

'Through science,' said Burford. 'The post-mortem showed her blood contained a very high concentration of nicotine poison.' He cleared his throat. 'In fact, double that ingested by the congregation in the chapel.'

44

Captain Fry and Major Rushton leapt to their feet again but their friends, Sir Stephen Lovell and Sir Oswald Clyne, managed to sit them back down.

'To be precise' – Dr Burford ran a finger around the inside of his collar nervously – 'Mrs Fry had received more than double.'

'In which case, how was it given to Mrs Fry?' said Major Rushton, flapping his hand at Captain Fry, seemingly willing to grasp at any hope. 'My wife was at my side during the service and nowhere near her.'

'I must admit, that had me stumped for a while,' said Mrs Bramble. 'I thought there might be an accomplice, especially after Esther died, until a piece of evidence came to light.' She turned to Captain Fry's maid. 'Beth, did Mrs Fry receive a gift with the card?'

'She did, ma'am,' said Beth. 'A small bottle of French scent. Exclusive, I'd say. For high-class ladies.'

'How can you, a housemaid, possibly know that?' said Inspector Cole.

'Mistresses wear perfume all the time and talk about the latest scents.'

'Would Mrs Fry have known its value?'

'She wasn't one for expensive perfume, but she was very pleased with it,' said Beth.

'Did she wear it often?' said Mrs Bramble.

'No, ma'am. It came on the day she died and she wore it for the first time to the reception.'

'Are you off on a tangent again, Mrs Bramble?' said Inspector Cole with a sigh. 'Have you something to show us? Anything that will prove your – our – case?' He glanced around to see if anyone had picked up on his mistake but no one appeared interested in whose case it was.

'Dr Burford,' said Mrs Bramble. 'In the post-mortem report, did you read about the red marks on Mrs Fry's wrists?'

'Red marks?' Dr Burford scratched his chin. 'Yes. I did.'

'And you recognised Mrs Fry's symptoms from another of your cases?'

'Yes. It was a while ago but I thought I knew what to ask my colleagues to focus on.'

'Beth.' Mrs Bramble smiled encouragingly at the housemaid. 'You have red marks on your wrists, don't you?'

Beth fidgeted. 'Yes, ma'am.'

'How did you acquire them?'

'I think I must be allergic to that perfume 'cause I sneaked a little spray of it this morning, just to try it, and then I got this.' Beth exposed her red wrists to those around the table, showing the effects of the perfume.

'Similar to the marks found on the wrists and neck of Esther,' said Mrs Bramble.

Beth gasped. 'I gave her a small amount to cheer her up on her birthday.'

Mrs Bramble nodded and showed everyone the tiny sample bottle given to Esther.

'Nicotine can be caustic, especially if concentrated,' said Dr Burford, nodding. 'Depending on how much is used, it might take a while for the irritation to manifest.'

'Exactly,' said Mrs Bramble. 'Dr Burford also mentioned

that he noticed Mrs Fry suffering from uncharacteristic facial twitching while in the chapel. This is an early symptom of nicotine poisoning, indicating she had received a dose *before* the service. Mrs Rushton knew Mrs Fry wouldn't be felled with one dose because she was fit and healthy, so she had to devise a way of giving her two doses close together. Her solution was daring but ingenious. She began overtures to lure Mrs Fry into believing an end to the feud might be possible. She then laced the bottle of perfume with nicotine concentrate and delivered it to Mrs Fry, hoping she would use the perfume that same day as suggested in the card. Skin absorption of the scent and oral consumption of the wine diluted with the heavily poisoned water provided the fatal combined dose that would kill Mrs Fry.'

Major Rushton leapt to his feet. 'I demand this charade be stopped,' he said, but he seemed less outraged than before. 'If the science of what you say is true, why has Captain Fry's maid not met her maker?'

'Because she did not attend the service, which meant she received only one dose, enough to make her ill but not prove deadly,' said Mrs Bramble. 'As for Esther, the chambermaid ...' She held up the packet of chloral hydrate sleeping tablets found in Esther's room. 'Doctor?'

'Eh?' said Dr Burford. 'Oh yes. It was obvious to me that she had used quite a lot of the perfume on her wrists and neck and gave herself a fatal dose.'

'But she was young and healthy,' countered Major Rushton.

'Unfortunately, no,' said Burford. 'The poor girl had been suffering from a bad cold and I had prescribed these sleeping pills to help her get a good night's sleep. She was run down and weak enough for that single large dose to incapacitate her.' He cleared his throat. 'That is why Esther collapsed on the stairs, hit her head during the fall and broke her neck.'

'The maid's death wasn't murder?' said Inspector Cole, looking in turn at Mrs Bramble, the chief and the doctor. 'Are you sure?'

'An unfortunate accident,' said Dr Burford. 'To which absolutely no blame can be attributed to Beth.'

Beth's eyes filled with tears and Jasper Chant held her close.

'To return to the chapel,' said Mrs Bramble. 'You will remember I said the anonymous figure I chased escaped wearing what sounded like clumpy boots. I heard those same boots later, after a conversation with one of you. Even after everything I discovered during this investigation, I wanted to be absolutely sure. That is why I suggested the trap.' She nodded at the major. 'In the vestry earlier tonight, Major Rushton was surprised to find his wife present, but I was not. Mrs Rushton was the odd one out, being the only one without an innocent reason for being there. She had not known the samples had been sent for testing and came back one last time to try to destroy any evidence.'

'And her boots are decidedly clumpy,' said Captain Fry.

'I-I must protest,' said Major Rushton half-heartedly.

Mrs Bramble could see the major buckling under the weight of evidence against his wife. After all those years of him keeping the feud suppressed enough for everyone to get on with their lives, she had caused her own downfall.

'Sit down, Edwin,' said Mrs Rushton, quietly but forcibly, her eyes red and full of tears. 'I'm afraid it's true. All of it. Just as Mrs Bramble has said.'

A wan smile came to her lips at the gasps and cries around the table, as though she knew their shock and pity was feigned. She dabbed beneath her eyes with a lace handkerchief as silence descended, and even Inspector Cole and the chief appeared reluctant to break its grip as everyone waited for more.

Mrs Rushton obliged.

'Too much had gone on between our two families for the feud to ever be resolved.' She dabbed her eyes again. 'My darling husband and Captain Fry refused to speak about the feud for many years, but it proved a scab neither I nor Catherine Fry could refrain from picking away at. This business of a dangerous posting abroad brought the whole affair to a head and I knew she thought the same as me, that something needed to be done. When Sir Oswald refused to act against Captain Fry in retribution on my behalf, in any capacity, I had it in my head to take matters into my own hands.'

'Even with such deep-rooted loathing, surely there were other ways than resorting to murder?' said Mrs Bramble.

Mrs Rushton shook her head sadly. 'Catherine Fry and I had descended too far into the abyss to climb out. I could not shake it from my thoughts and found myself working out a plan based on a warning I overheard issued to Reverend Dench by a gardener about how insecticides can cause sickness. It was mere fantasy at first but the seed germinated and took root until I could think of nothing else.' She sighed. 'I thought, if I could achieve my aim in front of everyone at the chapel service, poisoning everyone a little in the process, I would not be suspected.' She gave Mrs Bramble a sad, crooked smile. 'I did not account for the detection abilities of a Lady Housekeeper.'

Inspector Cole stiffened at the remark. 'I think you'll find—'

'Reverend Weaver,' interrupted the chief. 'Indisputably exonerated. A free man.'

'Mrs Margaret Rushton, I am arresting ...' Inspector Cole's words were drowned under a releasing tidal wave of pent-up emotion as everyone but Mrs Rushton sprang to their feet.

Reverend Weaver's cry of relief was cut off with a squeak as Reverend Dench gave him a sudden congratulatory slap on the back with such enthusiasm that he staggered forward.

Kitty rounded the table to hug Gwen while Jasper Chant and Beth embraced as though neither would ever let the other go.

Dr Burford had knocked over his chair again and managed to entangle his foot among the legs and spindles. This prevented the stony-faced Captain Fry from making the swift and dignified exit Mrs Bramble suspected he'd hoped for.

Major Rushton leant forward to console his shaking wife but veered away at the last second to stare out of the window.

Sir Stephen Lovell and Sir Oswald Clyne met at the near end of the table and eyed each other suspiciously. One gave a polite nod, the other reciprocated and both exchanged a gentlemanly handshake.

Inspector Cole cleared his throat theatrically. 'Ladies—'

'And gentlemen,' said the chief.

'I know,' Cole hissed out of the side of his mouth, turning back to address the gathering. 'You will need to sign the statements you gave throughout this investigation. And to clarify, I think you'll find the chief and I had the largest part to play in bringing this sorry affair to a satisfactory conclusion.'

Those around the table paid him no attention but Mrs Bramble patted him gently on the arm. 'Of course you did.'

Cole frowned.
The chief nodded.
She smiled.

Epilogue

A few months later, Kitty brought a copy of the *Daily Telegraph* to the breakfast table, an unusual occurrence because Mrs Bramble usually read in the evenings. Dodger had already had his morning treat – a crust licked clean of butter lay by the table leg – and retired elsewhere in the apartment. Similarly, Mrs Bramble had also finished her breakfast, having drained the last of her second cup of Earl Grey tea the second her housemaid had walked in.

The expression on Kitty's face told Mrs Bramble she should at least read the front page, and she realised exactly why the newspaper had been brought to her the moment she saw the headline.

MURDER AT THE TOWER — KILLER FOUND GUILTY

Although the outcome had been in no doubt, Mrs Bramble's heart sank a little. The whole affair was steeped in tragedy, more so because all the heartbreak could have been so easily avoided had the warring parties chosen to step back from the brink.

Mrs Rushton had been held at the Tower for one night before being handed over to Scotland Yard for questioning prior to her transfer to Newgate Prison. Major Rushton's request to remain in charge of the Royal Fusiliers at the Tower of London, at least until after his wife's trial for murder, was granted. In light of this, Captain Fry received the promotion to major that accompanied a posting to Suez in Egypt. He left the day after attending his wife's funeral.

Gwen elected to remain at the Tower in the service of Major Rushton but Beth and Jasper Chant, now engaged to be married, secured employment at Hillsborough Castle in County Down. Sir Stephen Lovell and Sir Oswald Clyne found they had more in common with each other regarding politics, business and art than they had ever suspected, and perhaps an unlikely friendship had begun.

Reverend Dench resumed his ministrations as resident Chaplain of the Chapel Royal of St Peter ad Vincula, delighted the chapel had reopened for worship. Dr Burford received an offer from Guy's Hospital to lead a small team researching the use of poisons in everyday products, which he gleefully accepted.

Detective Inspector Cole and Chief Yeoman Warder Stuart Treadle both received commendations from Scotland Yard and the Constable of the Tower of London, and personal letters from Her Majesty Queen Victoria for their part in the investigation. Once again, Mrs Bramble had allowed men to take the credit for her efforts, but she had no problem with doing so. She'd had her fill of adventures in the army and all she desired was a quiet life. At least, as quiet a life as the grace and favour ladies of Hampton Court Palace allowed her.

After the ordeal of being accused and arrested for murder at the Tower of London, Reverend Weaver had elected to take a leaf out of Mrs Bramble's book and keep a low profile. He had gone straight back to work as resident Chaplain of the Chapel Royal at Hampton Court Palace where the colour in his cheeks and spring in his step had soon returned.

Mrs Bramble went to place the newspaper on the table

but saw Kitty still hovering nearby, and raised an eyebrow. The housemaid stepped forward and tapped a small news item at the foot of the page. It took seconds for Mrs Bramble to read the one column inch and she looked up in surprise. Kitty smiled back. 'Shall I get our travelling coats?'

Acknowledgements

Firstly, I must thank my wife, Jane, who once again lost me to several days of research visits and the many months I spent beavering away in my writing room. My last book, *Murder at the Palace*, was crafted during the preparations for my daughter Laura's wedding to Tom. This time, my writing and editing coincided with the approaching birth of their son, Jane's and my first grandchild. Welcome to the world, George!

Secondly, thanks must go once again to my fantastic agent, Nelle Andrew, for getting me this gig, Leodora Darlington, Publishing Director of Orion Fiction, for being a joy to work with and for continuing to trust me with this project, and everyone at Rachel Mills Literary and Orion. At Historic Royal Palaces, I must thank Clare Murphy, Publishing and Asset Manager. She has a critical eye for historical accuracy and kindly arranged my private tour of the Tower of London.

I also have many to thank from within the walls of the fortress itself. Alfred Hawkins, Curator of Historic Buildings, pointed out many nooks and crannies, indulged my thirst for knowledge and provided me with a good deal of information.

Former chief Yeoman Warder Rob Fuller allowed me to badger his people outside of their usual interactions with the public. Of these, Yeoman Warder Tam Reilly sent me plenty of material regarding the historical drinking establishments of the Tower, and Yeoman Warder Darren Hardy VR took time to chat about the Tower and his duties, many of which are historical and traditional in nature.

I must say a big thank you to Yeoman Serjeant John Donald who not only showed me around the Keys pub, the Yeoman Warders' Club, and answered all my stupid questions but also invited me to take a drink there and witness the Ceremony of the Keys. It was a privilege to do both and something I will never forget. The barman that evening, Yeoman Warder Terrance 'Basher' Briggs, was a most interesting bloke to chat to and pulled an excellent pint of ale.

I reserve a special mention for Reverend Canon Roger Hall MBE, Chaplain of the Tower of London, who was very generous with his time. Not only did he stay behind after a Sunday service in the Chapel Royal of St Peter ad Vincula to chat about its layout and history, but he also showed me around the inside of his home at the Chaplain's House.

Finally, thanks go to Peter Atkinson and Colin Barwick, friends for most of my life and two of those to whom I can turn for an honest opinion. Their patience while I prattle on about fictional worlds is always to be commended, and I thank them for their company during my research visits to the Tower.

I had great fun being let loose in the Tower of London, a place I had visited with my father as a child and, many years later, took my own children to explore. As an author about to murder someone in the Tower, I was privileged to be given a private tour in the first instance and allowed to return again and again. It is amazing how much more is to be discovered than the surface detail most visitors digest during their fleeting visits. While I am conscious of slightly manipulating history, I make no apology for cherry picking the bits that enhanced my story. After all, it is for the noble purpose of entertainment. If you ever have the good fortune to include the Tower in your trip to London, I urge you to find out more for yourself by taking every opportunity to talk to those within, especially the Yeoman Warders, because they have a wealth of knowledge they are just itching to impart.

CREDITS

Orion Fiction would like to thank everyone at Orion who worked on the publication of *Murder at the Tower*.

Editor
Leodora Darlington
Clara Sokhn

Copy-editor
Francine Brody

Proofreader
Holly Kyte

Editorial Management
Anshuman Yadav
Clara Sokhn
Jane Hughes
Charlie Panayiotou
Lucy Bilton
Patrice Nelson

Inventory
Jo Jacobs
Dan Stevens

Audio
Paul Stark
Louise Richardson
Georgina Cutler-Ross

Contracts
Rachel Monte
Ellie Bowker
Tabitha Gresty

Design
Charlotte Abrams-Simpson
Nick Shah
Deborah Francois
Helen Ewing

Photo Shoots & Image Research
Natalie Dawkins

Finance
Nick Gibson
Jasdip Nandra
Sue Baker
Tom Costello

Production
Ruth Sharvell
Katie Horrocks

Marketing
Louis Patel

Publicity
Alisha Javaid

Sales
Dave Murphy

Victoria Laws
Esther Waters
Group Sales teams across
Digital, Field, International
and Non-Trade

Operations
Group Sales Operations team

Rights
Rebecca Folland
Tara Hiatt
Ben Fowler
Maddie Stephens
Ruth Blakemore
Marie Henckel

Make sure you join the palace housekeeper Mrs. Bramble, in the ultimate locked room mystery, *Murder at the Palace* . . .

When one of the ladies in residence at Hampton Court Palace fails to answer her maid's call in the morning, **Mrs Lydia Bramble**, palace housekeeper, is called in to investigate.

What Mrs Bramble finds sends shockwaves through the whole palace: **Miss Philomena Franklin, slumped over her desk, a knife in her back.**

With the police determined to bark up the wrong tree, Mrs Bramble decides to take up her own investigation with the help of her maid, Kitty. **After all, as servants, they know just how many dangerous secrets and secret squabbles the genteel residents of the palace apartments harbour.**

AVAILABLE NOW

RAISING READERS
Books Build Bright Futures

Dear Reader,

We'd love your attention for one more page to tell you about the crisis in children's reading, and what we can all do.

Studies have shown that reading for fun is the **single biggest predictor of a child's future life chances** – more than family circumstance, parents' educational background or income. It improves academic results, mental health, wealth, communication skills, ambition and happiness.[1]

The number of children reading for fun is in rapid decline. Young people have a lot of competition for their time. In 2024, 1 in 10 children and young people in the UK aged 5 to 18 did not own a single book at home.[2]

Hachette works extensively with schools, libraries and literacy charities, but here are some ways we can all raise more readers:

- Reading to children for just 10 minutes a day makes a difference
- Don't give up if children aren't regular readers – there will be books for them!
- Visit bookshops and libraries to get recommendations
- Encourage them to listen to audiobooks
- Support school libraries
- Give books as gifts

There's a lot more information about how to encourage children to read on our website: **www.RaisingReaders.co.uk**

Thank you for reading.

hachette UK

---

[1] OECD, '21st-Century Readers: Developing Literacy Skills in a Digital World', 2021, https://www.oecd.org/en/publications/21st-century-readers_a83d84cb-en.html

[2] National Literacy Trust, 'Book Ownership in 2024', November 2024, https://literacytrust.org.uk/research-services/research-reports/book-ownership-in-2024